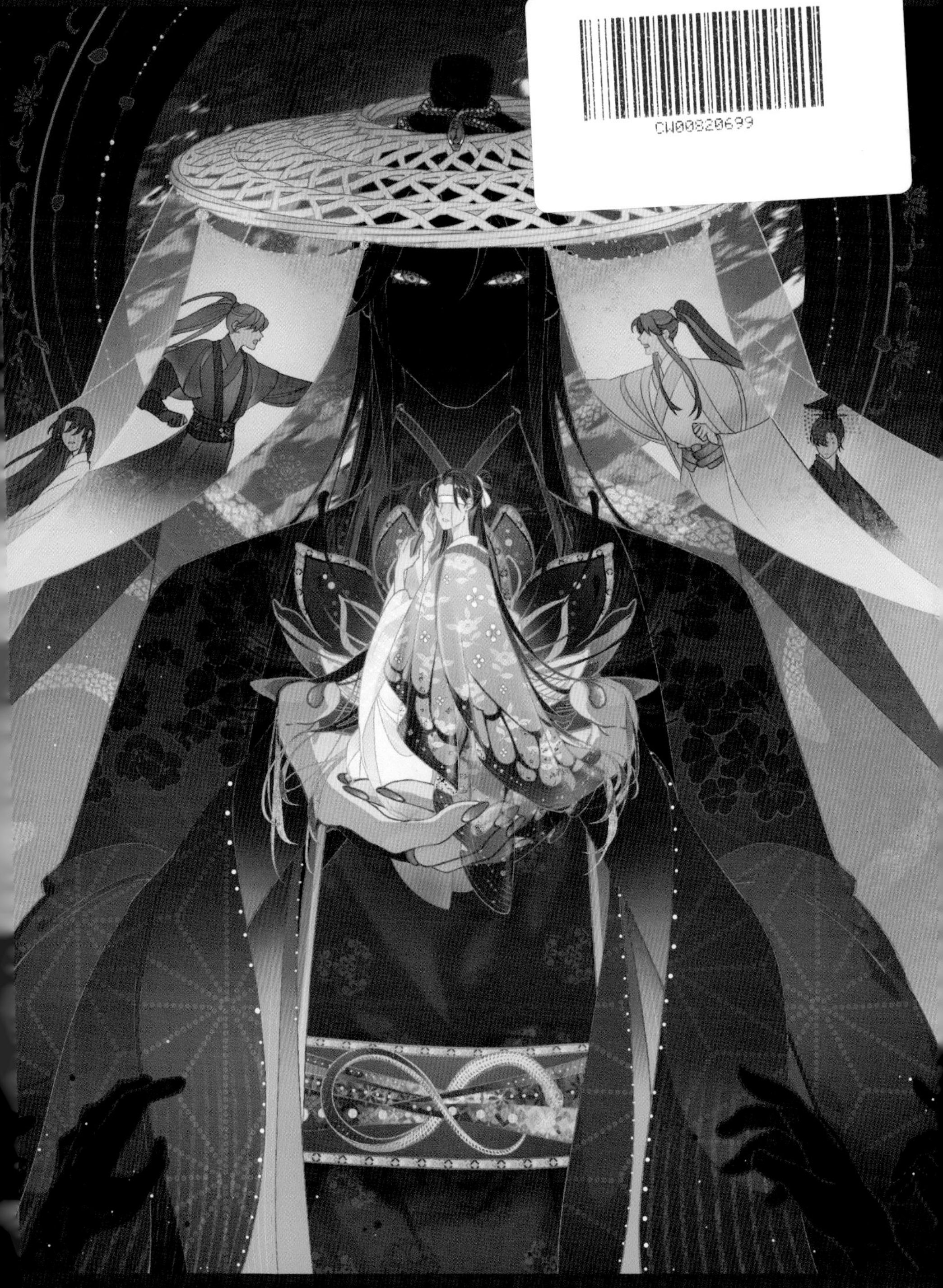

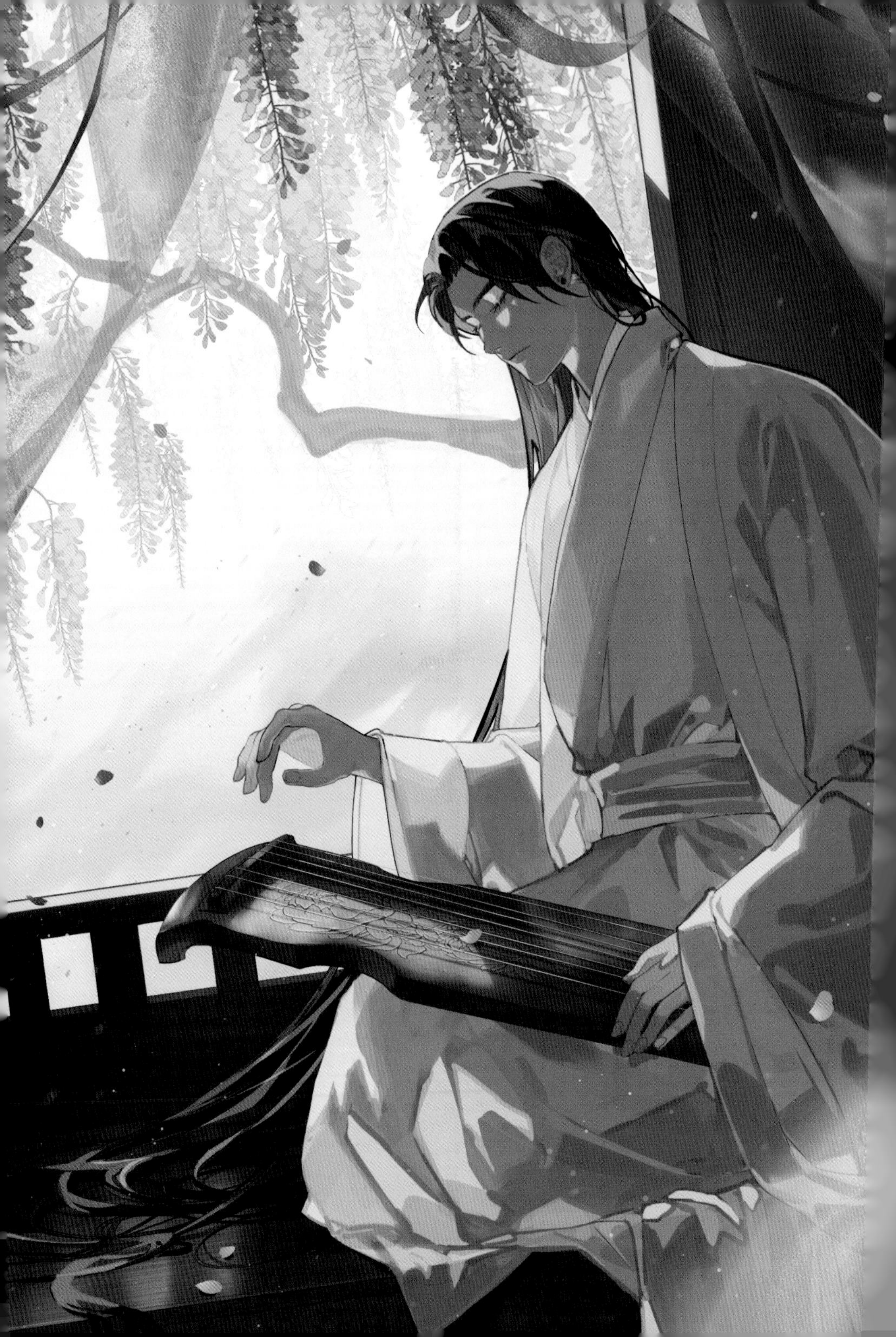

The HUSKY & His WHITE CAT SHIZUN

ERHA HE TA DE BAI MAO SHIZUN

8

WRITTEN BY
Rou Bao Bu Chi Rou

ILLUSTRATED BY
St

TRANSLATED BY
Jun, Rui, & Yu

Seven Seas

Seven Seas Entertainment

THE HUSKY & HIS WHITE CAT SHIZUN:
ERHA HE TA DE BAI MAO SHIZUN VOL. 8

Published originally under the title of 《二哈和他的白貓師尊》
(Erha He Ta De Bai Mao Shizun)
Author © 肉包不吃肉 (Rou Bao Bu Chi Rou)
English edition rights under license granted by 北京晋江原创网络科技有限公司
(Beijing Jinjiang Original Network Technology Co., Ltd.)
English edition copyright © 2025 Seven Seas Entertainment, Inc.
Arranged through JS Agency Co., Ltd
All rights reserved.

Cover and Interior Illustrations by St

No portion of this book may be reproduced or transmitted in any form without written
permission from the copyright holders. This is a work of fiction. Names, characters, places,
and incidents are the products of the author's imagination or are used fictitiously.
Any resemblance to actual events, locales, or persons, living or dead, is entirely coincidental.
Any information or opinions expressed by the creators of this book belong to those individual
creators and do not necessarily reflect the views of Seven Seas Entertainment or its employees.

Seven Seas press and purchase enquiries can be sent
to Marketing Manager Lauren Hill at press@gomanga.com.
Information regarding the distribution and purchase of digital editions is available
from Digital Manager Kristine Johnson at digital@gomanga.com.

Seven Seas and the Seven Seas logo are trademarks of
Seven Seas Entertainment. All rights reserved.

Follow Seven Seas Entertainment online at
sevenseasentertainment.com.

TRANSLATION: Jun, Rui, Yu
ADAPTATION: Neon Yang
COVER DESIGN: M. A. Lewife
INTERIOR DESIGN: Clay Gardner
INTERIOR LAYOUT: Karis Page
COPY EDITOR: Jehanne Bell
PROOFREADER: Kate Kishi, Hnä
EDITOR: Kelly Quinn Chiu
PREPRESS TECHNICIAN: Salvador Chan Jr., April Malig, Jules Valera
MANAGING EDITOR: Alyssa Scavetta
EDITOR-IN-CHIEF: Julie Davis
PUBLISHER: Lianne Sentar
VICE PRESIDENT: Adam Arnold
PRESIDENT: Jason DeAngelis

ISBN: 979-8-88843-483-3
Printed in Canada
First Printing: March 2025
10 9 8 7 6 5 4 3 2 1

</cite>

TABLE OF CONTENTS

TIANYIN PAVILION ARC

Snake-Shed

THE CULTIVATORS who had escaped Mount Jiao with their lives fled to Guyueye to recuperate. With the medicine sect's disciples' help, they extracted Hua Binan's heart-tunneler insects and bandaged their many wounds. The fog of dejection, however, proved harder to treat than any injury. The air itself seemed heavy and lifeless.

Xue Meng sat on the shore of Rainbell Isle with the scimitar Longcheng in his lap, staring blankly at the rise and fall of the tide. Footsteps sounded behind him, and he whipped around, eyes wide and filled with earnest hope. Yet when he saw who it was, the light in his eyes died in an instant; he dragged his gaze back to the boundless sea.

Mei Hanxue took a seat next to Xue Meng. "Your dad received a message and had to return to Sisheng Peak. He left in a hurry, so he asked me to inform you."

This statement was met with silence.

"You and your dad seem to be in a lousy mood," Mei Hanxue remarked.

"Since you've finally noticed, feel free to get lost."

Mei Hanxue did nothing of the sort. He tossed a wineskin to Xue Meng. "Do you drink?"

Xue Meng turned on him, furious, like a hedgehog with its quills raised. "Do I drink?! Like hell! I haven't fallen that far!"

Mei Hanxue smiled. His fine golden locks curled softly in the sea breeze, and his eyes were like pale jade, twin pools of teal flecked with fallen petals.

"What do you mean, 'fallen that far'? It's just a drink." Mei Hanxue smoothed a wisp of fair hair behind his ear. The silver bell around his wrist tinkled softly. "I heard Sisheng Peak forbids its people from visiting the pleasure districts, but surely the taverns aren't off-limits as well?"

At Xue Meng's lack of response, Mei Hanxue continued, "I also heard Chu-xianjun adores pear-blossom white wine. You're his disciple; have you not learned to hold your drink?"

Xue Meng glowered. His lips parted as if to curse Mei Hanxue out, but he simply twisted open the wineskin and took a generous gulp.

"Gutsy. This liquor's from Taxue Palace, it's quite str—"

"Pff—!" The gutsy Young Master Xue sputtered mightily, face ashen, and broke into a violent fit of coughing.

Mei Hanxue pressed his lips together, seemingly taken aback. "You really can't hold your drink?"

Now this, Xue Meng's pride could not take. He swatted Mei Hanxue's hand away as he reached for the wineskin and gulped down another burning mouthful. Not a second later, he turned his head aside and spat it out with a cry.

Mei Hanxue watched him in a rare state of bewilderment. "I didn't know you... Never mind, you've had enough."

"Get away from me!"

"Give me my wineskin back."

"Go *away!*" Xue Meng would nip at anyone who provoked him

whenever he got into a temper. Glaring daggers at Mei Hanxue, he snapped, "How would it make me look if I started and stopped whenever you told me to? What dignity would I have left?" He patted his own slightly flushed cheek, already slightly tipsy.

There was a saying on Sisheng Peak: Chu-zongshi could down a thousand cups, while one was enough to bring down Young Master Xue. As Mei Hanxue wasn't from Sisheng Peak, he'd naturally never heard such a thing. Otherwise, he would've known better than to pour liquor down Xue Meng's throat.

After Xue Meng was done spitting out his second swig, he picked up the wineskin again, this time managing four or five gulps. He gasped as he surfaced for air, his face alarmingly pale.

Mei Hanxue snatched back the wineskin and frowned. "All right, that's enough. Go home and rest. You've been sitting in this cold ocean wind for hours."

"I'm waiting for someone," Xue Meng replied obstinately.

Mei Hanxue blinked.

"I... I..." Xue Meng scowled at him for a long moment before surprising them both by bursting into tears. "You wouldn't understand. I'm waiting for my ge, for Shizun, for Shi Mei...got that? There're four of us, and all of us have to be here... It won't be the same if someone's missing..."

When it came to comforting women, Mei Hanxue was an expert: He'd put his arm around them and utter a few sweet nothings, make some pretty promises. It always worked like a charm. He'd never needed to comfort a man before.

Perhaps it was fortunate, then, that Xue Meng wasn't really in need of comforting. Rather, he had bottled up his emotions for too long, and once the liquor got to his head, they surged up and broke the levees. He wanted nothing more than to let them out.

"There were four of us, but I'm the only one left—my heart hurts. *Fuck.* Do you understand?"

Mei Hanxue sighed. "I do."

"Liar. You don't understand shit." Xue Meng bowed his head and wailed. He hugged Longcheng tightly to his chest, a piece of driftwood to keep himself afloat.

The liar didn't know how to convince him otherwise, so he agreed. "Okay, you're right, I don't understand."

"You heartless brute! Why can't you understand?" Xue Meng was too drunk to be reasoned with. He leveled a baleful glare at Mei Hanxue through the tears pooling in his eyes. "What don't you understand? It's simple!" He held up his fingers. "Four. Of. Us!" He put down one finger, then another. Before he got to the third, he dissolved into tears again, as if that trembling finger was a lever that opened the floodgates. "There's only one left—I'm the only one left. Get it now?"

Mei Hanxue didn't want to be a liar, and he didn't want to be heartless either. Since he couldn't say he understood, but he also couldn't say he didn't, he decided it was best to remain silent.

Xue Meng stared at him, then turned aside and vomited loudly.

The famed paramour Mei-gongzi was used to people staring at him, starry-eyed and besotted. Xue Meng was the first to stare and then throw up. Mei Hanxue's temples began to throb. "What's your problem? When you were little, I gave you fish mint and you threw up. Now that you're grown, I give you Kunlun wine and you throw up. You're fussier than a girl."

He watched Xue Meng's hunched-over figure as he heaved until he was dizzy and breathless, jade-green eyes exasperated. "Okay, enough cursing and puking—go back and rest," said Mei Hanxue. "None of them—your ge, your shizun, or your friend—would want to see you like this."

He stood to pull Xue Meng to his feet. After his spate of vomiting, Xue Meng felt weak, like his feet weren't planted firmly on the ground. He didn't even try to throw off the steadying hand Mei Hanxue placed on his arm.

Mei Hanxue escorted Xue Meng away from the shore and through the back entrance of Guyueye. He had intended to take him back to his room to rest, but before they made it through the gate to the garden pavilion, Mei Hanxue sensed danger. He quickly steered Xue Meng behind a column in the open-air corridor.

Xue Meng let out a whimper of protest that was swiftly cut off by Mei Hanxue's hand over his mouth. "Quiet."

"Let... Let go of me... I'm...gonna throw up again..." Xue Meng mumbled around his fingers.

"Swallow it."

This, at least, rendered Xue Meng temporarily speechless.

Still worried his intoxicated charge might stir up trouble, Mei Hanxue tapped a finger to Xue Meng's lips and cast a muffling spell. He turned and cast a swift glance into the pavilion—only to be struck dumb by the sight before him.

Mo Ran?!

By this point, most of the sect leaders and elders had returned to their own sects. After the chaos that had unfolded on Mount Jiao, all urgently needed to reinforce the barriers protecting their respective domains. But a number of injured cultivators still remained at Guyueye. These were currently gathered in the pavilion, staring at the man who'd appeared in their midst with looks of alarm.

"Tsk, tsk." Clad in a long, hooded cloak of black and gold, Mo Ran surveyed his surroundings with narrowed eyes. "Look at all these familiar faces. After so many years, I never thought I'd see you all standing here, alive and well."

One of the cultivators screwed up their courage and bellowed, "M-Mo Weiyu! What the hell's gotten into you? Have you been cursed?"

"What's gotten into me?" Mo Ran's thin lips curled in a sneer. "This venerable one should be asking what the hell's gotten into *you* to speak to me like that."

The crowd only saw the flash of a dark blur before blood spurted from the chest of the cultivator who'd yelled, splattering over the ceiling.

"M-murderer!"

"Mo Ran! What are you doing?!"

"Quick, get Jiang-zhangmen!" someone screamed. "Someone get Jiang-zhangmen now!"

"Oh?" Mo Ran languidly raised his gaze. "Jiang-zhangmen— Jiang Xi?"

When no one dared answer, Mo Ran continued. "He's got some skill, I'll give him that. Among all the people this venerable one has killed, he was in the top ten for sure."

"The hell are you talking about?!"

Something was not right. This man was nothing like the Mo-zongshi Mei Hanxue knew: Rancor and malevolence radiated from every fiber of him. Yet he looked and sounded exactly like Mo Ran. How could anyone have learned to mimic his appearance and voice so precisely, in such a short amount of time?

One of Guyueye's elders spoke up. "Mo-zongshi, I'm afraid you've been cursed by the demon dragon on Mount Jiao. Please have a seat so I can check your pulse—"

"What?" Mo Ran cut him off, eyes narrow. "Stop beating around the bush, you nitwit. Are you saying there's something wrong with this venerable one?"

The elder blinked in trepidation.

"Since you're so eager to treat someone, this venerable one will help you out. After all, without the sick and injured, you healers would starve—isn't that right?"

The cloaked figure leapt into the air like a shadow, and the pavilion was suddenly awash in scarlet. Mo Ran landed on the burgundy pollia-patterned carpet in the middle of the pavilion in a whirl of black robes as screams filled the air. The gathered cultivators were afflicted with a variety of gruesome injuries. Arms were hacked off, legs shattered; the most unfortunate died on the spot, their torsos ripped open in an instant.

Mo Ran gazed down at the elder who had spoken, now a crumpled heap on the ground. "Look, all these patients are for you. Aren't you happy?"

"Mo... Mo Weiyu..."

"Congratulations, and many happy returns." A brilliant smile unfolded over Mo Ran's face as he stepped over the cultivators, both the ones writhing miserably, and the glassy-eyed dead.

"Oh yes—one more thing." At the pavilion gate, he turned to look over his shoulder. "This venerable one almost forgot. The upper cultivation realm's been a stinking cesspool for centuries. Pass on a message to your sect leader for me—it's only a matter of time before this venerable one razes all the sects to the ground."

"Mo Ran, you coward!" one of the braver survivors rasped out. "You attacked a pavilion full of injured cultivators—are you scared of fighting the other sect leaders face to face?!"

"Scared? Of *them*?" Mo Ran gave the man a sharp look. "Even if you all held hands and formed a great big army, as long as I don't wish to die, none of you could touch a strand of hair on this venerable one's head."

"Mo Ran, have you gone mad? You and Hua Binan are working together! Wh-what do you want?!"

Mo Ran grinned, his dimples deep and his eyes distant. "You're asking what this venerable one wants?" he drawled. A strange look flitted across his handsome features, and he closed his eyes. "Even this venerable one isn't sure what it is exactly. But suffice it to say, it's not something those left in this world can give me. Nor can they hope to bring me any cheer," he said tonelessly. "For many years, this venerable one has been a dead man walking, without wants or desires. But if you insist on asking—" He chuckled and looked up, irises glinting scarlet. "Well then, I'd like to see you all dead."

Everyone's jaws dropped. Mo Ran swept his gaze over the crowd's ashen faces and couldn't help softly laughing. "It's been ages since this venerable one's seen anything so interesting. How fun."

"Mo Ran... You've truly gone mad..."

"That's the second time you've said that." His smile twisted into a leer. There was a loud *crack*; in the blink of an eye, Mo Ran had darted behind the speaker and bashed his head in. Gore splattered everywhere.

Amidst the horrified screams, Mo Ran lifted his gallant, blood-flecked face, revealing a pair of unnervingly bestial eyes. He leapt out of the crowd that chittered like panicked sparrows. "This venerable one wouldn't want to make a liar out of you now. So here's some madness, just for you, good sir."

This good sir had had his skull shattered, and his face was a torrent of blood. But Mo Ran barely spared him a glance. He surveyed the crowd coolly, as if he'd just finished a perfectly unremarkable meal.

"All right, this venerable one's killed enough idiots today." The corner of his mouth quirked up as he shoved the corpse over and kicked it aside. "It'd be a bore to get rid of everyone in one fell swoop. Besides, if all of you die, this venerable one will be lonely again. You can stick around a few more days." He paused. "Next time this venerable one's feeling fidgety, I'll take it out on your skulls."

The man strolled away from the mess of gore and through the main hall. At the gate, he glanced over his shoulder once more. "Before then, make sure to look after your heads."

He burst into laughter. With a swish of his cloak, he alighted upon the closest rooftop and vanished over the ridge.

In the cave on Dragonblood Mountain, Mo Ran and Chu Wanning were still sound asleep, recovering from the effects of the spell on the incense burner. Three days after those strange and gruesome events at Guyueye, the censer suddenly emitted a shrill whistle. The piercing noise echoed through the cave as black smoke and crimson blood spilled forth.

Mo Ran's eyes flew open.

His chest no longer ached, and he was otherwise uninjured. The mysterious tendril of smoke that had passed between him and Chu Wanning was nowhere to be seen.

"Shizun!"

He shot upright. Much to his surprise, he found that a third person had joined them in the cave.

The new arrival stood in front of the stone table with his back to Mo Ran, scrutinizing the smoking censer. Even from behind, his slender figure was unspeakably lovely. A pale, elegant hand opened the lid and plucked out a densely petaled, exotic-looking flower, holding it up to examine it in the low light.

"Totally destroyed," he said softly. Closing his fist, he crushed the flower into dust, which immediately began to glow with a faint pearlescence. He seemed pleased as he gazed down at the light with his hands tucked behind his back. "Ah. It's lucky I melded a piece of my own soul into this flower when I refined it. If not for that fragment, this cave would've been impossible to track down."

The light eddied around him, as though it knew he was talking about it. It grew fainter and fainter, until it vanished completely.

"Who..." Mo Ran rasped.

The man put down the censer and sighed. "You're awake?"

"Who are you?"

"Who do you think I am?" the man replied lightly.

He sounded terribly familiar, but Mo Ran was still groggy from sleep. He felt he'd been dreaming for ages and couldn't immediately place the voice. Who could this man be? Based on what he'd just said, he seemed to have a connection with the mysterious black flower. Refining magical flora and insects was Guyueye's specialty... so...was this Hua Binan?

The moment the name crossed his mind, Mo Ran thought of Shi Mei and felt his chest burn with hatred. But before he could attempt an answer, the man turned around.

The cave was dim, but the newcomer's face was so exquisite it seemed to light up the space. His hair, usually left loose down his back, was now bound in a high ponytail, with an embroidered ribbon tied neatly across his forehead. Below it, those peach-blossom eyes gleamed, as bright and clear as ever.

Everything about his appearance and aura was almost unrecognizable; not a trace of gentleness remained. Here was a beauty beyond compare, but Mo Ran felt as though a thunderclap had gone off in his head. His voice was like an arrow piercing the silence as he sputtered in terror, "Shi Mei?!"

Shi Mei... It was *Shi Mei*!

The breathtakingly lovely man before him tucked a stray lock of hair behind his ear. "A-Ran, are you so surprised to see me?" he asked mildly.

Mo Ran's mind seemed to stall as blood surged through his veins. His head buzzed. Why would Shi Mei suddenly show up here—why would he behave so strangely? He was rigid with shock, his throat clogged with a flood of words. At last, he tentatively managed, "Your eyes..."

"They're unharmed." With a small smile, Shi Mei walked toward Mo Ran. "I came here to see my beloved. Who'd like me if I were blind and ugly?"

As Shi Mei spoke, Mo Ran attempted to slowly gather his wits, but his astonishment was like a storm cloud obscuring his thoughts. "You..." he muttered. "How are you here. What about Hanlin the Sage?" He felt a surge of fury. At last, he understood how Xue Meng must've felt in the past life: There was nothing more painful than being betrayed and used by someone close to you. "What about Hanlin the Sage?!"

"Oh—about him." Shi Mei laughed. "There'll be plenty of time for me to explain later." He walked forward, step by step, until he was standing right beside Mo Ran. "After so many trials and tribulations, I'd rather have a heartfelt conversation with my beloved before I talk about Hanlin the Sage," he said with a smile.

Gripped by fury and dread, Mo Ran's face grew ashen. "What kind of conversation are the two of us supposed to have?"

That elegant man let out a silvery laugh. "Hm?" He fixed his eyes, softly shadowed as if wreathed in mist, on Mo Ran's face. "The two of us? The two of us are like oil and water. Indeed, we have nothing to say to each other."

Hem trailing over the ground, he stepped over to Chu Wanning.

Before Mo Ran could process what was happening, Shi Mei had extended a slender, well-proportioned hand to caress Chu Wanning's cheek.

Mo Ran's mind went blank; he couldn't seem to grasp what this action signified.

Gazing down at Chu Wanning, Shi Mei murmured to him as if Mo Ran wasn't there at all. "That oaf must've really hurt you. Poor Shizun... Then again, you'll remember your other life soon, won't you?" Shi Mei brushed a delicate finger over Chu Wanning's bottom lip and narrowed his eyes. His features were as lovely as ever, but he radiated danger, like poison wine. "No harm in remembering though. Even now, I'm not sure why you went to all the trouble you did. At least we can share strategies after you wake up."

He paused and smiled. "In the past lifetime, you stopped at nothing to achieve your goals and heartlessly bullied your disciple. Had anyone else tormented me so, I wouldn't be satisfied killing them a hundred times over. But though you opposed me, I adore you all the same."

He shot Mo Ran a glance, then leaned down and pressed a kiss to Chu Wanning's cheek. Lowering his gaze, he heaved a sigh. "Why did I have to fall in love with you, my dear shizun?"

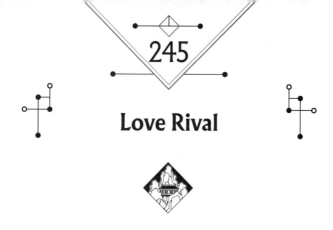

Love Rival

MO RAN STOOD UNMOVING, the shock going through him like a lightning strike. No way, no way... What was Shi Mei saying? What was Shi Mei *doing*? What the hell was going on?!

He was flabbergasted. It didn't seem real that Shi Mei had just kissed Chu Wanning—the sight was so horrifying he wondered if he'd hallucinated it. He brought a hand to his forehead, temples throbbing. Shi Mei's gentle smile from years ago flashed through his mind; he could almost hear him call out softly: *A-Ran.* But the man before him... He was actually...

All the hairs rose on Mo Ran's neck.

The one Shi Mei loved...was Shizun? But how?

Shi Mei had never shown any signs of having feelings for their shizun; it would be more believable if Xue Meng confessed he had a crush on Chu Wanning. How could Shi Mei be in love with him? He was polite and respectful, and hardly ever said a word more than necessary to Chu Wanning, much less clung to him or sought his attention. As soon as class ended, as soon as he finished his tasks, he promptly and properly took his leave...

How?!

Shi Mei straightened up. He cast a glance at Mo Ran and laughed softly. "I seem to have caused someone quite a fright."

"You're...completely...crazy..."

"Crazy?" Shi Mei's tone was conversational. "My dear shidi, you're calling me crazy? Was *I* the one who left Shizun in this sorry state?"

Mo Ran flushed with shame, his eyes swimming with fury and bewilderment. If it had been anyone else, he would've lunged at them without holding back. But the person who stood before him now was Shi Mingjing—the man he thought he'd loved for two lifetimes. All the words he wanted to say were stuck in his throat.

"To be fair, it's not like I've never done anything crazy," Shi Mei continued, unabashed. "For instance, pretending I returned your feelings, being nice to you for so many years. When you used Jiangui to interrogate me all those years ago, I even resisted the pain and lied through my teeth to say...*I like you*." He paused, eyes shining with ridicule. "Be serious. If I'd actually fallen in love with someone like you, with no merits besides a pretty face, I might as well gouge out my own eyes and die."

Met with Mo Ran's stunned silence, Shi Mei asked, "Why so quiet—are you upset?"

His was a beauty that could topple nations—even his sneer was a sight to behold. He shot Mo Ran another sidelong glance before reaching out to stroke Chu Wanning's chin.

Dizzy with rage, Mo Ran moved to summon Jiangui. But there was only a faint scarlet flash in his palm before his spiritual energy sputtered out.

Shi Mei didn't look up. "Don't waste your effort. The past life's Wanning used half his earth soul to uproot this flower for you. His plan succeeded: I'll never be able to control you again. But you'll need at least ten days of rest before you can access your spiritual energy. Trying to fight me now would be foolish."

"Who are you calling Wanning!"

"So you're allowed to take advantage of Shizun like this, but I'm not allowed to simply cherish him? It's hardly fair."

"You—!"

"You've had him so many times." Shi Mei laughed softly. "It's time for me to have a turn. In truth, I do think it's rather beneath me to fuck your secondhand goods. But I'll bear it for his sake."

Mo Ran had no holy weapon, yet he was so angry he started forward, fists raised.

"Ah... You know, there's nothing I despise more than an uncultured thug like you."

Shi Mei released Chu Wanning to block Mo Ran's blows. On the dim walls of the cave, the two men's long shadows flickered and swayed like dueling dragons spitting flames. Shi Mei had never been much of a fighter, and he knew he was no match for Mo Ran hand-to-hand. A flourish of his sleeve sent several spiritual snakes slithering out to bind Mo Ran in place. In that window of opportunity, Shi Mei leapt aside, gathered Chu Wanning in his arms, and dashed toward the mouth of the cave.

"Shizun!"

Mo Ran struggled free of those cold, scaly snakes and pelted after the other two. But when he burst from the entrance, Shi Mei had already leapt into a tree, the moon bright behind him.

"Don't bother," he said, smiling. "You've only just come to. You wouldn't be able to catch me if you killed yourself trying."

"Shi Mingjing, *why*... Why are you doing this?!"

"A-Ran," said Shi Mei, still smiling, "don't you know how much your shige hates the names Shi Mei and Shi Mingjing?"

Mo Ran blinked in confusion.

"If you don't mind, call me by my real name from now on."

"...What?"

"This humble one is surnamed Hua, no courtesy name, given name Binan."

Hua Binan?!

Seeing Mo Ran's eyes fly wide, Shi Mei's smile seemed to grow brighter. "Oh yes. As your shixiong, I'll give you an important piece of advice. Don't go to Guyueye—Jiang Xi will tear you apart. And don't try to follow me either. Be good now and go back to Sisheng Peak."

Mo Ran froze, his face drained of color. "What are you going to do to Sisheng Peak?"

"You're not as dumb in this lifetime after all." Shi Mei laughed. "Shige's prepared a little surprise for you. You'll see when you get there."

Mo Ran tasted blood at the back of his throat, and his eyes burned—whether with sorrow or rage, he couldn't have said. "Shi Mei, what are you trying to do?" he bellowed. "What are you plotting?! Didn't you tell me Sisheng Peak was your home? Didn't you tell me...that you owe your life to Uncle? Didn't you tell me we're the most important people to you in the world?!"

By the end, his voice was shaking, hands balled into fists, nails sinking deep into his palms. "Were you lying this whole time? All these years, in two lifetimes—" Mo Ran's voice caught, a bitter cold seeping into his bones. "Have you been scheming all along...for two whole lifetimes?"

Shi Mei said nothing. His wide sleeves fluttered as he stood high in the tree, gazing down at Mo Ran with a faint smile touching his lips. With his peach-blossom eyes curved into gentle crescents and his daintily pointed chin, he looked like a fox spirit amidst the mist-filled mountains.

"You..." The word rattled between Mo Ran's teeth. His thoughts were a hopeless tangle, his eyes wild with desperation. "Shi Mei, *say something...*"

This man had once consoled Mo Ran beneath the candlelight. They'd later spent so much time together they'd become inseparable.

"Say something!"

Ever since Mo Ran had first met him as a delicate youth, elegant as jade, until the moment he lay in Mo Ran's arms in the snow under the Heavenly Rift, he'd told Mo Ran, *Don't hold grudges, don't blame Shizun.*

Mo Ran was on the verge of shattering. "But you died... I saw it with my own eyes. I brought your body back to Sisheng Peak. You can't be Shi Mei... How could this be possible..."

"Because you're stupid," that refined voice answered at last, dripping disdain. "You imbeciles only ever cared about developing your spiritual cores and never took the medicinal arts seriously. You, the sect leader...even our wise shizun." Shi Mei laughed. "I misspoke—Shizun isn't an imbecile. But people like you have never shown proper regard for elixirs."

"Elixirs..." Mo Ran mumbled.

"It's difficult indeed to bring a dead person back to life," Shi Mei explained. "But there are plenty of ways to make a living person appear dead."

Had Mo Ran's mind been clear, he would've noticed the gaping hole in Shi Mei's story. Even if a substance existed that could simulate someone's death, Mo Ran had stood guard in Frostsky Hall for a full seven days in the past life, then watched as Shi Mei was lowered into the grave. He'd been laid to rest within three nested coffins, each sealed with longevity nails, then buried beneath a thick layer of dirt. How could any living person escape from such a grave by himself without attracting attention?

There were only two possibilities: One, Shi Mei was lying. Or two, that someone in the past life had snuck into Sisheng Peak's graveyard, opened Shi Mei's grave, and let him out after reversing the effects of that drug.

But Mo Ran was a complete mess. An invisible hand seemed to have scrambled his vital organs; he hadn't the strength to consider these details. When he heard Shi Mei's words, that bloodless, lifeless face swam before his eyes once more—

Shi Mingjing had perished in the flying snow. From that day forward, Mo Ran had felt nothing but hatred. Toward himself, for being weak and helpless, and toward Chu Wanning, for standing aside and doing nothing. From then on, he'd stepped into the abyss, falling into darkness.

How was he to know that it was fake—it was all fake!

On behalf of someone who'd faked his death, Mo Ran had spent the second half of his life as a madman, sinking into mindless obsession. He'd wrought carnage across the land and brought about the death of the man who'd loved him more than anyone.

Absurd. It was utterly absurd!

Rage and anguish stabbed through him, his scalp prickling and his pupils contracting. "How...how can you live with yourself?!" he roared savagely.

"Oh, I have no trouble with that," Shi Mei said with a smile. "How can *you* live with yourself, Emperor Taxian-jun?"

These words might as well have grabbed Mo Ran by the throat.

"No matter the reason you had for picking up the knife—whether out of resentment or unhappiness—your hands are covered in blood." Shi Mei tightened his hold on the unconscious Chu Wanning, as if flaunting his spoils of war. "Do you *really* think the blood-soaked hands of the Emperor Taxian-jun are fit to hold those of the immaculate Beidou Immortal?"

The last bit of color drained from Mo Ran's face.

Shi Mei knew his weakness exactly, injecting venom into tender flesh like the sting of a scorpion. He narrowed his eyes dangerously, his gaze finely honed. "Don't tell me you think you're worthy. Wouldn't you agree that you're too dirty? You're a thief."

The wind stirred the branches, and the lambent moon emerged from behind the clouds. Shi Mei's smile never faltered, but every word drew blood like a sharp blade. "Taxian-jun, every day you ever spent with him was stolen. You know better than anyone what scum you are. Surely I don't need to elaborate."

Mo Ran's lips were gray. Rage, sorrow, fear, regret, guilt, unbearable grief—no one could contain so many emotions without succumbing to insanity. "I..."

"Well, that's enough." Shi Mei heaved a long-suffering sigh. "What's the point? Did you really think spending a few years as Mo-zongshi, saving a couple of lives, would be enough to write off all of your sins?" Staring at Mo Ran's face, he laughed softly. "Please."

Mo Ran couldn't speak.

"Shizun has his memories from the past life now. He'll remember everything, all the monstrous things you did—the people you killed, the cities you slaughtered. He'll remember how you wronged him, how you destroyed the sect; he'll remember all the ways you broke his heart." Shi Mei paused, scrutinizing Mo Ran's expression. "Mo-zongshi, it's time to lower your head." He grinned. "Might as well confess to your crimes now and be done with it."

Lower your head. Confess to your crimes...

A lifetime of madness, of untold savagery—none of it justified.

Mo Ran's throat bobbed. He fixed scarlet eyes on the man in the tree, but as soon as he caught sight of Chu Wanning, limp in his arms, an uncontrollable anguish welled up in him. His gaze shrank back and withered, like a dry blade of grass. He jerked his head aside.

"Think about it. Once he wakes up and realizes how long you've been lying to him...how angry will he be?" Shi Mei stroked Chu Wanning's face, running a delicate finger over the corner of his mouth. "You know Shizun's temper—do you imagine he'll forgive you?"

Shi Mei spoke with deliberate malice, and Mo Ran felt like he'd fallen into an icy crevasse.

Forgive him?

Mo Ran's wishes had never been extravagant. Yet he'd always hoped his trial might never come; he'd never dared to think what this day might be like when it arrived. He squeezed his eyes shut, lashes quivering.

Shi Mei's voice was cool and ethereal over the hazy peaks and valleys, like a deity commanding a mortal to seek repentance. "Give up and go back to Sisheng Peak. When you get there, you'll find the surprise I've left for you." His words seemed to swirl around Mo Ran and echo in his ears. "Try to enjoy it; don't put up too much of a fight."

Then, as if something else had occurred to him, Shi Mei paused, fixing his peach-blossom eyes on Mo Ran standing below. "Besides, A-Ran, the two of us are not the same. You could never understand what I want." His tone was mild, no different than when he'd asked Mo Ran if the wontons were good, if there was enough chili oil. "I'm not as ruthless as you are; I wouldn't hurt my friends so rashly. But..." Shi Mei let his voice trail off.

Mo Ran's head jerked up. "What are you going to do?!"

Seeing Mo Ran's gaze flit over to Chu Wanning again, Shi Mei laughed. "Don't worry. I'll look after Shizun; I'd never hurt him. I know better than you how to cherish someone as pure and pristine as him." Every word was soaked in syrupy sweetness.

Mo Ran trembled from head to toe. If he'd had his spiritual energy, he would've long since torn Shi Mei limb from limb. But his spiritual energy was depleted, and Shi Mei knew he could do whatever he pleased.

Shi Mei snickered. "But as for my sectmates at Sisheng Peak, Aunt and Uncle...and the young master." Eyes gleaming, he said carefully, "If you don't deal with my surprise properly, I fear you'll bring about their deaths a second time. Consider this—if Shizun wakes up and finds out you let everyone die, that you put yourself first again, do you think he'll ever spare you another glance?"

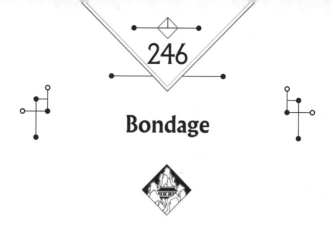

246

Bondage

"SHI MINGJING!" Mo Ran seethed, eyes blazing.

Shi Mei's sleeves fluttered gracefully in the moonlight. Perched in that tree, his handsome features were limned in silver. "Time to go, before Shizun wakes up. If he sees us fighting, he won't be happy." After a moment, he added with a smile, "Oh right. Next time we meet, A-Ran, remember to call me Hua Binan. Shigong[1] would also do. If there is a next time, that is."

With that, Shi Mei leapt nimbly into the air and vanished into the dense forest of Dragonblood Mountain. All that lingered was his lovely, chilling laughter, trailing behind him like a glittering web of gossamer.

"Shi Mei! *Shi Mingjing!*"

He didn't turn to look back at Mo Ran between the branches and the mist. Holding Chu Wanning in his arms, he flew swiftly through the craggy landscape, cloak whipping behind him and robes floating on the wind. His eyes shone as an indescribable satisfaction flooded his chest. He was like a hunter returning home, laden with his spoils and awaiting his victorious feast.

Yet as he leapt from the ground, he heard the man in his arms, besieged by the nightmares of another life, murmur hoarsely, "Mo Ran..."

---

1 *Husband of one's shizun.*

Shi Mei's smile stiffened. He lowered his lashes, his ardent gaze turning cool. "Why would you go to such lengths for his sake—what's so great about him?"

Chu Wanning couldn't hear. He was burning up with fever, his handsome face pale as ice, bluish veins visible beneath his skin. "Mo Ran..." he mumbled once more.

Shi Mei jerked to a stop. After holding himself back for so long, his eagerness and impatience were almost overwhelming. Yet after a moment's struggle, he again managed to restrain himself. Before the unconscious Chu Wanning, he was not nearly as cavalier as he'd been in front of Mo Ran. Staring down at Chu Wanning's face, he eventually said, "Stop reminiscing. Soon Mo Ran will be gone forever. In the future, you can keep me company instead."

After a pause, he continued, "I know your feelings for him run deep. It's all right if you can't forget him yet. Once my plans come to fruition and I can give you my full attention, you'll come around."

Again, Shi Mei flew skyward. Summoning his sword mid-leap, he sped toward the heroes' tomb on Mount Jiao.

The hour was late. In the silent burial grounds of Rufeng sect, the moonlight fell upon row after row of gravestones. Xu Shuanglin's Zhenlong chess pieces, no longer animated by spiritual energy, stood stiffly in place, never to move again.

Shi Mei opened the doors on Mount Jiao with the Nangong blood he'd collected in a vial. Glancing about, he spotted Nangong Liu woolgathering on a small hill.

Nangong Liu wasn't a complete pawn; he still retained some of his original personality. But his faculties of reason were gone; at best, he had the mind of a five-year-old child. Shi Mei had no plans to kill him. On the contrary, he thought the man might still prove useful.

"Dear friend-gege, you're back!" Nangong Liu broke into a sunny grin when he saw Shi Mei, his portly features seeming to glow with genuine delight. Since Xu Shuanglin had considered Shi Mingjing his dear friend, Nangong Liu had followed his lead, resulting in this childish moniker.

Shi Mei hesitated slightly, narrowing his eyes. "Don't call me that."

"Ah..." Nangong Liu was taken aback. "You don't like it?"

"I don't. Call me Hua Binan," Shi Mei said, sullen. "Come, walk with me and help me open the doors."

"Where does dear friend-gege wish to go?"

Shi Mei eyed him. Perhaps there was no point in bickering with someone who was mentally little better than a toddler. "Take me to the hidden chamber where Xu Shuanglin used to live," he answered impatiently.

Nangong Liu readily obliged. Shi Mei knew how to get to the hidden chamber, but there were many barriers along the way that required the blood of a Nangong to pass. It was a hassle getting the little vial of blood out each time with Chu Wanning in his arms— much simpler to let Nangong Liu take the lead.

After walking ahead of Shi Mei for some time, Nangong Liu suddenly turned around, apparently overcome by curiosity. "Dear friend-gege, are you having a sleepover with your friend?"

"A sleepover?" As if pleased by the word, Shi Mei's expression relaxed into a smile. "More or less, yes. But he'll spend many, many nights here in the future. You could say he'll be living here."

Nangong Liu's curiosity was further piqued. "Who is he?"

Shi Mei considered the question, then laughed. "You really want to know? I'm afraid it's not appropriate for a child's ears."

Nangong Liu's eyes grew round, the naïve expression on his middle-aged face at once comical and mildly revolting.

They arrived at the chamber and opened the door. The room inside was simply furnished, lit with everbright lanterns. A bed stood against one wall, spread with a thick tiger's pelt beneath a snow-silk canopy. The only other items were a small table and a harp beside the bed. Shi Mei settled Chu Wanning upon the bed, then took a seat on the edge of the mattress, gazing intently at his shizun's face. The bright glow of the lanterns fell over Chu Wanning's familiar features.

When he was awake, those sword-straight brows drew sharply down from his temples, and those phoenix eyes were proud and steely. Yet now, his features held a weariness, the curve of his jaw like a tendril of smoke from dying embers.

But Shi Mei didn't mind. Far more important was that, after two lifetimes of toil, both Chu Wanning and Mo Ran had fallen before his schemes. At that very moment, Chu Wanning was lying next to him, and Mo Ran had lost his spiritual energy and was about to obediently walk into the trap Shi Mei had laid. His plans were all about to succeed.

"Eh?" Nangong Liu piped up, shattering Shi Mei's reverie. "He looks so familiar."

Shi Mei shot him a sidelong glance. "Do you remember who he is?"

"Remember...?"

"This gege once scolded you," Shi Mei prompted. "He embarrassed you."

"Huh? Where?"

"In the main hall of Rufeng Sect."

"Ah, really?" Nangong Liu exclaimed in surprise. "Why don't I remember it at all?"

Shi Mei was silent for a moment, then smiled gently. "It's better that you don't."

The implication went completely over Nangong Liu's head. He gazed at Chu Wanning for a while longer, head cocked, then pronounced, "He's so handsome though. Even when his eyes are closed and he's not smiling."

"He's Emperor Taxian-jun's favorite consort," Shi Mei replied cheerfully. "How could he be anything but handsome?"

"Favorite consort... What does that mean?"

Shi Mei's eyes danced with amusement. "You'll understand when you grow up. Go pick some tangerines for me, and heat up some water. Knowing his temper, he'll be furious if there's nothing good to eat when he wakes up."

Nangong Liu went to the door, only to pause on the threshold.

"What's wrong?" Shi Mei asked.

"The tangerines..." Nangong Liu hesitated, biting down on his finger. "Dear friend-gege, do you know when His Majesty is coming back?"

He was referring, of course, to Xu Shuanglin. Shi Mei had no plans to tell Nangong Liu that Xu Shuanglin was dead. "Just be good and listen to me for now," he said with a smile. "His Majesty will be back very soon."

Nangong Liu's eyes lit up at once. Slinging a little bamboo basket over his shoulders, he left the chamber to pick tangerines.

Shi Mei gazed at the closed door; after a moment, he laughed. "Interesting. When he had his wits about him, he despised his brother, but now he's filled with brotherly affection... Just goes to show it's only kids who are pure. Once they grow older and begin to scheme and vie for power, they all become filthy."

He turned toward Chu Wanning and caressed his cheek. "See, the cultivation realm is full of people like this. They're not worthy of your protection." His fingertip traced over that handsome visage, and he sighed. "Why did you suffer so much for these people? Why did you toil endlessly, fracture your souls, rip open space and time, endure untold humiliation... Why did you battle me for two lifetimes, all for their sake?"

Chu Wanning, still fast asleep, did not answer. He was tormented by the anguish and nightmares of the past life, his cheeks burning, brow tightly furrowed. Shi Mei watched him with his chin in his hand. After a time, he took out a silver bottle of Tapir Fragrance Dew from his qiankun pouch.

"Drink some of this." Shi Mei uncapped the bottle. "I was certain you'd dream of the past lifetime. Back then, at Xuanyuan Pavilion, I knew you would come, so I instructed the auctioneers to bring out the Tapir Fragrance Dew... I merely wanted to soothe your discomfort without raising suspicion. See, isn't it nicer to be with me than Mo Ran? As long as you make me happy, I'll let you enjoy little trifles like this every day. What can he give you? He only knows how to knock people around."

He poured the sweet-smelling dew into a small porcelain bowl, then brought it to Chu Wanning's lips and watched him swallow. Shi Mei gazed at his war prize for a while, entranced. An idea occurred to him, and his eyes brightened. He rummaged around in his qiankun pouch and pulled out a pitch-black silk ribbon. He tied it around Chu Wanning's head and secured it with a binding spell so that his eyes were completely covered.

He slowly rose. Grasping Chu Wanning's jaw, he examined his face with an air of satisfaction. "Mn, beautiful indeed. No wonder Mo Ran liked to look at you tied up like this in the past life. I don't mind following his example from time to time—I admit he's got taste when it comes to such things."

Shi Mei's smile was as sweet as ever. His fingers trailed from Chu Wanning's chin up to his lips, then the bridge of his nose, finally landing on that black ribbon over his eyes.

"Shizun, wake up soon, won't you?" he said softly, his tone chillingly tender. "I just thought of a fun game. Once you're awake, we can play it together, okay?"

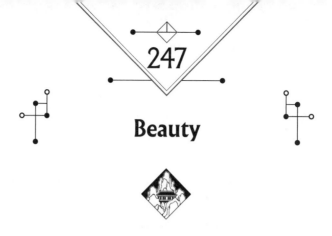

247

Beauty

CHU WANNING THOUGHT he was lying on a bed somewhere, his head heavy. At times his awareness would clear, only to soon grow hazy again.

He had seemed to hear two people arguing. It sounded like Shi Mei and Mo Ran. Then their voices faded, and his ears were filled with the whistling of the wind.

Later, he seemed to be lying under a warm blanket as someone spoke to him. Their fragmented voice sounded like it was coming to him across a vast ocean. He made out one word here and another there—something about a past life, and a shizun. He thought this person, too, sounded like Shi Mei, but he had no energy to ponder it further. Their speech quickly dissolved into nothingness, like morning mist.

Slowly, his memories filled out and sharpened. His recollections of the past lifetime swelled like rainwater flowing into a river, ultimately rushing into the sea.

The first place he dreamed of was a long, shady veranda on Sisheng Peak, behind the Red Lotus Pavilion. Flowering wisteria vines wound over the roof of the corridor, their fragrant petals falling like snow whenever the wind rose.

He was sitting under the awning, writing letters at a stone table. They were letters he had no way of sending. Emperor Taxian-jun didn't permit him contact with anyone outside the palace, nor was he allowed to keep pigeons or any other animals. The Red Lotus Pavilion was enchanted with countless alarm sigils to ward off any possible escape. Yet Chu Wanning continued to write.

It was a lonely existence. In this corner of the world there was only him, and he'd probably live out the rest of his days the same way. To say it wasn't depressing would be a lie.

He addressed his letter to Xue Meng. There wasn't much to write: He asked about recent happenings, whether Xue Meng was well, about circumstances on the outside, how his old friends were doing.

Although, to be fair, Chu Wanning really didn't have any old friends left.

He wrote slowly over the course of an afternoon, but the content of his letter amounted to nothing much. Toward the end, his mind began to wander. He found himself reminiscing about the peaceful days when he had three little disciples by his side. How he'd once taught them to hold a brush, to write poetry, and to paint.

Xue Meng and Shi Mei were both quick studies, but Mo Ran would still make mistakes after practicing a character three or four times. Chu Wanning had needed to guide his hand with his own to teach him properly.

What did they write back then?

As Chu Wanning sat lost in thought, his hand moved, and the ink flowed from his brush onto the fine writing paper.

First he wrote, *The body is the tree of enlightenment, the heart is the bright mirror's stand.*[2] Then, *The lives of mortals have no roots, floating about like dust on the road.*[3] One stroke after another, not a single line

---

2 Verse first attributed to the Tang dynasty Buddhist leader Yuquan Shenxiu.
3 From the first poem in a collection called *Twelve Miscellaneous Poems* by Tao Yuanming, a poet from the Six Dynasties period.

out of place. Regardless of what he wrote, his characters were crisp and carefully composed. He wanted to ensure those reading would be able to understand; he didn't want to set a bad example for his disciples. His handwriting resembled his person—straight-backed and proud.

He wrote, *I know not where those dear to me remain,* and *The seas are vast, the mountains distant.*[4]

The wisteria vines trembled in the wind, their petals landing on the paper. He didn't have the heart to brush them away. Gazing at those lovely scraps of pale purple, his brush moved again: *As late spring sheds the color of haitang, I remember the bygone warmth of gentle rain.*

The words rose and fell under his brush as the meter ebbed and flowed.

If I were a star and you a moon, we could shine together every night.[5]

As he wrote, his gaze unconsciously softened, as if he had returned to the serenity of yesteryear.

The wind picked up again, rustling his papers. The pages he hadn't weighed down flew into the air and scattered across the ground dappled with afternoon sunlight. Chu Wanning set down his brush and sighed. He knelt to collect the papers containing his letter and verses of poetry.

The pages had landed on the grass and steps, drifting over the fallen petals and withered twigs. He was about to reach for one among the scattered flowers when a strong, slender hand reached out and grabbed it first.

"What are you writing?"

---

4   *Two verses from the poem "Jade Butterfly" by the Song dynasty poet Liu Yong.*
5   *Verse from the poem "Chariot Journey" by the Southern Song dynasty poet Fan Chengda.*

Caught off guard, Chu Wanning straightened. Before him stood a tall, handsome man. Emperor Taxian-jun—Mo Weiyu—had at some point made his way into the pavilion.

"Nothing," said Chu Wanning after a pause.

Mo Ran was dressed in luxurious robes of black and gold and wore a nine-tasseled crown. On one of his pale, elegant fingers sat a dragonscale ring. He had apparently just returned from court. Mo Ran glanced coolly at Chu Wanning, then shook out the fine writing paper in his hand and scanned it. His eyes narrowed. "I hope you may greet these words with a smile, for writing is akin to reuniting'..." After a beat of silence, he looked up. "What does this mean?"

"Nothing really." Chu Wanning reached for the letter, but before he could take it, Mo Ran blocked him.

"Oh no you don't," Mo Ran said. "What're you getting all anxious for?" He looked down and read a few more lines, then said drily, "Oh, you're writing to Xue Meng?"

"I was only writing out of idleness." Chu Wanning didn't wish to implicate anyone else. "I wasn't planning to send it."

Mo Ran snorted derisively. "You couldn't even if you wanted to."

There was nothing for Chu Wanning to say. He turned to tidy away the ink and paper on the table. To his surprise, Taxian-jun followed him. With a snap of his black and gold sleeve, he slapped a hand over the page Chu Wanning was about to pick up.

Chu Wanning looked up, his phoenix eyes fixing on Taxian-jun's frowning face. He hesitated, then thought, *Forget it. Let him have it if he wants.* Chu Wanning reached for another piece of paper, only for Mo Ran to pin that one in place too.

Mo Ran continued confiscating all the pages Chu Wanning tried to take until Chu Wanning ran out of patience. Unable to guess what lay behind Mo Ran's bizarre antics, he lifted his lashes and said through gritted teeth, "What do you want?"

"'I hope you may greet these words with a smile, for writing is akin to reuniting.' What does it mean?" Mo Ran stared at him, eyes dark, thin lips parted slightly in expectation. "Explain."

Beneath the scattered light and shadow, as the blossoms and leaves swayed gently on the vines, Chu Wanning couldn't help but recall Mo Ran as he had been years ago, when he'd just become his disciple. Mo Ran had smiled and spoken so softly back then, asking him deferentially, *Shizun, what does "the body is the tree of enlightenment, the heart is the bright mirror's stand" mean? Shizun, could you teach me?* In comparison, the present Taxian-jun's brusque manner sent a twinge of pain through Chu Wanning's chest. He let his head fall and closed his eyes without answering.

Chu Wanning's silence served to further dampen Taxian-jun's mood. He lifted page after page from the table, his eyes narrowing dangerously as he read on. This man, who had come up with a reigning title that sounded like "Year of Cock," muttered to himself, exhausting all his wits as he peered at the words on the paper. At last, glum, he swept all the letters off the table onto the ground and looked up coldly. "Chu Wanning, you miss him."

"I do not." Chu Wanning had no interest in bickering with Taxian-jun and turned on his heel to leave. Before he could take a single step, he felt a hand yank his sleeve and another snap viciously around his chin. The world spun before his eyes.

When it righted itself, his back was flat against the stone table. Mo Ran's grip was so strong and unrelenting that bruises were already purpling across Chu Wanning's cheeks. Sunlight glimmered through the vines and into Chu Wanning's eyes, which reflected

Taxian-jun's distorted face. His features were handsome, bone-pale, and sparking with heat.

Emperor Taxian-jun knew not the meaning of shame; he began to paw at Chu Wanning's robes right out in the open. For him to pin Chu Wanning against the table could mean any number of things, but this forceful disrobing narrowed the possibilities to one. Chu Wanning's humiliation made him furious. "Mo Weiyu!" he yelled.

The rage and despair in his voice did nothing to quell the fire in Mo Ran's loins. On the contrary, they were like a ladleful of hot oil that sent the flames roaring higher. When Mo Ran entered him, Chu Wanning only felt a searing pain. He refused to cling to Mo Ran's back. He could only grip the edge of the table with spasming fingers, gasping roughly for breath. "You beast..."

Mo Ran's eyes seemed shrouded in bloody mist. He was unfazed at being called a beast, only leering down at Chu Wanning. "Fine, don't explain those words," he said. "This venerable one shouldn't have asked you anyway. You're no longer this venerable one's shizun these days—not by any measure."

His movements were quick and harsh. He chased his own pleasure with single-minded focus, sparing no thought for Chu Wanning's comfort.

"What does Wanning amount to these days?" he gritted out. "You're just a consort, another piece of my personal property... Spread your legs a little wider for this venerable one."

After a time, Mo Ran flipped him onto his stomach. Papers and ink tumbled from the table, and brushes clattered to the ground. Pinned against the tabletop, Chu Wanning's body throbbed with agony, and his eyes were filled with boundless chaos. He looked at those verses before him.

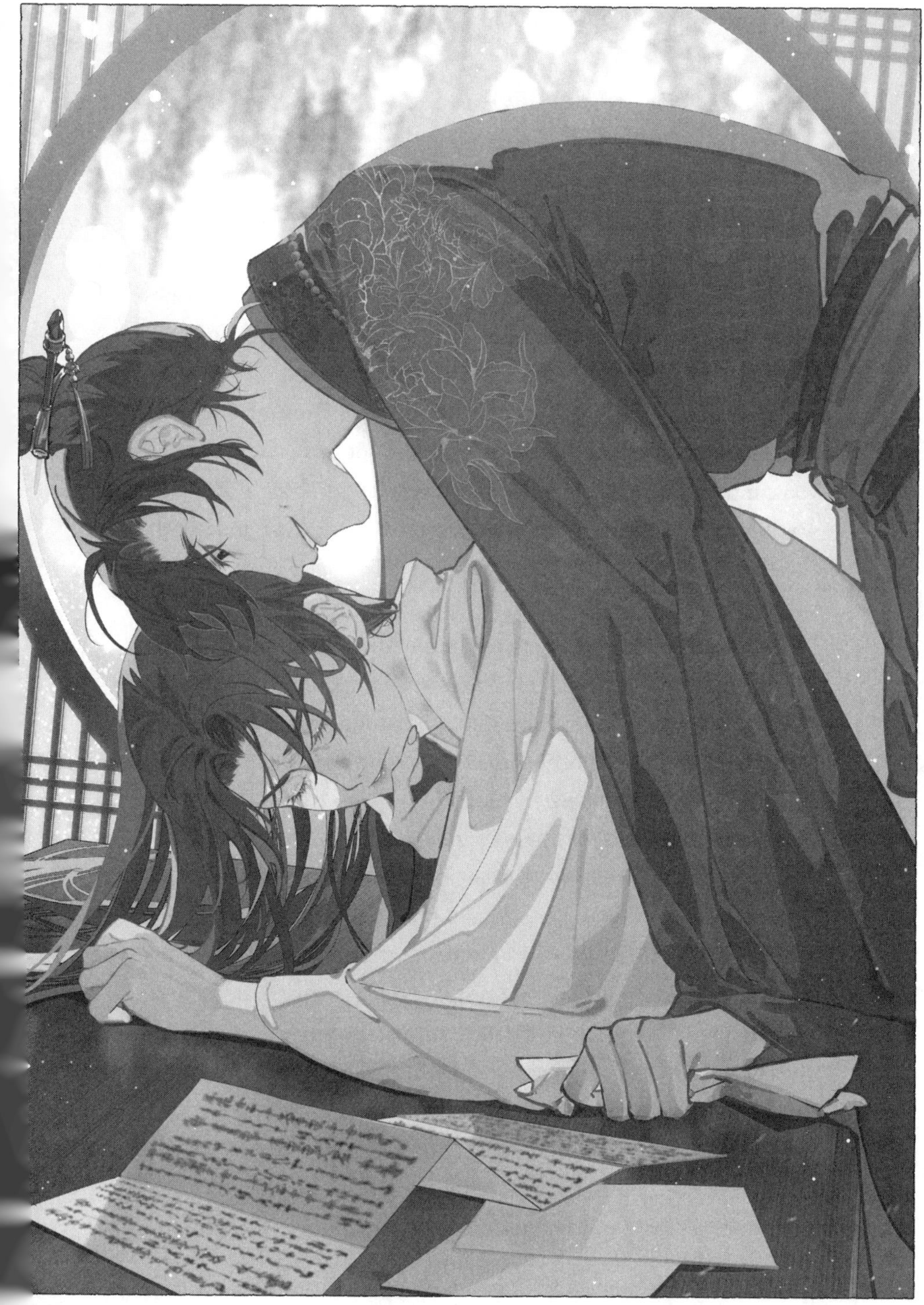

The body is the tree of enlightenment,
The heart is the bright mirror's stand...
I know not where those dear to me remain.
The seas are vast...the mountains distant.
The words were like a condemnation.

He saw Mo Ran as a youth, smiling at him, his dark lashes fluttering like butterfly pea blossoms stained black with ink. But all he heard were Taxian-jun's low pants as he defiled him, rasping: "Chu Wanning... Heh, does this venerable one's Consort Chu have someone else in his heart? What is this about 'If I were a star and you a moon, we could shine together every night'?" Mo Ran's voice was filled with lethal menace. "Did you think I wouldn't understand this?"

Chu Wanning gritted his teeth, splayed on the stone of the table. His flesh was bitten and pinched, red marks blooming across his skin, but his phoenix eyes were stubborn. "You don't understand."

He knew voicing any contradiction would worsen his predicament, but he still stubbornly insisted, *You don't understand.*

You don't understand what it means to have people dear to you. You don't understand why the seas are vast, why the mountains are distant.

You don't understand who's the star and who's the moon.

You...wouldn't be able to understand.

Eventually, that absurd entanglement came to its end, and Mo Ran released him. Chu Wanning's robes were in disarray. He lay sprawled amidst the wisteria petals, surrounded by ink and poetry. The ends of his eyes were stained red, like the lovely color of a rouge flower pinched from its stem. He had bitten his lips bloody.

He sat up slowly and straightened his robes. He'd been a prisoner for such a long time. In the beginning, the pain of captivity had been nigh unbearable. Now, his heart was largely numb. With his core broken, what could he possibly do? All that remained of his so-called dignity was his insistence on dressing himself after the deed was done. He refused to let anyone help.

Meanwhile, Mo Ran sat beside the stone table, poring over those pages of his writing. When he read *As late spring sheds the color of haitang, I remember the bygone warmth of gentle rain*, his hand paused for a moment on the words *gentle rain*—Weiyu, his courtesy name. He quickly flipped the page over. Voice mocking, he said, "You've rotted to the bone, yet your handwriting's still so neat."

He tucked that sheaf of papers into his robes and stood. The breeze whispered over his hems, the gold-embroidered imperial motifs glimmering against the dark fabric. "I'm off."

Chu Wanning said nothing.

Mo Ran looked at him askance. His black eyes, framed by the purple blooms on the vines, seemed even darker than usual. "You won't see this venerable one off?"

Within the shifting shadows, Chu Wanning's voice was hoarse. "I taught you this before," he said slowly.

Mo Ran blinked. "What?"

"'I hope you may greet these words with a smile, for writing is akin to reuniting.'" Chu Wanning finally lifted his lashes to look at that man who stood at the apex of the world. "I taught you how to write it. You're the one who forgot."

"You taught me how to write it?" Mo Ran knitted his brows. He no longer seemed to be toying with Chu Wanning; he looked as if he genuinely had no recollection of such a thing. He had meant to leave, but Chu Wanning's words had stopped him in his tracks. "When?"

Watching him, Chu Wanning said, "A very long time ago." With that, he turned and walked back to the Red Lotus Pavilion.

Mo Ran stood rooted to the spot, neither leaving nor following Chu Wanning inside. When Chu Wanning glanced out the window, he saw that Mo Ran had walked back over to the table and was reading the pages left under the paperweights.

Chu Wanning closed the window.

After the torment he'd endured, coupled with him not knowing how to clean himself properly afterward, he soon caught a chill. His illness wasn't serious, and he didn't think Mo Ran would have cause to find out. When Liu-gong came by, he mentioned Song Qiutong had made a bowl of wontons earlier in the day and somehow managed to send Taxian-jun into a towering rage. Not only did he refuse to stay in the empress's quarters, he had stormed out without touching his dinner.

Deep in the night, a heavy rain began to fall, and a servant came to the Red Lotus Pavilion.

"His Majesty has requested that Chu-zongshi rest in the palace tonight."

All these retainers were more than aware of the relationship between Mo Ran and Chu Wanning, yet they still addressed him as *Chu-zongshi* on Mo Ran's orders. If it wasn't out of some vestigial kindness, then it was out of cruelty.

Chu Wanning felt dreadful. His complexion was wan, and his mood was low. "I won't," he said.

"His Majesty has—"

"I don't care what he has. I'm not going."

The servant had little choice but to leave in silence.

It was no fun going to bed with someone who was unwell. In the past, Mo Ran had never forced himself on Chu Wanning when his health was especially poor. But before long, the same servant returned. While Chu Wanning was beset by a fit of coughing, the servant bowed and said flatly, "His Majesty has requested that Chu-zongshi wait upon him tonight in Wushan Palace, in sickness or in health."

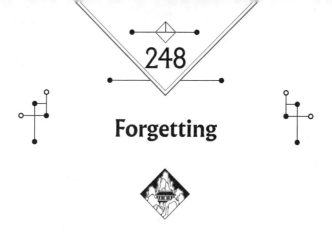

248

Forgetting

CHU WANNING HAD NO CHOICE but to go. He threw
on a thick fox-fur cloak, opened an oilpaper umbrella, and
went to Wushan Palace.

The hall was lit by a forest of branching lamps cast of bronze inlaid
with silver. Ninety-nine flames flickered like a river of stars, filling
Wushan Palace with their radiance. The servants on both sides were
familiar with Chu-zongshi's overnight stays. As he entered through
a side door, they bowed respectfully with eyes lowered. Stony-faced,
Chu Wanning strode down the covered corridor toward the sleeping
quarters in the rear of the palace. When he reached the carved
red-lacquer door, he raised a hand and pushed it open.

The room was stifling—a world apart from the torrential rain
outside—and the air was heavy with the scent of alcohol. Mo Ran
occupied the bed, lying indolently on his side and drinking from a
small jar of red clay that he gripped in jade-white fingers.

"You came." Met with silence, Mo Ran went on, "Sit."

Chu Wanning walked to the bamboo mat farthest away from
Mo Ran and sat down. He closed his eyes.

Mo Ran didn't demand he move closer. He was already several
cups in, his pallid cheeks tinged faintly with pink. His dark irises, so
black they seemed purple, glimmered as he looked sidelong at Chu
Wanning. He took another swig of wine and tilted his head back,

studying the carved dragons and phoenixes on the ceiling as he drummed his fingers against his knee.

"Do you still know how to make wontons?" he asked.

Chu Wanning's lashes quivered minutely. "Not anymore."

"You made them before," Mo Ran said, as if unwilling to accept his answer. "The year... The year he left."

"I didn't make them well." Chu Wanning's expression was impassive. "You weren't wrong to call me a piss-poor copycat."

Mo Ran narrowed his eyes. "Do you hold a grudge against this venerable one?"

"No."

"So, what if this venerable one ordered you to make some right now?"

Chu Wanning didn't answer. Mo Ran stared at him, eyes blazing. "I'm asking you a question. If I told you to make me a bowl of wontons right now, would you?"

"If I did." At last, Chu Wanning opened his eyes and looked coolly at Mo Ran. "Would you eat them?"

The retort caught Mo Ran by surprise; he flushed at once. Whether from the alcohol or rage, his gaze slackened, his eyes losing focus. Jaw clenched, he tossed the wine jar to the floor in front of the table, where it broke, sending exquisite pear-blossom white splashing over the stone. When he got to his feet, his expression was dangerous, like a mountain lumbering upright. Stepping over the shards of broken pottery, he stalked over to Chu Wanning and grabbed him by his collar.

"You're no different from Song Qiutong," Mo Ran said through gritted teeth. "All you do is cause this venerable one displeasure."

He released Chu Wanning and paced like a bird of prey, circling, footfalls roving to and fro until they abruptly came to a stop. He turned to pin Chu Wanning with a glare. "When did you teach me the phrase 'I hope you may greet these words with a smile, for writing is akin to reuniting'?"

Taxian-jun was drunk. There was no rhyme or reason to his questioning; he simply said whatever came to mind. "Why don't I remember it at all?"

An ice-cold hand closed around Chu Wanning's wrist. Mo Ran hauled him upright and dragged him over to the desk. He readied a brush, then unfurled a scroll with a snap. "Write it for me. Teach me again."

Chu Wanning had been feverish when he arrived, and Mo Ran's infuriating demands added to the uncomfortable pressure building within his skull. He sputtered and coughed, face reddening.

Mo Ran thrust the brush into his hand. "Write," he snarled. "Hurry up."

Chu Wanning's health had been fragile since he shattered his core in that decisive battle against Mo Ran. As he doubled over in another fit, he began to cough up flecks of blood. Only then did Mo Ran pause. Staring at those drops of scarlet sinking into the paper, he slowly loosened his grip.

Finally, Chu Wanning took a shuddering breath. "It's a common greeting in a letter," he said. "It doesn't mean anything else." He wiped the corner of his mouth with a handkerchief and, exhaling, looked up at Mo Ran. "You used to begin every letter with this phrase. I suppose you haven't written anything for so long that you've forgotten."

"I...used to write letters?" Mo Ran turned those dark eyes on him. "To whom?" His voice took on an indignant edge. "Who'd I write to? Who in the world could I possibly write to? What a load of rubbish... Bullshit!"

But Mo Ran sounded agitated and despondent, a scattered light jumping in his eyes. It was at that moment that, for the first time,

Chu Wanning had a vague inkling that something was amiss. He didn't linger on the thought—Mo Ran's forgetfulness could be chalked up to his inebriation. He only furrowed his brow without replying.

In the library of Wushan Palace, there was a qiankun box in which all of Sisheng Peak's letters had been filed away. Mo Ran paced in circles like a caged beast until he suddenly remembered that box. Dragging Chu Wanning along with him to the library, he dug out the dusty case and ripped open letter after faded letter.

The majority of the letters had been written by disciples, organized according to the elders they'd studied under. Most of the writers had perished when Mo Ran betrayed the sect. Among all the elders of Sisheng Peak, the Yuheng Elder had had the fewest disciples—only three. Their letters were easily found. Quickly, Mo Ran pulled out a thick stack of pages and tore it open, fingers trembling.

It was indeed his handwriting—immature and crooked, but shockingly earnest. He flipped through letter after letter. On each one was written *I hope you may greet these words with a smile, for writing is akin to reuniting.* Every single letter, without exception.

Mo Ran's hands were shaking, his eyes flashing with an inconstant light.

Mom, I hope you may greet these words with a smile, for writing is akin to reuniting.

Xun-jiejie, I hope you may greet these words with a smile, for writing is akin to reuniting.

Those bygone greetings sent a shiver down his spine. His face took on a dangerous cast, his handsome features shadowed by dark storm clouds.

Chu Wanning stood to the side, indifferent, until Mo Ran's turbulent expression finally began to make him uneasy. At last, he couldn't help fixing his gaze on that man frantically riffling through old letters before the writing table. Chu Wanning felt a twinge of foreboding, as if a tiny bird pecked at his heart. He slowly paced closer, studying Mo Ran's bewildered, manic expression. Something wasn't right.

But what?

"My mom was already dead..." Mo Ran mumbled, looking up at Chu Wanning. "Why would I write letters to her?"

Chu Wanning scrutinized him carefully, that pricking sense of dread now boring through his chest, like a terrible darkness ready to blot out the sun and swallow him whole. It was bizarre that Mo Ran would forget a common salutation, yet it wasn't impossible. But for him to have no recollection of writing any of these letters was truly inexplicable.

Mo Ran was still skimming through those pages. *I hope you may greet these words with a smile... I hope you may greet these words with a smile...* His violet-black irises glinted with torment. He seemed to be missing an entire swath of memories.

Chu Wanning could almost hear the sound of something shattering in his ears. He held his breath, spine tingling. In the silence of the deserted library, Chu Wanning hesitated, then asked softly: "Don't you remember? Back then, you said even though your mom couldn't get your letters, you still wanted to write to her."

Mo Ran jerked his head up. Chu Wanning felt as though his blood was slowly turning to ice in his veins. "The first thing you learned to write wasn't your own name," he said.

Staring at him blankly, Mo Ran asked, "What was it?"

"The first word you had me teach you was 'Mom.'"

The thunderstorm raged overhead, the shrieking wind like devils dragging their talons over the windows, rattling the latticework. A forking bolt of lightning threw their surroundings into sharp relief.

"You taught me?" Emperor Taxian-jun mumbled. "Why don't I remember... I don't remember that at all."

The trees creaked and swayed in the wind. Vengeful ghosts seemed to swarm over the mountain and through the courtyards. Chu Wanning's face was deathly pale as he watched Mo Ran like a hawk. "You don't remember anything?" His heart drummed relentlessly in his chest.

A brief silence. Then Mo Ran answered him with a baffled question of his own: "Anything about what?"

The drum halted. In that minute, fear broke through its shell at last. An all-consuming terror roared toward him, a dark tidal wave bearing down on the only person in the room who was truly awake. Chu Wanning's scalp was prickling. *He forgot? How could he possibly forget?* Not only had Mo Ran said he wanted to write to his mother—he'd written more than three hundred letters all told. He'd said he wanted to write a thousand, which he would burn during the Ghost Festival[6] so they could reach his mother in the underworld... How could he forget three hundred letters, just like that?

Chu Wanning's lips quivered as a terrifying thought rose in his mind. "Do you remember...what you said when you saw Tianwen for the first time?" he asked hoarsely.

"What I said?" repeated Mo Ran. "That was so long ago. How could I remember something like that?"

"You said you wanted a holy weapon just like it," Chu Wanning said. "You wanted your own Tianwen..."

"What would I want a Tianwen for?" the drunken man asked mockingly. "To murder people, or to interrogate them?"

"The earthworms," Chu Wanning murmured.

---

6 Traditional holiday featuring ritualistic offerings from the living to the deceased to pay respects.

Outside the Red Lotus Pavilion all those years ago, that tender youth had held up an oilpaper umbrella and said to him cheerfully, *I can use it to save the earthworms.*

Yet tonight, Taxian-jun narrowed his predatory eyes and asked, uncomprehending, "What earthworms?"

Lightning tore the sky into purple-edged shreds, and thunder cleaved the earth. Chu Wanning pressed his lips together, his dark eyes wavering, pupils contracting. He felt cold—bone-chillingly cold.

Mo Ran didn't touch Chu Wanning that night. After drinking himself drunk, he merely sat, blankly staring at the letters in his hands. At some point, he drifted off at the table, muttering under his breath, "What earthworms...? There were no earthworms..."

A gust of wind blew the window open. Cold wind and rainwater rushed in, extinguishing several lamps near the sill and plunging the room into darkness. Chu Wanning stood beside Mo Ran, teeth chattering, watching him as he slept. The unformed idea coalescing in his mind began to solidify.

How could Mo Ran fail to remember these parts of his past? Why would he willingly forget those innocent days of his youth? Was it because he was drunk? Was it a coincidence?

Or...had someone purposefully erased those memories of kindness from his heart?

Slumped on the table, Taxian-jun muttered, "Cold..."

Chu Wanning's blood was thoroughly chilled; his entire body had gone numb. At this murmured complaint, he automatically walked over to the window. He pulled the shutters closed, blocking out the wind and rain. But he didn't immediately walk away. Still dazed, he pressed his forehead to the window frame carved with bats and deer, his clenched knuckles white as jade.

After a long while, he drew a wrinkled talisman from his robes—the Rising Dragon Talisman.

Chu Wanning's core was gone; Mo Ran hadn't bothered to confiscate his old paper talismans, assuming he couldn't use any magic. He wasn't altogether wrong. Chu Wanning had to squeeze more than a dozen drops of blood from his bitten fingertip onto the talisman—until the paper was nearly soaked—before the little dragon stirred sluggishly to life.

As its weakly glowing form emerged from the talisman, it feebly raised its head. "Ah... Chu Wanning... Long time no see..."

The little dragon could barely stand upright. After taking just a few steps on its flimsy dragon claws, it crumpled to the paper. "Why's it been so long since you've summoned this venerable one?" it asked, sounding hurt and confused. "Why'd you provide this venerable one such a paltry amount of spiritual qi... Hmph, it's really just qi... Not even real spiritual energy... What's going on with you?"

"It's a long story. There's too much to explain." Chu Wanning gently plucked the dragon from the talisman and placed it in his palm. "I'd like to ask a favor."

"Ah, you only ever remember me when you need me," the little dragon wheezed. But its energy was tied to Chu Wanning's; it had no strength to spare for complaints. Head drooping, it said, "Go on—what can this venerable one do for you?"

Chu Wanning carried the dragon over to Mo Ran and placed it on the sleeping man's temple. He clenched his fists, nails digging into his palms as his complexion somehow grew paler still. "Please check if there are any strange spells on him," he said.

The boy who'd once been so easy-going and cheerful, who couldn't bear to see even an earthworm come to harm, had become a monster. As his shizun, why had Chu Wanning never questioned this?

He'd watched with his own eyes as his disciple slew Xue Zhengyong and Madam Wang, and then Jiang Xi and Ye Wangxi. As he massacred Rufeng Sect and crushed the bones of a thousand beneath his heel. He'd watched Mo Ran commit slaughter upon slaughter, blood streaming from his hands, his robes soaked in hot scarlet. Mo Ran, standing upon a pile of corpses, flashing him a hateful grin over his shoulder.

He had grieved it all. But had he ever thought it strange? Mo Ran had never been that kind of person before.

The little dragon toiled over its paper, diligently sketching a spell diagram. Though Chu Wanning thought he had steeled himself for anything, the finished drawing stupefied him.

An affection spell. Mo Ran had been bewitched by an affection spell?

The little dragon had exhausted its last ounce of energy. Its tiny paper form vanished in a puff of dark smoke and reappeared on the talisman. Chu Wanning clutched the diagram, his head ringing as if a rock slide had just crashed through his skull.

He forced himself into calmness and looked over the drawing repeatedly. Something was wrong with the diagram of this affection spell: It was reversed from left to right.

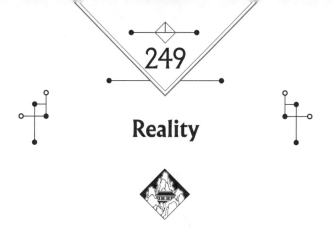

249

Reality

WHEN MO RAN WOKE the next morning, he remembered little of what had happened after he'd started drinking the night before. But what Mo Ran couldn't remember, Chu Wanning couldn't forget.

After that day, he began indirectly probing Mo Ran. He found that Mo Ran had indeed lost many of his memories. Chu Wanning's anxiety compounded. After a long and arduous search, he uncovered a dusty medicine manual in Sisheng Peak's library that identified the spell in question. Beneath the sunlight spilling in from the window, he read, "Flower of Eightfold Sorrows…"

His fingers brushed over the inked drawing in the book. Chu Wanning reached for the little dragon's diagram and laid the pages side by side. They were identical: a black heart, easily mistaken for an affection spell. Only upon close inspection might one notice that the affection spell's heart had a tiny spot of white space on its left side. This one had the same spot, but on the right.

The paper dragon's spell diagrams were meant to reflect the technique's effects. Were this gu flower's effects like those of an affection spell, but likewise reversed?

The book he had dug up was an ancient text of the demon tribe, long abandoned in a corner of this deserted library. He had some cursory knowledge of the script, but reading it was by no means straightforward. He waded through the text a word at a time, a slow and painstaking process. With every sentence he understood, his alarm deepened.

"The Flower of Eightfold Sorrows, a plant of the demon tribe." Chu Wanning's pale lips parted softly around the words. "Legend has it that Gouchen the Exalted brought this flower to the mortal world from the demon realm."

Between the passages a strange-looking seed was depicted, with a drop of blood and a wisp of smoke pictured alongside it.

"The seed is exceedingly difficult to cultivate. It must be nourished on demon blood for ten years, then integrated into the souls of its chosen host to germinate," Chu Wanning muttered. "It requires demon blood and a host soul to grow? But...there shouldn't be any pure-blooded demons left in this world." Perhaps this account wasn't entirely correct or comprehensive.

He continued reading. Painted on the silk was a human heart with a lush flower growing out of its right side. Next to this, in the intricate script of the demon tribe was written: *This demonic flower cannot grow in soil or water; the presence or absence of sun is immaterial. Only a human heart can sustain it.*

Chu Wanning blinked in surprise. This blossom could only flourish when planted in a person's heart?

The further he read, the greater his horror grew. After the Flower of Eightfold Sorrows was sown in the heart of a host, its effects took hold in three stages. In the first, the host would display an inclination toward melancholy and tend to assume the worst of others' intentions, but their behavior would be mostly unchanged otherwise. At the same time, their recollection of their happiest memories would gradually begin to fade. Although the Flower of Eightfold Sorrows was difficult to extract from a host completely, if discovered at this stage, its influence could be suppressed. In the best case, the flower would go dormant and no longer affect the host.

If the flower was not detected during this period, it would take root within the host and progress to the second stage. This could take as long as a decade, though it could be accelerated by a traumatic event. This stage was marked by a rapid loss of the memories associated with innocence, kindness, and hope. The host would ruminate on the obstacles and setbacks they'd encountered, as well as any mistreatment or humiliation they'd suffered. There were eight sorrows in life, and it was for these the flower was named: birth, death, aging, illness, unfulfilled wishes, clashes with enemies, separation from loved ones, and the worldly trappings of the self.[7] The host would dwell on all these, etching their suffering into their marrow.

By the time he came to this passage, Chu Wanning's face was white as frost. Was this not exactly what had happened to Mo Ran? He'd forgotten the dreams of his youth, forgotten every word of the letters he'd written. Even his memories of his own mother were no longer clear.

He read on to the description of the third stage: The host would become bloodthirsty and violent, increasingly irrational... They would seek to avenge all the suffering they had endured a thousand times over.

A figure swam before Chu Wanning's eyes: Mo Ran in Rufeng Sect's sea of blood. Face distorted in a sneer, Mo Ran funneled spiritual energy into his hand and thrust his bare fingers into a cultivator's chest. Blood sprayed as he pulled out the cultivator's heart and crushed it in his grip. He was surrounded by the dead and dying, the air thick with cries for mercy. But Mo Ran threw his head back

---

7   The concept of Duḥkha (suffering, sorrows, unhappiness) is central in Buddhism as one of the three marks of existence, alongside impermanence and "no-self."

and laughed, his eyes flashing with frenzied light. The only thing he said, over and over, was: "Beggars can't be choosers... Beggars can't be choosers!" He was ruthless and deranged, barely human.

How had Mo Ran come to this? In the past, Chu Wanning might have had fleeting moments of doubt, but they had been easily brushed aside. The Flower of Eightfold Sorrows acted gradually, its effects deepening imperceptibly over time. Just as the text described, its violence wasn't senseless or unfounded—this demonic seed magnified the host's own grievances and desires.

In other words, those grievances and desires belonged indisputably to Mo Ran. No one else was responsible for them.

Mo Ran had truly wanted to massacre Rufeng Sect, to rule all under heaven; he'd truly hated and resented Chu Wanning. But these emotions should've lasted a fleeting instant, or else been buried and forgotten as flights of fancy. The Flower of Eightfold Sorrows dug out every scrap of hatred hidden in the crevices of his heart and made them real. Onlookers would think the flower's host insane, but the host's hatred would appear justified. Their personality, too, would undergo no dramatic shift, at least not to the point of seeming like a different person altogether. Those around them would inevitably assume it was their hatefulness that had twisted them, not some outside enchantment. No one would have had reason to suspect that Mo Ran had been implanted with the Flower of Eightfold Sorrows. By the time anyone might have discovered it, the enchantment would likely have progressed to the second or third stage, at which point it was impossible to excise or even suppress the flower.

When he'd read the entire entry, Chu Wanning sank into thought for a long time. What did he feel? Surprise? Regret? Rage? Fear? Or was it grief... He didn't know.

He sat on the dilapidated floorboards in the long-neglected library. The afternoon sunlight streamed in, but it seemed unable to warm his skin. Sitting in his nest of scrolls and volumes, he felt as if someone stood behind him, a person he could neither see nor touch. They were laughing quietly, infiltrating his world like a vengeful spirit, watching his every movement from behind a curtain.

He lowered his head to reread that sentence inked upon the silk cloth—

Although the Flower of Eightfold Sorrows is difficult to uproot, during the first stage, it can be suppressed if discovered in time. If suppressed successfully, the host's heart will remain unchanged.

Chu Wanning recited this sentence to himself many times over. He was startled to discover a few splotches of wetness on the silk, slowly soaking into the fabric. He extended an ice-cold hand, thinking to wipe away those drops. But before his fingers touched the silk, he flinched back; instead, his hand reached up to cover his damp, quivering lashes.

It was he who was no good; it was he who was at fault. He'd always been too aloof, prizing his reputation above all else. He'd never been willing to initiate difficult conversations.

If discovered in time...their heart will remain unchanged.

But he hadn't noticed anything in all those years. The man they called Yuheng of the Night Sky, the Beidou Immortal, had failed to discover the demonic flower planted in his own disciple's heart. Because Chu Wanning was so withdrawn, so bad with words, Mo Ran had been forced onto this lonely road. He had walked into an endless night, into a bloody ocean of vengeance.

How could Chu Wanning have the gall to act as his elder? How could he bear to hear Mo Ran call him *shizun*?

If discovered in time.

That sentence was like a nightmare echoing in his ears—like a curse. He felt as if a thicket of brambles was stabbing into his spine, as if a sharp bone was lodged in his throat, as if his heart was jumping out of his chest—he didn't deserve to be Mo Ran's teacher.

Looking back now, how long had something been wrong with Mo Ran? They'd spent so much time together, not just a matter of one or two years. Mo Ran had once been a bashful yet brilliant boy. Bit by bit, darkness had swallowed him; crimson rain had soaked him to the bone. And Chu Wanning, as his shifu, hadn't realized that anything was amiss until today—not until it was already too late to turn back, too late to change a thing... Chu Wanning's heart was tarnished, his body unmoored, his pain and regret all-consuming— he didn't deserve to be Mo Ran's teacher!

Chu Wanning didn't know how he'd pulled himself together that day, how he'd managed to leave the library and walk into Sisheng Peak's silent bamboo forest. He didn't know how he made his way back to the Red Lotus Pavilion. Beneath the blooming wisteria vines, everything was a mess. He sat by himself until the brilliant day turned into golden sunset.

Someone walked into his field of view.

It was a man's figure, stately and proud, with broad shoulders and a narrow waist. He strolled over the sun-dappled ground, a gleaming wine cup in his hand as he made his way toward the lotus pond. Chu Wanning, lost in his thoughts, couldn't immediately place who he was, or *when* he was. In his eyes, the image of that tall, handsome man overlapped with that of the youth from his memories—

Barely a month after Mo Ran became his disciple, he had cheerfully hurried over to the Red Lotus Pavilion to look for Chu Wanning. He was slightly out of breath from running, his cheeks flushed, eyes startlingly bright. In his hand, he carried a little clay jar in a sling of woven bamboo.

"Shizun, I tried some really delicious wine at the bottom of the mountain. I've brought some back—will you drink with me?"

"You haven't received any assignments yet," said Chu Wanning. "Where'd you get the money?"

Mo Ran grinned. "I borrowed from Uncle."

"Why go to such trouble?"

"'Cause Shizun likes me." Mo Ran smiled and held out the jar in both hands. "I like Shizun too."

Chu Wanning still remembered the awkwardness and embarrassment he'd felt then. This young man expressed himself too ardently. Chu Wanning didn't want to reciprocate; he feared reaching out would get him burnt. He flicked his sleeves and replied curtly, "What does liking me have to do with anything? Don't say such things."

"Oh... All right." Mo Ran scratched his head. "But if I eat or drink something good, I'll definitely think of Shizun. I'll want Shizun to taste it too."

Chu Wanning paused. "I've never had wine before."

This made Mo Ran laugh. "Then you've gotta try it at least once! Who knows, maybe you'll be able to drink everyone under the table."

Chu Wanning pressed his lips together and took the jar. Removing the stopper, he took a tentative whiff. His eyes widened slightly.

"Does it smell good?"

"Mn."

"Ha ha—come on, take a sip!"

So Chu Wanning swallowed a mouthful of wine. It was strong and heady, its rich, complex flavor flooding his tongue. Chu Wanning couldn't help taking a second sip. "Not bad. What's it called?"

Mo Ran broke into a grin. "This is pear-blossom white wine."

It was the first wine Chu Wanning had ever tasted. "Pear-blossom white..." he repeated softly. "A fitting name."

Mo Ran was delighted. "If Shizun likes it, as soon as I start taking missions and getting paid, I'll buy it for you every day!"

Chu Wanning took another sip of wine. Expression perfectly neutral, he turned his phoenix eyes upon Mo Ran. "Then you'll never manage to build up any savings."

"I don't need to," Mo Ran cheerfully replied. "I'll use all my money to buy things for Shizun, and for Uncle and Auntie."

Chu Wanning didn't answer, but he could feel a tiny crack forming in his heart, into which sweetness trickled. He didn't want Mo Ran to notice his happiness, lest he get the impression that the Yuheng Elder could be bribed with a simple cup of wine. He gripped the jar and continued to drink as impassively as ever.

This chatty new disciple often flummoxed Chu Wanning. To everyone else, his cool indifference was like a formidable wall. But this boy happily clambered over this barrier, and was now rubbing the back of his head and looking around in apparent unconcern. Maybe he was an idiot, Chu Wanning mused.

Entirely oblivious, Mo Ran was contemplating what sorts of presents would best demonstrate his respect for his teacher. "Shizun, do you like osmanthus cake?"

"Mm-hmm."

"What about lotus crisps?"

"Mm-hmm."

"Sweet osmanthus lotus root?"

"Mm-hmm."

Cheeks dimpling deeply, Mo Ran laughed. "So Shizun has a sweet tooth."

This time, Chu Wanning was silent. It belatedly occurred to him how his penchant for sweets must appear at odds with his icy demeanor. He took another gulp of wine, a bit too enthusiastic in his irritation. Although the wine was smooth and sweet, it was still quite strong—he choked.

Chu Wanning valued his dignity above all, and choking on wine was too great a humiliation for him to bear. He held back his coughing, but the burning itch in his throat made his eyes and nose redden against his will.

"In the future I'll bring back all the sweets for Shizun." Mo Ran was still waxing poetic about his grand plans, which were becoming increasingly far-fetched. "I'll put together a book of the yummiest food from all over, and then take a trip with Shizun to try everything! And then..." Turning to look at Chu Wanning, his laughter turned into a hiccup of shock. "Shizun, are—are you okay?"

Chu Wanning blinked through watering eyes. Wouldn't it be too ridiculous for a teacher to choke on the wine his disciple had given him? *Stay strong. Don't cough*, he thought to himself. But this only caused his eyes to mist over, and their ends to grow visibly redder.

"Did I say something wrong?" Mo Ran asked helplessly. "Shizun, why do you look like you're about to cry?"

Chu Wanning glared at him, his lashes quivering with silent rage, but Mo Ran was oblivious to Chu Wanning's ire. Struck by a realization, he asked, voice going soft, "Shizun, is it because no one's ever bought sweets for you before?"

At this, Chu Wanning's fury multiplied.

"Actually," Mo Ran continued heedlessly, "there was a time I couldn't get enough to eat and almost starved to death. I ran into a xiao-gege who fed me some sweet congee... I like sweets too, but no one's ever bought them for me either."

The boy had a real gift for projection; somehow, he'd convinced himself Chu Wanning's eyes were red because he was greatly moved. Mo Ran grabbed Chu Wanning's hand.

This was totally outside Chu Wanning's expectations. In all his years—other than touching others' hands to teach them spells—he'd only ever held hands with Huaizui as a child. For this new disciple to grab his hand without warning or inhibition gave him quite a shock. He was on the verge of blowing his top when he looked up and saw his little disciple's handsome, naïve face.

"Shizun," said Mo Ran, all earnestness. "Once I make a name for myself, I'll get so many sweets for you, mark my words." His eyes shone with tenderness. "I'll buy you all the best candy. My mom always told me I have to repay kindness."

Mo Ran had no schooling, and he'd grown up in an entertainment house. His word choices were a bit strange, and sometimes even laughably awkward. All Chu Wanning knew was that Mo Ran's passion had scalded him. He glanced at Mo Ran, then lowered his lashes without a word.

As the wine's sting dissipated, Chu Wanning gingerly cleared his throat. "Don't babble on like this," he said flatly. "Also..." A spark of curiosity. "I want to ask you something."

"Shizun can ask me anything."

Chu Wanning hesitated, then asked with some embarrassment, "There were so many people at the Heaven-Piercing Tower that day. Why did you pick me?"

The boy Mo Ran opened his mouth and said—

But at that moment, Chu Wanning's reverie was broken. Taxian-jun stood facing Chu Wanning, wine jar in hand. Seeing Chu Wanning lost in thought, he reached out and poked him in the forehead. "What's wrong?"

Chu Wanning's pupils slowly refocused upon the Mo Ran before him. This man's complexion was white as bone, his eyes narrowed in a predatory leer. He was handsome as ever, but his good looks couldn't hide the violence etched into his bones. No longer was he that brilliant youth from those early days. All those things were already in the past.

Suddenly, Chu Wanning felt so very tired. In the long years of his imprisonment, he'd never known such debilitating confusion and pain. He was impossibly conflicted; he had no idea how to face the man before him. He turned his face away.

A large, cool hand gripped his chin, forcing him to look forward once more. Chu Wanning's phoenix eyes reflected the last rosy blush on the horizon, the dense shadows of twilight, and Taxian-jun's glowering face.

"You're still angry?"

Chu Wanning closed his eyes and didn't reply for a long beat. "No," he said hoarsely.

"Your fever broke?" Before Chu Wanning could answer, Mo Ran released his jaw and placed a palm against Chu Wanning's forehead. "Mn, it's gone," he muttered under his breath.

Helping himself to a seat, Mo Ran broke the seal on the wine jar and continued, "Now that you've gotten over your fever and your hissy fit, you'll drink with this venerable one tonight."

Chu Wanning couldn't speak. There was an invisible mastermind standing behind Mo Ran. Despite Sisheng Peak's outward serenity, dangers lurked around every corner. He couldn't afford to draw the enemy's attention; he couldn't reveal a single thing.

Mo Ran poured the wine. "Pear-blossom white," he said carelessly. "Your favorite."

Chu Wanning's thoughts stalled as the fragrance of the wine wafted up, a diaphanous barrier between worlds. It was the first wine he'd ever tried. A memory he could never forget. He raised his eyes, watching the man pouring wine. Mo Ran surely wouldn't remember that anymore. Chu Wanning's chest ached dully, and his throat stung. He raised his cup and downed it in one draught.

The wine was fiery. After such a mighty gulp, of course he would choke. He found he no longer cared a whit—in fact, he embraced it, as though grabbing onto a piece of driftwood amidst pounding rapids. He coughed violently, until the rims of his eyes turned red, and finally, until hot tears slipped out from between his damp lashes.

Mo Ran paused, his eyes momentarily widening in alarm. He quickly schooled his expression, lips curving in a methodical grin. "Shizun, what's wrong? What're you crying for?"

Chu Wanning pulled himself together. It didn't matter how painful or unbearable things were; it didn't matter that he knew the truth. There was nothing he could do. As long as he hadn't extracted the Flower of Eightfold Sorrows or found the villain behind the scenes—as long as he was still alive—he had to endure his situation. He had to pretend ignorance, to feign hatred and fury.

He closed his eyes and forced his spine to straighten. "The wine," he rasped.

"The wine's too strong?" Mo Ran asked slowly.

In lieu of answering, Chu Wanning drank another cup. The wine burned a trail of fire to his belly.

Why did you pick me?

His misty eyes drifted open, gazing into the distance. Amidst the evening haze, the Heaven-Piercing Tower rose as tall and regal as ever. But the youth who'd once grinned and replied, *Because I like you—you look the gentlest* was gone forever.

In life, there were eight sorrows. Birth, death, aging, and illness. Separation from loved ones. Unfulfilled wishes. Clashes with enemies. The worldly trappings of the self. Thus eternal regret was born.

There had been so many opportunities for him to uncover the truth, but he'd missed them all. Now that he finally saw how Mo Ran's heart had been corrupted, he was hobbled; he couldn't do a thing.

That night, Chu Wanning watched Mo Ran sleep beside him. His once-innocent face was shrouded behind cold shadows, his skin white as paper.

Chu Wanning had hated him, resented him. When Mo Ran had turned his sword on him, his blood had run cold. When Mo Ran had forced him to submit on his knees, his heart had withered. But in that boundless night, beneath the gloomy bed canopy, Chu Wanning felt that, in the face of the truth, his hatred and resentment, his deadened heart, were so very ridiculous. A gu flower had been planted in Mo Ran's heart. None of the things he'd done reflected his true intentions. The almighty Emperor Taxian-jun had long been shackled and bound.

And although Chu Wanning was his shizun, he was completely powerless. He didn't know how many eyes watched him from behind—he couldn't tell anyone the truth. He couldn't show Mo Ran the slightest hint of compassion or warmth. He had to keep hating and resenting, had to keep his heart walled off and numb.

Deep in the night, behind the curtains in the still and silent Wushan Palace, Chu Wanning waited for Mo Ran to fall into sound slumber. Only then could he sit up and touch Mo Ran's bloodless face. Only then could he whisper, ever so softly, "I'm sorry. It was your shifu who didn't protect you properly."

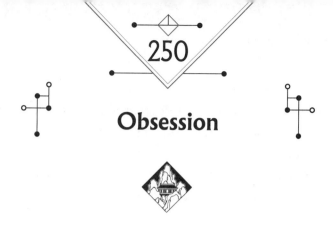

250

Obsession

I'M THE ONE who didn't protect you properly. I let you become someone else's pawn. I let you become a monstrous tyrant.

No one knows who you really are. No one knows you were once kind and innocent. No one knows how you once fretted over the earthworms you couldn't save on a rainy day, how you once smiled brilliantly before a pond of lotuses in full bloom.

Everyone thinks you're cold-blooded and heartless. They don't know you once scratched your head and said bashfully, "It—it's not like I can do anything special. But when I was little, I didn't have a place to stay. When I have money to spare in the future, I'll build lots of houses so people like me have somewhere to live. Wouldn't that be nice?"

Everyone hates you for being a ruthless butcher, but they don't know you once told me, "Shizun, I want a holy weapon like Tianwen. It can tell lies from truth, and it can save lives."

Everyone curses your existence, wishes you'd meet a terrible end. And even though I know the truth now, I still can't give your dignity back to you.

Perhaps Mo Ran was sensitive to being watched, even while sleeping. His eyelids twitched. Before Chu Wanning could react, his eyes snapped open. "You..."

Their gazes met.

"What are you looking at?"

Chu Wanning's emotions were strained to the breaking point. He didn't know how to answer, so he flipped over to avoid Mo Ran's eyes. "Nothing."

Mo Ran didn't reply. After a beat, Chu Wanning found himself drawn into a heated embrace, a broad, firm chest pressed to his back.

In the darkness, Chu Wanning opened his eyes. The canopy fluttered idly before him, while Taxian-jun's body was warm against his back. "You're so cold," Mo Ran remarked. His tone was indifferent; whether out of scorn or indolence, it was hard to say. "But you're sweating."

He nuzzled his face into the crook of Chu Wanning's neck and inhaled. "Did you have a nightmare?" Mo Ran laughed softly, his words slow with drowsiness. "I can smell the fear on you."

Chu Wanning said nothing, but he could feel himself trembling. Not out of fear, but because he was about to shatter under the weight of his pain and guilt. He summoned all his strength, willing himself to keep calm.

At last, Taxian-jun's interest seemed to wane. Mo Ran yawned, gradually growing more alert. He sniffed at Chu Wanning's shoulders and temples, then hummed in satisfaction. "Come to think of it, why do you smell like flowers even when you're sweating?" He sounded amused. "You're like a plant spirit that's cultivated into a human."

Such ridicule would usually earn him a furious retort. But on this night, Mo Ran waited, yet got no reaction at all. Bemused, he sat up and flipped Chu Wanning onto his back. Mo Ran climbed on top of him, his solid bulk pinning Chu Wanning to the bed.

When their eyes met, they left no room for anything but each other.

The hall was lit by only a single guttering candle, its light blurring as it wound its way through layers of gauze. In the gloom, Mo Ran stared down his nose at Chu Wanning's handsome features. Those sword-straight brows remained forbidding above his upturned phoenix eyes and regal nose, as haughty and proud as ever they had been. Yet for some reason, there was something queer about his expression tonight.

"What's wrong with you?" Mo Ran reached out and cupped Chu Wanning's cheek. He felt a tremor ripple through his fingertips. The man beneath him closed his eyes, suppressing an onslaught of unknowable emotions.

Mo Ran found himself jolted fully awake by his own arousal. Whether it was Chu Wanning's knitted brows or his pale, delicate lips, or that face like brittle porcelain... Everything fed the burning hunger in his chest, stoking his urge to conquer. Even so, a gnawing sense of unease stayed Mo Ran's hand. "Seriously, what's wrong with you?"

Chu Wanning opened his eyes, irises glimmering unsteadily beneath lowered lashes. He had no outlet for any of his pain and frustration. At last, he said hoarsely, "How did the two of us...come to this?"

Silence.

"If I could've stopped you earlier, would things be different now?"

Mo Ran didn't answer. He found Chu Wanning's question laughable. After all, he'd triumphed over Chu Wanning so long ago. He'd forced Chu Wanning to wed him, made him his consort, turned him into his plaything. All this was set in stone. What would possess Chu Wanning to suddenly ask such outlandish questions?

Wushan Palace was deserted save for that pair of adversaries lying naked together in bed. The soothing smell of flowers drifted in through the window, dulling Mo Ran's desire to snarl at this insubordinate man. He'd always had far more patience for his Consort Chu than his empress.

He peered down at Chu Wanning's pained expression with renewed interest. The burning itch in his heart sent heat radiating through his chest like a tiny flame. He usually wasn't one to joke, but now he said languidly, "If Wanning had discovered sooner that this venerable one intended to take the throne, how would you have stopped me?" Taxian-jun's fingers trailed downward. Voice alluringly husky, he drawled, "With your body?"

An inscrutable mixture of emotions flitted through Chu Wanning's eyes. Mo Ran's gaze darkened. After a moment, he swore under his breath. He was powerless to resist any manner of temptation from Chu Wanning, intentional or not. There was no warning or foreplay. Like a beast in heat, Mo Ran only lifted one of Chu Wanning's willowy legs and swiftly thrust forward—

His opening was still slick from the last time they'd made love, and his body seemed to remember the sensation of it. Mo Ran slid in easily. Both of them couldn't help a low groan.

Chu Wanning's eyes were misty with unshed tears. He looked at Mo Ran's broad chest and at his handsome face, suffused with fervent arousal. The lovely shape of his full lips parted slightly around his sharp gasps of pleasure...

The eight sorrows, eternal regret—all of these were born of desire. If not for their influence, could this broken body of his still rouse Mo Ran's passion?

He didn't know.

As he and Mo Ran twined their limbs between the sheets, Chu Wanning's heart tied itself in knots. He couldn't muster the strength to struggle as he usually did.

Mo Ran seemed to find the strangeness of his reactions all the more enticing—or perhaps it was simply because Chu Wanning felt even hotter inside than usual from his fever. Mo Ran gathered Chu Wanning in his arms as he buried himself greedily into his pliant body, kissing Chu Wanning's lips over and over. He gripped Chu Wanning's ass, then raised one of Chu Wanning's legs, snapping his own hips fast and hard.

Chu Wanning's emotions were in tatters, and his usual self-control was nowhere to be found. His throat bobbed, low moans leaking unbidden from his lips. This thrilled Mo Ran. Tangled within the disheveled bedding, his labored breaths were low and sensual. "Is it here?" he rasped.

After all the times he'd taken him, Mo Ran should have been intimately familiar with Chu Wanning's most sensitive spots. But Chu Wanning's willpower was such that he rarely made any noise in bed—Mo Ran was not completely certain. He shifted angles and positions several times, gazing down at Chu Wanning's frowning face each time. "Where does it feel best when I fuck you?"

Chu Wanning's world was in shambles. He heard Mo Ran whisper questions into his ear, kissing him, his breaths heavy with an aching urgency, as inescapable as a tempestuous downpour. For the first time, he felt as though he was duckweed floating in a vast river, unable to grasp anything or chart his own course, unable to change a thing. He had never been as helpless as he was on that night.

Though Chu Wanning said nothing, from the trembling of his limbs and the look in his eyes, Mo Ran could tell which position overwhelmed him most. His motions were sharp and forceful, lighting up those nerves within Chu Wanning with every thrust. At first, he bit his lip and stayed silent. Mo Ran began to move with renewed vigor, his balls slapping loudly against Chu Wanning's ass. Fluid seeped from where they joined, making a mess of the sheets...

Mo Ran grabbed his jaw. His hips never stopped moving as his lips sought Chu Wanning's, capturing his mouth in another ravenous kiss.

Chu Wanning's eyes welled with tears. He tried to—wanted to—resist, but for some reason, with that kiss, his willpower evaporated. Helpless, he groaned and panted to the rhythm of Mo Ran's conquest, grabbing at the sheets beneath him as if they were pieces of his shattered pride.

But Mo Ran was relentless. Chu Wanning's legs were shaking, his opening a sloppy mess; he couldn't hold back the whines and soft moans that escaped his lips. As Mo Ran pounded into him with unbridled ferocity, Chu Wanning lost himself completely. He spread his legs wide, toes curling, gasping uncontrollably under the onslaught. "Ah... Nngh... *Haaa...*"

Mo Ran's eyes grew darker still. The louder and more desperate Chu Wanning's cries, the harder Mo Ran fucked him. In the chaos of their joining, the bedframe creaked in protest, and the pillows tumbled to the ground. Neither of them spared a thought for their surroundings. Their lovemaking was too engrossing, almost soul-stirring. They made such a racket that the guards on duty could scarcely look at Chu Wanning the next day without blushing, their gazes furtive with prurient curiosity.

When Mo Ran at last came inside him, it sent Chu Wanning careening over the edge. The sheets were soaked, the air heavy with musk. In all the years he'd been Mo Ran's prisoner, it was the first time Chu Wanning had come just from Mo Ran's cock, without the use of any aphrodisiacs.

Dazed, he heard Mo Ran say, his voice a low rumble, "It's inevitable that we came to this. Do you know why?"

When Chu Wanning said nothing, Mo Ran continued, "Because I've wanted to fuck you for ages." He ran his fingers through Chu Wanning's long, inky hair. "I hated that pretentious, indifferent look on your face. No matter what I did, you never had a single good word to say about it."

Chu Wanning's lashes quivered; Mo Ran's words were like a sharp thorn in his side. Mo Ran had been the ultimate victor, yet he somehow sounded like a jilted bride as he murmured resentfully into Chu Wanning's ear. "No matter how well I did, how hard I worked, you never spared me a glance."

No. That's not true. There was once warmth between us. We shared a jar of wine in a garden; we huddled beneath an umbrella in the rain. But you've forgotten it all, and I can't remind you it happened anymore.

"Don't you see—you're only lying obediently beneath me because I snapped your bones and pulled out your claws." Mo Ran pressed a kiss to Chu Wanning's lips, a manic edge rising in his voice. "I had to become Emperor Taxian-jun to abuse and torment you, to trample you underfoot."

His spent cock throbbed within Chu Wanning, still thick with arousal.

"I don't mind going to hell for the sin of lust if it means I can see you like this right now," Mo Ran said softly. "For such a tantalizing sight, it's worth every torment." He stroked a hand over Chu Wanning's hair, his cock still buried to the hilt in him.

That night seemed to stir something in Mo Ran—afterward, he developed a habit of refusing to pull out, despite knowing Chu Wanning would get sick. An insatiable fire burned in his heart, a beastly desire that couldn't be suppressed. Chu Wanning was the only water that could quench the flames, his only safe harbor.

He wanted to ravage him, then retrace the ruined wreckage of his body with kisses.

As for Chu Wanning, he slowly extricated himself from his debilitating sorrow. Working in secret, he gathered up clues. He knew someone had planted the Flower of Eightfold Sorrows in Mo Ran—but what were they plotting, and what did they hope to accomplish?

Although the demon tribe's text said the flower couldn't be excised in the third stage of its development, Chu Wanning didn't intend to give up. As ever, he was obstinate and unwilling to concede defeat. He refused to bend to fate.

The days passed like this, one after another. Ever since the loss of his spiritual energy, Chu Wanning found himself tiring easily. Having to make sure nobody else discovered his investigations made it worse. It would be nigh impossible to find the mastermind behind the scenes, and the thought of uprooting the flower was pure fantasy. At the same time, the goal of whoever was controlling Mo Ran became more and more clear, for Mo Ran began to study the Space-Time Gate of Life and Death.

"This venerable one won't be able to learn the Rebirth technique."

Chu Wanning remembered watching Mo Ran as he stood before a window, hands behind his back, gazing at a twittering oriole outside. "I looked at the scrolls—only people with a heavy yin aura can use it," he'd said calmly, then glanced over his shoulder at Chu Wanning. "I'll learn the first forbidden technique instead."

"The Space-Time Gate?"

"Naturally."

"...You can't master it."

Mo Ran had merely smiled. "I have to at least try before conceding defeat. Who are you to say what I can or can't do? What do you know?"

Chu Wanning shook his head. "The first forbidden technique defies the natural order of the world. It will rip open a portal between two unconnected universes. The will of heaven has never permitted—"

"What's so great about the will of heaven?" Mo Ran retorted, his eyes languid and unconcerned. "Why would I need its permission? This venerable one has never believed in fate."

Mo Ran thus embarked upon his research. Knowledge regarding the first forbidden technique had been lost for a very long time. Even with all his resources as an omnipotent emperor, Mo Ran managed to secure, after much difficulty, merely a fragment of the ancient scrolls, and even this was still missing the most important passages. Without complete instructions, Mo Ran could only create a Space Gate. He was unable to command both space and time.

More and more, Chu Wanning began to understand why the flower's architect had planted this curse in Mo Ran. Vanishingly few people possessed Mo Ran's astonishingly potent reserves of spiritual energy, which would be necessary to accomplish their objectives. Whoever it was didn't want to rule the world. Instead, Chu Wanning suspected that their ultimate goal was to open the Space-Time Gate. And they were seeking more than a small rip in space-time—rather, they very probably intended to fuse two separate universes into one.

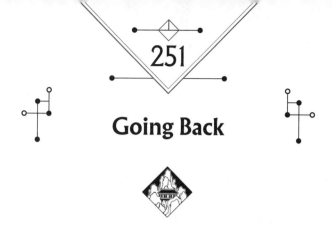

Going Back

"**W**HAT ARE YOU GOING to use the first forbidden technique for?"

Chu Wanning wasn't sure how many times he'd asked this question. But on that particular day, Mo Ran was in a good mood. He answered slowly at last, "To go back to the past."

"To do what?"

Taxian-jun raised his eyes. "I'll save him."

Whom he meant was obvious.

Chu Wanning was standing before Mo Ran in robes as white as snow. "If you've read all the records on the first forbidden technique, you should know all of its practitioners died horrific deaths. The last zongshi who mastered it tried to bring back his daughter from a different universe. He and that world's version of himself ended up killing each other. You can't be ignorant of this case."

Mo Ran frowned and shifted in his seat. Crossing one leg over the other, he propped his cheek against a hand and looked up at Chu Wanning. "Actually, this venerable one is ignorant indeed."

Chu Wanning blinked.

"What's the point in studying a failure?"

"No one's ever succeeded," said Chu Wanning.

"Then this venerable one will be the first."

"You cannot foresee the consequences of disturbing space-time," Chu Wanning warned.

Mo Ran snorted. "Whatever chaos or destruction comes of it, how does it affect this venerable one?"

"Even if you were really able to bring Shi Mingjing from another universe into this one, what about your other self?" Chu Wanning persisted. "Would he allow it? If it comes down to a fight like the one between the two zongshi in the tale, what will you do?"

Mo Ran grinned. "Who cares about some other version of myself? If he tries to stop me, I'll kill him."

Chu Wanning's mouth snapped shut as goosebumps rose over his skin. Mo Ran had truly lost his mind.

"So, if..." Chu Wanning continued woodenly. "If history were to repeat itself, and something went wrong when you tried to take Shi Mingjing from your other self, then the other world's Shi Mingjing might get crushed by the rift in space-time. You—"

A loud crash cut him off. Mo Ran had shot to his feet, flipping the table of fruit in front of him. Grapes, tangerines, and dried lychees tumbled everywhere, rolling about like the heads he'd so wantonly hacked off.

Taxian-jun stalked over with great strides, his dragon-embroidered shoes crushing grapes and lychees beneath their soles, juices splattering like blood and brains. Amidst the sweetly scented carnage, he yanked Chu Wanning up by the lapels. His eyes were savage. "I know you always looked down on him—you wanted him to die," Mo Ran growled. "How could you be so cruel? No matter what, he was your disciple too; he chose you as his teacher; he trusted you. Yet you curse him this way, Chu Wanning."

"I'm not cursing him. Everything I'm saying is the truth."

"Who wants to listen to your truth?" Mo Ran roared. "If this venerable one wants someone, it doesn't matter if I have to tear apart space-time, if I have to turn the universe upside-down—I'm going to save him; I'm going to bring him back! If the world tries to stop me, I'll destroy the world. If I try to stop me, I'll kill myself. If *you* try to stop me, I'll—"

He stopped, chest heaving. His frantic eyes seemed to go distant. What would he do? Trample him into the dirt? But he'd already snapped Chu Wanning's spine beneath his feet. Humiliate him? But he'd already forced Chu Wanning to bow to heaven and earth alongside him.

Then—kill him?

An ache tore through his heart. He couldn't say it; he didn't know how to finish that sentence.

Mo Ran stormed out, leaving Chu Wanning standing in the desolate hall by himself. Darkness pressed in on him on all sides. All of this was part of someone's plot. Both Taxian-jun and the Beidou Immortal had already been ensnared. What was he supposed to do?

Should the first forbidden technique be performed again, it wouldn't be a problem if the rift was small. Just as a small wound could scab over, space-time should also be able to heal itself. But if the rip was large, bringing about many changes as the two worlds collided, the outcome might be the chaos alluded to in the ancient scrolls. Nothing would be left intact.

There is an order to the mortal realm. Should the order collapse, the heavens will render their judgment. All shall return to primordial chaos.

Chu Wanning didn't remember where exactly he'd read this, but the words had left an indelible impression on him. They referred precisely to the consequences of opening the Space-Time Gate. The heavens would visit retribution upon the mortal realm: The two entangled universes would both be reduced to nothingness.

If the first forbidden technique spiraled out of control, the cost would be the annihilation of two worlds. Chu Wanning couldn't let such a thing happen. He could not let Mo Ran continue.

That night, Mo Ran was occupied tidying up the scrolls Kunlun Taxue Palace had thrown into disarray and didn't torment Chu Wanning further. Chu Wanning took a lantern and headed to the library.

Chu Wanning was practically powerless, and as such, Mo Ran didn't bar him from any areas of Sisheng Peak unless he was particularly angry. This was a tiny show of mercy on Mo Ran's part. Chu Wanning could freely access the library, the backwoods, and even the holy weapon arsenal. Mo Ran kept him as he would a cat: It was enough to file down the animal's fangs and clip its claws; there was no fun in breaking its legs, shackling its wild nature, and preventing it from roaming free.

Within the library, Chu Wanning sat and organized his various clues. After putting everything he had learned in order, he ascertained two things:

Firstly, the mastermind behind the scenes had an excellent command of medicine, but their spiritual power was weak. If this person had been gifted with copious amounts of spiritual energy, they wouldn't need to exploit a pawn like Mo Ran to achieve their ends.

Secondly, this mastermind must have plotted Shi Mei's death with the goal of rousing hatred in Mo Ran's heart. When Chu Wanning had painstakingly deciphered the demon tribe's ancient text, he'd learned of this strategy:

The Flower of Eightfold Sorrows will erase all the kindness from the heart of its host. However, it may preserve their fond memories of one person in particular. To this end, the spellcaster will often ensure that the host's memories of them remain intact. The host will develop affection for the spellcaster and come to rely on them, willingly facing death and mortal danger for their sake.

Chu Wanning had personally witnessed Shi Mei's death; he trusted there was no deception there. Shi Mei therefore couldn't be the spellcaster. Yet Mo Ran still retained his good memories of Shi Mei. It seemed the mastermind had used this bit of lingering warmth to draw Mo Ran toward the three forbidden techniques. From the Zhenlong Chess Formation, capable of controlling all under heaven, to the death-defying Rebirth technique, to the Space-Time Gate, which could warp the very fabric of the universe: Mo Ran had indeed tried them one after the other, regardless of whether he had ultimately succeeded in their execution.

Who would have such a pressing need to master all three forbidden techniques? Who would want to rip open space and time, risking the existence of two separate universes, in order to satisfy their personal ambitions?

To this, he had no ready answer. But as he considered his next steps, finding the mastermind seemed the least important. What Chu Wanning needed to do was stop Mo Ran before he could learn the Space-Time Gate. After careful thought, he saw that there was one path before him.

He must kill the Emperor Taxian-jun. Then he needed to return to the past, to a time before the Flower of Eightfold Sorrows took root in Mo Ran's heart, and find a way to nip the vile blossom in the bud. According to the texts, the flower couldn't be planted in the same person's heart twice. Thus, even if the mastermind opened the Space-Time Gate after Taxian-jun's death, they would never again be able to control Mo Weiyu at the height of his power.

He had to kill Emperor Taxian-jun...

Moths fluttered about in the dark library, drawn to Chu Wanning's lantern. One flew in, then the other, each instantly engulfed by the flame, leaving nothing but the faint scent of ashes. Chu Wanning watched that lonely light, those oblivious moths. The fire was very bright, but his heart was freezing cold.

He had to kill Emperor Taxian-jun... To kill Mo Ran.

He had to kill that man who'd been manipulated and exploited, who'd suffered, unknowingly, so very much. In the past, as his shizun, he hadn't properly protected him. Now, he needed to scheme against him. He needed to execute him.

Chu Wanning's eyes squeezed shut as he let his head fall back against a bookshelf. The lantern light flickered and swayed. He too was a moth, throwing himself toward a brilliant flame.

He had to kill Mo Weiyu.

It had begun to rain, a mist so soft it could sink into one's bones. Chu Wanning woke from shallow sleep beside the man who kept him as his concubine.

Mo Ran's desire and stamina had always been astonishing. Chu Wanning didn't know if he coupled with Song Qiutong the same way he did with him, if he unleashed the same primal lust onto her—or if that insatiable appetite was reserved for him alone. It wasn't important.

At that moment, Mo Ran was lying right next to him, sound asleep—no different from countless previous nights. Of late,

Mo Ran had become more and more insatiable. After sex, he often refused to pull out, and the next morning, he'd demand a second round before he went to court.

Kill him.

Chu Wanning was no match for Mo Ran's raw strength. He doubted he had any chance of succeeding, even while Mo Ran lay defenseless next to him.

Not yet—wait a little longer, he told himself.

He had set himself two tasks. He had to commit murder, and then he had to open the Space-Time Gate before his opponent got the chance and stop Mo Ran from being devoured by the Flower of Eightfold Sorrows in the past. As he had no way of completing the first, he poured his efforts into the second: He would realize the first forbidden technique, the Space-Time Gate of Life and Death.

For some reason unknown even to himself, he possessed a vague intuition regarding this technique. He'd been piecing together the scroll fragments Mo Ran had found; after untold struggles and failed attempts, he finally recovered the form of the original spell.

Yet without his spiritual core, it was exceedingly difficult for Chu Wanning to use any magic. The endeavor would've been impossible if not for his innate connection with his holy weapon Jiuge, which allowed him to summon the guqin even without a core. Even so, Chu Wanning's progress was painfully slow, and he encountered innumerable setbacks.

Drawing on Jiuge's power, he was at last able to rip open a tiny crack in space-time—one that would allow him to return to the past.

He heard a haunting whistle from within the breach as he approached. It was just as the legends said: This whistle marked both the opening and the closing of the gate.

An eerie, distant voice asked: *"Where do you wish to travel?"*

At first, his heart had pounded like a drum, but now that he had reached the threshold at last, he was suddenly, surprisingly calm.

"Where do you wish to travel?" the voice repeated.

Chu Wanning glanced back at Wushan Palace, which was hosting a spectacle of song and dance. He had made certain to send Mo Ran into a towering rage that day, and Mo Ran had summoned Song Qiutong to his side instead. He figured Mo Ran wouldn't seek him out again soon. He took a deep breath, phoenix eyes glinting. "I wish to return to the year when the Flower of Eightfold Sorrows had just been planted in Mo Ran." And clarified: "Back when the flower was still in its first stage, when everything could still be turned back." He hesitated. "Do you understand?"

No answer came from the rift, but just as Chu Wanning felt his hope begin to wane, there was a flash of light, and the breach slowly opened. He stepped in, and the world spun giddily. When it had righted itself again, he opened his eyes. Peach-blossom petals floated before him.

He... He'd truly gone back in time.

Sisheng Peak was bathed in the limpid moonlight of late spring. Chu Wanning stood in silence, struggling to bring his emotions under control. At last, he swept aside the flowers and walked out of the rift.

He found himself in the sect's backwoods. He could smell Madam Wang's various magical flowers and herbs and see countless pinpricks of light twinkling in the distance, where the lamps from thousands of disciples' rooms merged into a silver river like the Milky Way.

To find himself back here again felt like a dream.

Chu Wanning's face betrayed nothing, but a million emotions surged within his chest as he stood frozen. Slowly, he took one step forward, then another. He saw little disciples giggling as they ran past. He saw the Xuanji Elder comparing notes with the Lucun Elder upon the Dancing Sword Platform. When he turned a corner, he even spotted Madam Wang's fat cat, Veggiebun. The kitty was perched on a low wall, craning his fuzzy head to sniff a flourishing Bengal rose.

No—it wasn't like a dream. Even in his very best dreams all these years, he had never been able to return to a Sisheng Peak like this.

Drinking in every detail, he proceeded onward. He had never had the habit of leaving the Red Lotus Pavilion at night, and so wasn't worried about running into his other self from this timeline. Suddenly, he caught sight of two young men walking toward him. One was as lovely as a blooming lotus, while the other was bright as a bird with splendid plumage.

Chu Wanning's steps, already slow, came to a stop. These youths were none other than Xue Meng and Shi Mei.

Soul-Splitting

THE TWO YOUTHS were engrossed in conversation, smiling easily as they chatted. At one point, Xue Meng reached up to tuck a little white and yellow flower in Shi Mei's hair. Shi Mei, simultaneously exasperated and amused, reached up to pluck it out again, sending Xue Meng into a fit of laughter.

"Ah—Shizun?"

It was too late to avoid them. When Xue Meng turned, he'd already seen Chu Wanning out of the corner of his eye. After a moment of shock, he hurried forward and exclaimed, "I didn't expect to see Shizun out so late!"

Shi Mei followed with a gentle smile. "Good evening, Shizun."

Chu Wanning found himself unable to speak. He'd intended to answer as if it was the most natural thing in the world, but before he could open his mouth, the rims of his eyes reddened. Luckily, the night was dark enough to hide it.

Xue Meng's eyes shone with a kitten-like curiosity. "Where are you going, Shizun?"

"Just..." Chu Wanning's voice came out as a hideous rasp. He cleared his throat, but it was a moment before he could continue. "Just taking a walk." After another beat, he couldn't help asking, "What about you two?"

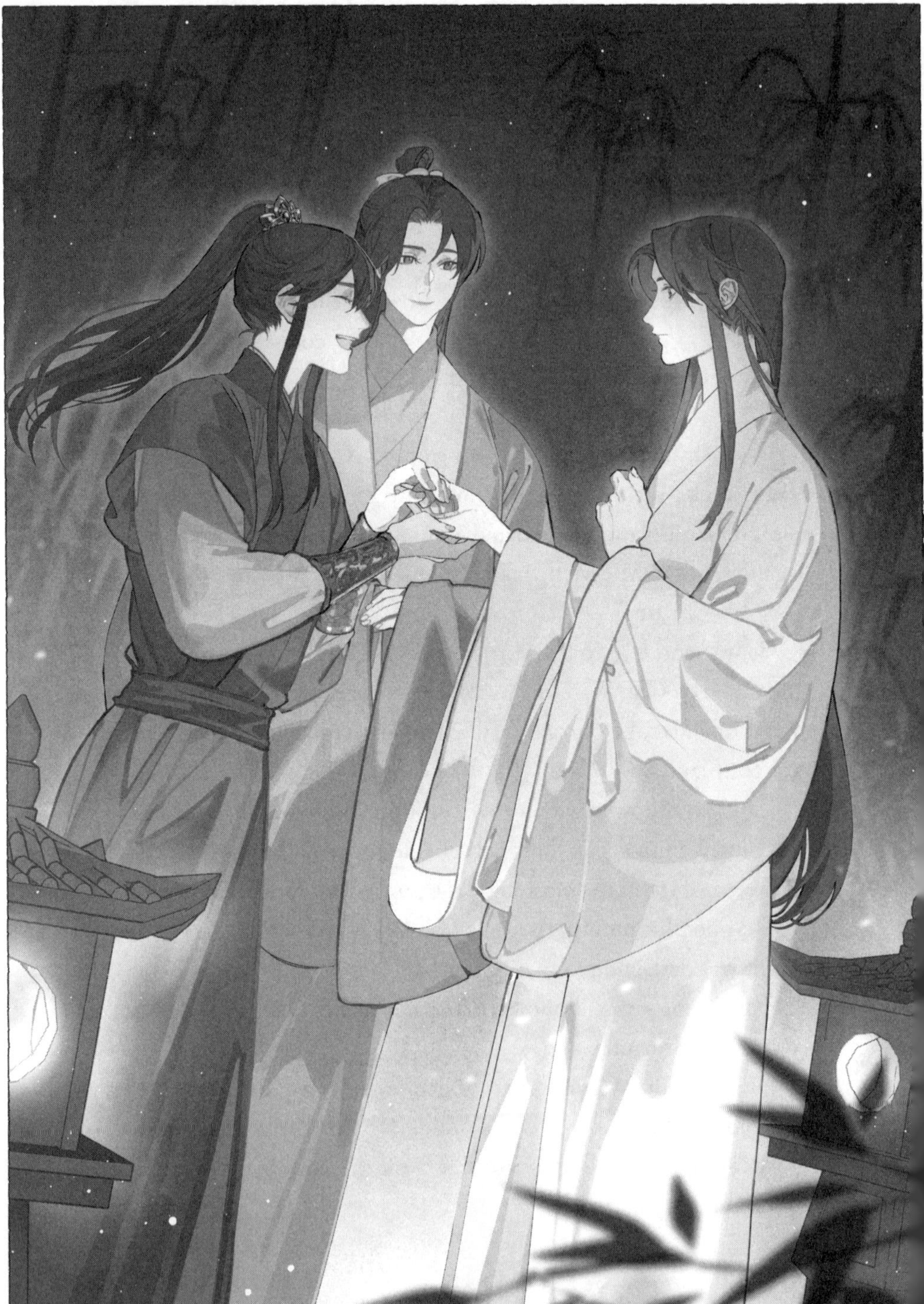

"Us? We just got back from Wuchang Town. We brought back loads of delicious snacks." Xue Meng was in high spirits. "There was a temple festival today; it was tons of fun."

Had they been talking to the Chu Wanning from this timeline, the conversation would've ended there. He wouldn't have cared to know more about these boys' amusements, what delicious food they'd eaten, why they were so happy. At that time, he'd been cool and distant with everyone. He'd never liked to pry into anyone's personal business.

But the Chu Wanning who had traveled back in time found every word, every smile, every twinkle in the eyes of Xue Meng and Shi Mei to be unspeakably precious. He wanted one more glimpse of them, wanted to listen to them talk a little longer. After all, he no longer had any such opportunities in his world.

So he asked, "What did you get?"

"Does Shizun wanna see?" Plainly delighted, Xue Meng drew a handful of items from his qiankun pouch, presenting them like precious baubles. "Hawthorn rolls, pine-nut pastries, sweet osmanthus candies..." He rattled off a list, then grabbed a fistful of osmanthus candies and thrust them into Chu Wanning's empty hands. "I got too many. These are for you, Shizun."

Shi Mei also rummaged through his pouch, but it seemed he hadn't bought much. Unable to find anything worth giving to Chu Wanning, his ears turned faintly pink.

"I don't need any more," said Chu Wanning. He took a few candies and handed the rest back to Xue Meng. His eyes glimmered softly beneath the moonlight. "This is plenty."

He knew the Space-Time Gate could close at any moment. He was already overdrawing Jiuge's power; it would be tremendously difficult to open a second rift. Besides, he only had this single stolen night; Taxian-jun might become suspicious if he was gone for too long.

Quashing the tumult in his heart, he asked, "Where's Mo Ran? Didn't he go out with you?"

Xue Meng and Shi Mei exchanged a glance. "We haven't seen him since lunch," said Xue Meng.

"He hasn't spent much time with us recently," Shi Mei added. "He's probably busy with his own things."

Chu Wanning went to the disciples' quarters and then the temple festival, but Mo Ran was nowhere to be found. As the hours passed, Chu Wanning grew more and more anxious. Brow furrowed, he pondered all sorts of possibilities—until he suddenly remembered.

Surely Mo Ran wouldn't have gone to...

Chu Wanning didn't complete the thought. Even the memory made him rather uncomfortable. His face darkened, fingers curling into fists.

There was one place in particular that Mo Ran frequented often when he'd first started going astray.

An hour later, Chu Wanning stood outside a building of red and purple lacquered wood. Above its doors hung a scarlet plaque that read MAY YOU FEAST ON THE PEACHES OF IMMORTALITY.

This was a well-known entertainment house in the nearby Black Bamboo Town, the Immortal Peach Pavilion. It was now deep in the night, yet here, things were just beginning to get lively. Guests streamed through the doors, most of them either greasy-looking older men or dolled-up youngsters. And then there was Chu Wanning, sticking out like a sore thumb with his austere expression and rigid posture.

"Welcome, welcome—please come on in." An attendant called out at the door. "Take a look around—today we have a famous dan singer[8]

---

8   A female role in many genres of Chinese opera.

from Xiangtan. She sings like Xun Fengruo and dances like Duan Yihan. Come see the show, just eighty copper coins, ten more for a front-row seat..."

A sophisticated-looking gongzi waving a calligraphed fan jeered as he walked by. "How shameless. Who are you calling a famous dan? You dare compare her with the bygone goddesses Duan Yihan and Xun Fengruo?"

"That's right! Eighty coins, and they have the cheek to mention her in the same breath as Xun Fengruo. Even eight hundred gold couldn't buy you one of Xun Fengruo's performances."

"This old circus is scamming people again!" A passing night watchman chimed in with a guffaw, scratching his armpit.

Now curious, Chu Wanning lifted the curtain and walked in. Silk lanterns were strung up across the bustling hall, which was filled with people watching shows and drinking wine, losing themselves in a billowing sea of rouge and paint. The singers' voices had the luster of gold, and the rent boys' muscles flexed alluringly beneath jade-like skin.

Onstage, a woman dressed as an imperial consort was drunkenly sprawled within a lush tableau. The opera singer's every gesture was heavy with sorrow, moving many in her audience to tears.

"Amazing!"

"One more song, one more song!"

Chu Wanning knit his brows at the cloying scent of powder and perfume. His phoenix eyes scanned the crowd, but there was no sign of Mo Ran. Had he come to the wrong place?

The brothel madam, busy with the crush of guests, chose that moment to notice Chu Wanning amidst the crowd. She swooped over like a glittering butterfly, vermilion lips parting in a coy smile. "Gongzi, please step up to watch the show, or head inside if you're seeking other pleasures."

Chu Wanning shot her a cool glance. "I'm looking for someone."

"Looking for..." The madam paused, her smile icing over. "You're on your own."

Chu Wanning sighed and reached down for a pendant hanging from his belt. It was a gift from Taxian-jun, made of the finest jade, smooth and warm to the touch. He handed it to the madam and repeated, "I'm looking for someone."

The madam peered down at the pendant, her eyes reflected in the luminous jade. She coughed softly and tucked the little trinket away. Flashing an even more radiant smile, she asked sweetly, "Now who is the gongzi looking for?"

"A young man, about fifteen or sixteen," said Chu Wanning. "Surnamed Mo."

They climbed the stairs to the third floor, which was decorated with elegant carvings, and stopped in front of a sign that said *Feirong Boudoir*. Chu Wanning's feet sank into the luxurious carpet. Small wonder so many were willing to drown themselves in drunken pleasure here—they could exchange their coin for a fantasy as clustered with beauties as a field filled with poppies. How many heroes had rotted away in such a place? With its tender glow to chase away the endless dark of night, precious few would be willing to face life's devastating realities.

"This is the room." The madam flipped over a wooden placard on the door carved with the name *Rong Jiu*, her cardamom-dyed nails a pinkish blur.

She looked up, giving Chu Wanning a thoughtful once-over. "Gongzi, please wait a moment—I'll fetch Jiu-er out so you can go in and speak with your friend."

Chu Wanning blinked, then closed his eyes. Even a brothel madam could tell how he cared for Mo Ran. "Thank you for your trouble."

She entered the room. Chu Wanning heard some indistinct snatches of conversation. Some moments later, she stepped out again, a young male prostitute behind her. Chu Wanning glanced at him. Rong Jiu's face was still faintly flushed from wine. As he turned aside, Chu Wanning found he looked very familiar, though he couldn't quite place the resemblance.

The youth bowed deeply to Chu Wanning, then left with the madam.

Chu Wanning pushed the door open. Inside was a garish vision of red and purple; the sight made Chu Wanning's scalp tingle. No incense had been lit, but the room smelled unmistakably of wine.

Mo Ran was sprawled on the bed on his side, cheek propped in one hand. His long fingers toyed with the red tassel of a clay wine jar. The bed was a sea of disheveled crimson; Chu Wanning preferred not to think how it'd gotten into that state. He swept like a frosty gust of wind into this sensual scene a world apart from him.

"Mngh... Shizun's here?"

When Chu Wanning didn't answer, Mo Ran asked, "Wanna sit down and have a cup of wine? It's pear-blossom white—good wine. Bet you never tried it before."

"You're drunk," said Chu Wanning.

Mo Ran giggled as he watched the man in white approach the bed. He really was drunk. His hand shot out, and he boldly grabbed Chu Wanning's waist sash. "It's nice to be drunk, nothing can faze me like this. Come on, the night is young—let's have some fun."

Without a word, Chu Wanning hauled Mo Ran up from the bed, yanking him out of that scarlet sea of desires. The veins on his hands stood out from the strain. Even so, his bearing was solemn, as befitted a respected zongshi. All that betrayed his anxiety was the minute trembling of his fingertips. He closed his eyes. "Mo Ran," he whispered.

The drunken youth grunted in acknowledgment and let slip another mindless giggle.

"I'm already too late," Chu Wanning rasped.

He pressed his forehead to Mo Ran's. With a twitch of his fingers, a terrible pain bloomed in Chu Wanning's chest, and a holy weapon materialized: a black guqin with an upswept tail. Haitang blossoms unfurled along the body made of sacred wood, and its seven strings glowed softly in the dimness of the room.

Jaw clenched, Chu Wanning channeled the holy weapon's bountiful spiritual energy into his own body. This kind of power wouldn't stand a chance against Taxian-jun, but it was enough for him to cast many spells.

Holding Mo Ran's forehead tightly against his own, he closed his eyes. After just a moment, he felt it... The aura of the Flower of Eightfold Sorrows within Mo Ran. He could almost see it, a black blossom with many petals, its roots twining along Mo Ran's arteries to drink from his heart.

Here was the source of his endless hatred, the root of all the evil he'd done.

Chu Wanning inhaled deeply. Following the instructions in the ancient text, he slowly mouthed an incantation. Then, with all the strength he could muster, he cried: "Fracture soul!"

His eyes flew open. A cold light flooded his vision.

The Flower of Eightfold Sorrows could only be suppressed using part of a spellcaster's soul. Just as the book described, he'd cleaved his earth soul in two. He transferred one half into Mo Ran where their foreheads met.

A gale rose within the room, and Jiuge emitted a cry like a phoenix's shriek as spiritual energy blazed to life.

Mo Ran, Mo Ran... Back then, it was your shifu who didn't protect you properly. Now, I'm here to save you. I'll set you free.

The fragmented soul transformed into a wisp of white smoke that issued from Chu Wanning's body. Mo Ran had lost consciousness, and Chu Wanning was in agony. But he didn't let Mo Ran go for a moment, keeping their brows pressed together.

I'll save you...

When the last ray of light faded, both of them reeled backward. Chu Wanning released his grip, and Mo Ran crumpled onto the bed. Jiuge disappeared, melding back into Chu Wanning's body. After tearing away half of his earth soul, he could no longer control the holy weapon.

He settled at the edge of the bed, letting his eyes drift shut. His face was deathly pale, his lips drained of their color. But relief flooded his chest. At last, he'd taken the first step toward rewriting destiny. Using the power of his soul, he had arrested the flower's development. Mo Ran's heart would remain unchanged. He'd swum upstream through the river of time and, finally, he had been able to protect him.

Chu Wanning couldn't tarry here. His first errand—to stop Mo Ran from being devoured by the flower—was complete. Now, he needed to turn his attention to the second.

He didn't know how patient the villain behind the scenes would prove to be. They couldn't yet tear open a rift in space-time, but caution was always prudent. He needed to impart his memories to this world's version of himself—should the worst come to pass, his self here should be equipped to mount a resistance.

Thus, the second thing he needed to do was to find himself.

The alarm sigils on the Red Lotus Pavilion were naturally useless against him; he got inside without a hitch. Standing before the open window, he looked at the white-robed man slumped over the desk inside, fallen asleep in the middle of painting the half-finished Holy Night Guardian before him.

If only dealing with little ghosts and devils was still the worst of his worries—how nice that would be.

Chu Wanning transferred the remaining half of his earth soul to his sleeping other self. This soul was his to begin with, and the slumbering man's body readily accepted it. Chu Wanning watched the silvery radiance curl through the air, wreathing his other self in a gentle glow until it gradually faded. A breeze rose, blowing some of the blueprints from the desk onto the floor.

"If another crisis arises, Mo Ran won't make you his enemy again," he said softly, leaning against the windowsill. "My spiritual core is broken, and I've now split one of my souls in two. This is all I can do. I can no longer change my own world, but you can still change yours."

The man in the room slumbered on.

"My earth soul is the weakest among my three ethereal souls. I gave half of it to you, and the other half to Mo Ran. If your life-times remain peaceful, these souls won't affect you. But in case the Flower of Eightfold Sorrows takes root despite my efforts, or if the mortal realm is plunged in chaos, I'll leave a spell to fuse the two halves back together."

If everything went as planned, the Flower of Eightfold Sorrows would be fully uprooted from Mo Ran's heart when those two soul fragments reunited. His other self would also receive the memories from his own timeline.

"Don't resent me for passing this responsibility onto you," Chu Wanning continued. "If it were possible, I'd rather you didn't have to know what I do. But..."

He sighed quietly and said no more.

At last he set about his third and final errand here: He went to Huaizui and entrusted him with a censer he had been working on all this time, on which he'd cast a soul-fusing spell. The spell would take the memory that had left the deepest impression on him and use it to stitch the two halves of his soul back together. What that memory would be, Chu Wanning didn't know. There were too many possibilities, he thought. Perhaps it would be the great battle at the Heavenly Rift, or the experience of being turned into a blood hourglass when Mo Ran took him prisoner, or that agonizing moment when Mo Ran had first defiled him.

Out of so many options, he couldn't guess. Sometimes, people didn't know their own hearts.

He asked Huaizui to seal the censer in the cave on Dragonblood Mountain. He warned Huaizui that, in the event of a great upheaval, he was to bring both Chu Wanning and Mo Ran from this world to the cave.

And then Chu Wanning's time was up. The fabric of space-time had the power to heal itself. Even deliberate tears like the one Chu Wanning had created would eventually knit back together. He wanted badly to remain, to stay in this pristine, peaceful world where all was still well. But he didn't belong here. He wouldn't defy the limitations of the first forbidden technique just to selfishly seek out a little warmth.

So he left. He departed from this world that was like a lovely dream. He didn't look back.

Chu Wanning stepped out of the rift into the backwoods in his own time. Just as he finished concealing the residual traces of spiritual energy, he spied a servant in red robes approaching.

"Chu-zongshi," the newcomer respectfully said. It was the elderly eunuch Liu-gong, one of Mo Ran's personal attendants. "Zongshi, where have you been? His Majesty's been looking for you."

"Where is he?" asked Chu Wanning.

"In the Red Lotus Pavilion."

Chu Wanning found Mo Ran sitting beneath the wisteria vines with his eyes closed. As he heard Chu Wanning open the door, he slowly looked up and beckoned him over. "Come here."

Chu Wanning pressed his lips together, face impassive as ever. "Was the music not to your liking? You dismissed the performers so early."

"It's got nothing to do with *liking*," said Mo Ran. "All the songs sound the same after a while. So tedious."

He spread his sleeves wide and pulled Chu Wanning into his arms. He didn't bother asking where Chu Wanning had been. After all, Chu Wanning had always possessed an intractable personality. It would be stranger if he idled about in the Red Lotus Pavilion all day long.

Mo Ran made Chu Wanning sit in his lap, then kissed him on the cheek before burying his face in his neck. "This venerable one had a dream just now."

"Hm?"

"I dreamed you were holding my hand, teaching me how to write."

Chu Wanning's heart skipped a beat. But Taxian-jun, lost in his own memories, didn't notice. He continued, speaking smoothly yet with a faint note of sorrow even he failed to discern.

"There was a character I couldn't get right, even after five tries. You were so mad. But you didn't give up on me," said Mo Ran. "You took my hand in your own. Some petals floated into the room through the window. I saw..."

He was so engrossed in recounting his dream he'd forgotten to call himself *this venerable one*.

Mo Ran paused, suddenly wistful and young again. "I saw on the paper, 'I hope you may greet these words with a smile, for writing is akin to reuniting.'" His face split into a grin, equal parts joyful and menacing. "I can only ever see these things in my dreams."

He raised his head, meeting Chu Wanning's troubled gaze. When he next spoke, his voice contained Taxian-jun's usual coldness once more. "Do you know why this venerable one wanted to see you?"

Mo Ran reached up, touching Chu Wanning's cool cheek. "You looked so beautiful in that dream," he said placidly. "So beautiful this venerable one couldn't forget it. This venerable one wanted to come take a good look at the real you."

Chu Wanning lowered his lashes.

"I'm afraid of not hating you. I need to hate you," said Mo Ran. "Otherwise, I..." His throat went dry. *Otherwise what?*

Otherwise, I'd never be able to forgive myself? Otherwise, I wouldn't know how to carry on? Otherwise, I wouldn't know how to keep dragging out this sorry existence?

I have to hate you. I haven't changed my mind, and I've never been wrong to hate you.

"Wanning." At length, he sighed and closed his eyes. "At the end, you and I are the only ones left."

Chu Wanning felt like a knife was pushing through his heart. He was about to speak when he felt the ground give out beneath him. He was tumbling through empty air—

He startled awake.

His eyes flew open, but everything was dark. He could hear his racing heartbeat and feel cold sweat soaking his back. Emperor Taxian-jun's leering face seemed to hang before him. He shook all over, gasping for breath. The memories of his other lifetime washed over him, and he trembled with uncontrollable dread as those images of the past surged in wave after frantic wave.

Chu Wanning swallowed thickly. Where was he? Where was he… Why couldn't he see anything? Why was there only darkness? His thoughts were a hopeless jumble. It was a long time before he remembered what had happened at Dragonblood Mountain.

"Mo Ran…" he mumbled absently, trying to gather his fragmented consciousness.

Without warning, a cool hand, smooth as silk, touched his cheek. The hand took hold of his jaw to turn his face, and a thumb ghosted over his lips. A voice obviously warped by a voice-changing spell laughed softly. "Finally, you're awake. I've been waiting for ages."

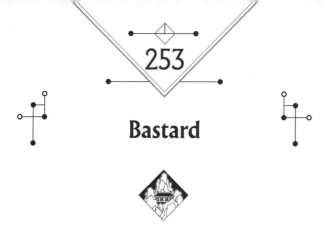

253

Bastard

THAT UNSETTLINGLY DISTORTED voice broke the stillness of the room. Had Chu Wanning been able to see, he would've discovered Shi Mei sitting at his bedside, gazing at him cheerfully—as if he was a spider, and Chu Wanning a creature that had haplessly stumbled into his web.

"How are you feeling? Did you sleep well?"

Chu Wanning didn't immediately answer. He shifted slightly and found that his spiritual energy was still woefully depleted. His wrists were bound with an immortal-binding rope and his eyes by a black silk ribbon.

Panic would be futile at this juncture. Chu Wanning had always been dauntless; he had a clear idea of his goals, and he knew how to meet any challenge with a steady heart. Across two lifetimes, only one man had ever put him off-balance. No one else could so much as ruffle his composure.

Chu Wanning silently combed through his disjointed memories and impressions from before he'd lost consciousness. He'd heard fragmented conversations and movements around him while he'd been drifting in and out of awareness. He now endeavored to piece together this information.

As he thought, the door to the hidden chamber rumbled open. Nangong Liu had returned with a basket full of fresh fruit.

"Dear friend-gege, here are the tangerines," he said. "I picked the ones with little circles on the bottom. They're the sweetest..." He paused as he caught sight of Chu Wanning on the bed. "Huh? The favorite consort-gege's awake?"

Hearing such an epithet directed toward himself, Chu Wanning's bloodless face instantly grew stormy. Favorite consort...as in Consort Chu? So then this "dear friend-gege" could only be...

Shi Mei took the tangerines from Nangong Liu and patted him on the head with a smile. "Good job. I have to talk to Consort Chu about a few things. Go outside and play by yourself, okay?"

"Can't I stay? I can peel the tangerines for you."

"No, you shouldn't stay," Shi Mei replied. "Some things aren't fit for children's ears."

Nangong Liu grumbled dopily and left the way he'd come.

The room was now quiet, filled only with the sounds of their breathing and the occasional sputter of the candles. Shi Mei selected a tangerine, peeled it with practiced movements, and removed the stringy pith. As he worked, he spoke to Chu Wanning in a tone one might use to chat about the weather. "Could you tell who that was—the person who just left?"

Met with silence, Shi Mei prompted, "I'm sure you recognized his voice."

He brought the freshly peeled tangerine to Chu Wanning's lips. "Try this—it's a tangerine from Mount Jiao. Xu Shuanglin planted it himself, and he knew what he was doing. It should be very sweet."

Chu Wanning turned his face away.

"Look at you," Shi Mei said slowly. "In a temper the moment you wake up."

After sitting silent a minute, Chu Wanning said coldly, "Where is he?"

"Who?"

"You know who I'm talking about."

Shi Mei arched a brow. "You mean Mo Ran?"

When Chu Wanning didn't reply, Shi Mei laughed softly. "Looks like you really do care for him. See how his whereabouts are the first thing on your mind—you haven't even asked who I am. Surely someone who humiliated you all those years isn't worth your concern?"

The blindfolded man pressed his lips into a thin line, his strain showing in the set of his jaw.

As Shi Mei stared, a maddening heat flared to life in his chest. But he still feigned calm, as if nothing fazed him. A proper meal should be eaten with elegance. It wouldn't do to bare one's fangs or leave bloody drippings. Taxian-jun's style of wolfing everything down, bones and all, was too rash. His bowl was empty before he could appreciate the flavor. Shi Mingjing felt nothing but disdain for that reincarnated starving mongrel. Though a burning heat was pooling in his own belly, he would still take the time to gently massage the meat, to baste the delectable dish before him in aromatic juices. He would braise this delicacy until it was meltingly tender before savoring every last bite.

"Let me ask you another question: You won't eat a tangerine that's held right up to your lips?" Shi Mei chuckled. "With this obstinate personality of yours, how did you ever manage to keep Emperor Taxian-jun happy?"

"Take it away."

"I still think it best if you eat it. You haven't drunk any water in days; your lips are starting to crack."

"Where is Mo Ran?" Chu Wanning said between gritted teeth.

Shi Mei fixed his gaze on Chu Wanning, his smile slowly fading. "Whether in this lifetime or the last, whether you have your memories or not, Mo Ran's the only person you ever think about. Sh—"

Before he could finish saying *Shizun*, Shi Mei realized his mistake and promptly shut his mouth. But Chu Wanning caught the tiny wobble in his act.

Shi Mei narrowed his eyes. "Tell me, what's so great about Mo Ran?" he demanded, watching the last bit of color fade from Chu Wanning's compressed lips. "He's impulsive, dense, laughably naïve, and morally questionable. What is there to like about *him*?" He waited. When no answer was forthcoming, he asked derisively: "His face? His spiritual power? His charm?"

His voice was a low growl by the end, those long-suppressed carnal desires rearing their head. When he saw Chu Wanning biting his bottom lip as he controlled his emotions, Shi Mei felt his mouth grow dry. His questioning veered in a more obscene direction. "Or is it because he's good in bed?"

Chu Wanning's pallid face colored with fury. "Shut up."

Of course Shi Mei didn't listen to him. He'd gone to no end of trouble to get his hands on this man. He wasn't going to stop before he'd had his fun. Grinning, he asked, "Perhaps Consort Chu doesn't know that Mo Ran left the posthumous title of 'Esteemed Consort' on your grave in the past life?"

Shi Mei trained his gaze on Chu Wanning's face, taking in every minute change in his expression. His eyes curved into generous crescents. "It sounds silly to call a bed warmer *esteemed*, but I guess it's fitting. In both lifetimes, no one sullied your honor but him. But that also means you have no one to compare him to," Shi Mei mused. "Of course you'd think he's the best if you've never tried anyone else."

A slow fingertip traced Chu Wanning's features, sliding from his nose to his lips, his jaw, the jut of his throat. Chu Wanning vibrated with anger, tendons bulging from his wrists as he strained against the immortal-binding ropes. But his efforts were futile.

"Don't waste your energy," Shi Mei advised. "If Consort Chu wants to be unbound, if you want to know where Mo Ran is, I can grant your wishes. But—as my war prize, won't you at least play a little game with me first?"

A tense pause. "What do you want?"

Shi Mei laughed. "I just want to take a little bit of your heart from the person you gave it to. I want you to stop thinking about him and think fondly of me instead—how about that?"

"You're the one who planted that gu flower. Why would I think fondly of you?"

It was impossible for Chu Wanning to completely hide the despair and pain in his voice. Despite a mighty effort to quell his emotions, they were still on the verge of flooding out.

"Indeed I am." Shi Mei chuckled softly. "But, Consort Chu, do you know who I really am? Why don't you take a guess?"

"If there's something you want to say, get to the point."

"Ah, you're as ferocious as ever." Shi Mei sighed. "All right then. Consort Chu once said that small bets beget cheer and large bets beget ruin—you might as well go for ruin if you're going to bet at all. So why don't we have a little wager between us?" After a beat of silence, Shi Mei added, "If you don't mind, let me first see how many articles of clothing you're wearing."

Chu Wanning didn't make a sound, but his jaw spasmed uncon-sciously. Shi Mei's spirits rose yet again. He counted five separate articles of clothing on Chu Wanning including his robes and belt sash.

"I'll give you five chances. If you guess right, I'll tell you where Mo Ran is." Shi Mei paused thoughtfully. "But for every time you guess wrong, I'll take off a piece of clothing. If all your clothes are gone, but Consort Chu still hasn't guessed correctly, then..."

Rather than finish the thought, Shi Mei's pale pink tongue flicked out to moisten his lips. He returned to his seat, waiting for Chu Wanning to make his first guess. If Chu Wanning refused to speak, that too was fine—Shi Mei was in no rush. If there was one thing he had plenty of now, it was time.

Yet as minute after minute slipped by without a peep from Chu Wanning, Shi Mei's brows inched higher. He had plenty of time, it was true, but not necessarily the patience to go with it. "Come, take a guess," he urged.

Chu Wanning replied at last: "Fuck off."

Shi Mei's lip curled. "Don't forget—you're at my mercy right now. Don't push me." A pause. "Chu Wanning, you have nothing with which to bargain with me. Emperor Taxian-jun isn't right in the head; he might have let you have your way when he couldn't figure out how to win the argument, but I'm not like him." He coldly continued, "When you're in my hands, you'll need to be a little more obedient."

He waited a while longer, but Chu Wanning said nothing. "Don't make me resort to force," Shi Mei warned, voice hardening. "Keeping silent won't make things any easier for you."

He reached for Chu Wanning's sash with one long, slender hand, his fingers trailing along the fabric like a knife slicing through the tender meat of a fish. "Listen now. I'm going to count to three. If you still refuse to speak, the consequences will be yours to bear."

Shi Mei's eyes gleamed faintly. He wasn't sure if he wanted Chu Wanning to guess correctly or not. Either way, it didn't really matter. They were long past the point of no return. He wondered how he should reveal his true identity. Whatever method he chose, it had to be both sufficiently thrilling and visceral. He had traded moves with the man before him over two lifetimes. Now that he'd come away victorious, he deserved to savor his triumph.

"One."

The world seemed to shimmer with excitement in Shi Mei's eyes. "Two."

How would Chu Wanning feel? Angry? Sad? Scared? He waited, lips parted in expectation.

"Three. I see Consort Chu intends to take his esteemed chastity to the grave. No wonder Taxian-jun was so addicted to you," said Shi Mei, only half-joking. "Since you refuse to guess, we'll move on to harsher methods. You—"

"Hua Binan." Chu Wanning's voice was cold as ice.

Shi Mei's hand stilled on its way to pulling open Chu Wanning's sash. He let out a small laugh. "You got half of it. Go on?"

A foxlike smirk appeared on his face. Such cunning would be disagreeable on most people, but Shi Mei's elegance was such that he still resembled a pure lotus blooming over the water. He was certain Chu Wanning wouldn't be able to tease out that innermost kernel of truth. Self-satisfaction surged in his chest—

"I wish you'd truly died."

Shi Mei's smile froze. It was several breaths before he managed to ask: "What did you say?"

The man on the bed spoke without the slightest hint of warmth. "In the past lifetime, during that Heavenly Rift in the snowstorm. I wish you had truly died."

Shi Mei gaped at him. Words of jubilation had been on the tip of his tongue, but now, he found himself speechless. His hand remained suspended above Chu Wanning; he didn't know where to put it or what to do.

"Shi Mingjing." Chu Wanning's sigh was soft, but it left Shi Mei suddenly numb, as if stung by a wasp. "It's you, isn't it."

It was phrased like a question, but Chu Wanning's voice was sure.

Shi Mei let his lashes fall, hiding his eyes. Finally, he chuckled. "That's right—I didn't die. Sorry to disappoint you." He wouldn't admit he'd lost, but the elation had faded from his voice. "I'm the Shi Mingjing who came here from the past lifetime," said Shi Mei. "From your other life; from Taxian-jun's world. Don't get me mixed up with that kid who's been tagging at your heels in this lifetime." He hesitated. "I'll untie you like I said I would."

He unknotted the immortal-binding rope and tugged the ribbon from Chu Wanning's face. Peach-blossom eyes met phoenix ones, both pairs as calm and unfathomable as an ancient well.

"Greetings, Shizun."

Chu Wanning had expected this; he felt deeply grim but not surprised. "So you do remember I'm your shizun," he remarked, fixing his eyes on Shi Mei.

Shi Mei smiled even more sweetly. Only now did Chu Wanning see how finely honed the dagger lurking beneath that sweetness was. "Mn, of course I remember," answered Shi Mei. "You once held an umbrella over me. I've never forgotten."

As utterly spent as Chu Wanning was, even this couldn't negate the innate stubbornness in his features. He glared at Shi Mei, then said, clipped and cold: "You bastard."

"You flatter me," Shi Mei said with a laugh. "Shizun, when did you guess it was me? Was it in the past life?"

Chu Wanning merely pinned him with that icy gaze. His eyes contained fury, to be sure, but most prominent was disappointment.

"No, it can't have been," Shi Mei mused. "If you'd known I was Hua Binan then, you would've told Huaizui when you opened the Space-Time Gate." His long lashes flicked up. "It was in this lifetime. Maybe not long ago." He paused. "You heard some of the conversation between me and Mo Ran at Dragonblood Mountain."

Faced once again with Chu Wanning's silence, Shi Mei smiled. "Forget it—it doesn't matter. You're in my hands now. And you'll never escape."

Chu Wanning's gaze seemed to shutter. Of his three disciples, Shi Mei had always been most mysterious to him. He'd accepted him as a student because he was gentle and respectful. He could empathize with the pain and worries of others, and he treated everyone kindly. Chu Wanning admired all these qualities, even more so because they were qualities he himself did not possess. Thus he had agreed to be Shi Mei's teacher.

But more than once, he'd felt that something wasn't right. For instance, Xue Zhengyong told him Shi Mei was an orphan he'd rescued from a war-torn area, yet little inconsistencies would often crop up when Shi Mei talked about his life before Sisheng Peak. It was exactly what one would expect from someone who'd made up a story and then forgotten the details. And sometimes Shi Mei's behavior would inexplicably change for an instant, like a well-trained beast who looked docile but couldn't stop his eyes from flashing at the scent of blood.

But after watching him closely all these years, Chu Wanning had never seen Shi Mei act disgracefully. He'd eventually concluded he was seeing things, that the flower before him was so splendid he'd mistakenly taken its dazzling colors for warning signs.

Chu Wanning was like a hedgehog. His whole body was covered in sharp quills, save for his soft underside. But he took in his disciples, took in all the people who showed him kindness, and tucked them under his velvety belly. He'd doubted whether he should trust Shi Mei. He'd had his reservations and tested the waters. But he'd still chosen to put his faith in him in the end. The knife plunged into the hedgehog's soft stomach from beneath, blood streaming over the ground.

"How much of the past life do you remember now?" Shi Mei asked.

Of course, he was answered yet again by silence. Shi Mei continued his interrogation: "You were getting along perfectly well staying out of it. Why'd you put yourself through all that suffering to stop me?" He had manifold grievances from the past lifetime. Now that Shi Mei finally had a chance to get answers, he couldn't pass up the opportunity. "You spared Emperor Taxian-jun's life. You even helped him transmigrate and be reborn. Why?"

At this last question, Chu Wanning at last looked up. "He's not like you."

Shi Mei hesitated. "How so? Perhaps I'm ruthless, but aren't his hands covered in blood?"

Chu Wanning stared at Shi Mei. "You know what you planted in his heart."

"So what? I might've planted the flower, but he's the one who killed all those people," Shi Mei retorted. "You saw it with your own eyes in the past life. He laid waste to the land. Xue Zhengyong, Wang Chuqing, Jiang Xi, Ye Wangxi... Who slaughtered them all in cold blood?"

Shi Mei lifted a languid hand, peering at his slender fingers and his neat, rounded nails. Those hands were clean and refined, unmarred by a single speck of dust. He slanted Chu Wanning a glance and laughed. "Surely, it wasn't *me*?"

Red-hot fury blazed up in his chest, rendering Chu Wanning temporarily speechless.

"*I* never wished to massacre Rufeng Sect or kill Xue Zhengyong. No one would come to me to avenge them," Shi Mei continued. "What have I done? I merely gave him a gu flower. I've never killed anyone as long as I've lived."

Shi Mei cheerfully concluded: "The knife was in his hands, and he drove it into their chests. It really has very little to do with me. The Flower of Eightfold Sorrows doesn't create new grudges. The curse can only amplify what was already there. All those desires were his own. It would be too unfair to blame me for his crimes."

Every word Shi Mei spoke heightened Chu Wanning's disgust. At the word *unfair*, Chu Wanning's eyes flashed, glacially cold. "What do you find unfair about it?"

"Those were all his actions. Why should Shizun blame me?"

"Don't you know what kind of person he really is?"

"Of course I do," replied Shi Mei. "I'm afraid Shizun's the one who's confused."

A thread of tangerine pith was stuck between two of Shi Mei's fingers. He produced a white silk handkerchief and gingerly wiped it away, then intoned, "Why did Mo Ran raze Rufeng Sect to the ground? Because his heart held hatred. Why did Mo Ran kill Xue Zhengyong? Because his heart held fear. Why did Mo Ran defile you? Because his heart held lust."

His gaze flicked over to Chu Wanning. "If someone stabbed him once, he could never forgive them. If someone gave him an inch, he'd take a mile. If a beauty stepped toward him, he'd have to have a taste. That's the kind of person he is."

"Shi Mingjing," said Chu Wanning through gritted teeth. "You erased all the kindness from his heart and amplified his grudges and impulses by a thousand, ten thousand times. Can you really say with a straight face that he wished to do all those things? Who wouldn't wish to destroy the world if they were consumed by hatred? You?"

"Whose fault is it that he held grudges? That he had greed carved into his bones? That he had those impulses in the first place?" Shi Mei laughed. "If his heart were pure, with no ill intentions, the Flower of Eightfold Sorrows would've had no effect. What happened was because his heart was filthy. He's simply a vulgar man."

The expression on Chu Wanning's face grew deeply ugly. Just as he drew breath to respond, Shi Mei added, "People are responsible for their own desires. That's an undeniable fact."

Chu Wanning had been ready to argue with him, but at this, he suddenly felt that there was nothing more to say. He turned away.

Shi Mei shook his head. "Shizun, you're always on his side. You think there's a reason, an explanation, behind everything he does."

"Tell me, then—whose explanations should I believe?" Chu Wanning asked icily. "Yours?"

Shi Mei was quiet for a turn, then chuckled. "So Shizun still likes him?"

Chu Wanning's eyes were like a frozen lake reflecting the cold moon.

"I've been trading blows with Shizun across two lifetimes. I still can't compare to him, even when I've won?"

"What is there to compare between the two of you?" Chu Wanning replied coolly.

Shi Mei narrowed his eyes. "Is that really what you think of me? Is there nothing else you wish to say?"

Chu Wanning didn't reply right away. He seemed to ponder the question in earnest. Then he lifted his lashes. "There is," he answered evenly.

Shi Mei broke into a smile. "What's that?"

"There's no need for you to compare yourself to Mo Ran," Chu Wanning said expressionlessly. "You aren't even worthy of comparison to Xu Shuanglin. He at least had real passion, and wasn't afraid to act on it. He wasn't like you, Hua Binan." He didn't even bother calling him Shi Mingjing anymore. "You're just a bastard."

254

Missing You

SHI MEI FELL SILENT, his fair cheek twitching as if he'd been slapped. At last, he pursed his lips, then said, "You're determined not to leave me the slightest bit of dignity."

He reached for Chu Wanning's jaw again, but this time, Chu Wanning flinched away like he'd felt the touch of a snake.

Shi Mei's eyes narrowed. His face clouded over, yet a second later, he'd rearranged his features into a mask of serenity. "Enough," he said, his countenance gentle as ever. "You've always been hard-headed. In the past life, you intended to kill him, did you not? But in the end, you couldn't bear to. Just before you died, you even transferred your broken souls into his heart."

He was correct. During that terrible final battle in snowy Kunlun, when Chu Wanning had touched Mo Ran's forehead for the last time, he'd channeled the fractured remnants of his souls into Mo Ran's body. By the end of his previous lifetime, his souls had been splintered and separated from each other. He had left one fragment in the body of the teenaged Mo Ran, and given another to his slumbering other self. He'd taken everything that remained, along with his final, precarious hopes, and bequeathed it all to Emperor Taxian-jun.

Chu Wanning hadn't known what effect this might have on the Flower of Eightfold Sorrows in its third stage of development.

But he knew the gu flower received its first nourishment from the soul of its spellcaster. If he channeled his own souls into it, perhaps something would change.

At that point, he was no more than an empty, battered shell. He'd exhausted his strength doing all that he could, all that he had to do. He had always been iron-willed and decisive; Mo Ran was his first and only weakness. Because he'd held tight to a thread of hope that Mo Ran could be saved, he hadn't killed him. He didn't mind offering up his shattered souls, whether or not it would be of any use—he just wanted to bring the old Mo Ran back to the world of the living.

Shi Mei laughed, as if he understood everything Chu Wanning hadn't said. "Your last-ditch effort couldn't pull the gu flower out of Mo Ran's chest, but you did succeed in influencing his emotions. He found himself caught between good and evil, ultimately succumbing to madness and dying by his own hand."

Chu Wanning's expression flickered as he looked up in silence.

After crossing paths on Mount Jiao with that Taxian-jun without a heartbeat, he had guessed Mo Ran had met such an end. But he still felt a dull ache in his heart upon hearing Shi Mei say so bluntly that he'd taken his own life.

Watching him closely, Shi Mei continued, "Shizun, you did it— you protected him. I don't know how, but his souls transmigrated to the past." He sighed. "I still don't understand even now. You were an invalid then; how did you manage to dash my plans? Ah you... You always manage to surprise me."

He lowered his dark lashes, downy as cattail fluff, and drew closer, as if to kiss Chu Wanning's lips.

Chu Wanning jerked back to reality. Lightning-fast, he grabbed Shi Mei by the throat, veins bulging on the back of his hands.

Shi Mei's expression didn't waver. He calmly reached up to grip Chu Wanning's wrists, as though he'd anticipated such a reaction. "Really, Shizun?" He chuckled. "Ruining me once isn't good enough for you? Unfortunately, you're too late."

With a soft hiss, a gold-and-black banded krait slithered out of Shi Mei's wide sleeves and clamped its jaws around Chu Wanning's arm. Who knew what kind of magical tempering the snake had undergone, but the single bite was unbelievably agonizing. Chu Wanning's hands immediately went limp. Maneuvering him easily by the wrists, Shi Mei bound him against the bedpost in an even more humiliating position than before.

"Don't worry, the snake isn't venomous." Shi Mei tied Chu Wanning's hands together, then sat up and stroked the banded snake with snow-white fingertips. He narrowed his peach-blossom eyes. "I raised this snake just for you. Its bite will sap you of strength. Out of respect for Shizun, I'll leave it at this."

Shi Mei raised his hand, and the snake slithered back into his sleeve. "Speaking of the past life—in truth, I never wanted to leave you with Mo Weiyu for so long." Shi Mei stood up. With unhurried movements, he removed his cloak, then his outer robe, then...

All the color drained from Chu Wanning's face. *"Shi Mingjing—!"* he thundered, revolted.

Shi Mei flashed an agreeable smile and paced closer. "Shizun, I'll tell you a secret. When you two were married in the past life, I came to the wedding banquet as Hua Binan."

Chu Wanning's eyes flew wide in shock.

"Emperor Taxian-jun draped you in red silks, selfishly preventing the guests from seeing your face. They only knew he'd married a Consort Chu, but I knew it was you. When the banquet ended, I didn't leave. I slipped into the Red Lotus Pavilion—and then he walked in."

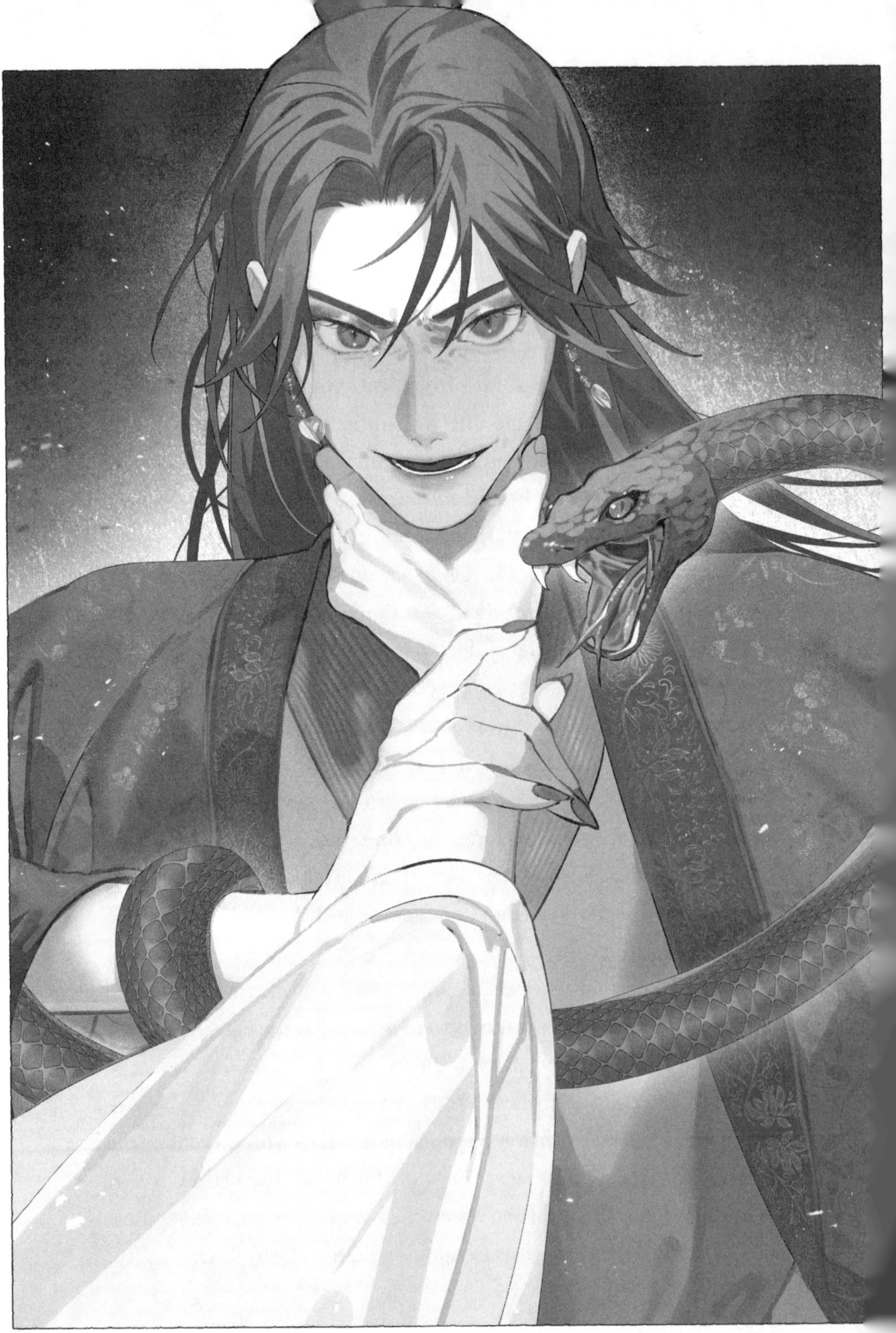

Shi Mei's eyes glittered. "He was under the control of my flower, but his thoughts and emotions were still his own. I hid—I couldn't let him detect me—but I didn't leave."

Overwhelming fury and disgust sent tremors through Chu Wanning as he looked back at him.

Shi Mei took a seat on the bed, laying cool hands on Chu Wanning's chest. "Did you know?" His voice had become slightly hoarse, his eyes glimmering hungrily. His fingers trailed downward and paused at Chu Wanning's waist. He began to untie Chu Wanning's sash. "The sight of you that night, mad with lust from the aphrodisiac, as he fucked you till you screamed... *Tsk.*" The rims of Shi Mei's eyes were reddening with desire. "It's fueled my fantasies for two lifetimes."

This humiliation was almost too much to bear. But Chu Wanning was exhausted from receiving the memories from his other lifetime, and the snake bite had left him without any strength in his limbs. "Shi Mingjing," he gritted out, "get the fuck out of here!"

Shi Mei let out a tinkling laugh. "It's just sex; no need to be so touchy. Besides, haven't you already let one of your disciples fuck you? Enough with the sanctimonious act."

"Get *out*!"

"What's the difference between getting on your knees to satisfy one disciple versus two?" Shi Mei asked blithely. "*I* don't mind. So why don't you just lie back and enjoy it? You never know, my skills might be better than his."

"Get. The. F—"

Before Chu Wanning could finish, he heard a frigid voice from the door. "Get the fuck out."

Chu Wanning jolted as if struck by lightning, whipping his head around. Without his notice, someone had opened the stone door from outside. At its threshold stood a man with his face in shadow, holding a long black-and-gold blade to his chest. He loomed imposingly with the door ajar behind him, a stern and upright silhouette lit from behind.

Shi Mei's brows knit together. "It's you...? Back already?"

The man strode into the room, frigid air gusting in his wake. The candles swayed and flickered. Their light seemed somehow cold as it landed on his slim-fitting combat robes and leather armor, illuminating him fully at last. His long legs were wrapped tightly in a pair of black military boots, and he wore a belt with a silver dragon's-head buckle around his slender waist, with a weapon compartment of pure silver hanging from it. His thorned vambraces flashed above a pair of black dragonskin gloves. Above it all was a handsome, chiseled face, his features impossibly gallant.

Emperor Taxian-jun.

He emanated a terrifying cold, and the coppery scent of blood lingered on him, as if he'd just come from the battlefield. When he looked up, his pale cheek was still marred with a few flecks of blood. His dagger-like gaze honed in on the two men upon the bed. His eyes skimmed over Chu Wanning then bored into Shi Mingjing, glinting like shards of ice. "Fuck off."

A chill settled over Shi Mei's features at the sight of him. He slowly sat upright. "Did you kill all those people at Guyueye like I told you?"

"It wasn't enough to satisfy this venerable one's appetites." As he crossed the room, he tore off his gloves with flashing white teeth, revealing fine-boned hands beneath. He tossed the bloodied dragonskin onto the table, then fixed Shi Mei with a glare. "Watch yourself. This venerable one won't hesitate to make you another vengeful ghost who's died by my hand."

Shi Mei's expression was unsightly. "Don't forget to whom you're speaking."

"This venerable one only cares whether or not I'm having a good time," Taxian-jun shot back coldly. "You're in the wrong bed. Out."

"Since when do you have the right to use that tone with me?"

"This venerable one has always had it," Taxian-jun said, voice laced with threat.

Shi Mei seemed on the verge of losing his temper. "I am your master!" he cried, eyes flashing.

"So what? Mount Jiao is this venerable one's territory, and on that bed is this venerable one's property." Taxian-jun loomed over Shi Mingjing, the corner of his mouth quirking with mockery. "Master. Kindly fuck off."

Taxian-jun and Shi Mingjing continued to fling insults back and forth, neither giving an inch. Chu Wanning watched from the sidelines in silence, rather lost.

Shi Mingjing had said Taxian-jun was dead, so what was this man before him? A pawn? A puppet? Plus, the gu flower he'd neutralized had resided in the body of the present timeline's Mo Ran. Emperor Taxian-jun's flower had been rooted too deeply; his heart could never recover. As such, he should've been hopelessly in love with Shi Mei—but judging from his tone, he didn't give a rat's ass about him.

And why did he call him his master?

Shi Mei glared at Taxian-jun, then scoffed and rose to his feet, draping a robe over his shoulders. Naturally, he was well acquainted with the answers to these questions that stumped Chu Wanning.

Mo Ran's suicide in the past lifetime had cost Shi Mei his most formidable weapon. He'd used medicine to revive Mo Ran's physical body and rouse the cognizance soul that remained within it, turning the dead man into a revenant. The result was similar to a Zhenlong pawn—

Taxian-jun would obey Shi Mei's orders while retaining his original consciousness.

There were, however, several outcomes that Shi Mei had not foreseen. Perhaps he had made a mistake somewhere, or perhaps Mo Ran had suffered too much trauma while alive, or perhaps the unnatural modifications to Mo Ran's body—first in life, then death—had caused some irreversible damage. At any rate, the revenant Taxian-jun's memories of Shi Mei were hopelessly confused. He'd think Shi Mei was alive in one moment and dead in the next. Sometimes, he'd forget who Shi Mei was entirely. Even though Taxian-jun was presently staring Hua Binan in the face, he didn't recognize this person before him as the man whose memory he'd long cherished. He only saw him as his master, whose orders he often ignored.

"You're impossible to deal with." Shi Mei walked up to Taxian-jun and prodded him in the forehead. "Scatter Soul!" he commanded.

Taxian-jun stiffened. His sharp gaze went slack, his pupils losing focus.

"You're a puppet I made, but you're getting more and more defiant, always talking back to me and trying to undermine me." Shi Mei patted Taxian-jun's ice-cold cheek. "It's fine, I don't blame you. You're a mere scrap of a person, after all."

Taxian-jun stared straight ahead in uncomprehending silence.

"Try to bear with it a little longer," Shi Mei advised. "Once I get my hands on the item we talked about, I'll refine it for you. Then you'll behave."

Yet just as he said this, his control over Taxian-jun again began to fray. Shi Mei's face turned somber as he saw how quickly Taxian-jun was recovering. In no time at all, Taxian-jun's eyes were once more bright and focused. If anything, they were even colder and more determined than before.

Taxian-jun turned that oppressively cold gaze on Shi Mei. He squinted slightly and wrinkled his nose, like a panther peering at its meal. "Hm? Why haven't you fucked off yet?" His slender fingers closed around Bugui's hilt. "Do you want to become one of this venerable one's sword practice dummies?"

Shi Mei didn't bother answering. Taxian-jun was too pigheaded; even as his so-called master, Shi Mingjing knew the rope around his neck would have no effect no matter how hard he yanked it. If this lord of darkness truly gave his wildest impulses their heads, the outcome would be frightful.

In the end, Shi Mei had little choice but to leave. As the door closed behind him, Taxian-jun stared at Chu Wanning on the bed. His expression was subtly strange, as though he was trying with all his might to hold back, yet was overcome by a longing he couldn't suppress.

He sat down and reached for Chu Wanning, grabbing him by the waist.

"I..." His voice faltered. He didn't know how to continue, so he pressed his lips together and changed tack. "You..."

Chu Wanning looked back at him steadily, but even after more than a moment, Taxian-jun didn't finish that thought. He blinked several times, his eyes swimming with undisguised bitterness. "Ahem. This venerable one has something important to tell you."

"Go on."

Taxian-jun hesitated again, then backpedaled. "Actually, it's not that important. No need to say it."

Met with silence, Taxian-jun spoke up again in an even more decisive manner. "It doesn't matter whether or not it's important. If you want to hear it so badly, this venerable one will tell you."

This left Chu Wanning at a loss for words.

"This venerable one wants to say..." Taxian-jun took a deep breath and closed his eyes. "This venerable one wants to say," he repeated stiffly, "that after all these years, it's almost like...this venerable one might have missed you somewhat..." He added hastily, "Not very much though. Just a little bit."

That handsome, bone-white face instantly clouded over with regret at having voiced such a sentiment.

Chu Wanning stared at him blankly, the souls and memories from two lifetimes bleeding together in his mind. He wasn't sure how he ought to feel about this man.

But Taxian-jun didn't leave him time to ponder. Almost distraught with impatience, he unknotted the rope from around Chu Wanning's wrists and tugged Chu Wanning toward him, bringing a broad palm to the back of Chu Wanning's head. Agitated and infatuated, he pressed a fervent kiss to his lips.

Taxian-jun's lips were cold as ice, but the flames of his passion were red-hot. In the space of this impetuous, frantic kiss, a flood of memories from a bygone life seemed to merge and overlap. Their lips once again met across two lifetimes of fickle fate. These two people—two sets of fragmented, imperfect souls—kissed and intertwined their limbs once more.

When Taxian-jun clutched him to his chest and kissed him, Chu Wanning's mind seemed to be simultaneously inundated and yet utterly empty, thoughts slipping through his fingers like water. But in the end, he could tell his eyes were wet.

Right and wrong, good and evil—none of it was clearly divided; none so easy to discern. But as he kissed this man whose body would never again be warm, Chu Wanning knew one thing: Taxian-jun wasn't lying. Mo Ran wasn't lying. He really had missed him.

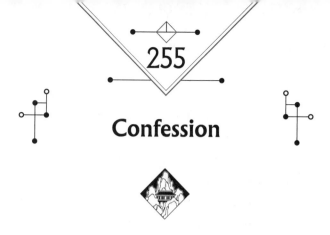

255

Confession

CHU WANNING DIDN'T KNOW how long the kiss lasted before Taxian-jun released him. He thought Taxian-jun had had enough, only to feel their lips come together once more.

It took several more aborted attempts at stopping before Taxian-jun was finally sated. He licked his lips, black pupils fixed on Chu Wanning's face. "It's you. You haven't changed."

After all that had happened, there were too many questions to ask. Chu Wanning was still for a moment, then spoke up in a hoarse voice: "Do you still remember the past?"

"Of course."

"Do you remember how you died?"

Taxian-jun's face darkened. "The ten great sects joined forces and surrounded me. This venerable one was sick of it."

"Do you remember how I died?"

The storm clouds slowly cleared from Taxian-jun's brow, only to be replaced by a different kind of shadow. "You stood in my way at Taxue Palace. This venerable one wouldn't allow it."

"Then do you remember how you came back to life after you died?"

"Hua Binan revived me."

"How did he do it?"

"Naturally, he..." Before he could explain, a strange blankness came over Taxian-jun's face. He closed his eyes, but only for a moment. When he opened them again, they were clear and bright once more. Taxian-jun knit his brows. "What were you saying just now?"

Chu Wanning didn't reply. He had more or less guessed what Shi Mei had done to Taxian-jun's body. A person's heart was the most difficult thing to control. After Mo Ran had died, Shi Mei wasn't powerful enough to rule this revenant's turbulent emotions, and he didn't dare touch Mo Ran's already fractured memories. He had thus opted to prevent Mo Ran from defying certain orders by erasing the relevant memories. This Emperor Taxian-jun really was no more than a walking corpse.

Chu Wanning closed his eyes. Eventually, his lips parted again, as though to speak. But before he could get the words out, he tasted iron at the back of his throat and began to cough violently.

"Mo Ran..." he choked out between blood-stained lips. He raised his watering eyes. "Stop working for him. You're just an empty shell; you should've been laid to rest long ago. You—" He was cut off by another spate of coughs.

His vision flashed dark, shattered memories threatening to engulf him once more. *You should go back to the past. You've already entered your eternal rest; you don't belong here.*

But Chu Wanning didn't have the strength to say this. His lips twitched one last time as his awareness began to fade. The last thing he saw was Taxian-jun's frowning face, his pallid, handsome features tense with worry as his lips formed a name.

"Chu Wanning." He hazily heard Taxian-jun calling to him, just like in the past life. "Wanning..."

He closed his eyes. The agony of his souls knitting back together rushed up again, and he knew no more.

Many mountains away, the leaves rustled in a forest in Sichuan. In recent days, misty rains had fallen continuously over the region. Even the wooden window lattice of the delivery outpost was beginning to darken with a faint layer of mildew. From its little window, one could watch drops of water falling one by one from the bamboo leaves outside, like beads rolling off a string. As they dripped into the puddles below, gentle ripples rose in their wake.

Without warning, a pair of shoes splashed through the water, shattering the peaceful reflection of the clouds.

Mo-zongshi had arrived before the winding path leading up to Sisheng Peak.

Since descending Dragonblood Mountain, his spiritual energy had yet to recover; he couldn't travel by sword. Yet so anxious was he about Sisheng Peak's safety that he'd rushed from Dragonblood Mountain entirely on foot, making the journey in a scant four days.

Along the way, he'd had time to think about many things. He thought about why he had been reborn, and why the past life's Chu Wanning had left that spell in the cave on Dragonblood Mountain. He thought about Shi Mei.

He pondered it all over the four days of his journey, but arrived at no satisfactory answer to any of his questions. He'd never been a clever person. In his current state—beset by torment and worry—he found himself unable to see anything clearly. Shi Mei knew him too well: Chu Wanning was his weakness. If Chu Wanning remembered his past life, it was tantamount to a death sentence for Mo Ran. His heart twisted in knots.

The rain fell faster. Mo Ran stood in the wind at the bottom of the steps leading up to Sisheng Peak. He lifted his head, rain-silvered locks framing his face. The stone stairway unfurled before him, winding its way up to the summit wreathed in mist.

He'd walked this mountain path through all the joys and sorrows of life and death. Across two lifetimes, he'd ascended these stairs countless times, from his naïve teen years to this final reckoning today, as he returned to answer for his crimes.

The day was cold, with bits of sleet mixed in with the rain. His black robes were slowly soaking through, his temples sodden and icy. These days of his youth should have been carefree, but the chill north wind turned his hair white with snow...

Mo Ran closed his eyes. He stepped onto the long staircase, climbing toward the top of the mountain. At last, he pushed open the red-lacquered doors of Sisheng Peak's Loyalty Hall—a fugitive walking straight into a well-laid trap.

The door creaked as it swung ponderously open. For two lifetimes, all of his madness and glory, his nightmares and sins, had been tied to this place. In his past life, at the age of twenty-two, he'd changed Loyalty Hall's name to Wushan Palace. He'd smashed the sign hanging above the door, reducing it to billowing dust. Standing before those ruined words, he vowed to trample the world's cultivators underfoot, to rule over all under heaven.

In that lifetime, he'd tumbled into the abyss here. In this lifetime, he would likewise meet his end beneath this roof.

Loyalty Hall was packed with people. The crowd contained even more notable figures than the group that had trekked up Mount Jiao to apprehend Xu Shuanglin. All of them turned at the creak of the door. They saw a tall man standing before the threshold. His complexion was wan, his bedraggled hair plastered limply to his forehead. Behind him, icy rain swirled down from the leaden sky.

Nobody had expected Mo Ran would appear so suddenly. Was this the hero who'd led everyone to safety on Mount Jiao, or the monster who'd slaughtered so many at Guyueye? Who was he, really?

For a moment, no one spoke. Every pair of eyes was fixed on the travelworn man who'd reappeared in their midst. Those who trusted him found him pitiable. He was wet and cold, like a dog who'd trudged home through the rain. Those who distrusted him found him terrifying. He was forebodingly wretched, like a ghost who'd crawled out of hell.

The rain pummeled the roof and its dark eaves, seeping into the cracks in the stone walkway and running over the moss growing on the shingles. Mo Ran looked up, his night-dark eyes wet beneath dense lashes like two black fans. "Uncle, I'm back," he said softly.

"Ran-er! Why—why are you by yourself?" Xue Zhengyong was sitting in the sect leader's seat. His face was lined with anxiety, and he wasn't dressed as neatly as usual. His iron fan had been haphazardly tossed onto the table, the words *Others Are Ugly* shimmering faintly, as if offering commentary on this farcical scene. "Where's Yuheng?"

Mo Ran took a step into the hall. He was like a drop of water landing in a pot of roiling oil, sending up a raucous splatter. Almost everyone simultaneously drew back from the doors.

"Mo Ran!"

"You monster! The nerve of you to show your face now!"

"You killed so many at Guyueye, yet you dare return here!"

Mo Ran ignored these shouts. He'd heard news of the bloody massacre at Guyueye on his way to Sisheng Peak. He knew better than anyone that Taxian-jun was deranged—what were a few dozen lives to him? Even the deaths of a hundred or a thousand hardly tipped the scale. To his mind, all the world's inhabitants amounted to no more than a swarm of walking corpses. Taxian-jun would think nothing of slaughtering all of Guyueye.

"Lunatic... You and Hua Binan are working together!"

"What are you trying to pull? The best fighters from every sect are here right now, and the master of Tianyin Pavilion is on her way. No matter how slippery you are, you won't be able to worm your way out of this one!"

"You really had us, Mo Ran—playing the hero one moment and the villain in the next. Do you think your schemes will succeed if you confuse the hell out of everyone? You're despicable!"

Accusations and taunts rushed toward him like a tide; faces etched with fury pressed in. But Mo Ran ignored them all as he continued forward.

By now, he'd understood what Hua Binan intended for him. Hua Binan—for Mo Ran didn't wish to call him Shi Mei—had dug a grave for Mo Ran. He'd already inscribed his name on the tombstone. Hua Binan was certain Mo Ran would jump into the grave of his own accord. The instant Chu Wanning remembered the events of the past life, Mo Weiyu had sentenced himself to death. He was beyond saving. Everything was over.

"No matter how many masks you wear, the heroes assembled here today will expose your true face."

"We'll send you to Tianyin Pavilion for sentencing!"

The crowd shouted and jeered. Over and over, their most frequently repeated refrain was *Tianyin Pavilion.*

Mo Ran hadn't expected Hua Binan to involve Tianyin Pavilion. Was it coincidence? Or part of a larger plot?

The lofty Tianyin Pavilion was an ancient sect established in the cultivation realm thousands of years ago. Their first leader had been the son of a god and a mortal, and the mantle of the pavilion master was thereafter passed down through his bloodline. Although the divine blood flowing through each new master's veins grew thinner with the generations, their spiritual energy remained bountiful.

Tianyin Pavilion did not often meddle in mortal affairs, but just as commoners believed in the power of cultivators, so too did cultivators believe in the righteousness of Tianyin Pavilion.

The longer any authority was enshrined, the harder it became to overthrow. In the past life, Taxian-jun had aspired to rule all the vast lands of the realm, but he'd left Tianyin Pavilion untouched. This maneuver of placing Mo Ran's sentencing in the hands of Tianyin Pavilion was an astute one. No one would—or could—challenge the verdict.

The noisy crowd parted before Mo Ran as he walked down the pollia-embroidered carpet. When he reached the front of the hall, he came to a stop. "I..."

With this single word, the hubbub died down. Everyone trained their eyes on him, many of their stares hateful and wary. They were waiting for him to talk back, to panic, to misstep. They were craning their necks in anticipation, ready to throw themselves at this evil monster and tear him to shreds. They didn't know if this man was good or evil, or what, precisely, he had done. But they would rather kill the wrong man than let him go; they would stop at nothing to—

"I've come to confess my crimes."

A hush fell over the crowd, a fuller silence than before. The assembled cultivators were like soldiers sharpening their sabers amidst the thunder of war drums and savage cries of battle—only to receive the sudden news that the enemy general had killed himself in his tent rather than fight. How utterly absurd.

"What did he say?"

It was a moment before someone finally reacted. Unable to believe this villain would admit his guilt so easily, one woman quietly asked her neighbor, "Did he say he's here to confess his crimes?"

Lashes lowered, Mo Ran knelt before his aunt and uncle and a deathly pale Xue Meng. The hazy lamplight fell upon his handsome, gaunt face. He intended to bare his neck for the executioner's blade, yet he was also unwilling to comply so readily with Hua Binan's schemes. Before his own reckoning came, there was one more thing he needed to do.

He hadn't much strength remaining, but he would exhaust it all to protect the man he'd never be able to protect again.

Mo Ran began to speak, slow and somber. "My hands are indeed covered in blood. Because of a personal grievance, I killed many people. For years, I've wanted to repent, but my crimes are unpardonable. Chu Wanning has already learned of this matter... I wish to lay bare my wrongs before you all today, and also to make another declaration."

Here he paused before letting the next words fall like a knife carving out his heart. "Chu Wanning and I are no longer master and disciple."

Most of the crowd gaped in astonishment. "What's going on?"

In the cultivation realm, it was considered a major scandal for a teacher and student to publicly part ways; such a falling out damaged the reputations of both parties. As such, a master and disciple would strive to maintain the outward appearance of harmony even if their relationship was uncomfortably strained, so long as the grudges between them weren't impossibly bloody or deep.

Once the initial shock passed, many began to mutter among themselves. "Weren't they getting along just fine before? What changed so suddenly? He'd better not be trying to trick us."

"Look at him—it doesn't seem like he's faking. Did something happen on Mount Jiao?"

"It's possible... Chu Wanning doesn't seem to place much value in his disciples. When Hua Binan captured Shi Mingjing, didn't he dawdle instead of rushing over to save him? Shi Mingjing was blinded... If I were his disciple, I'd be disillusioned too."

Their murmurs ebbed and flowed like a tide.

Voice rising over the chatter, Mo Ran continued. "He didn't tolerate my crimes, but that's not the main reason I wish to sever our ties. He has always treated me coldly and insulted my dignity. He speaks constantly of his compassion for the common people, yet he's so cruel to his disciples—a hypocrite! If it weren't for him, I would've never walked down this path."

It hurt too much. Mo Ran paused, his teeth chattering. But he had to press on; he had to keep dragging this blade across his skin.

"He mistreated me and misunderstood me. He and I don't share the same goals, and I'm ashamed to have chosen him as my teacher. From now on, Chu Wanning and I have nothing to do with one another. If anyone refers to me as his disciple after today..." He raised his eyes—Taxian-jun's eyes. "The very thought makes me sick. I beg of you all to never speak of it again!"

"Ran-er!" Xue Zhengyong gasped in horror.

"Ge, are you crazy?" Xue Meng cried, his face ashen. "Do you know what you're saying?"

Mo Ran closed his eyes. He couldn't bear to look at anyone in Xue Meng's family. Even that single cry of *Ge* was like a talon piercing his chest.

"There's one more thing I want to announce," Mo Ran said.

"A confession is a confession. What's with all these announcements and declarations? You—"

Before the protester could finish, Jiang Xi, the cultivation world's current leader, raised a hand for silence. Eyes on Mo Ran, he commanded, "Please continue."

"I have indeed committed terrible crimes and deserve to be punished in accordance with our laws," said Mo Ran. "However, what happened at Guyueye had nothing to do with me."

Many of the cultivators present had come to avenge debts of blood. Their emotions had been running high since they arrived. Hearing Mo Ran deny his involvement in Guyueye's murders, they could no longer restrain themselves.

"Bullshit!" someone shouted. "How do you think you can argue against eyewitness testimony?"

"That's right—who else could it have been?"

"I was never at Guyueye," answered Mo Ran. "During that time, Chu Wanning and I were both on Dragonblood Mountain. Someone else is the culprit. If I'm not mistaken, it's..."

He hesitated to name Taxian-jun. It wasn't that he feared the crowd's fury—rather, he was certain no one would believe anything so absurd as a second Mo Ran coming into this world through the Space-Time Gate.

"Who?" someone piped up.

Mo Ran pressed his lips together, resolving to wait a little before mentioning Taxian-jun. "I'll get to that later," he said instead. "At any rate, he is working with Hua Binan. One of them appeared at Guyueye to frame me, while the other abducted Chu Wanning."

Two types of cries rose up from the crowd: The first was weaker, yet still possible to make out, and came mostly from Sisheng Peak's disciples.

"What happened to the Yuheng Elder?!"

"Where did they take the elder?!"

The second was voiced by those who'd come to condemn and criticize. "Mo Ran, did you think we'd believe such a ridiculous story?"

"What the hell are you smoking? How could someone else be responsible—you're on the same side as Hua Binan! You two put on quite the performance on Mount Jiao. Killing so many people didn't faze you at all. Shi Mingjing is your own shixiong, yet you didn't hesitate to maim him! You—you heartless liar!"

At Shi Mei's name, Mo Ran slowly raised his head. He looked up at Xue Zhengyong, then glanced at Xue Meng. "About Shi Mei, he..."

Sick with worry, Xue Meng staggered forward a step. "What happened to Shi Mei? Is he okay?"

Mo Ran found himself unable to meet Xue Meng's eyes. He'd seen that kind of shattered expression on his face once before; once was more than enough.

"Shi Mei *is* Hua Binan," Mo Ran said, eyes still closed.

The entire hall fell silent. A moment later, Xue Meng dropped back into his seat. "Stop joking. How's that even possible..."

If he hadn't seen it with his own eyes and heard it with his own ears, Mo Ran would've thought the same. Shi Mei was gentle and good. The three of them had been through so much together. Shi Mei was the first real friend his own age he'd ever had. But this friendship turned out to be a sham, like the lovely reflection of the moon on water. It was a travesty from beginning to end.

The onlookers began to mutter among themselves. "What kind of nonsense is this?"

"He's lost his mind. How could that little cultivator be the world's foremost medicinal sage?"

"If Shi Mei was Hua Binan, why would he help us with the heart-tunnelers on Mount Jiao?"

One of the people Shi Mei had rescued was deeply grateful toward their savior. Heedless of any consequence, he pointed a shaking finger and cried, "Mo Ran, the gall you have to tell these brazen lies to clear your name! This is slander!"

Jiang Xi, who'd been listening with his brow furrowed in silence, now spoke up as well. "What evidence do you have that Hua Binan is Shi Mingjing? Hua Binan has worked in my sect for many years. During that time, he hardly ever left Guyueye. If he, like you say, is actually Shi Mingjing, how do you explain how he can appear in two places at the same time?"

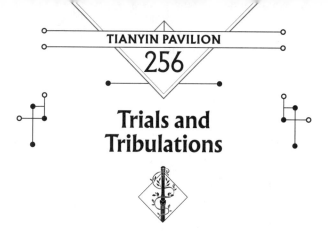

Trials and
Tribulations

"**H**ANLIN THE SAGE spends most of his time in his pill-refining workroom and rarely makes public appearances. When he does, it's with a veil," said Mo Ran. "All he'd need to do is control someone who could pass as a body double, and we'd be none the wiser."

"So what you're saying," Jiang Xi said, brows furrowed, "is that the Hua Binan at Guyueye is a fake?"

"Not always. The real one and fake one might have switched places as needed."

"To do that, Shi Mingjing would need to be able to wield the Zhenlong Chess Formation," Jiang Xi said, following his line of logic. "Our medicine master lacks the spiritual strength necessary for such a technique."

"Jiang-zhangmen is not wrong. The Zhenlong Chess Formation does require a prodigious amount of spiritual energy from its wielder. Hua Binan might know it in theory, but be unable to use it himself with his weak spiritual energy. That's why he needed Xu Shuanglin—"

"That makes no sense," Jiang Xi said with a shake of his head. "Xu Shuanglin called the person behind the scenes an ally; he was unwilling to betray them. All the way until his death, he refused to reveal his co-conspirator's identity. If, as you say, Shi Mei is Hua Binan, then Xu Shuanglin would've recognized him. But if that's so, when Hua Binan destroyed his Rebirth array, why didn't Xu Shuanglin turn on him?"

"Because Xu Shuanglin had no idea that Shi Mei and Hua Binan were one and the same," Mo Ran answered.

Master Xuanjing, the abbot of Wubei Temple, stroked his beard. "They must have been working closely together. How could Xu Shuanglin not know something so important?"

"Xu Shuanglin considered Shi Mei a friend, but there's no way Shi Mei held him in the same regard. To him, Xu Shuanglin would've been nothing more than a piece on the chessboard." Mo Ran thought it over. "Back when Hua Binan was injured on Mount Jiao, he removed his veil to reveal a disfigured face, with a raised, spiny texture to the skin. In retrospect, that was likely some kind of sophisticated skin mask. Perhaps Xu Shuanglin only ever saw the original face of this friend of his—that is, Shi Mei's face. He wouldn't have made the connection between Hua Binan and Shi Mei on sight alone. He died never realizing he'd been set up, used by someone he considered a friend. He never knew the truth."

"So according to this theory," Jiang Xi said, "when Shi Mingjing and Hua Binan were both on Mount Jiao at the same time, one of the two was actually a Zhenlong pawn?"

"That's my guess. But there's another possibility."

"What?"

Mo Ran shook his head. "I'll come back to it in just a moment."

"Let's say Mo-shizhu's first explanation is correct," Master Xuanjing said. "This humble monk still feels there's something we're missing—why did Hua Binan disrupt Xu Shuanglin's Rebirth array? Does he have some grudge against Xu Shuanglin? Some reason to deprive Xu Shuanglin of his wish to see Luo Fenghua reborn?"

Mo Ran sighed. "Does the great master recall what Xu Shuanglin's array turned out to be?"

The old bald donkey shook his head, taken aback.

"The rift that appeared wasn't Rebirth," Mo Ran explained. "In fact, Shi Mei didn't actually teach the Rebirth technique to Xu Shuanglin at all."

"Ah..."

"He was lying to Xu Shuanglin the entire time. Xu Shuanglin made all that effort, believing he was planting the seeds for his Rebirth technique, but all he did was grow a garden for the use of Hua Binan and his weak spiritual power."

"Then which technique did Hua Binan teach him?"

"The foremost of the forbidden techniques." The next words seemed to stick in Mo Ran's throat as he spoke them. "What Xu Shuanglin learned was the technique for the Space-Time Gate of Life and Death."

Murmurs ran through the crowd. Those who had been at Mount Jiao couldn't help but recall that black rift torn in the sky and the thousands of mysterious cultivators who had poured out. *That* had been the Space-Time Gate?

"This would be the other possibility I raised earlier," Mo Ran said. "Using the Space-Time Gate, it would indeed be possible for Shi Mei to be in the same place at the same time. One from this world, and the other from an entirely different world from our own."

The silence was broken by someone slapping their thigh and guffawing. "Mo-zongshi, what kind of bedtime story is this? Legendary forbidden techniques? Two Shi Mingjings?" The man was gasping with laughter. "You can't be serious!"

"Right? How would that even be possible, we're talking about a forbidden technique that's been lost for thousands of years… How would anyone even learn it?"

"According to legend, the most important scroll relating the Space-Time Gate technique was sealed within the Flame Emperor's sacred tree long ago. Even if somebody wanted to learn it based on the surviving texts, they would be able to master the space aspect at best. There's no way they could tear a rift in time—if one world's timeline were to overlap with another's, both worlds would be thrown into chaos!"

Mo Ran didn't bother to refute their objections. This was likely the very last opportunity he, as Mo-zongshi, would have to reveal everything. After today, the odds that these people would listen to anything he said were slim to none. He would use the pretext of confessing his crimes to hold their attention, to make them think, just long enough to share what he'd deduced. Whether they believed him or not, he would have said his piece. It was all the warning he could give them. If things got worse from here, perhaps some few might recall what he'd said today, and it wouldn't be too late.

"Everyone, please just imagine it. Pretend I'm Hua Binan, and I've grasped the fundamentals of both the Zhenlong Chess Formation and the Space-Time Gate, yet I have neither the spiritual strength to wield them, nor the status or authority to take reckless action. What would I do?"

Most of the crowd in the hall had already written Mo Ran off and were unwilling to hear him out. Jiang Xi, however, held some measure of esteem toward him after their previous interactions. He also had his own suspicions about the slaughter at Guyueye. He considered Mo Ran's question and concluded: "You'd get someone to help you."

"Who would help me?"

"Nobody."

"Right." Mo Ran nodded. "Truly, nobody would help. And so, as Hua Binan, I'd have no option but to deceive someone into helping. Someone with a powerful ambition or goal—someone like Xu Shuanglin. I'd befriend him, and I'd pretend to help him with his plans."

"Mo-shizhu is being absurd," Master Xuanjing scoffed. "What makes you so sure the array was the Space-Time Gate? The Gate is not a feat achievable by just anyone. In thousands of years, *nobody* has managed it. The most important scroll for the technique is lost. Who would be able to accomplish this?"

"Exactly," someone else piped up. "This is pure fantasy!"

"Why not say Fuxi's descended to walk this world again; it's about as likely as a Space-Time Gate opening."

"A ludicrous idea—even tavern storytellers would find this too much of a stretch."

Concurring murmurs filled Loyalty Hall. Eventually, someone said scornfully, "Mo-zongshi, you've laid it out so nicely. Surely you're not about to tell us that the one who killed those heroes at Guyueye wasn't you, but another version of yourself who came through the Space-Time Gate?"

When Mo Ran made no response, the crowd burst into laughter. "Incredible, incredible. To think Mo-zongshi would go to such elaborate lengths to exonerate himself."

"All that imagine this and that, and in the end he just wants to blame his crimes on a tall tale?"

Unable to bear the incessant chatter any longer, Jiang Xi shook out his sleeves and turned to glare at the hecklers. "If you've something to say, then out with it. What are you insinuating?"

"Jiang-zhangmen, it is not that these bystanders are insinuating anything untoward, but rather that Mo-zongshi's tale is far too fantastical." Master Xuanjing pressed his palms together piously. "In this humble monk's opinion, it would be best to invite Tianyin Pavilion to do a thorough investigation before any decision is made."

"That's right, Tianyin's pavilion master should be arriving any moment. Once she's here, let Mo-zongshi try and take her for a ride."

Before Jiang Xi could reply, Xue Zhengyong cut in. "Ran-er's reasoning makes sense. Perhaps the Space-Time Gate really *did* open. Tianyin Pavilion's investigations are reserved for only the most heinous crimes." Though his emotions were in disarray, his voice was firm. "Until we've cleared things up here, you're not taking him anywhere."

"That's right!" A Sisheng Peak disciple stepped forward. "When things were at their worst on Mount Jiao, it was Mo-shixiong who saved you. Would you be standing here today if not for him? If he really wanted to destroy the cultivation realm, he could've just left us trapped on Mount Jiao!"

"W-well..." Master Xuanjing sputtered.

"It's true," another person chimed in. "Back then, it was Mo-zongshi who opened the way. If he wanted to kill us, he could've done so right there."

The truth of this statement gave a few people pause. For a moment, the roiling crowd seemed to settle, but the matter was not so easily put aside. Many in the crowd had donned mourning colors for the friends and family they'd so recently lost, and for whom they were still grieving. The survivors of the massacre in the garden pavilion had witnessed Mo Ran's slaughter with their own eyes. Only Mei Hanxue had found something off about the situation;

every other survivor was fully convinced the killer had been the man standing before them now. For them to put aside their lust for vengeance would take much more than some fantastical tale of the Space-Time Gate.

It didn't take long before someone voiced new disagreement. "Something's still not right. All of you remember, don't you? On Mount Huang, Mo-zongshi displayed a profound understanding of the workings of the Zhenlong Chess Formation. He's saying Shi Mingjing knows the Zhenlong Chess Formation, but isn't he the one who knows too much about this forbidden technique?"

"That's right," another dissenter chimed in. "You know what else is odd? How did Mo Ran open the seal on Mount Jiao when he's not a Nangong descendant?"

"Nothing odd about that." A clear female voice answered from the entrance of Loyalty Hall. "After all, Nangong blood runs through Mo-zongshi's veins."

The crowd turned as one as a cadre of guards marched in arrayed in silvery green armor, each with a tassel dangling from their waist bearing a silver token embossed with the word *Tian*. At their head was a beautiful young woman who looked to be in her late twenties. With her bright eyes, clear features, and thick, inky hair, she could have rivaled the cultivation world's number-one beauty, Song Qiutong, if not for the iciness in her demeanor that underscored her striking looks.

Her appearance sent ripples through the crowd, and a few sect leaders stood up a little straighter. Only Jiang Xi remained unmoved, nodding as she strode across the threshold. "Pavilion Master, you've finally arrived."

This armored woman was none other the reclusive master of Tianyin Pavilion, Mu Yanli.

As the leader of Tianyin Pavilion, investigations into the most monstrous crimes committed in the cultivation realm all fell under her purview. Still, cases that required Tianyin Pavilion's intervention were few and far between, and thus Tianyin Pavilion's leader had rarely made any public appearances, or indeed stepped outside Tianyin Pavilion at all, in the past several decades. Her reclusiveness was evident in the fairness of her skin, so exceedingly pale one could see the faint traceries of veins beneath.

She took a few deliberate steps into the hall, then stopped and said evenly, "Apologies for my tardiness."

"Did something delay the pavilion master?" Master Xuanjing asked.

"Not quite," Mu Yanli answered with a shake of her head. "Tianyin Pavilion makes it a point to be thorough in its investigations before making any arrests. Before I came, I made several inquiries into the background of Sisheng Peak's Mo-zongshi." Her almond eyes were cold as she regarded Mo Ran, red lips parting around her next words. "These inquiries unearthed a rather complicated web of connections between this Mo-zongshi and a long-cold case in Xiangtan."

Everyone exchanged confused glances. "What long-cold case?" someone asked.

But Mo Ran had gone pale, his palms clammy with sweat. He'd never expected *this* to come back to haunt him.

Mu Yanli cast a cold glance over at the man kneeling in the front of the hall, her words falling like an executioner's axe: "Mo-xianjun, let's cut to the chase. You and I both know what happened in your past. Would you like to confess to it yourself, or shall I call in the witnesses?"

Mo Ran closed his eyes.

In the early days, after he'd just been reborn, he'd known that if he truly wanted to live freely, there were certain people he would need to get rid of or he'd risk regretting it later. At the time, he had neither power nor opportunity to do so. Later, when he had both the power and the opportunity, he was no longer inclined to take another's life for his own selfish reasons. After all, in the past life, he'd killed more than his fair share of people, either to conceal his past, or to keep bargaining chips in his hands.

Mu Yanli spoke into his silence. "It appears Mo-zongshi does not wish to confess." Undisguised scorn twisted the cold beauty of her features. Shaking out her sleeves, she turned to face the crowd. Her voice was bell-clear, resonating through the crush of assembled cultivators. "Then it falls to me. Heed my words—before this famed zongshi entered Sisheng Peak, he had already taken more than a dozen lives. This vile, despicable monster should have long been brought to justice!"

"What?!"

"He killed a dozen people before even entering the sect?"

"Ge...?" Xue Meng's eyes were wide with shock.

Though his voice wasn't loud, it reached Mu Yanli's ears. She glanced over at the young master of Sisheng Peak, and said mildly, *"Ge?"*

Xue Meng did not reply.

The sleeting rain pelted down outside, the skies overhead growing darker and darker, until even the candlelight within the hall was not enough to lift the chokingly oppressive atmosphere.

The contempt that filled Mu Yanli's gaze when it rested on Mo Ran turned to cold mockery when she looked upon Xue Meng. Her lips were like two sunset-stained clouds as she said, "Mistaking killer for kin? Truly Young Master Xue is to be pitied."

Xue Meng had no idea what she meant, yet the words crackled through him like a lightning strike, reverberating in his skull.

He stumbled back, eyes growing wider still. "What...what do you mean, mistaking killer for kin?" His entire body shook with fine tremors. "What nonsense are you..."

Mu Yanli turned away, losing interest in him. "Mo Weiyu is not Xue-zhangmen's nephew. In fact—" She paused, her pitiless gaze slicing like a dagger across Xue Zhengyong and Madam Wang's faces. Her voice rang with both righteousness and cruelty. "Eight years ago, Xue-zhangmen's real nephew was slain by Mo Ran."

257

Goddess of the Riverbanks

THE HALL ERUPTED into chaos—all save for Mo Ran, who remained calm, eyes still closed.

"How can that be?"

"What cold case in Xiangtan?"

"Why would he want to kill..."

Mu Yanli spoke over them. "It's a long story, and one that happened many years ago. Many of those who witnessed those events are no longer living, but as they say, the truth will out. Despite the difficulty, Tianyin Pavilion's investigations managed to unearth irrefutable evidence."

The tension in the room rose like smoke around them, yet Mu Yanli cut through, continuing without hurry. "Have the people I dispatched you to find in Xiangtan arrived?"

Her attendant excused himself to check outside the hall before returning with his answer: "Yes, Pavilion Master. They're waiting outside."

"Invite the first one in."

The first to enter the hall was an elderly tradesman, his back stooped with age, tremulous and quivering. At the sight of the hall filled with cultivators, he fell to his knees, kowtowing frantically as the words tumbled from his mouth. "Greetings, honored cultivators... Greetings, honored cultivators..."

"It's been a long, hard journey for you, sir, but there's no need to be anxious," Mu Yanli assured him. "I merely have a few questions. All you need to do is answer them."

The old man continued to tremble upon the floor until a monk from Wubei Temple brought over a seat and helped him onto it. Even then, the man was too terrified to seat himself fully; more than half his rear hung over the edge of the seat as he made himself as small as possible.

"I'll ask two questions to start. Where are you from? What do you do?"

The old man's teeth chattered as he answered in a strong accent, "I...I'm from Xiangtan, and, and, I just...sell lanterns...by the roadside..."

The crowd eyed him curiously, from the sparse white hair on his head down to his ratty shoes. How could this lantern seller be connected to such horrific events?

"And how long have you been selling lanterns, sir?"

"Most of my life...fifty or so years; it's hard to remember..."

"That's all right, what I want to ask you about happened much more recently than fifty years ago." Mu Yanli raised a hand to indicate Mo Ran. "Do you recognize this man?"

The old man glanced at Mo Ran and caught a glimpse of a tall, strapping young man, imposing in his magnificence. Hesitant to look in the first place, he barely glanced before tearing his eyes away. After a few moments, he snuck another look, then another, before eventually announcing, "No... No I don't."

"Not surprising," Mu Yanli said. "Let me ask you this then. When you sold your lanterns near the House of Drunken Jade in Xiangtan, was there a child who liked to stand by your stall and watch you work?"

The old man's memory of this was as sharp as his eyes were rheumy. "Ah... That's right," he said, nodding away. "The child who came nearly every night. He loved to watch me make my lanterns, but he was too poor to buy one for himself... I remember speaking to him a few times. A quiet lad—timid."

"And do you remember this child's name?"

"Hm...I think it was...Mo? Mo Ran-er?"

The crowd, now hanging on the old man's every word, turned as one to stare at Mo Ran.

Lost in memory, the old man mumbled, "Was there an 'er' at the end? I dunno...but he was from the House of Drunken Jade."

"Ran-er is indeed the child of my brother and the house's madam." Xue Zhengyong said, his brows drawn low. "Pavilion Master Mu, what are you trying to accomplish by inviting this gentleman here to tell his tale?"

"Madam?" Startled, the old man waved his hands in the negative. "Nah, that's not it. The madam's son was also Mo, but his name was Mo Nian, the little tyrant of the area." The old man lowered his head to gesture at a faded scar on his forehead. "That kid was vicious; I still have this scar from where he hit me with a brick. A right little terror, that one."

Xue Zhengyong's face paled. "Mo...Nian?"

"Sir, are you absolutely certain?" Madam Wang chimed in, anxious. "The names do share a character after all. Was the name of the madam's child Mo Ran, or Mo Nian?"

The old man considered the question carefully, then nodded again. "It was Mo Nian. No mistake about it; I wouldn't forget this. It was definitely Mo Nian."

Xue Zhengyong had been leaning forward intently. On hearing this, he stiffened, then slumped back in his seat, dazed. "Mo Nian..."

Mu Yanli pressed ahead. "The child who liked to watch you make your lanterns. Do you remember what he did at the House of Drunken Jade?"

"Ay, I'm not too sure about the specifics. Maybe helping in the kitchen? I do know he had a bad reputation. Rumor was the boy was light-fingered, especially around guests." The old man racked his brain, then his face lit up. "Ah, that's right. Nothing good came of that kid. He grew worse as he got older. I remember he raped a virgin—the girl killed herself for shame."

If the reveal of the identity swap had been astonishing, it was nothing compared to the shock that resounded through the hall at the revelation that Mo Ran had ruined an innocent young woman. A number of the cultivators in the hall, parents themselves, took it especially hard. One man growled through clenched teeth, "Who knew...the upright Mo-zongshi is actually a beast disguised as a man!"

"How vile!"

"Make him pay with his life!"

Mo Ran said nothing, silently watching the old tradesman. In his previous life, the bloodbath he'd made of the cultivation world had caused Tianyin Pavilion to step in as well. Back then, this very same old man had been brought forward by Mu Yanli to identify him.

And what had Mo Ran done back then?

He'd laughed in their faces, uncaring. He'd turned to Xue Zhengyong and Madam Wang, the mirth on his face twisting into a sneer. "And?" he'd said. "Do you hate me? Detest me? Will you turn on me, just like my good shizun did? Gonna tell me I'm vile by nature, beyond remedy?"

By then, Mo Ran had long been studying the Zhenlong Chess Formation. All his plotting had more or less been dragged into the open, yet Xue Zhengyong had still believed in him. Only after hearing the man's tale did Xue Zhengyong jump up, so enraged he was ready to spit blood, his tiger-like eyes bulging and teeth bared as he shouted, "Bastard! You...you *bastard*!"

The word *bastard* drew another guffaw from Mo Ran, deranged in his delight. He laughed so hard the corners of his eyes began to mist with tears. Raped a virgin? Xue Zhengyong believed he'd done that.

Xue Zhengyong seriously believed *he'd* done that.

Mo Ran's laughter had wrenched to a stop as he relinquished the last of his hope. His handsome face distorted like a candle melting into a warped mess of wax. "That's right. I committed every single one of those terrible crimes. I killed your nephew, I sent that pitiful girl to her death—and so what if I did? If Uncle wants to act as judge and jury, just go ahead and ki—"

Pain seared through his chest.

Xue Zhengyong was an impulsive man. Before Mo Ran had finished his sentence, he was already lunging forward, tears of hatred bright in his eyes, the sharp edge of his fan slicing across the skin above Mo Ran's heart.

Mo Ran had frozen where he stood. Then the corners of his mouth lifted. He lowered his head to look at the fresh blood dripping from his chest, then sighed. "Uncle... You've raised me for so many years now—yet you doubt me?"

"Shut up!"

Mo Ran smiled, but there was a quiver to the set of his shoulders. "Fine, whatever. When it comes down to it, we're not related by blood after all. So this sham of a family, this Sisheng Peak... There's nothing left for me to be sentimental about!"

Blood splattered hot and crimson across his face.

Numbly, Mo Ran watched as Xue Zhengyong crumpled at his feet. He hadn't wanted to kill him—but Xue Zhengyong, rash as ever, had been the one to strike first... He'd practically asked for it.

After a long moment, Mo Ran lifted his bloody gaze to the horror-struck Madam Wang. Licking his lips, he stepped over his uncle's body toward his aunt.

Xue Zhengyong reached out with the last of his strength to grip the hem of Mo Ran's robes, refusing to let go. There seemed to be a genuine distress and heartache beneath the fury of this middle-aged man. But Mo Ran, lost in his madness, had no idea how to interpret such an emotion in his uncle's eyes, or the tears welling up in them—nor did he want to.

"Don't..." Mo Ran heard Xue Zhengyong say. "Don't hurt..."

"She's a witness. I can't let her go." Mo Ran's voice was calm, even amiable. "At least Xue Meng's not around. In exchange for all those years you spent raising me, I'll spare his life."

What could Madam Wang do against Mo Ran? She couldn't fight him; she could only weep and repeat her husband's words. "Bastard..." As the blade slid in and blood spilled out, as her consciousness faded, as she looked at Mo Ran for the last time, she mumbled, "Ran-er... why...?"

In truth, Mo Ran's hands had trembled, unsteady, as he'd stabbed her. When he pulled out the dagger and looked down, they were slippery with blood. The dagger gleamed filthy and crimson in his grasp, still warm, but the warmth soon faded to nothing. Just like his home, like every single person he could call his kin. He'd lived with an undercurrent of unease all these years—deep down, he knew Xue Meng, Xue Zhengyong, and Madam Wang...none of them were related to him. Their real nephew had long died at his own hands.

"Ridiculous!"

The shout broke Mo Ran out of his reverie. His head shot up, but in his confusion, he looked left and right before realizing it was Xue Zhengyong who had cried out.

"I've raised this kid. I know better than anyone, there's no way he'd do that to a young maiden! This is a blatant lie!"

Mo Ran stared, stunned. A strange, acrid bitterness surged in his heart as he closed his eyes, lashes trembling.

It was different this time.

Between these two lifetimes...so much was different.

The old craftsman was so startled he tumbled off his seat and began to kowtow, knocking his head against the floor. "N-no, I'm not lying—Xianjun, please calm down, I just... I really... I'm not lying..." He was but a pitiful craftsman, completely out of his depth. To be shouted down by a sect leader so alarmed him that his complexion went a muddy gray. He couldn't even stammer out a full sentence.

"Get out." Xue Zhengyong's low command held a leashed fury. When the old man didn't move at once, it was followed by a sharp *"Out!"*

The old tradesman finally scrambled up but was stopped by men from Tianyin Pavilion. Trapped, he dropped to the floor, shivering, and mumbled over and over, "What the hell, why is this happening..."

"Xue-zhangmen," Mu Yanli warned. "Kindly keep your temper in check. Sir, there is nothing to be afraid of. Tianyin Pavilion only seeks to right wrongdoing, we do not stoop to making false accusations or harming innocents." Helping the man up, she gestured. "Please sir, continue."

"I dunno what else there is to say..." The old man was well and truly frightened; he didn't dare continue reminiscing. "Xianjun, venerable monks, I beg you all to let me go, I really have nothing else to say, my memory's terrible, it's really really terrible."

Amidst this deadlock, Mo Ran, who had been silent all this time, suddenly turned to Xue Zhengyong and dropped into a deep kowtow. His reaction left no doubt in anyone's mind.

"Ran-er?"

Xue Zhengyong and Xue Meng were both speechless, unable to manage a single word. That soft, disbelieving murmur had come from Madam Wang.

"Back on Mount Jiao," Mo Ran said, "I said I would tell Uncle about everything once we got back. I never expected things to turn out like this." His gaze was serene—so serene it seemed almost hollow as he continued to speak into the stunned silence. "Pavilion Master Mu, I assume you've gathered evidence and witnesses over the past few days. There's nothing much left for me to say, is there? Yes, that's right. I'm not the second young master of Sisheng Peak."

His next words drifted into the hall on the back of a soft sigh, featherlight. "My father is the city lord of the ninth city of Rufeng Sect's seventy-two cities, Nangong Yan."

"What?!" Someone in crowd blurted in shock.

"You wanted to hear the full story, didn't you?" Mo Ran closed his eyes before continuing. "The fire at the House of Drunken Jade that year was indeed my doing. The people who lost their lives in that fire died because of me."

"Ran-er, why..." Madam Wang choked out through tears. "Why would you..."

"But that year in Xiangtan, the tofu-seller's daughter who was violated and died—"

He fell silent. In his previous life, nobody had been willing to hear him out. They'd rebuked him, they'd scorned him, and so he had lost any inclination to explain himself. He was such a reprehensible monster in their eyes; what was one more bloodstain on his record? But in this life, he finally had the chance to speak.

"I did not harm that girl."

Loyalty Hall was silent as a tomb, all eyes fixed on Mo Ran as they waited for him to continue recounting those bygone events whose truths had been lost to time.

Mu Yanli raised a brow. "Oh? Is there more to that case?"

"Yes."

"Do go on," Mu Yanli said. "I'm all ears."

But Mo Ran shook his head. "Before I get to the story of how the tofu-seller's daughter met her tragic end, there's someone I must introduce first."

"Who?"

"A songstress." As Mo Ran spoke, his gaze went distant, looking past the shutters of the open window off into the horizon beyond. "In those days, there was a pair of pipa players in Xiangtan. One was named Xun Fengruo, and the other... Duan Yihan."

The names were familiar to quite a few in the crowd, and their eyes widened in recognition.

"Xun Fengruo... Duan Yihan...ah! Those famous pleasure house musicians?"

"That's them! I remember—the two were musicians from Xiangtan, hailed as the twin goddesses of the riverbanks, after their hometown's geography."

"Yes, how did it go now? 'Fengruo's singing heralds the arrival of spring, Yihan's dancing fills the skies with flowers' was it?" One man stroked his beard with a sigh. "I was in my thirties then, and those two were all anyone could talk about. They were highly sought after, and their performances were very exclusive. Supposedly, wherever

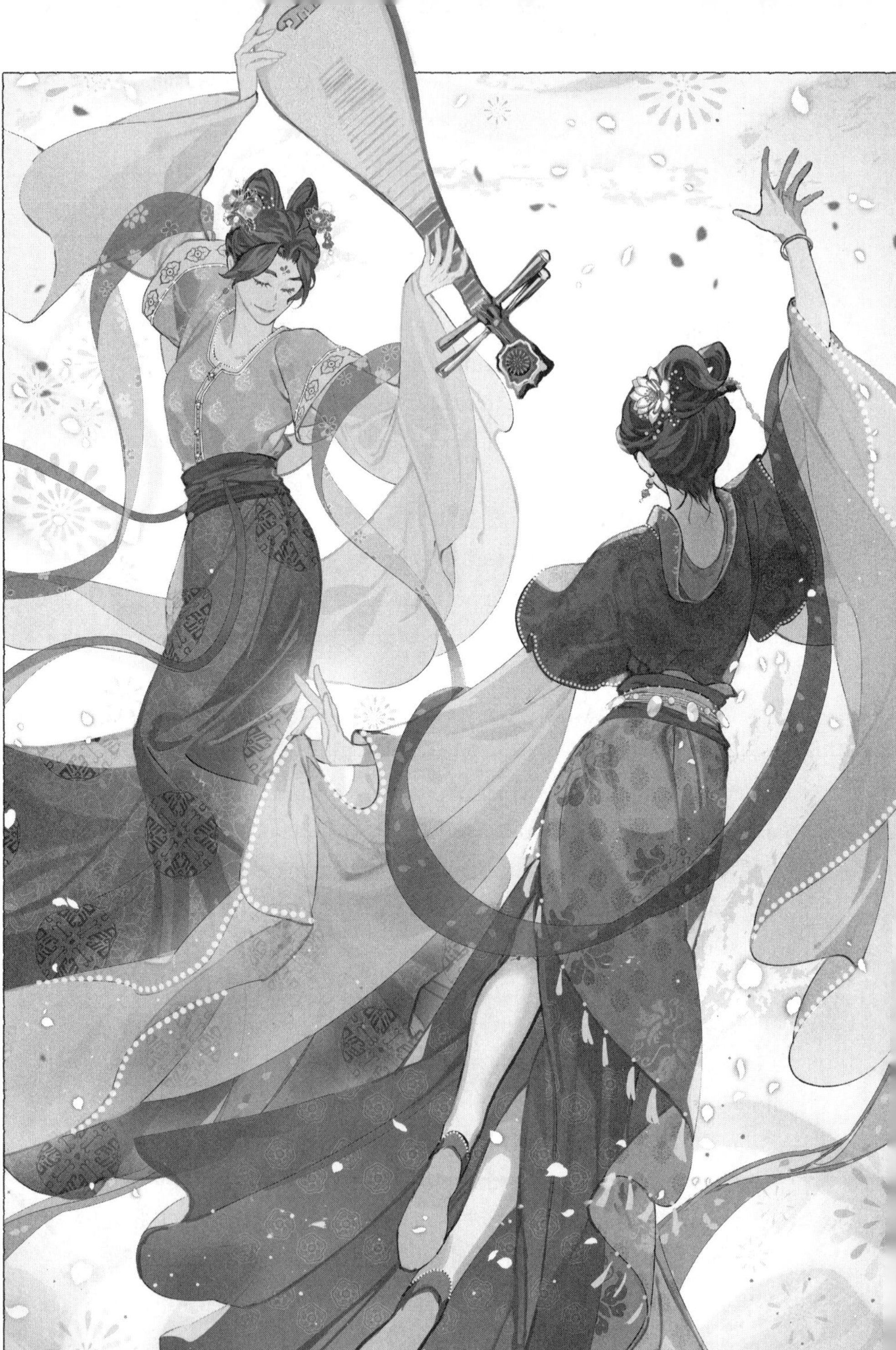

they performed, the pleasure houses would be filled to capacity and beyond—they were that popular."

"Didn't those two legendary musicians duel at some point?" another voice chimed in.

"They did," Mo Ran confirmed. "Xun Fengruo was two years younger than Duan Yihan, and accordingly joined the pleasure house she worked at two years later. Her youthful arrogance wouldn't allow her to tolerate Duan Yihan as a rival in fame, and she threw down a challenge, inviting Duan Yihan to a competition at the House of Drunken Jade. Three songs played, three songs danced, to see whose skills were superior."

"Who won?"

"It was a tie," Mo Ran said. "But it was the start of a fast friendship between the two. Though Xun Fengruo and Duan Yihan worked at different pleasure houses, they frequently crossed paths and became as close as sisters."

One impatient listener cut in: "What's all this got to do with anything?! Why bring these women up now?"

Mo Ran flicked a glance over at the speaker, then said, "Duan Yihan was my mother."

258

Pride
Unyielding

HIS DECLARATION was met with shocked silence. The mere sight of Duan Yihan stepping out with her pipa in her arms cost extravagant sums of silk and coin. That celestial goddess of music was Mo Ran's *mother*?

"My mom happened to cross paths with Nangong Yan, the ninth city lord of Rufeng Sect, in the entertainment houses. He had some skill at poetry and song, as well as a silver tongue and good looks to boot." Mo Ran paused. "My mom made the mistake of falling for him."

Xue Meng shook his head. "How could this be...?" he murmured.

"In what world would Nangong Yan refuse a beauty falling into his lap? But he was mindful of his rank and status, and didn't dare reveal his true identity to a songstress. He told my mom he was a businessman from Linyi who was visiting Xiangtan."

"Um...they were lovers, after all. If they spent their days together, how did your mom not find out?"

Mo Ran scoffed. "If she did, many things would've been different. Nangong Yan was a consummate liar, and he was only in Xiangtan for a short while. My mom had no time to discover the truth. While he was there, a letter came from Linyi. As soon as Nangong Yan received this mysterious note, he left Xiangtan in a rush."

"Did your mom not ask where he was going?"

"He left in the middle of the night without even saying goodbye. They'd been together for months, yet Nangong Yan merely left a stack of silver leaves and a slip of paper with the words *Yearn not for me* before disappearing into thin air."

A female cultivator sighed. "Dancers and singers at these places are always hoping for true love. How pitiable." Unable to contain her curiosity, she inquired, "What then? Did his abandonment leave your mother so devastated she sent someone after him?"

Mo Ran shook his head. "My mom was kind, gentle, and timid. She kept her suffering to herself even after being abandoned." He paused. "But soon, she found she was with child."

Madam Wang gasped. Her eyes were filled with grief; she had no idea what to say to Mo Ran.

"The entertainment house was willing to keep her on the condition that she get rid of the child. A mother did not dance as beautifully as a maiden, and they were not in the business of losing money."

Mo Ran closed his eyes. "My mom refused, but the madam asked for a huge sum for her freedom. She took all the savings she had, every valuable thing she owned down to the embroidered slippers on her feet, and bought herself the freedom to seek my dad in Linyi."

"How did a penniless woman travel all the way from Xiangtan to Linyi?" whispered Madam Wang.

"Someone helped her," Mo Ran said.

"Who?"

"Xun Fengruo. When Xun-jiejie heard my mom had left the entertainment house, she rushed out in the dead of night. She gave my mom all the coin she had and said that if she couldn't find my dad, my mom should come to the House of Drunken Jade in search of her, and they'd live happily together."

Master Xuanjing sighed. "Such tender sisterhood. I underestimated these women."

"What then?" asked Jiang Xi. "Did your mom find Nangong Yan?"

After a beat of silence, Mo Ran burst into laughter. "She did. Nangong Yan had faked his name and identity, but my mom still found him with no trouble at all."

"Huh?" someone gasped. "No way!"

"Yep," answered Mo Ran. "Through pure coincidence."

The audience members exchanged confused glances. "How can that be?" someone asked. "The city lords of Rufeng rarely show themselves in public."

"That's true." Mo Ran's features took on a darker cast. "But...at weddings, and at the first-month celebrations for their children, Rufeng Sect always hosts a banquet and accepts well-wishes upon the city towers, do they not?"

Comprehension dawned upon the crowd. "Was the letter Nangong Yan received a command for him to return home to be married?"

Someone else burst out, "I remember now! Nangong Yan's wife was the daughter of a rich family—was he forced to give up the songstress he'd pledged himself to and go home to marry the rich maiden?"

Apathy was written all over Mo Ran's face. "He wasn't forced to give her up, nor did he go home to be wed. The mysterious letter he received was actually a piece of good news—the leader of Rufeng Sect had informed him that his wife was about to give birth, and he should hurry home to be at her side."

Xue Zhengyong had been listening in pale-faced silence, but at this, he couldn't help blurting, "So, when Nangong Yan was having his fun in Xiangtan—he was already married?!"

"Mn." Mo Ran lowered his lashes. Surprisingly, he didn't seem remotely upset. "Nangong Yan had gone traveling to take his mind off the fact his wife was pregnant yet so sickly she stood to lose the child. When he met my mom, he liked her, so he lied and said he was unmarried to win her over."

Someone stomped a foot in fury. "What a beast!"

"Going off to have his fun with his pregnant wife at home, and getting a child on another woman too!"

"Poor Duan Yihan. Did Nangong Yan even acknowledge her?"

Of course, the answer to this final question hardly needed to be said. After the waves of castigation, the eyes on Mo Ran were growing more sympathetic.

Mo Ran didn't care what they thought of him. He continued his mother's sad tale. One secret, kept across two lifetimes. This was the first time he was speaking these words out loud, and there was relief in the telling amidst the pain.

"A banquet was held in Linyi to celebrate the birth of the city lord's son. When my mom arrived at the ninth city, she saw Nangong Yan atop that richly decorated tower with his arm around his wife, giving his thanks to the people below and tossing out treats. My mom...never sought him out. She'd spent every coin she'd had to get there—she couldn't even make her way back to Xiangtan. After a few months, she gave birth to me alone, in an abandoned woodshed in Linyi."

"Did she take you back to the House of Drunken Jade?" asked Jiang Xi.

Mo Ran shook his head. "When I was born, I was weak. I fell terribly ill before I was even a month old. There was no way she could travel with me. She went begging at the door of every doctor in the city, but no one would help her. Eventually, she had no choice but to go to Rufeng Sect with me in her arms in search of Nangong Yan."

Thus had that frail mother and her kitten-like newborn appeared, travel-worn and weary, before her bygone lover.

That man had felt no joy upon seeing them—only endless shock and fear that soon turned to anger. He had a wife and son of his own, and his bride was the distinguished daughter of a powerful family. His son was a cute and chubby baby; their family was peaceful and whole. In his eyes, Duan Yihan was like rat droppings on his doorstep, an unwelcome sight that threatened his reputation and family. Surely this woman had come with some motive in mind. Why on earth would he acknowledge them?

Afraid she'd make a scene, Nangong Yan gave her sufficient coin and told her to get the hell out of Rufeng Sect. Clutching at the last of her hopes, Duan Yihan spoke through her tears: "The child doesn't yet have a name. Could you—"

Nangong Yan's face was gray with fury. "Get out! Get the hell out! This child is no son of mine. You'd better figure out what's good for you and get the hell away from here!"

She was crudely shoved out the door. Yet she had no time to grieve—the babe in her arms could barely whimper, and his hands and feet were freezing cold. He lay curled in her arms like a dying kitten. When she called to him, he squinted one eye open and gazed at her blankly. He wasn't mischievous at all; he was well-behaved and very quiet.

Blinking back tears, she brought her child again to a healer's hall. The doctor cried out at the sight of her. "How many times have I told you? We're not a charity, we don't take patients for free! If you have no money—"

She hastily dug out the dirty cash Nangong Yan had shoved at her to pay her off, terrified the doctor would frighten the baby in her arms. Misery shone in her eyes; she bowed and scraped before the doctor. "I do have money, Doctor, I do. Please, please do a good deed and help my son. Look, he's...he's still so small..."

The doctor wasn't cruel. His harsh manner was only because children's medicines were expensive, and this woman had bothered him too many times before. Now that she could afford treatment, his attitude changed.

So began weeks of herbal concoctions, acupuncture treatments, and an extended stay in the healer's hall. Mo Ran was sick on and off for months before he finally began to grow stronger. By then, Duan Yihan hadn't much coin left. She thanked the doctor and took her leave, carrying her child in her arms.

By this time, winter was coming to Linyi. Fearing the babe would take ill once again, she used the last of her money to buy a small cotton jacket and a set of blankets. She had nothing left with which to return to Xiangtan, but as Duan Yihan sat in that abandoned woodshed and looked at the little rascal sucking his thumb and gurgling up at her, she was happy and serene. She had an easy nature, content with small joys.

"What should I call you?"

The baby gurgled again. Duan Yihan started a fire, teasing him as they warmed themselves by its glow. When the child laughed, so did she. The flames flickered brightly. Though the shed was dilapidated, the fire warmed her to her core. She pinched the baby's small cheeks, playing with him until he kicked his chubby feet and laughed with joy.

After some thought, she said, "Why don't I call you Ran-er?"

Sucking on his fingers, Mo Ran watched her with his dark eyes shining.

"I don't know what your last name should be." Sadness stole over Duan Yihan's face. "You can't be a Nangong, but you can't take my surname either. Mine was chosen by the madam at the entertainment house; it'd be strange if you took it... I'll just call you Ran-er, after the flames, okay?"

Mo Ran released his finger with a wet smack. He looked up at her calmly.

"Little Ran-er, once spring comes, we'll go back to Xiangtan." Duan Yihan stroked his downy hair. "Mama knows how to play the pipa, and to dance. Miss Xun is there, and Miss Xun is Mama's best friend. I'm sure she'll love you. You should be good, and quickly learn to call her Aunt... Mm, forget it. With her temper, you're better off calling her Jiejie. Say 'Xun-jiejie' as soon as you see her, or you won't get any candy. Okay?"

Holding his soft hands, Duan Yihan whispered, "Ran-er, wait a little longer. When winter is over, when the flowers bloom, we'll go home."

But that winter lasted far too long. It was a year of disasters; the lower cultivation realm was overrun by demons, and Linyi reinforced its defenses by putting severe restrictions on the movements of commoners. Duan Yihan couldn't leave the city. She sought out work at a bun stall, trying to earn enough money to live on—but nothing stayed secret forever. Someone must have whispered to Nangong Yan's wife about her husband's misbehavior, and soon after, the stall Duan Yihan worked at drove her off for no reason at all. Afterward, Duan Yihan was given no more chances. She could find no work, no matter how little it paid, and was reduced to begging for scraps and performing on the street with her child at her side.

Often, she'd be singing softly as Nangong Yan rode past, garbed in finery and followed by his entire retinue. He avoided her out of shame, though there was no real need. Although Duan Yihan was weak, she was proud. She merely sang her songs of Xiangtan; she wouldn't spare her past lover a glance, let alone cry out to him on the street and ask why she'd been abandoned. Nangong Yan had never understood how proud this pipa-girl really was.

"Look how she cries; dressed in tattered cloth, unrecognizable to her kin—so why does she stare?"[9] she sang.

When someone threw a copper coin her way, she again became that beautiful goddess of music. Lowering her lashes, she'd bow and murmur, "Thank you for the kindness, good sir."

Months passed in this manner, then years. Ghosts and fiends continued to devastate the lower cultivation realm, while Linyi watched and did nothing. The evil-repelling walls stayed erected for five full years.

Mo Ran was now five.

One day, after arguing with his wife, Nangong Yan left in a huff to wander the city and clear his head. It was a beautiful day at the west market; he stood dispirited with his hands behind his back, looking down streets lined with bakeries and jewelry stores. Beneath a banyan tree, two old men played chess.

Linyi had always been a land of riches. No matter how many perished in the lower cultivation realm, what did it have to do with them? Here, cheer and prosperity had reigned for centuries.

Nangong Yan watched the chess match with interest. He had stepped out in casual clothes, unrecognizable to strangers. He stood there chuckling and throwing out suggestions until the men grew annoyed and shooed him off.

Miffed, Nangong Yan strolled along until he found himself under the shade of a great tree. A golden birdcage hung from its branches, holding a chirping canary.

---

9   Duan Yihan's verses are all from the song "Meeting by the Well" from the opera The White Rabbit, which tells of the reunion between a long-lost mother and son.

Perhaps the sunlight was so beautiful it cleared his heart. As Nangong Yan stood beneath the tree, lost in his own thoughts, he remembered that gentle girl who'd sung in Xiangtan. Cocking his head, he teased the canary. "My dear, do you know any Xiangtan melodies?"

The bird trilled its song, heedless of Nangong Yan's request. He sighed, humming under his breath the song Duan Yihan had sung countless times as she sat beside him.

A clear voice cut through his daydream. Someone behind him was singing: "Clouds gather low as the winter storm approaches; a world of snow freezes the well." That voice was like the tinkling of jade or pearls, transporting him to another time.

Nangong Yan whirled around. He'd avoided her for so long, yet out of nowhere—through the bustle of the city and the rushing passersby—he caught sight of that delicate woman, just as he had in those dreams he never dared mention to his wife.

They met once more.

Duan Yihan stood on the street with a fragile child by her side. Eyes lowered, she sang those songs that had once been impossibly dear, hoping to garner some little sympathy from the gentlemen walking past. Enough, at least, for a meal.

"Whether the broad road before the mountain or the narrow path through the backwoods, thousands pass by this way..."

People streamed past in droves. No one stopped for her. The song was beautiful, but it was only a pleasant sound. She was singing of her own free will; no one wanted to pay her for it.

"...Farewell is easy but reunion is hard; I look into the empty distance alone."

Shoes inlaid with jade and embroidered in gilt thread appeared in her vision. A man's voice finished the verse: "Countless letters left unsent, my sorrows gathering as I wait for you to read them."

Duan Yihan slowly lifted her eyes.

She saw Nangong Yan again, as handsome and refined as he'd been five years ago. He seemed not to have aged at all; time had left no trace of its passage on his face.

In his eyes, Duan Yihan saw her own reflection. That beauty from five years ago had grown miserably faded and worn. But Nangong Yan's gaze on her was soft. He'd been married for years, stuck with a woman who'd found out what he'd done and, not daring to voice her displeasure outright, had taken to expressing it in other ways. She lost her temper at the drop of a hat, and his son was likewise spoiled and ill-behaved. Now as he stood before Duan Yihan and saw her sorry state, guilt and compassion surged in his heart.

Duan Yihan fell silent. She lowered her lashes. The song was over.

"Mom?" Confused, Mo Ran turned to look at her.

"Mom's tired," she said. "Let's go home."

Mo Ran nodded, smiling. "Let's go back. I'll figure out how to get dinner."

Hand in hand, mother and son turned to leave.

"You..." Nangong Yan called after her. His gaze fell upon Mo Ran. This boy was skinny and his clothes were tattered, but he was clever and handsome. Nangong Yan realized—this was *his son*. His own flesh and blood.

He reached out to touch Mo Ran's head. Bewildered, Mo Ran squinted, allowing this stranger to muss his hair. "Hm?"

Nangong Yan recalled then how Duan Yihan had come to his door with a sickly babe in her arms, begging for help, telling him the child was not yet named.

"What's your name?" Nangong Yan asked.

"Ran-er."

"What's your surname?"

"I don't have one."

Nangong Yan turned a heartsick gaze upon Duan Yihan. Something compelled him to say: "Why don't you both—"

Before he could finish, he caught sight of a group of Rufeng Sect cultivators. He flinched as if woken from a trance. Nangong Yan met Duan Yihan's gaze once more. Those eyes that had once curved in sweet smiles for him were now hard, with no hint of girlish fantasy. Her gaze was cold and clear, even in the moment he'd nearly acknowledged them. She'd taken the measure of this man a long time ago.

In this light, Nangong Yan seemed pathetic, even disgraceful. He cleared his throat and magnanimously reached for his wallet, stuffing the bag full of gold and silver and precious baubles into Mo Ran's hands in an attempt to hide his own churning emotions. He patted the boy's head once more. "Your mom sings beautifully. These jewels should be hers."

A slender hand took the pouch from Mo Ran. Duan Yihan removed one copper coin and placed it in the bowl Mo Ran held, then gave the hefty pouch full of treasures back to Nangong Yan. She said nothing else. All she offered was a gentle bow, the same she'd make to any passerby who gave her coin. "Thank you for the kindness," she said in tones of perfect cordiality. "Good sir." With that, she turned to leave.

She'd been the music goddess of Xiangtan; her admirers had been as numerous as stars to her luminous moon when she danced. She had not been haughty when the masses gathered for a glimpse of her, and now that her shine had faded and she was reduced to singing by the street, she did not feel shame.

But her behavior that day made Mo Ran suspicious, and after all sorts of questioning and his own small investigations, he discovered the truth of his birth.

"I'm telling you this because I don't want to lie to you," Duan Yihan had said when she finally explained. "But—little Ran-er, you must remember not to hate, yet nor should you beg before him." She poked his little head. "Once the crisis in the lower cultivation realm passes and Linyi lets commoners through the walls, we'll go back to Xiangtan."

Mo Ran was silent for a very long time. "I won't beg him for anything," he said with a nod. "I'll go to Xiangtan with Mom."

Duan Yihan smiled. "I don't know if Xun-meimei will even recognize me. I'm not pretty anymore."

This comment deeply upset Mo Ran. "Mom is pretty."

"Hm?"

"Mom is the prettiest."

A smile bloomed over Duan Yihan's face, and that faded beauty did indeed reappear once more. "What a charmer," she teased. "You'll make your future wife happy for sure."

Embarrassed, Mo Ran pouted and fell silent. Yet those sharp little canines reappeared in his grin as he said, "When I grow up, I'll marry a wife as beautiful as a goddess, and then we'll stay with Mom forever."

"Aiya, keep dreaming. What kind of goddess would marry you?"

Twin chimes of laughter spilled into the shed as the firewood crackled beside mother and son. Wrapped in such perfect warmth, it was easy to imagine that every day that followed would be just as peaceful. The fire in the night conjured a beautiful illusion for the penniless pair; neither could have imagined that Duan Yihan was already running out of time.

"It was in the autumn of the year I turned five," Mo Ran continued. "The Mid-Autumn Festival had just passed. Rufeng Sect had closed itself off for so long there wasn't enough food for everyone in Linyi, so they put out an order to raise the prices. In truth, they meant to have the poorest among them fasting instead of fighting the rich for food."

The tale thus far had already wreaked havoc on Xue Zhengyong's heart, but at these words, he sunk into thought. He nodded. "Yes, I remember. Rufeng Sect only lowered the prices after the starving citizens rose in revolt. It lasted...maybe a year?"

"Six months or so," said Jiang Xi.

Mo Ran closed his eyes. "It wasn't that long. Just over a month—it was only thirty-five days."

At Your Side

"I T'S BEEN SO LONG! How can you remember?" someone asked.

But of course he remembered. In the upper cultivation realm, in Jiang Xi's memory, it had been an ordinary six months. In the lower cultivation realm, in Xue Zhengyong's recollection, it had been a year of sorrow.

But for Mo Ran, it'd been thirty-five days of sinking despair. Every morning had felt as long as a year; every day was torment, and every night was hell.

When the new prices were announced, everyone worried for themselves. No one would spare anything for Duan Yihan and her son on the street, so they had no choice but to dig through the trash for rotting vegetables and moldy bread. As more and more people went hungry, even the rotting vegetables grew scarce. Under these circumstances, Mo Ran couldn't help asking, "Mom, why don't we go to Rufeng Sect and ask him for food?"

But Duan Yihan mumbled, "Anyone but him."

Singing on the streetside, nodding her head and bending her back, hawking her wares and smiling—all this was work she did to survive. But begging before Nangong Yan was different. No matter how dire their straits, Duan Yihan couldn't bring herself to cross that final line.

Since she wouldn't bend, Mo Ran didn't bring it up again.

The little boy was unobtrusive and extraordinarily nimble. On the ninth day after the prices were raised, he managed to steal a white radish out from the dirt. Duan Yihan hid it very carefully. Every day, they'd boil a piece the length of a fist and share it. By the eighth meal of radish, the remainder was rotting, but there was still no food to be had. Duan Yihan cut it in half once more, in hopes of stretching it just a few days longer.

On the twenty-first day, they finished the last of the radish. Nothing edible was left.

On the twenty-fifth day, there was a great storm. Worms crawled out of the mud, and Mo Ran caught them and boiled them in a little rainwater to eat. Their sliminess was disgusting. Mo Ran apologized over and over to the tiny creatures, explaining that there was really nothing else. If he survived this, he promised, he'd honor the worms as his saviors. He prayed to the heavens, begging not to have to eat his saviors anymore... Begging for this nightmare to pass...

On the twenty-eighth day, Mo Ran fell sick with a fever. No child, no matter how quick or clever, or how strong their spiritual energy, could endure such privation.

Duan Yihan had no more strength left, her eyes two hollow pits. That day, as Mo Ran slept, she made up her mind. She rose and left the woodshed that was their home, turning her steps toward Rufeng Sect's lofty towers. She had her line in the sand; she'd rather die than beg Nangong Yan for food. But her child had done nothing wrong. He was so little—how could she bear to let him die with her?

Compassion shone on the faces of the listening crowd. Regardless of whether Mo Ran had sinned or not, these events of the past were all too tragic. Someone carefully asked, their voice a sigh, "Did she manage to get any food?"

"No," said Mo Ran. "Unfortunately, Nangong Yan was in the middle of a fight with his wife when she got there." He paused. "The madam had a fit the instant she saw my mother. Never mind showing her charity—she ordered her beaten and chased out of Rufeng Sect."

"What about Nangong Yan?"

"I don't know," said Mo Ran. "My mom never said."

He might've tried to stop them, or he might've stood there, helpless. Mo Ran would never know what happened that day, except that his mom returned covered in injuries. She lay curled up in the woodshed, holding him in silence—later, she began coughing, spitting out bloody foam and filling the room with the sour stench of copper and bile.

By the thirty-fourth day, Duan Yihan was close to death. She could barely speak, and she'd stopped crying. On that day, she woke from her stupor, having regained some measure of strength, and saw Mo Ran curled into her side, trying to use his body, all skin and bones, to keep her warm. Ever so softly, she whispered: "Little Ran-er, if you can, go back to Xiangtan."

"Mom..."

"Go to Xiangtan and find Xun-jiejie. Repay her." Duan Yihan patted Mo Ran's hair. "Go back to Xiangtan and repay her, don't stay in Linyi for revenge... Listen to Mom, be good. I owe your Xun-jiejie a lot of money... I can't pay it back... Go to her and stay with her, help her with her work and be sure to make her smile. When someone does you a kindness, you must remember it."

Holding back his tears, Mo Ran looked up into her emaciated face. Duan Yihan's eyes were so dark they seemed to gleam faintly purple. "And pay them back."

Such was the path Duan Yihan laid out for Mo Ran before she died. She feared her child would take a dark road after her death, so she gave him a thousand reminders to do otherwise. She exhorted him over and over again to leave this place of tragedy.

Someone with a firm purpose in mind wouldn't overthink; they wouldn't fall into the prison of hatred so easily. So she gave him that purpose: Go and repay her kindness. Do not seek revenge.

On the thirty-fifth day, that absurd price order was finally abolished in the wake of revolt. It had only lasted a month and five days. To the wealthy, it was as if a farce had ended. Smoke was rising from the ruins of Linyi, but they in their silken canopies only stretched lazily as day broke over the city, taking the fragrant dew offered by their handmaidens and rinsing their mouths. At news of the price order being abolished, they groused a bit, then yawned. None of it mattered overmuch.

But to Mo Ran, this was the best news of his life.

Now that they didn't have to worry about filling their own stomachs, kind people reappeared on the streets. Mo Ran was given a pancake and a battered bowl of pathetically thin gruel flavored with shreds of meat. He couldn't bear to take even a sip of it for himself. Cradling it with utmost care, he rushed back home to his sick mother.

Meat porridge is amazing—surely Mom will get better as soon as she has some?

He rushed to save his mom's life with that porridge, but he couldn't run. The bowl had a crack in its side; wouldn't it be a shame if any spilled as he ran? He burst into the woodshed with mingled delight and impatience. "Mom!"

Holding the broken bowl in his hands, he nudged open the shoddy door with his head like a particularly grubby dog. A smile spread over his face, his features creased with anticipation for the future. It was such a good day. They had meat porridge, his mom would get better; spring was finally here, and they'd go back to Xiangtan together. It would be peaceful there—they wouldn't go hungry, and there was someone named Xun-jiejie; they'd finally stop wandering and begging for food. What a wonderful thing it would be, to go home together.

The door creaked open.

"She was lying there," said Mo Ran, voice steady. Some of the onlookers were shocked at his calmness, others disturbed by his callousness. This man was serene even while describing his own mother's death. There was no warmth, emotion, nor even a glint of tears. No one gave any thought to how many years of haunted nightmares and agonized sorrow it took to smooth those scars into a peaceful mask.

"I called for her, but she didn't wake. She never would. She never had any of the porridge."

Silence settled over the hall.

"Then...afterward." It was Madam Wang, her voice quavering. "You returned to Xiangtan alone?"

Mo Ran shook his head. "I went to Rufeng Sect."

Someone exclaimed. "D-did you go to get revenge?"

"My mom told me to repay kindness, not to take revenge." Mo Ran was still unnervingly calm. "I didn't go for revenge. I just wanted to bury my mom properly. But I had no money, nor any time to raise it. I went to his manor to beg for some coin for a coffin."

"Did he give you any?"

Mo Ran almost smiled. "No."

"N-no? But you said Nangong Yan still felt something for your mom. Couldn't he at least spare something for the funeral...?"

"When I arrived, his wife had died by her own hand not long ago."

"What?!"

Jiang Xi narrowed his eyes. "Nangong Yan's wife did die young, and it *was* a suicide..."

"When that woman was pregnant, her husband was out getting bastards on other women. After she had their son, she and her husband fought constantly. Her life was a deeply unhappy one. When she caught my mom begging for food at the manor, she was furious—I heard she stabbed Nangong Yan with a knife, and he threatened to divorce her." Mo Ran paused. "She couldn't bear it. In the dead of night, she hung herself. Actually, she died just a few days before my mother did."

No one knew what to say. A dissolute young master's careless dalliance had left one woman in ruins and his own family destroyed. Perhaps it was karmic retribution.

"I showed up just as the sect leader was berating Nangong Yan. His wife's family was there too—all powerful merchants in Linyi. They'd already given Nangong Yan the sharp end of their tongue up and down, and all he felt was resentment. Of course he wasn't happy to see me."

Madam Wang had the softest heart of any in the room. Though she knew Mo Ran wasn't kin, she still wept and murmured, "Ran-er..."

These were not memories he wished to relive. The sight of Nangong Yan's face, the faces of all those there to pay their respects in Madam Nangong's memorial hall. That woman had everything—gilt paper, silver flowers, paper dolls and piles of spiritual tools, brocade soul flags and a gleaming casket of goldwood. Hundreds wept, kneeling in vigil for a woman who'd taken her own life. The everbright lamps were filled with scented whale oil, and those ninety-nine coils of incense burned in silence, scattering fragrant ash at the soft touch of the breeze. It was a busy scene of mourning.

But what of his own mother? Duan Yihan, the music goddess of Xiangtan, only had rags unfit to wear and a son who was skin and bones. She lacked even a straw mat to wrap her body in.

"Beggars can't be choosers"—these were the words Nangong Yan hurled at Mo Ran in his fury and his despair. Before the watching eyes of his sect leader and in-laws, he shoved his bastard son out the door and out of his life.

Of course Madam Nangong's funeral had a lacquered coffin, agates and fragrance pearls; there was frostcloth to preserve her body, silk to hide her face, and brocade to cover her eyes as she embarked on her final journey. Duan Yihan's death was marked by just one corpse and one mourner. It was an eternal farewell and nothing more. According to Nangong Yan, she didn't even deserve a casket of cheap board.

Who dared to say all were equal in the face of death? They were unequal from the very beginning. In the end, one was borne up like pristine jade, while the other sank into putrid mud.

"I dragged her to the burial mounds and buried her there." Mo Ran kept this part of the story brief, his voice carefully level. He didn't mention how he'd begged passersby to help him, or how he'd spent two weeks carrying that rotting corpse to the city outskirts. Nor did he describe how he dug through gravel and stone with his bare hands to cover his mother's wasted form.

Mo Ran wasn't used to giving voice to his suffering. He'd always been someone who buried his past deep inside; he never brought it up of his own will. In the first decade and more of his life, he'd experienced all there was of humiliation, malice, scorn, and slander. His heart was hard as iron; he cared nothing for what others thought of him, and wanted their compassion not at all.

"And then I went to Xiangtan."

After burying his mother, he couldn't bear to remain in Linyi. He hid in a basket stowed in the back of a Daoist's cart and snuck out of the city, planning to do as his mother bade him and go to Xiangtan.

It took him six months, from high summer to the beginning of winter. When his shoes fell apart, he went barefoot. Thick calluses covered the soles of his feet. He walked on and on, asking and asking for directions. Just outside Wubei Temple, hunger and cold finally defeated him. He collapsed into a heap of dried grass.

"Mom..." The little boy lay curled on the ground, eyes dull beneath scraggly hair. He looked up at the sky. It was snowing; the first snow of winter. "I'm coming to see you... I'm sorry... I can't do it anymore..."

Snowflakes fell, whisper-light, covering his eyes.

There came the sound of rustling footsteps, followed by a pair of hands reaching into the grass. He heard a boy's voice ring out. "Shizun, come take a look—what's wrong with him?"

After a moment, the rustle of straw sandals drew closer. A man said, "Don't worry, let me take a look at him. You go back first." This deeper voice was calm and indifferent.

Instinct made Mo Ran afraid. He liked the youth better; the man seemed cold as ice. He shouldn't have had the strength to do it, but his desire to live drove him to lift his hand and grab weakly at the young man's hem. Tears streamed down his little face before he could form the word: "Food..."

I'm so hungry. Please, I want some food.

The youth was precisely the young Chu Wanning, who'd come down from the mountain with Huaizui. Chu Wanning froze. "What?"

Mo Ran struggled to lift his filthy face, hands shaking as he mimed eating. Bitterness stung his throat, and darkness blotted his sight. His ears were ringing. Weeping, he begged the youth in front of him for mercy. If this xiao-gege abandoned him like so many lords and young masters had before, he'd die. He would die for sure. He finally fell apart. "Hungry..."

Chu Wanning fed him a flask of congee, and that congee saved a starving boy.

Mo Ran left Wubei Temple, nearly delirious. All he remembered of his savior-gege was that he had sharp phoenix eyes, swept up at the ends, and that his lashes were very long and thick. Nothing else. But every day on the trek from Wubei Temple to Xiangtan, he wore the cloak his savior-gege had given him.

He had been very small back then; a young man's cloak on his tiny body was conspicuously oversized. When he pulled up the hood, it more or less covered his whole face. Along the road, well-fed children snuggled against their parents would see him and laugh. "Mom, Dad, look at that little beggar boy! What the heck is he wearing? Ha ha ha!"

But Mo Ran wasn't angry. What was a stranger's mockery to him? He was merely thankful this ill-fitting cloak could shield him from the wind and rain, that it could give him some small share of warmth. Snowflakes wouldn't land on him when it snowed, and in the dark, the shadows wouldn't touch his heart.

Every day at nightfall he lit a fire and sat beside it, his arms tight around his knees. He put up his hood, tucking his entire body within the cloak and staring into the orange flames from beneath its fur trim.

The cloak was warm like his mom's embrace, or his savior-gege's gentle phoenix eyes. The little boy fell asleep like this, and in his dreams, he breathed in the light fragrance that lingered on the cloak and felt as if he was leaning against the trunk of a haitang tree in full bloom.

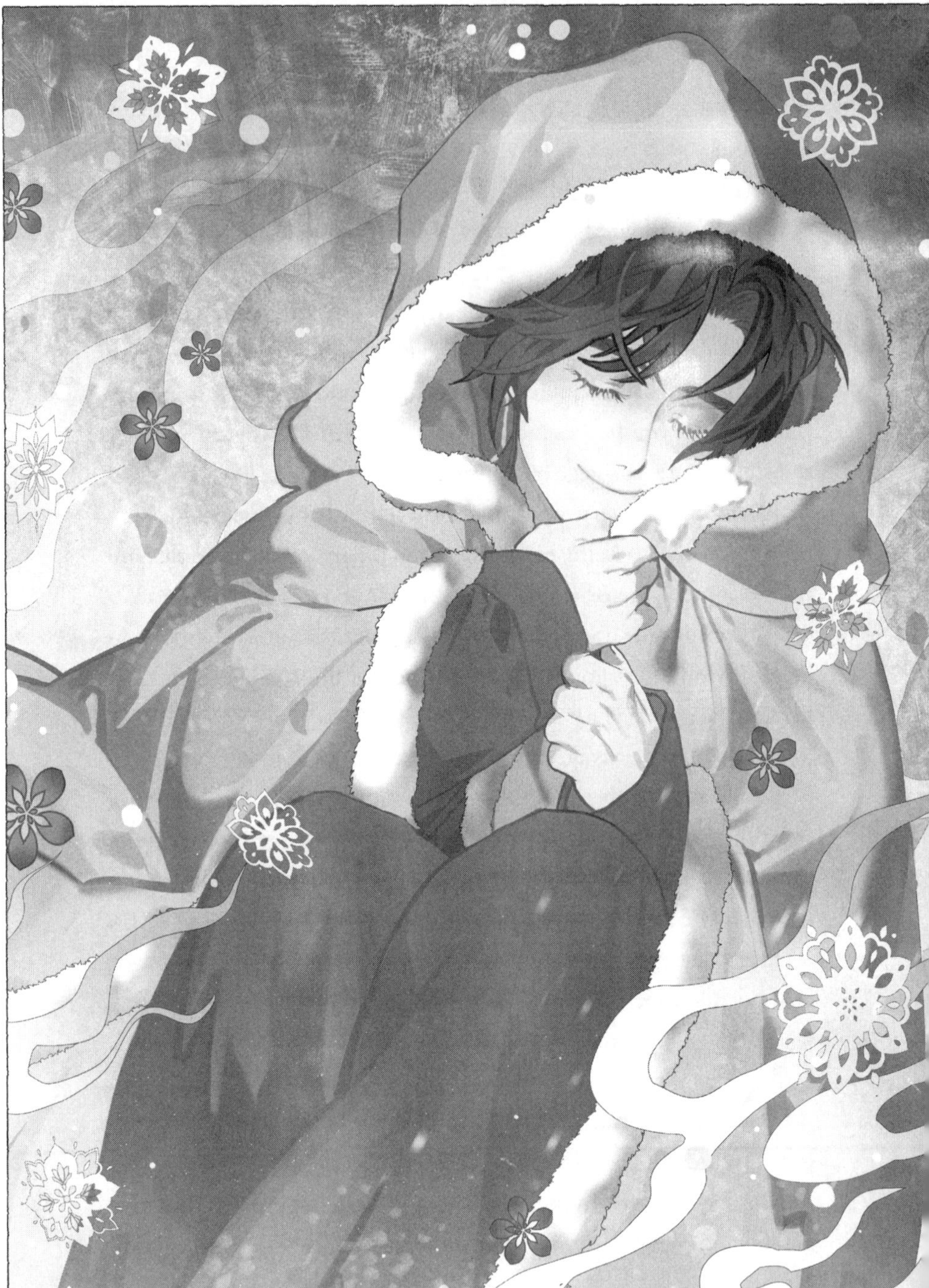

In hindsight, of course he found Chu Wanning's scent delicious. Of course he'd always sleep peacefully if he smelled it on his pillows. Of course he'd found those lowered phoenix eyes gentle when he first saw the Yuheng Elder beneath the Heaven-Piercing Tower. No wonder he felt as if he'd seen them before.

Perhaps everything was predestined. He and Chu Wanning had spoken long ago. Had touched, long ago—he'd even licked Chu Wanning's palm. It turned out he'd smelled the floral scent of Chu Wanning's clothes long ago. It turned out that savior-gege he'd always sought was right by his side, never leaving in life or in death.

Mo Ran looked down at the floor. In that freezing Loyalty Hall, he felt a small curl of warmth. But that was a secret between the two of them. Mo Ran allowed himself to dwell on it for a moment, lingering on its bittersweet ache. Then he hid that secret in his heart; he wouldn't tell another soul, let alone this staring crowd.

He took a breath. "Once I arrived in Xiangtan, I fulfilled my mom's dying wish and sought out Xun Fengruo."

Five-year-old Ran-er had stood there, wrapped in the thick cloak that once belonged to Chu Wanning. Its filthy hem dragged on the ground. The little boy's dark hair looked like a bird's nest poking out from beneath the fur trim, his thin and sallow face upturned. "May I ask..." he said quietly. "Is Xun Fengruo-jiejie here?"

"Xun Fengruo?" The girl he'd asked burst out laughing. "Our star? We ply our talents here, not our bodies, but which of Miss Xun's admirers are here for her singing and not her face? Xiao-didi, how old are you? How do you know her name?"

Mo Ran blinked, expression earnest. He hadn't understood a word of her chatter, but it was obvious she was making fun of him. Embarrassed, Mo Ran clutched the edges of his cloak and flushed. "Please, I want to find Xun-jiejie. M-my mom told me to..."

"Huh? Who's your mom?"

"Her surname's Duan, Duan Yihan..."

"Ah!" The girl paled, taking a step back and covering her mouth with a handkerchief. Those languid peach-blossom eyes had rounded in shock. "Y-you're the goddess's son?"

Even at the height of Duan Yihan's fame, she'd never put on airs and always shared extra coin and jewelry with aging sisters whose looks and voices had faded. The second the girl heard this little boy was Miss Duan's son, her attitude changed completely. She hustled him into the inner room to see Xun Fengruo.

The instant the door closed behind his guide, Mo Ran knelt before Xun Fengruo and told her everything. Xun Fengruo's tears soaked her silks. She summoned the madam at once and said she'd keep Mo Ran by her side. The madam was loath to do it, but she couldn't refuse her star performer's repeated entreaties. After looking Mo Ran up and down and deciding he was strong enough to work, she agreed with great reluctance. But a beggar moving in was thought to be bad luck—he was required to burn all his clothes and scrub every inch of his skin.

The bath was no problem, but Mo Ran burst into tears when she said they'd burn his clothes.

"What are you crying for? It's not like we won't buy you new ones!" The madam smacked him in the head with her pipe. "Smarten up! I'm giving you room and board—anyone else would be celebrating, but look at you whining instead!"

Mo Ran didn't want to make any trouble for Xun-jiejie. She'd already done all she could. He bit his lip and willed himself to silence, rubbing his scarlet eyes and standing beside the fire as his shoulders shook with soundless sobs.

Back then, he didn't understand why things had to be this way.

He'd only wanted to keep his cloak, but because he was weak, because he was lowly, because he was a filthy beggar, because he didn't want to bring bad luck or cause trouble, he had to let them yank it off his shoulders. Why couldn't he fight back, why couldn't he say *no*, why did he not even have the right to cry? The cloak had been his source of warmth and safety; it'd been his shelter in so many storms. It was so dirty no one could tell what its original color had been. Now that he had somewhere to stay, he might not need it anymore. But even if he couldn't wear it again, he wanted to wash it clean and fold it neatly. He would be satisfied with simply storing it at the bottom of a chest. It was his *friend*, not some old rag.

But he wasn't given a choice.

That filthy cloak met the flames with a crackle. The servant doing the burning didn't care; he only thought the cloak dirty. But to Mo Ran, it was a cremation, a burial. He watched unblinking as the flames licked into the air and blurred the edges of the world with their heat.

Slow down...there's more...

Where did you come from...?

That young man's gentle voice seemed to echo in his ears, one of the pitifully few times someone ever showed him kindness in his lowly life. Now, it was ash.

Mo Ran took the madam of the House of Drunken Jade for his adopted mother and received her surname: Mo. From then on he worked in that house and finally enjoyed some peaceful days.

But the peace didn't last. Xun Fengruo was no longer young, and although the entertainment house wasn't billed as a brothel, women above a certain age were still required to earn enough to pay a dignity fee. If they came up short, their first night might be auctioned off by the madam.

Xun Fengruo wasn't worried; she'd already earned lavish sums for the House of Drunken Jade. "Only a hundred fifty thousand gold left," she said to Mo Ran with a smile. "Little Ran-er, once your jiejie earns enough, I'll be able to buy my freedom. Jiejie will take you somewhere nice."

Mo Ran had been sent to work in the kitchen and saw her very rarely. The madam was intent on keeping her workers from commiserating, so Xun Fengruo and Mo Ran always met covertly.

She reached out and pinched his cheek, then handed him a sweet. "Shh, take this. Too bad I can't give you any money. Mother's too sharp with that, heh."

Mo Ran gave her a gap-toothed grin. "Mn, thank you, Xun-jiejie."

But the madam knew just as well as Xun Fengruo did that her star was a mere hundred fifty thousand gold away from freedom. Though she looked unconcerned, deep down, she was terrified. If they lost Xun Fengruo, the House of Drunken Jade's profits would plummet. She was determined to get one last payout before Xun Fengruo left her.

There was no shortage of wealthy clients who wanted Xun Fengruo; any of their bids would be enough to keep the madam in luxury for the rest of her life. Thus the woman hatched a plan—she made an agreement with one of the richest merchants in the city. During the Lantern Festival, when Xun Fengruo was playing music in the hall, the madam served her a cup of drugged tea and brought her to her room.

That night, Mo Ran had carefully prepared a bowl of tangyuan, which he carried to the inner room for Xun-jiejie. The sound of coarse panting stopped him at the threshold. Stunned, Mo Ran pushed open the door and was hit in the face with the smell of resin incense, so thick it turned his stomach. In the darkness, he saw a greasy merchant with spit dangling from his mouth and his lapels hanging open, gasping atop a weakly struggling Xun Fengruo.

The bowl of tangyuan crashed to the ground as Mo Ran darted inside. With preternatural strength—he'd always been powerful—he knocked the merchant off her. Keeping the man pinned, he yelled at the stunned and sobbing Xun Fengruo, "Jiejie, run!"

"But—"

"Run! I can't go, I have to keep him down! If you stay, we're both doomed when the madam comes! Run! Run! Don't worry, I'll be right behind you!"

Xun Fengruo was his savior. Mo Ran wanted her to flee Xiangtan and never come back. That day, he finally got to play the hero.

Xun Fengruo made him a final tearful bow and ran, but Mo Ran was not so lucky. The madam came upstairs as soon as she heard the clamor, whereupon she found that Mo Ran had not only beat up an important client but also let their star performer escape. She nearly spat blood in anger, her features twisting in a mask of rage.

The madam had a son about Mo Ran's own age, a boy who was malicious by nature. Seeing his mother furious, he came up with an idea both naïve and cruel, in the way only children could be. Because Mo Ran had angered his mother, the boy punished a fellow child like an animal—he found a dog kennel and ordered someone to lock Mo Ran inside.

The kennel was narrow and cramped; Mo Ran could only crouch, unable to either lie down or stand up. They fed him table scraps like a dog and left him like that for seven days.

For seven days, Mo Ran was trapped in Xun Fengruo's old room. The haze of the incense and the stink of the man's sweat mingled in his nose, inescapable. He crouched, stooped over, breathing in that syrupy miasma. Wanting to puke, for seven whole days. After this incident, he developed an aversion to the scent of incense—a fear etched into his very bones.

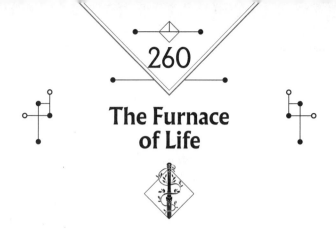

260

The Furnace of Life

NONE OF THE CULTIVATORS in Loyalty Hall knew what to say. Many had lowered their heads, incapable of speech. "Ah...bitter fate," said Master Xuanjing. "So much bitter fate."

"Every bitterness has its source; every grievance has its cause. Much of the world is linked through action and consequence, harm and retribution," said Mu Yanli. Here, she changed her tone. "But Mo Ran, you must know that suffering does not justify venting your resentment on others."

"Of course not."

An elder of Huohuang Pavilion sighed. "Mo-xianjun, the trials you went through are certainly worthy of pity, but they were the result of your poor birth and unfortunate fate. Everyone has their own path to walk; you cannot terrorize other people simply because you yourself were terrorized. You've done good and suffered harm, but based on what we know, you also killed... All things must be accounted for."

This time, it was not Mo Ran but Jiang Xi who responded, "How so?"

"Um..."

"Who can account for it all? Whose lives are considered worthy of praise and whose should be condemned—who can be that fairest arbiter?" Jiang Xi was strong and willful; he'd never considered those of Tianyin Pavilion to be gods. "I don't intend to be partial toward Mo Ran, but I want to ask a question. We stand here today declaring we want to settle things with Mo Ran, that we want to make him pay. Then—what about what Mo Ran has suffered? What about the injustice he's been made to bear?"

No one had imagined that Jiang Xi, who had endured the heaviest losses during the slaughter at Guyueye, would be the one to speak up on Mo Weiyu's behalf. They looked at him wide-eyed.

"Jiang-zhangmen, Tianyin Pavilion has always been fair," said Mu Yanli. "My tribe has guarded the Divine Scales of Justice for generations. When the time comes, we will use the scales to measure his sins and virtues before ascertaining his punishment. You needn't worry."

"What does he have to do with me? Why would I be worried?" Jiang Xi replied. Tianyin Pavilion irritated him to no end. His sect upheld the power of medicine—they believed any mortal man could live forever as long as an elixir was refined with enough sophistication. Guyueye had never held any superstitions regarding these descendants of gods.

"But I *am* curious." He narrowed his almond eyes, voice cold. "Once you've finished Mo Ran's trial, shouldn't Tianyin Pavilion look for the others involved? Shouldn't you scour the earth and check whether Nangong Yan is still among the living? Shouldn't you go off to Xiangtan in search of that merchant who debased Miss Xun? If it's right for Mo Ran to pay for murder with his life, then what about the time he was locked in a cage, beaten, or forced into penniless famine, his savior disgraced and his mother starved to death—who will you be punishing for these crimes?"

"Jiang-zhangmen," mumbled Master Xuanjing, "why do you speak for a criminal?"

"I don't," said Jiang Xi. His thin lips curled in a sneer. "I simply recall how we treated Nangong Si and Ye Wangxi at Mount Huang. I do not wish to see such a scene reenacted."

"This is completely different," someone protested.

"How so?" retorted Jiang Xi. "Yes, the situation has changed— Nangong Si is dead and Ye Wangxi lies bedridden at Guyueye even now. But did we not force their hands in the same way, telling them that the sins of Rufeng Sect must be repaid with their lives?" He turned toward the speaker, brown eyes sharp as a hawk's. "Where was Tianyin Pavilion then? Where was justice?"

Those of Bitan Manor were still furious at Rufeng Sect over the matter of the sword manual. Li Wuxin's disciple Zhen Congming cut in: "Jiang-zhangmen is biased. Nangong Si was the heir to Rufeng Sect, and every grievance has its source. Unless all of Rufeng Sect is gone, those debts must be paid. No one wants to be the one getting the short end of the stick."

Jiang Xi scoffed. "That's right. You understand this perfectly, don't you? No one wants to be the victim who can't fight back."

Zhen Congming fell silent.

"You think this way, Xu Shuanglin thought this way, and Mo Ran is allowed to think the same." Jiang Xi swept his sleeves back. "When it happens to others, it's easy to say these things, but when you're the victim of injustice and violence, you see only the cruelties of the world and wonder why you're the one to suffer."

"So Jiang-zhangmen believes we were unfair and cruel to Nangong Si and Ye Wangxi, and that the matter of the Bitan sword manual should be forgotten?"

"Nangong Si is dead," Jiang Xi said. "Whom are you hoping to pursue?"

Zhen Congming exploded. "Then my shizun died for nothing?!"

Nangong Si is dead, but doesn't Ye Wangxi still live? She was the leader of Rufeng Sect's shadow city—does *she* know nothing about the sword manual?"

Everyone fell silent; Jiang Xi was notorious for his irascible temper. To openly fight with Jiang Xi... Indeed, the "very smart" Zhen Congming did not live up to his name in the least.

Jiang Xi gave him a look that spoke volumes. "On Mount Jiao, Nangong Si was grievously injured when he fought Nangong Changying." He paused. "Back then, he conveyed a message to me through the barrier."

"What did he say?"

Jiang Xi closed his eyes, the scene rising before him once more. Nangong Si, near death beneath Nangong Changying's sword, mouthing each word for Jiang Xi to read from his lips through the barrier. "'I wish for all the wealth of Rufeng Sect to be spread across the lands, leaving nothing behind.'"

"This..." The crowd looked at each other in embarrassment, the monks of Wubei Temple even more so—they lowered their eyes, hands clasped as their mouths moved in silent chanting.

Zhen Congming colored. "He didn't even leave a corpse behind. All the treasures of Rufeng Sect are in their secret chamber," he gritted out. "Who can open it? Let's be honest—he didn't mean it."

"Nangong Si didn't think he would die in such a way," replied Jiang Xi. "Also, I'd prefer to believe that his dying words were sincere."

Zhen Congming's mouth wobbled; it took him a moment to retort. "*This* is why Jiang-zhangmen is taking Mo Weiyu's side? You want lenience so you don't have to see a second Nangong Si?"

"I merely think that true justice is difficult—perhaps impossible—to achieve. I hope that those of you passing judgment on others don't put yourself on too high a pedestal. Do not assume that you represent all that is good or righteous." He cast a glance at Tianyin Pavilion. "Even the highest court is not infallible."

At last Xue Zhengyong lifted his head. He looked exhausted, as if he didn't know how to face Mo Ran. But although he hesitated, he still spoke.

"Jiang-zhangmen is right," he rasped. "There have been many conflicts over these years of trouble in the cultivation realm; every sect has done things they're not proud of. Who can decide what's truly fair? Ah, to be honest…" He sighed, closing his eyes. "To be honest, do we limit murder to killings done by one's own hand? How many innocents were killed by Rufeng Sect's decision to raise the price of food? I've lived more than forty years and achieved little of note. But what I did wasn't in pursuit of ascending to immortality or leaving my name in history—I just hoped to lessen some of the suffering in the world." His eyes dulled. The leader of Sisheng Peak—no matter how he tried to stay composed—was still stunned by the revelation that the child he'd raised was not his kin. "I just wanted there to be less suffering," he murmured. "Even for just one person."

"Xue-zhangmen is magnanimous," Mu Yanli said, her tone once again icy. "But have you not considered how your leniency toward a criminal is an act of disrespect to the innocent civilians he harmed and an offense to those mortals who had no part in his crimes? Tianyin Pavilion does not have the power to account for every wrong under the sun, to punish everyone by law—but we *can* make an example of him. Sect Leader, please be aware of this: As the matter of Mo Ran was handed over to our pavilion, it will not be hastily addressed."

Xue Zhengyong fell silent.

Mu Yanli turned back to Mo Ran. "Mo-gongzi, you've finished your tale of woe and received your share of pity. Why don't we now move on to a different subject?"

"What does the pavilion master wish to discuss?" asked Mo Ran indifferently.

"You say the incident where the tofu-seller's daughter was disgraced and died was not your doing. I believe you. But there is another death you cannot be excused from."

Mo Ran closed his eyes. "The pavilion master is certainly thorough."

"Let's hear it," Mu Yanli replied coolly. "How did you kill Mo Nian—Xue-zunzhu's *real* nephew?"

"Enough!" A furious shout cut her off. Xue Meng stood with teeth gritted, eyes shining with tears and hatred. "Shut up!"

Mu Yanli shot him a glance. "Attempting to avoid the subject," she pronounced. "Disappointing to see from the darling of the heavens."

She was answered by Longcheng's shrill cry of warning. The scimitar flew by her face and into the column behind her, sending splinters raining down.

Mu Yanli didn't flinch or even blink. Her beautiful eyes pinned their frozen stare upon Xue Meng.

Xue Meng clenched his jaw, muscles twitching in his face. "Real nephew this, fake nephew that... Have you had *enough*?"

He strode forward and yanked Longcheng out of the column, his chest heaving. He didn't look at Mo Ran or anyone else. He resembled nothing as much as a trapped beast, driven insane where he stood—driven to despair. "Have you said enough?! Have you had a good time? Had your fill?"

"Meng-er..." Madam Wang sighed.

Xue Meng ignored her. He looked around with scarlet-rimmed eyes, gripping Longcheng's hilt. "Seeing a zongshi become a murderer," he said mockingly, both himself and the audience objects of his scorn. "Watching the brothers of Sisheng Peak turn on each other—

watching as members of a family become enemies—you're enjoying yourself, aren't you?" His voice was so hoarse it whistled in his throat, each syllable shivering into the air. "Did you really come here for justice? For the truth?" He paused, teeth clenched. "Or was it for your own personal, petty vendettas?"

Jiang Xi narrowed his eyes. "Young Master Xue, you forget yourself."

Xue Meng whirled on him with eyes like flames. "What gives *you* the right to rebuke me?"

"Meng-er!" Xue Zhengyong reached out to pull Xue Meng back but froze upon touching him. Xue Meng was furious, but his entire body was trembling fit to shatter.

"I don't want to hear it." He bit the words out. "It's all fake. All wrong... You're all liars!"

Before Xue Zhengyong could try to speak to him, Xue Meng had already shoved his way through the crowd and out of Loyalty Hall.

Throughout it all, he never once turned to look at Mo Ran. In fact, Xue Meng knew perfectly well what the truth was, and who the liar was. But there were many things in the world that were easily known yet impossible to accept. Xue Meng had lived two decades in carefree ease. He'd never experienced any devastation besides Chu Wanning's death. His easy life meant he was still in many ways like a child, yet this was only to his detriment. One like a child would have a child's pure heart, but would also have a child's naïvete, recklessness, and brash temper.

Xue Zhengyong stared in the direction Xue Meng had gone for a long moment before slowly sitting back down. The time of his youth was long past. He was nearly fifty, and white had begun to feather his temples. He didn't know if he could endure what was to happen; he had to sit down. This, at least, would allow him some small measure of composure.

Mu Yanli's face seemed sheened in frost, devoid of any warmth. She cared about the matter at hand and nothing else. "Mo Weiyu, will you speak, or should I find another witness?"

Mo Ran was as calm as any prisoner on death row. "No need," he said. "If there are any witnesses still alive, I don't wish to see them." He slowly looked up. Weak sunlight streamed down upon his pallid face. "I'll tell you myself."

At a gesture from Mu Yanli, Tianyin Pavilion's servants brought a chair. She sat down with a flourish, resting her chin on one hand in preparation to attend to his tale. "Proceed."

Mo Ran closed his eyes and drew in a breath before beginning. "It started with a businessman."

"Who?"

He hesitated. "I'm sure many of you have heard of the investigator's market."

Ma Yun of Taobao Estate knew this business best. He raised a hand. "Oh yes, our sect works closely with these investigators. They roam the cities, making their living investigating old stories and events of the past."

"That's right. Back when Uncle was looking for his brother's orphan, he engaged just such an investigator."

Xue Zhengyong said nothing. Of course he remembered this; they'd found Mo Ran using the information provided by the investigator, who'd told them only one boy survived when the House of Drunken Jade went up in flames. He still remembered the look on the man's face as he exclaimed, *What god-given luck! That your brother's son survived such a calamity must mean prosperity lies in his future!*

"The investigator accepted Uncle's commission. After a few failed attempts, he found a lead and went to the House of Drunken Jade in search of a woman surnamed Mo."

"Who?" someone asked.

"Xue-zhangmen's brother's lover, known as Madam Mo. She was the baseborn daughter of a large family."

Realization broke over the assembly. "Madam Mo? Wasn't that the name of the brothel madam?"

"But she sounded like a vicious shrew."

"She wasn't always so," said Mo Ran peaceably. "My mom said Madam Mo had gone through an experience similar to hers, and that she too was to be pitied. She'd had a lover when she was young—a penniless wandering cultivator. He said he was going to the lower cultivation realm to establish a powerful sect, so Madam Mo gave him all her coin and jewelry so he could realize this dream."

"It was my dage..." mumbled Xue Zhengyong.

"Before this cultivator left, he swore Madam Mo an oath. Once he accomplished his goals, he said, he'd marry her with all pomp and circumstance and bring her home. He even wrote her a line of verse—*Through the river mists do the pipa notes float, he listens in silence to the goddess on her boat.* That was how the investigator later made certain of her identity."

Star-crossed love stories like these were by far the most popular fare. A female cultivator sighed. "Did the former sect leader of Sisheng Peak abandon his lover—just like Nangong Yan?"

Xue Zhengyong's eyes widened. "Nonsense!" he cried. "My gege was nothing like that! My gege never forgot Miss Mo..." Tears sprang to his eyes at the mention of his deceased brother.

The Xuanji Elder took up the explanation. "Miss, please mind what you say. The former sect leader lost his life in a terrible battle not long after the sect was founded; he never intended to go back on his word. Before he passed, he spoke often of Miss Mo to the sect leader. He always said he'd seek her out as soon as the sect had stabilized. He and Nangong Yan were nothing alike."

"Indeed," sighed Mo Ran. "She was much luckier than my mother. Her lover passed, but there was still someone thinking of her and wanting to bring her home. Whereas Nangong Yan was still alive, but he never had the courage to acknowledge my mom and me."

"I see now!" another voice cried. "This made you jealous, so you pulled a prince-and-pauper conceit, killing Madam Mo and burning down the House of Drunken Jade so you could pass yourself off as the real goods!"

At this uncharitable conjecture, Mo Ran shot the genius cultivator who'd spoken a glance. "I never attempted to pass myself off as anything."

Unfazed, the cultivator scoffed. "Then what was it? Did someone force you to become young master of Sisheng Peak?"

What was it? Mo Ran found himself wondering the same. So much of this world had once been something entirely different, until a butterfly flapped its wings and stirred a breeze that became a whirlwind, which changed the skies themselves. Just as he'd never intended to take Xue Zhengyong's nephew's place, Madam Mo hadn't always been that cruel mistress of the entertainment house. She too had had days of gentle youth. She too had once stood at the window hoping for her lover to return. She'd joyfully written to her distant love about the child growing in her belly and received his letters in reply, the excitement and delight of a soon-to-be father inked clear across the pages. She'd had all of that happiness, once.

It didn't matter that she was baseborn. It didn't matter that people mocked her because her man was a nameless cultivator; it didn't matter that she was pregnant out of wedlock. Someday, he would make good on his promise and come in glory to bring them home. She believed this faithfully.

But as the days wore on, the letters that had come every three days began to come once a week. They dwindled from once a week to once a month, and then there were none at all.

Eventually, Madam Mo gave up hope. She was a willful young woman; she'd hidden her relationship from her parents, and after she had the child, she'd hesitated for ages before bringing the boy home. When she finally worked up the courage, her father flew into a rage, and the mistress of the house heaped abuse upon her. Furious, Madam Mo ran away from home. The years flew by, and the young woman became the madam of the House of Drunken Jade.

Such were the ups and downs of fate. Life was like a furnace— some who entered its tempering flames would emerge entirely unrecognizable. Mo Ran had experienced this first-hand, and so too had Madam Mo.

When the investigator found her at last, it had been fourteen years since those days of her girlish youth. The man Xue Zhengyong had hired helped himself to a seat in the entertainment house. Snapping open his fan, he smiled. "Where's the madam? Call her over."

She arrived wearing a jacket patterned with peach blossoms and a shawl of yellow silk. Peeking through the doorway with pipe in hand, she lifted the tinkling bead veil and tittered. "Hello Gongzi, here for music so early in the morning? Do you prefer the pipa or the yangqin? My girls are skilled in all manner of instruments—as the first customer of the day, I'll be sure to give you a good price."

This was the nature of life. When her lover had left fourteen years ago, she'd sat by the bead veil with tears on her lovely cheeks, watching him leave. Fourteen years later, when her lover's brother finally found her, the veil of time was brushed aside once more.

She pushed away the dangling jewels to reveal a face marked by time. That maiden bashful as a doe was dead and gone, and the one in the position of command in the House of Drunken Jade was a sly-eyed matron with a long-stemmed pipe in her hand.

The investigator didn't care much for sorrow, only money. Fanning himself, he smiled. "No thank you. I've come to ask the madam about a certain person."

The woman's smile stiffened. "A certain person?" she asked, tone cool. "Who?"

The man clearly enunciated each syllable of the words he had memorized: "Through the river mists do the pipa notes float, he listens in silence to the goddess on her boat."

Before he'd gotten halfway through, Madam Mo had paled. By the time he finished his recitation, she was white as paper. Her lips quivered, her sharp brows twitching as she clutched a handkerchief to her chest. "Who... Who *are* you?!"

The investigator smiled. "If I'm not mistaken, I've finally found Xue-xianzhang the right person. Madam Mo, how have you been?"

Madam Mo swayed and sat heavily on the round stool before the table. She gasped for breath, face flushing then going bloodless once more. When she recovered, she sent everyone away, leaving only the investigator in the hall. She stared into the man's face, eyes shining with joy, grief, and everything in between.

The investigator was unbothered. He lifted the pot of tea and poured her a lukewarm cup, then passed it over. "Have a sip."

She picked it up with a trembling hand, taking one sip, then two. Even after finishing the cup, she sipped on nothing before looking up. "Did...did Xue-lang send you here?"

The man sighed. "Unfortunately, the Xue-xianjun you speak of has long since passed."

"What?!"

"It was his younger brother who sent me on a search for his lost lover. More than a decade ago, the Xue brothers went to the lower cultivation realm to found a sect. Their fortunes rose, and they were no longer those helpless wandering cultivators anymore. But because Xue-xianzhang was crucial in building up the sect, he couldn't step away—and when he was on an exorcism mission, he unfortunately..."

He didn't need to finish. Madam Mo buried her face in her hands and burst into tears. The investigator consoled her for a long time before she managed to master herself.

"Before Xue-xianjun passed, he spoke often to his brother about you. All these years his brother has been looking for you, in hopes of finding you and bringing you home."

Madam Mo grasped the investigator's hand, mumbling in disbelief. "Say—say those words again! I refuse... I won't believe he's dead..."

Those words were the key to this whole enterprise; the investigator spoke them easily. "Through the river mists do the pipa notes float, he listens in silence to the goddess on her boat."

Tears swam in Madam Mo's eyes. "H-he didn't come back for me, because—because...and I thought... I blamed him..."

The investigator sighed. "It's been so many years. Madam, please rest easy. By the way, do you happen to have a son?"

"Y-yes, I do!" Madam Mo wept harder, mopping at her face as she called up the stairs. "A-Nian, A-Nian... Mo Nian! Hurry! Come downstairs!"

The door opened, but the boy who emerged was not Mo Nian. It was a scrawny child holding a pile of dirty laundry, poking his gaunt face out from behind the clothes. Cuts and bruises marred his cheek, and his eyes were smudged with exhaustion.

The investigator hesitated. "Is this...your son?"

"Ah—no, no." Wiping her face, Madam Mo answered, "This is just one of our kitchen boys."

Relieved, the man smiled. "I see."

Madam Mo turned. "Mo Ran, where is the young master?"

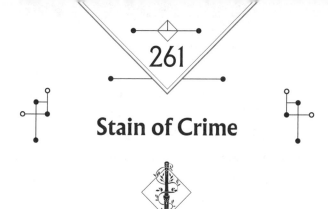

261

Stain of Crime

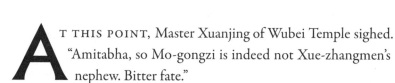

A T THIS POINT, Master Xuanjing of Wubei Temple sighed. "Amitabha, so Mo-gongzi is indeed not Xue-zhangmen's nephew. Bitter fate."

Someone in the crowd had connected the dots. "Ah... So that was *him*, then?"

A nearby cultivator didn't understand. "Who?"

"The boy who came up with the idea of locking Mo Ran in the dog kennel. The boy about Mo Ran's age, Madam Mo's son." As if experiencing an epiphany, the man slapped a hand to his forehead and cried, "I see now—you killed them and took his place not out of jealousy or greed, but because you held a grudge against him!"

This logic made sense to many in the crowd, who turned looks of both scorn and pity upon Mo Ran.

"That lines up."

"Ah, of course. Even the despicable have reason to be pitied."

Mu Yanli cleared her throat, and the murmuring settled down. "Mo-gongzi, I heard you were starved and abused at the House of Drunken Jade, and that the madam beat and swore at you. Is that true?"

"Yes," Mo Ran replied.

"Then her son was that boy who locked you in a kennel, correct?"

"Yes."

The guesses of the crowd were confirmed. The murmurs swelled again as they nodded to themselves. "See, of course his motive came out of that grudge. He must've hated them both."

They were right. How could Mo Ran not hate them? Mo Nian was his own age, but much healthier and stronger. No one dared raise a hand to him because he was the madam's son. The boy had been cruel since he was little, and Mo Ran was his favorite punching bag. Whenever he got into trouble, he made sure Mo Ran took the fall. Mo Ran was framed for all sorts of nasty mischief Mo Nian had caused.

But Mo Ran was an extremely obedient child. Despite his suffering, he never dared take revenge on Young Master A-Nian. He was only given one flatbread a day as it was. If he spoke up, that single mouthful of food might be taken away from him. It didn't matter if he was beaten or wronged—he never said a word. When he truly couldn't take it anymore, he'd curl up in the woodshed where he slept to sob quietly. Even there he couldn't make too much noise; he was sure to be beaten again if he woke anyone up.

"Did you hate them very much?" asked Mu Yanli.

Mo Ran looked up, disdain in his eyes. "Who wouldn't?"

"But your surname was given to you by her. If you despised her, why didn't you change it?"

"Mo was the adoptive name used in the House of Drunken Jade. Lots of servants sold to the house had that surname. We called Madam Mo 'Mother' or 'Ma'am.' Everyone did it, so I got used to it. No point in changing my surname."

"And did she treat all of you so poorly?"

Mo Ran hesitated. "No. But she'd never liked me, and after I let Xun Fengruo go, she couldn't stand the sight of me."

"How poorly did Madam Mo treat you?"

It was an easy question. In all the years Mo Ran spent in the House of Drunken Jade, the only time he was allowed meat was on New Year's Eve, when he could gnaw on a half-eaten piece of gristle that a patron left behind. On any other day, he only ever had that single flatbread. He was always given the hardest work, and the slightest mistake earned him a whipping.

But he didn't want to say all that. "I'd rather not talk about it," he replied simply.

"That's fine. Let's talk about something else. She treated you poorly. When she asked you where Mo Nian was that day, did you lie? Had you already begun to scheme to take Mo Nian's place?"

"No," said Mo Ran.

Of course he wouldn't dare to. His shelter, food, and safety were all in the madam's hands. The young Mo Ran had reacted to her question like a dog accustomed to being hit—flinching, he whispered, "Nian-gongzi went to his lessons..."

Madam Mo had no illusions about her son; she knew this was impossible. That boy hated studying. It was vastly more likely he'd gone off on a wild lark somewhere. But the investigator was right there, so she only cleared her throat and nodded. "Oh, that child of mine is so mature. Look, sir, he's...gone to school again."

The man laughed. "Ah, a studious child is a blessing. How about this? I'll write a letter to the sect leader of Sisheng Peak and call him here. He'll meet the boy soon enough—there's no point rushing things now."

Madam Mo rose just to fall down to her knees in front of him, overwhelmed with emotion. "Thank you, sir. Even in future prosperity, I will never forget what you've done for us."

When the investigator had left, Madam Mo sat in a daze for a long time, lost in fanciful thoughts and old sorrows. Every so often, she'd burst into laughter or tears. Hours passed before she noticed Mo Ran watching her fearfully from a corner.

Perhaps it was because she saw her own shame in Duan Yihan's past, or the simple fact that Mo Ran had dared set her golden goose free. Regardless, Mo Ran's impression of her was correct. She disliked the boy, and her resentment had grown more intense over time. "What are you looking at?" she said, glaring at him.

Mo Ran lowered his long lashes. "Sorry."

"You say that, but I bet you think my laughing and crying is ridiculous, don't you?"

Mo Ran said nothing. His meek obedience made Madam Mo shoot him a glance and sneer, "Forget it, I won't bother with you. What would you know, anyway? Faithless, ungrateful cur."

He was used to such epithets from her. Silent, he kept his head down.

"Don't just stand there. I'm in a good mood today; I won't beat you. Go find Nian-gongzi—don't try to fool me, I know he's not at his lessons. Bring him home. I have something important to tell him. Hurry."

At the mention of the young master, Mo Ran couldn't help flinching again. But still he nodded and mumbled, "Yes, Mother."

"Don't call me that anymore." Madam Mo wrinkled her nose. "Soon, I'll be out of the House of Drunken Jade... Forget it, I've said enough to you. Hurry and go."

That evening, Mo Ran apprehensively set out to look for Nian-gongzi. He didn't know if he'd rather find the boy sooner or later—the young master was certain to yell at him for ruining his day just as soon they crossed paths, but if he went back empty-handed, Madam Mo was sure to do the same over his incompetence.

His slight silhouette wandered helplessly through the fading light.

At that moment, Mo Ran had no idea he and Nian-gongzi would swap places. He looked hither and thither, just as he was told. He went to every one of Nian-gongzi's regular haunts—the riverside, the gambling hall, the brothel, the cockfighting rings...only to be chased from each with derision.

Finally, after asking around, he learned that Nian-gongzi and his friends had gone to an old mill on the outskirts of the city with a large sack in tow. Mo Ran thought nothing of it before rushing off.

The mill had been abandoned for years, and the only landmark nearby was a cemetery. Very rarely did anyone come here. Mo Ran jogged the whole way, but before he reached the building, he saw a group of half-clothed youths scrambling from it. Nian-gongzi was in the lead, still pulling up his pants.

"Gongzi, Mother wants you home," Mo Ran hastily cried. "She says—"

His voice died in his throat. There were expressions of terror on the boys' faces; some were in tears, shaking as they cowered at the side of the group.

Mo Ran froze. Years of abuse had honed his instinct for danger. When he saw Nian-gongzi staring fixedly at him with red-rimmed eyes, Mo Ran's hair stood on end. He whirled around and ran.

Nian-gongzi reacted quickly. "Grab him!" he shouted.

How could Mo Ran be a match for them? The other boys had him pinned in moments and dragged him before Nian-gongzi.

"What do we do?" someone whispered. "A-Nian, we're in big trouble."

"It's too late to run—this brat saw us."

"Why don't we..."

Mo Ran had no idea what they were talking about, but the youthful faces around him were all dark with malice. This was his earliest impression of the word *monster*.

Nian-gongzi narrowed his eyes. He was the calmest and cruelest among them, and after some thought, he said, "Don't kill him."

Mo Ran's head jerked up. *Kill?*

They'd beaten him, cursed him, and abused him, but he'd never imagined he would hear the word *kill* from the mouths of a group of teenagers. His mind went blank.

"Lock him up in the mill," Mo Nian said.

The group exchanged glances. One boy with a pinched and narrow face was the first to catch on. Eyes shining, cheeks red, with snot still streaming from his nose, he exclaimed: "Yes! What a good idea!"

One by one, the others also saw his intent. "Ah! I get it! A-Nian, you're a genius!"

Moments ago they had looked at Mo Ran as if he was their ultimate enemy. Now the eyes pinned on him were those of starving wolves eyeing a fatted lamb.

The boys shoved Mo Ran into the mill. He pounded on the door with both fists, thrashing, but it was swiftly barricaded shut. There were no windows; the only light came in through the cracks between the wooden boards of the walls.

"Let me out!" he yelled. "Let me out!"

Someone outside cried, "Report him! Report him right now!"

"Hurry up! We'll keep an eye on him, you guys go run and tell the officials!"

Mo Ran shouted and pounded on the door, but it was no use. He let his hands fall, turning around dizzily. In the thin bars of light, he saw the room's other inhabitant sprawled upon the ground.

It was a girl with familiar features. Upon further thought, he realized she was the daughter of the tofu-seller on the eastern street, whom Nian-gongzi had been pursuing for some time. Her clothes were torn away, leaving her body bare on the ground. Her limbs were askew, her skin mottled with purpling bruises, and between her legs...

She'd been raped to death by these beasts. The tears on her face had yet to dry, and her wide, sightless eyes stared blankly at the doorway where Mo Ran stood.

It took Mo Ran a moment to understand. When he did, he screamed. His back hit the door with a thud, his pupils contracting as he finally grasped what they had done and what they were going to do.

After being rebuffed, Nian-gongzi had come up with a terrible plan for the girl. She was a soft target—weak-willed and from an unimportant family. He and his friends had tricked her and dragged her to the mill, where they had taken turns defiling her. The girl was frail to begin with, and the brutes were so rough with her that she died partway through their fun.

"No...no!" Mo Ran cried. He turned, crazed, slamming against the doors. "Open the door! Open the door! It wasn't me! *Open the door!*"

As if in answer to his prayers, the mill doors opened.

Mo Ran tried to run, but the boys grabbed his wrists and pinned them. Once again, Nian-gongzi led the group. "Nearly forgot," he said mercilessly. "You have to look the part."

He directed the boys to rip off Mo Ran's clothes, then smeared blood and fluids from the girl's corpse over his skin. Mo Ran wept the whole time, thrashing with all his might, but they were too strong. Desperation to save their own skins took precedence over all else; they ignored Mo Ran's begging and sobbing, their eyes flashing like the eyes of beasts. One of the boys backhanded Mo Ran across the face after Mo Ran bit him. "Shut the fuck up," he spat. "You're a murderer! Rapist! With so many witnesses, how could you possibly defend yourself?!"

"It...it wasn't me! It wasn't..."

But what could he do? They roughed him up and threw him in the mill, locking him in with that dead girl's naked body before running off to falsely report the crime to the officials. There was nothing Mo Ran could say for himself. The court punished him with thirty strikes of the rod, leaving him bruised and bloodied, then locked him up to await sentencing. The other prisoners mocked and swore at him, and those with daughters held nothing back as they beat him. One of them was ready to defile him in retribution, and was only stopped because the head jailer wanted to minimize fuss.

Madam Mo came to the prison that very night. Of course she knew what had really happened, and resented her son's base nature. But what use was resentment? A mother would always protect her child first and foremost. Her greatest fear was that the truth would come out during the hearing. If it came to light that Mo Nian was the real culprit, how would the two of them move up in the world? The investigator's letter had already gone out, and Sisheng Peak was sending people to bring them home. She'd waited for this so long her hair had gone gray at the temples. She and her son deserved that glory and status. Nothing would stand in their way.

So it was that she rushed through the night and bribed both jailer and the county officials. *Don't look too closely*, she'd pleaded—just make it all Mo Ran's fault. But perhaps her conscience wouldn't let her rest, for she went to the prison afterward to see Mo Ran. She even brought him a bowl of braised pork.

"It's not poisoned. I wouldn't poison you."

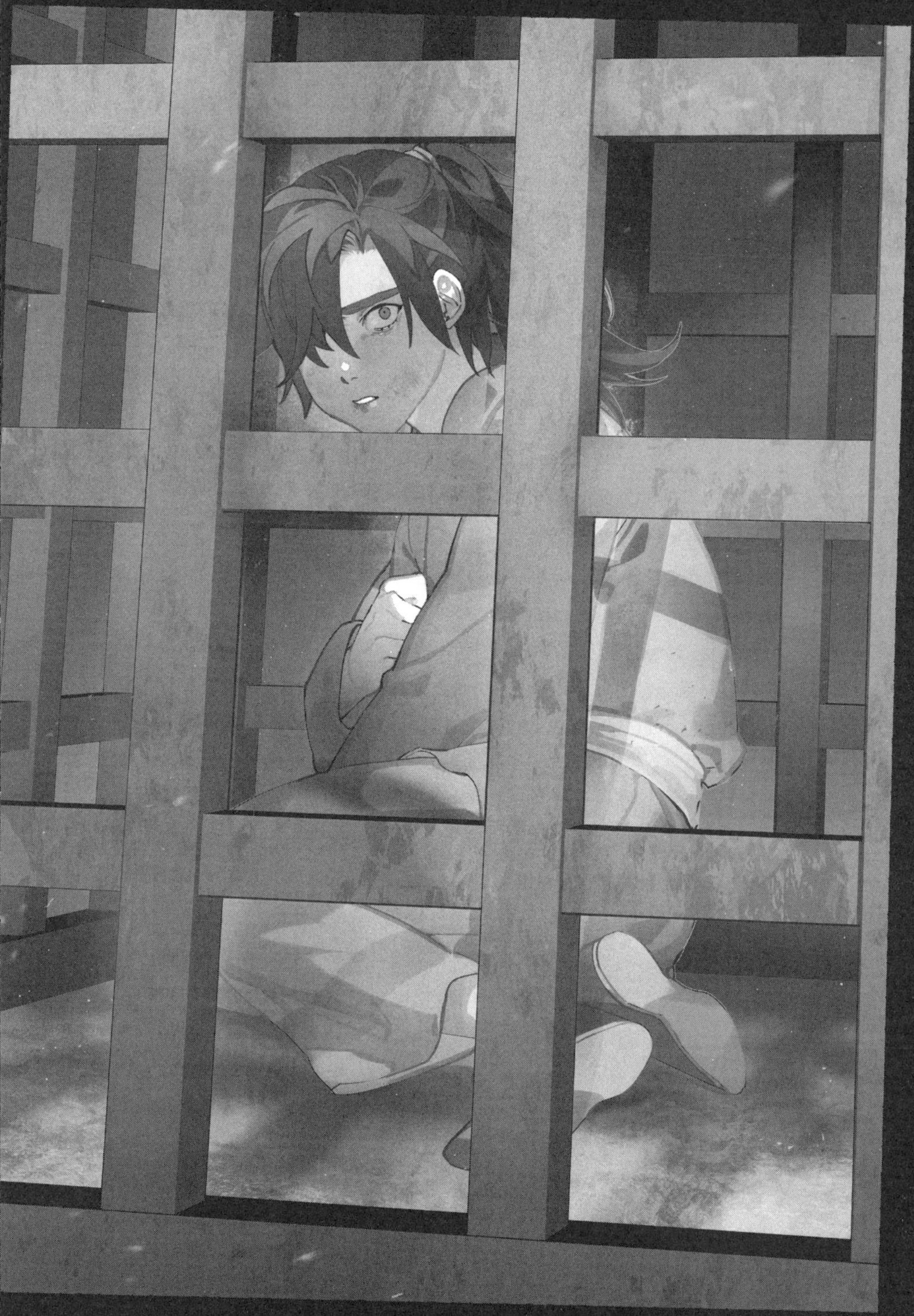

Mo Ran watched her from the corner where he was curled, his eyes—so dark they looked purple—glimmering with helplessness and hurt. He looked like an animal lined up for slaughter: upset and fearful, yet docile with despair.

Something quavered in Madam Mo. Terrified by her own reaction, she rose quickly to her feet. Hardening her heart and her voice, she said, "You're an orphan, after all. It's sad, but no one will mourn your death. I've kept you alive for so many years—it's high time you repaid the favor."

Mo Ran looked silently back at her.

Madam Mo gritted her teeth. "Consider this bowl of pork your compensation. Once you eat it, don't blame me in the underworld... I didn't have a choice either."

With a flare of her skirts, she was gone.

Mo Ran had never eaten braised pork. Now that a whole bowl sat before him, he stared at it but did not touch any of its contents. He knocked it over, watching as the red sauce spilled into the dirt of the cell. The sight reminded him of the blood that had pooled beneath the girl's body, filling him with a revulsion so sharp he turned and heaved, clutching the wall for support. There was nothing for him to throw up. Mo Ran was fed a flatbread a day, and his last meal had long since been digested. He brought up only bile.

That night, he couldn't sleep. The blood smeared over his skin had hardened into a shell that flaked into rusty powder at the slightest touch, sloughing off onto the ground. He sat in silence. No one knew what he was thinking; no one knew if he was even alive.

Huddled in on himself, he slowly came to realize many truths.

In that dark and filthy prison, in that cell reeking of bile and braised pork, the obedient Mo Ran died. Born in his place was

Emperor Taxian-jun, feared throughout the realm by commoners and cultivators alike—Emperor Taxian-jun, at his inception.

This was the root of the all-consuming hatred brought to life by the Flower of Eightfold Sorrows.

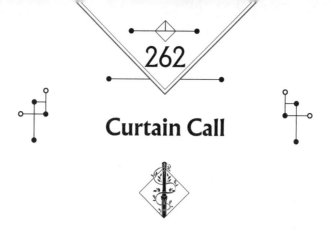

262

Curtain Call

THE JAIL IN XIANGTAN was old and shabby; none of the doors were secure. The next morning when the guards were busy calling in a prisoner, Mo Ran seized his chance and snuck out.

The first thing he did upon regaining his freedom was return to the House of Drunken Jade. When he entered the backyard, he saw A-Nian standing smugly in its middle, freshly attired in black cultivator's robes. His mistakes had fallen upon the head of that orphan Mo Ran, just as they always had in the past. Within a day, he was sure he'd gotten away with it.

You're an orphan, after all. No one will mourn your death.

I've kept you alive for so many years—it's high time you repaid the favor.

This was their justification for sending an innocent young man to the gallows. How pompous. How self-satisfied.

Mo Ran hung back in the shadows, spying on the carefree and confident Nian-gongzi. Was this how it felt to be loved and cared for? To have a mother's protection, someone to keep you safe even if the sky fell?

Mo Ran was the only one whose death didn't matter.

That morning, Mo Ran watched Nian-gongzi for a very long time. The boy had already purchased robes and dressed himself

224 o-• THE HUSKY & HIS WHITE CAT SHIZUN

up like a cultivator. Once his mother sold the House of Drunken Jade, they would set off for the lower cultivation realm, where he would be a rich young master. He waved a sword around in the yard, surrounded by the same boys who'd framed Mo Ran.

"Great moves, A-Nian!"

"You look so good! You'll definitely be a famous swordsman when you go to the lower cultivation realm!"

"I've heard lots about your uncle's Sisheng Peak these past few years. You're going to be living the high life! Don't forget your bros!"

"That's right," another boy added. "A-Nian, you'd better not forget us. We grew up together, and we've been there for you through thick and thin. Even the death of that little tofu-seller's bitch, even then—"

A-Nian was already putting on airs befitting his new status. He couldn't allow anyone to learn of the rape; he whipped out his sword and pointed it at the speaker's throat. "Mo Ran killed that tofu-seller's girl. We all saw it!" snapped Mo Nian. "He defiled her like a rabid beast—how many times do I have to say it before you guys remember?!"

The youth held at sword point shivered. "Y-yes... My memory's bad—I misspoke!"

Everyone else hastened to soothe A-Nian's ruffled feathers. "It was all done by Mo Ran, a brute in human skin!"

"Yes, yes—raping an innocent girl before killing her, we all saw it. I'll never forget the evil look on his face."

They spoke over each other in their haste, adding details to their story. When it came to lies, this was the nature of such people: Repeated a thousand times, they would begin to feel it was the truth. The young men grew more and more self-righteous, happily absolving themselves of all responsibility.

A-Nian burst into laughter, his sword glinting as he slashed wildly at the straw dummies on the field. Once he had struck them all down, he brandished his blade at the straw and cried, "Once I'm a master swordsman, I'll kill all monsters, punishing...punishing something..." He hated school and often skipped his lessons, so he stuttered, unable to continue.

One of his friends came to his rescue. "Punishing evil and upholding righteousness! Standing for justice! Bringing good to the land! Having the world at your feet!"

A-Nian snorted. "You sure know a lot of big words," he said disdainfully.

Having missed the mark, the toady lapsed into an embarrassed silence. A-Nian waved his sword once again. "It takes power to have everything in the palm of your hand, not a clever tongue. If I ever see a rutting beast like Mo Ran again, I'll cut off his head with my sword. What are you gonna do, read poetry at him? Ha ha ha—"

He was still laughing when the crisp sounds of applause drifted into his ears. "Nian-gongzi, you do look like a young master of Sisheng Peak... How impressive."

A-Nian started and brought the sword up before him, face paling. "Mo Ran?!" he cried.

A dark cloud rolled by overhead, obscuring the blazing sun and plunging the yard into shadow. That youth in ragged clothes, who had arrived without their notice, looked up from where he stood on the pile of firewood.

Despite the gauntness of his face, Mo Ran's features were very fine. His eyes blazed, and lash-marks from the whip were still vivid across his face. He hadn't washed since he'd escaped the prison, and blood was caked on his skin.

For all that it had Mo Ran's familiar features, A-Nian felt this face belonged to a stranger. It was the boy he knew, yet there was something different about him. Mo Ran held a machete in his hand, eyes curved into smiling crescents. There seemed to be something sinister in the depths of his dimples, like the swirl of a gathering storm; his expression was mild and yet indescribably eerie.

"Bringing good to the land, having the world at your feet? Mo Nian-gongzi, future master swordsman, young master of Sisheng Peak. Since when have you had such ambitions? What a joke." His smile widened, features warping.

This kitchen boy had been meek and obedient since he was small, always obliging and rarely speaking. Although he'd been away for a single night, he seemed like a moth that had emerged from its cocoon: glittering with life, his grin brash and wild.

In the past, the boy seldom smiled; at best he bent his mouth into a timid curve. But he'd been driven to madness.

The youths shrank back in fear. A-Nian's hand shook as he clutched the hilt of his sword. He swallowed hard and hollered, "Mo Ran, what do you think you're doing?! How dare you escape prison? On behalf of the people and the law, I'll end your worthless life today!"

"Sure." Mo Ran smiled. "I don't want to live like this anymore. If you're strong enough to take this worthless life of mine, go right ahead. But if you're not—"

A metallic glint flickered in his eyes as he leapt forward. With a flash of shadow, his machete struck true. The sword in A-Nian's hand clanged to the ground—an instant later, his head dropped next to it, eyes wide and unseeing. Blood sprayed into the air. The headless corpse swayed for a terrible moment before slumping to the ground.

There was a ringing silence. Blood had splattered over Mo Ran's face; those tattered rags hung from his form, fluttering in the coppery wind as seaweed sways in water. When he raised his head, the smile on his face broadened. Eyes bloodred, he licked the blood from his lips and quietly finished his sentence: "Then I'll take your head off instead."

The other boys were frozen in fear, unable to make a sound. Mo Ran looked at them with eyes like chips of ice. "Aren't you all so powerful? Aren't you all great at passing the blame? All so good with your fists? Punishing evil, upholding righteousness... Go ahead! *Come at me!*"

Of course they didn't dare to. They stood shaking, scared out of their wits. *This* was Mo Ran? The same Mo Ran who was so timid and shy he'd bear the greatest suffering in silence?

Mo Ran looked up and sighed. Dragging the machete on the ground behind him, he approached them with slow strides, the point of the blade scrawling a line of blood across the ground. "How modest you've all become." He chuckled, blade flashing as the corners of his mouth hooked up. "Since you won't make the first move, I have no choice but to do the honors."

In the blink of an eye, that yard became a hell on earth: a scene of wanton slaughter.

The hall was closed at this early hour, and most of the House of Drunken Jade staff were asleep. After Mo Ran dispatched the boys in the yard, he went to the side rooms and took care of the others one by one. Some had their throats slit in their sleep, while others woke just to be silenced with a flash of metal.

By the time anyone realized what was going on, it was too late. Mo Ran had set the hall ablaze, reducing the House of Drunken Jade to a towering inferno. The song girls and servants screamed and sobbed, but no one dared run into the flames to save them.

By the time he reached the last few victims, Mo Ran was no longer satisfied with dispensing quick deaths. He took his machete to their legs and allowed the fire to claim them. In the sea of flames, he calmly sat down in the middle of the hall and laid the naked blade across his knees, watching those he'd immobilized with a smile. Among their number was Madam Mo, his adoptive mother. Face hidden by smoke, Mo Ran gazed at them writhing like maggots, convulsing and sobbing in the blaze.

He raised the machete again and extended his arm, but not to hack at his victims. He used the sharp tip to pick up a bunch of grapes from a table nearby. Slowly, he plucked the fruit from the stem and peeled them. Then he popped them into his mouth, one by one, savoring their sweetness with his cheeks bulging.

"Oh? These are so good." Mo Ran grinned again. "I've never tried grapes from the western territories before. All this time you were eating such tasty things." He looked down, chuckling to himself. "I'm jealous."

One of the beams overhead buckled, crashing down in a cloud of sparks. The dying on the ground screamed pitifully; only Mo Ran sat with his chin propped in his hand, legs crossed and machete in his arms. He took his time eating those grapes, as if the sky could fall without disturbing his peace.

"The fire's so big. None of us are getting out of here." Done with the grapes, Mo Ran picked out a peach. "Why don't we sit here and have a nice long chat?"

"Who wants to chat with you? You brute! You beast! You're no better than an animal!" shrieked Madam Mo.

"No?" Mo Ran spat out some grape seeds, grinning. "Then let's talk business. Mother said so herself last night; I owe all of you for your companionship and Mother's thoughtful care. Of course I have to do my filial duty and send you on your way."

He stood and walked around them, making a polite bow. "Don't walk too quickly on the road to the underworld," he said with a smile. "Wait for me."

As the others sobbed, Madam Mo yelled, "Mo Ran! You cur! I never should've let that Xun girl talk me into taking you in! You're a scourge, a curse! You—you're a depraved beast!"

"And you are not worthy of speaking Xun-jiejie's name," said Mo Ran flatly. "I rushed here from Wubei Temple to fulfill my mom's dying wish and repay Xun-jiejie's kindness. She knew I'd lost my mother, so she gave you a whole year's earnings to allow me to stay. She was my savior. But you? What are you to me?"

"I never should've said yes! I never—who cares about a year's worth of earnings? You went behind my back and set her free! She was the star of the House of Drunken Jade! Do you have any idea how much money she made us with a single song?! But you...you dared..."

"She was my mom's savior, and mine. She sold her skills and not her body, yet you took that merchant's bribe and sold her—you forced her to take a client. Tell me, why *shouldn't* I have let her go?! All these years, you've hated and tormented me, but I never spoke up or fought back. My mom told me anyone willing to give me food couldn't be truly evil." Mo Ran closed his eyes. "So I endured it... I endured everything..."

"Pah! How dare you?! Ungrateful brat—*I'm* the one who housed you, *I* took a beggar like you off the streets! You beast, you bastard son of a dog-bitch mother!"

"Hm, what a coincidence. A bastard son of a dog-bitch mother?" Mo Ran smiled, his face bathed in the amber glow of the firelight.

"Don't you think your poor dead son will think you're calling for him?"

Mo Ran stepped forward and grabbed the madam's powdered face. "But Mother, you did remind me. Thank you very much for giving me food to eat and a place to sleep. I'll send you on your way first."

"You—!"

"To lighten the mood, why don't we play a game? What do you think of guessing pictures?" Mo Ran asked eagerly. He picked up a bit of wood still smoldering at the end and traced the shape of a sun around the madam's eye. Her flesh burned in the wake of his movements, but her hysterical screams only made Mo Ran smile. "Mother, do you know what I'm drawing? If you can't guess it, you lose, and I'll draw something else."

That night, he slowly tortured everyone in the building to death. In one blow, he retaliated for a decade of accumulated malice and helplessness, reducing the House of Drunken Jade and its inhabitants to corpses and scorched earth.

He lay down in the flames among those twisted bodies, watching as the exquisite building began to crumble. He shoved fruit and sweets into his mouth, smiling all the while.

"Delicious." He grimaced as tears began to stream down his grinning face. He reached up to cover his eyes, laughing as he cried. "Too bad I'll never get to have it again..."

The ebony tablet inscribed with the House of Drunken Jade's name came crashing down, splintering upon the ground. Smoke billowed into the sky, and the building and all its carved pillars collapsed with a thunderous *boom*.

That hall had seen all there was of song and dance, gauzy skirts and spilled wine. Once, it had prospered, its glory endless. Now that majesty was dead and gone, its opulence turned to ash.

Those bygone love affairs of men and women went up in smoke with the burning wooden beams. Amidst the blazing inferno, the sound of two goddesses in duet seemed to drift from the cracks in the wood and the seams in the roof tiles.

"Beautiful as a flower in bloom—" sang Duan Yihan.

"All given over to these wretched wastes—" cried Xun Fengruo.

Thus the curtain fell on the tale of a famous Xiangtan pleasure house. Within a sea of roaring flames and the fading strains of song, its storied history of tragedies and triumphs culminated in one last majestic finale.

263

Return of an
Old Dream

M O RAN'S TALE came to an end. No one spoke in Loyalty
Hall. What was good and what was evil? Who was right,
and who was wrong? They all had their opinions, but no
one could make a definite judgment.

Mo Ran didn't look at the faces of the Xue family. He lowered
his lashes. "I thought I would die in that fire. But when I woke up,
I was lying in a room at Sisheng Peak with that investigator sitting
by my bedside. He grabbed me as soon as I woke up and said—he
said I would be the young master of Sisheng Peak from now on." He
paused, then laughed softly. "Uncle's nephew."

The carpets of Loyalty Hall were embroidered with pollia flowers.
Mo Ran trained his eyes on their beautiful patterns, his face serene.
"The investigator didn't want to lose his commission. When Uncle
pulled me out of the wreck of the House of Drunken Jade and asked
if this was the boy he was looking for, he nodded. That one nod
changed my life."

Master Xuanjing sighed. "Amitabha. Mo-shizhu, how could you
rest easy? Have you never thought of confessing to Xue-zunzhu?"

"Of course I have. When I first woke up, I couldn't bear it.
I wanted badly to confess the truth." Mo Ran's gaze was distant, as
if looking into the past. "But when they heard I was awake, Uncle...
immediately came to see me, and Auntie made me a bowl of noodles.

There were three poached eggs in it, with runny yolks, all covered in meat sauce. She...told me she was afraid I'd have trouble keeping it down since I just woke up, and had minced it finely to help. Xue Meng also came by and brought me a whole box of sweets."

His eyes drifted shut. "I ate that bowl of noodles, and those cakes, and I couldn't form the words. They smiled at me and treated me so well... If I'd said I was the one who set fire to the House of Drunken Jade, I killed your nephew, your sister-in-law...what then?" Mo Ran murmured. "I couldn't do it. I swallowed the words down, and as time passed...I could no longer say them at all."

Master Xuanjing heaved a sigh.

"I knew what kind of person Mo Nian was—lazy and careless. In the beginning, I didn't know how much Uncle knew of him, so I tried my best to act as his copy. When I realized Uncle didn't know him at all, I stopped doing things as he would." Mo Ran was silent a beat. "Ultimately, I owed a blood debt to Mo Nian and his family, but I ended up taking advantage of their kin."

The members of Sisheng Peak were stunned; many of the disciples and elders who'd known Mo Ran were frozen stiff, their hearts in turmoil. Madam Wang and Xue Zhengyong were speechless, staring blankly at Mo Ran's lonely silhouette. They'd watched this boy grow up from a young and immature child to a once-in-a-generation zongshi. And now he was telling them it'd been a mistake from the very start.

Mo Ran wasn't their nephew; they shared no blood. Rather, what lay between them was only death and hatred. What could they say? What could they do? Neither Madam Wang nor Xue Zhengyong knew. They'd never met the real Mo Nian. They had poured all of their regret and yearning for Xue Zhengyong's dead brother into this boy named Mo Ran. Mo Nian was a stranger, but they'd patted

Mo Ran's head, held Mo Ran's hand, and answered his cries of "Uncle" and "Auntie."

Xue Zhengyong had no idea what to think.

Mu Yanli shattered the silence. "Mo Ran, you may be pitiable, but your crimes are many and cannot be lightly excused. Do you know exactly how many major offenses you've committed?"

Mo Ran had never liked Tianyin Pavilion. He closed his eyes and said nothing.

Mu Yanli shot him a glance, her voice ringing like a bell. "Murder, arson, theft of identity. On Mount Jiao, you knew you had Nangong blood, but you looked on, acting in your own interests. At Guyueye, you committed a bloody slaughter—all for what?"

"I'll say it once again: I wasn't responsible for the murders at Guyueye. The Space-Time Gate has reopened and two worlds have comingled. That man was not me."

"The Space-Time Gate is the first forbidden technique, unused for millennia. Do you not find this excuse ridiculous?" Mu Yanli was unmoved. "Is it not that you are, in truth, dissatisfied—that, as a Nangong descendant, your own ambition drives you to throw both the upper and lower cultivation realms into chaos?"

"Pavilion Master Mu oversteps." Jiang Xi frowned. "I don't see how Mo Ran has any motive for overturning the cultivation realms. If that was his goal, he could've pulled off any kind of scheme at Mount Jiao. The ten great sects would've been decimated. None of this is adding up. Before the truth is revealed, please be careful what you say."

Mu Yanli cast him a scornful glance. "Jiang-zhangmen need not speak on his behalf. Even if he had no intent to overthrow the cultivation world, his past misdeeds are more than sufficient to place him in Tianyin Pavilion's custody." She gestured toward her retinue. "Seize Mo Ran. Take him away."

"Wait!"

Mu Yanli turned to Xue Zhengyong. "Does Xue-zunzhu have something to add?"

Xue Zhengyong looked ill, as if he himself didn't understand why he'd called out to Mu Yanli. After all these years of seeing Mo Ran as his own flesh and blood, it had become second nature for him. He couldn't stand by as Tianyin Pavilion dragged him off. But what could he do? Urge them not to?

He closed his eyes, teeth chattering. He felt cold, his chest hollowed out, as if something crucial had been carved away. He buried his face in his palms. This man, who had always been bursting with vitality, suddenly looked old and frail.

"Does Xue-zunzhu wish to bid his nephew farewell?"

These words were cruelly chosen. Xue Zhengyong shook harder when she said the word *nephew*, shuddering like willows in the wind. "I..." Xue Zhengyong rasped. "Ran-er... Mo Ran..." He didn't know how to address him anymore.

It was Mo Ran who moved to ease things—closing his eyes, he stepped toward Xue Zhengyong and knelt, kowtowing again and again in the most formal bow.

"Aren't they just wasting time?" came a murmur.

"Putting on airs..."

Mo Ran ignored them. When he had completed the bows, he rose and made ready to leave.

Yet before he could start forward, Xue Meng rushed back into Loyalty Hall. Black blood dripped from Longcheng as he shouted in horror, "There's—"

"What's going on?"

"There's an army of Zhenlong pawns outside—tons of them are cultivators from Rufeng Sect's Mount Jiao!"

Terror shook them. The crowd rushed out of the hall and saw countless cultivators aloft on their swords outside Sisheng Peak, their robes fluttering in the wind. Half were like the cultivators who had streamed from the rift, wearing those same black robes with masks over their faces, but the others were dressed in crane robes with a ribbon over their eyes—corpses from the heroes' tomb of Rufeng Sect.

"Wh-what's going on?!"

"Didn't Nangong Si suppress them? How are they back?! Who countered the spell?"

The answer was self-evident. Who could counter a suppression spell cast by a member of the Nangong family? Furious eyes swung to fasten on Mo Ran.

Even if he knew who was behind it, there was nothing Mo Ran could say in his own defense. Worse still, his spiritual energy was still depleted. He couldn't stop the pawns from attacking; he could only watch as thousands of undead soldiers swarmed toward them.

Just as in the previous life, Sisheng Peak would be swept up in a bloody maelstrom. It seemed the surprise Shi Mei spoke of wasn't over yet.

"Fight them!"

"Drive them off first! Drive them off!"

The crowd rushed up to meet them, but they had been caught badly off-guard, and there seemed to be no end to the enemy's numbers. Chaos reigned.

Mo Ran stood before the hall, watching the pawns land. They crossed swords with the Sisheng Peak disciples and met the other cultivators with spells. Blue robes and silver armor whirled around black cloaks, an impenetrable mass of dark color.

He stood on the jade steps, temples throbbing. The sight before him seemed to mirror his past life. Back then, it was he who'd sent an army of pawns, both dead and alive, into Sisheng Peak to kill all who dared stand in his way. He'd grown used to killing without mercy, to slaughtering thousands without a care and leaving mountains of corpses in his wake. He remembered standing just like this before Loyalty Hall, the traitorous disciple Mo Weiyu looking down on the charging soldiers and grieving crowd with a smile on his lips while the bodies of Xue Zhengyong and Madam Wang lay at his feet.

"Your blood will pave me a path that begins at Sisheng Peak."

His deranged cackling from that bygone lifetime seemed to echo in his ears. Mo Ran's eyes twitched. "Stop, you can't win!" he shouted at Xue Meng. "Run, all of you—*run!*" But the din was too great, and Xue Meng was too far away to hear.

Mo Ran took in the clanging blades and frantic struggles of the cultivators. He saw Jiang Xi fending off a dozen pawns and remembered how the other Jiang Xi had fallen before Mo Ran's own blade.

"You won't kneel?"

"No."

"You won't accept this venerable one as emperor?"

"No."

The blade descended, blood splashing across the ground.

They couldn't win...

Mo Ran watched the leader of Taxue Palace play her ocarina, its sound piercing the skies and sending the pawns swaying. He recalled how this palace master's fingers had been shattered, her tendons snapped—

"Why resist?"

"As the leader of Taxue Palace, I will not run, even if I cannot ensure its safety."

The ocarina had shattered, never to sound again.

They couldn't win.

In the mayhem, Mo Ran looked toward Madam Wang and Xue Zhengyong in the distance, fighting together—yet what he saw was their dead faces, grief and fury frozen in their sightless eyes. They stared at him across lifetimes, hate-filled and accusatory.

It was cold. So cold.

Mo Ran was shivering, his fingertips numb. To think Shi Mei had gone so far... Shi Mei had done this!

He'd known the threat Shi Mei made as he'd taken Chu Wanning was not an idle one. It was because of this that he'd so resolutely returned to Sisheng Peak. But now, he felt a prickling over his skin. If he'd ignored Shi Mei's warning and chased him down to save Chu Wanning, what would've happened? The leaders of the cultivation realm were all here. If they died in mysterious circumstances at Sisheng Peak, what would have happened?

Shi Mei's interlocking schemes allowed him no moment of rest. Mo Ran looked up and saw a field of Zhenlong pawns, living dead that feared no pain and needed no rest, a writhing, endless mass of bloody corpses and rotting bones...

They couldn't go on like this.

Shi Mei said this was a surprise for him, so it must have been set up with specific intent. Since he'd returned here as Shi Mei wanted, there must be something he could do to stop it. He couldn't let those remembered tragedies play out again; he couldn't see Sisheng Peak destroyed again, couldn't bear watching his aunt and uncle die in front of him again. If the past repeated itself, how could he face himself—how could he face Chu Wanning?

Mo Ran jolted back to awareness. He shoved his way past the crowd and sprinted toward his aunt and uncle. "Stop fighting! Retreat, get out of here, stop fighting! There's no way we can win!"

His voice tore out of his throat. His face was twisted into a mask of desperation; he was a drowning man struggling for the opposite shore, a dying man running to those still alive. He was a moth throwing himself toward the flame, one life chasing down the other.

"Stop fighting! Run—run away! You can't win!"

You can't win. I've watched you die once before. Run, I'm begging you.

A blade appeared before him, flashing silver as it blocked his path. Mu Yanli's icy visage came into view. "Trying to take advantage of the chaos to flee?"

"Step aside!" Mo Ran shouted.

"You're a criminal of the cultivation realm, I have every right to—"

Mu Yanli felt air stirring behind her and turned to see a masked pawn descending on her with sword extended. She met the pawn's blade with her own, face dark with murderous intent. "Mo Ran!" she shouted. "So it *is* you behind this!"

Her voice was as crisp as a frozen spring, ringing out over the din of the crowd. Many around them turned, watching as the pawn engaged Mu Yanli in bitter combat while ignoring Mo Ran entirely. In fact, all of the pawns on Sisheng Peak seemed to take Mo Ran for one of their own. They avoided him in their attacks, never touching a single hair on his head.

"So it *is* that bastard Mo Ran's doing!" someone snarled.

"They're on the same side!"

Angry faces turned in his direction, ears tuned to those whispers and growls of accusation, eyes red-rimmed with rage fixing upon him. Past and present overlapped. In those hateful eyes, he was once again a murderous monster. He was the emperor who'd trampled all these cultivators underfoot in another lifetime—undefeated in battle, beholden to no principles, scornful and wholly insane.

"Take him down!" someone cried.

"Don't let him escape!"

"Let's see how long he can keep up his act!"

His ears rang with those same shouts, filled with the same wrath, castigation, and condemnation.

These sights were too familiar. He could almost see his and Chu Wanning's decisive battle. Mo Ran had used Zhenlong chess pieces to take control of both the living and the dead, along with beasts of both the land and air. His army had spilled onto the peak like ink, their weapons shining like snow upon a high mountain. From his lofty vantage point, he'd lowered his gaze and smiled thinly, watching as the skies flipped and daylight turned to dusk.

Then, it was Chu Wanning who'd stopped him. Chu Wanning who had given all he had against the tens of thousands of pawns, wielding Tianwen, then Jiuge, then, finally, Huaisha.[10]

Huaisha. Mo Ran would never forget the grief and agony in Chu Wanning's eyes as he summoned his longsword.

"I heard this is the blade Shizun uses to kill. It seems today I finally get to see it."

"Mo Ran," Chu Wanning had said. "What will it take for you to stop?"

Mo Ran had thrown his head back and laughed. "I can't, Shizun. My hands are covered in blood. I killed Aunt and Uncle, I killed my own sect siblings... Now I only have to take your head and I'll be the ultimate tyrant. No one will be able to stand in my way."

Chu Wanning looked like he had been run through.

---

10 Tianwen, Jiuge, and Huaisha take their names from poems in Verses of Chu written by the poet and statesman Qu Yuan during the Warring States period. The poem "Huaisha" expresses grief, idealistic resolve, and acceptance of death; it is commonly interpreted as Qu Yuan's suicide note. Its title, which means "embracing sand," is thought to be a reference to Qu Yuan's chosen means of death: exiled and distraught over the fall of his state's capital, he drowned himself in the Miluo River by clutching a stone to his chest.

Yet Mo Ran remained unsatisfied; a malicious impulse beat in his heart. "Once I kill you," he bit out, each syllable crushed between his teeth, "there will be no one on earth I cannot kill."

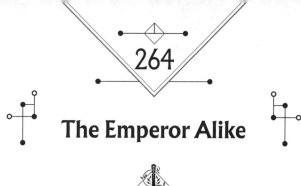

264

The Emperor Alike

A T LAST, master and disciple turned upon each other. It was a battle for the ages, but in the end, Chu Wanning's fragile core was no match for Mo Ran's raw and youthful strength.

"Stop struggling." The young fiend had grown increasingly formidable as they fought. He leered behind his blade as Bugui and Huaisha met and flashed. Huaisha's golden glow flickered and dimmed, while Bugui's green flames filled the eyes of teacher and student.

Mo Ran took in the sight of Chu Wanning's bloodless face, then flicked a glance at Huaisha's fading light. Derision rose in his gaze. "You're out of spiritual energy. If you keep going, your core will shatter. You'd rather die than become a commoner. Am I right?"

Chu Wanning clenched his jaw and said nothing, his lips devoid of color.

When Huaisha went completely dark, Mo Ran knew Chu Wanning was well and truly spent. He burst into wild laughter. "What else can you use against me? Yuheng of the Night Sky...my most high and lofty shizun?"

Chu Wanning fell to one knee, bracing himself with his sword to keep from collapsing, his white robes splattered with blood. He looked up. Back then, Mo Ran had been so full of spite that all he saw was the determination in Chu Wanning's eyes, and not the sorrow buried beneath. Many years later, when Taxian-jun swallowed the poison that would end his life, his mind had drifted back to that defining battle. Chu Wanning had truly been willing to die just to stop him.

Putting the people before the self.

He'd derided Chu Wanning as a coward who spoke in empty platitudes. But Chu Wanning was indeed a man of his word.

"Choose compassion," his shizun said. "Don't hold onto hatred."

A flash of gold.

Mo Ran saw that final serenity in Chu Wanning's eyes an instant before a brilliant light rose from Chu Wanning's palms. This was how the Beidou Immortal, a man with no friends or family in the cultivation world, sacrificed his spiritual core to summon his three holy weapons once more.

Jiuge, Tianwen, Huaisha. Was there no end to Chu Wanning's prideful stubbornness? Mo Ran's massive army fell before the bright power of Chu Wanning's spiritual core. In the light of those holy weapons, those black and white chess pieces had crumbled to dust.

It was funny—Mo Ran had been standing right in front of Chu Wanning, inches away. He had seen this desperate man, nearly delirious with blood loss, and did nothing. He had only watched, mildly surprised and a little curious. He wanted to know how far this callous man would go for the sake of *the people* of whom he so often spoke.

He watched as Chu Wanning spent the very last of his spiritual energy. The roaring river quieted; the crows blocking the sun scattered. The living who had been made puppets regained their minds, and the dead closed their eyes and returned to their eternal sleep.

Mo Ran watched. Watched as the Beidou Immortal's core splintered, watched as the golden glow of it faded, watched as his shizun sank to his knees before him and collapsed in the dust.

Throughout it all, Mo Ran's face was impassive. He seemed to hear his mother's dying words in his ears, the sound of that kind-hearted woman stroking his cheek and telling him to repay others for their kindness instead of seeking them out for revenge. Despite the years that had gone by, here again were those same familiar exhortations. Before Chu Wanning sacrificed his core, he'd said: "Choose compassion. Don't hold onto hatred."

But Mo Ran had failed. His heart held endless loathing; only spilling blood gave him a moment's respite—

He destroyed Sisheng Peak, slaughtered Rufeng Sect, killed his aunt and uncle along with thousands of cultivators and dozens of sect leaders. He dyed the world red and built mountains of white bone until the very end, when he was surrounded at Wushan Palace and took his own life before the tower.

He'd lived through all of it himself. Those colossal crimes had been the work of his own hands. He was the perpetrator of those atrocities; Bugui had soaked in the blood of hundreds, and the Zhenlong Chess Formation had taken tens of thousands of lives.

It was all him.

Mo Ran's vision went dark. He could scarcely breathe.

A nearby groan yanked him back to his senses and out of the mire of memory. Mu Yanli had been stabbed in the shoulder, and her blood was hot on his face.

"Pavilion Master!"

"Pavilion Master, watch out!"

Members of Tianyin Pavilion rushed up to protect Mu Yanli, who panted but gritted out, "I'm fine."

The pawn in front of her flourished its blade. Before all those watching eyes, he knelt to greet Mo Ran. Bowing his masked face, he said, "This subordinate deserves to be punished for failing to rescue Master."

Gasps of shock raced through the crowd.

"Mo Ran's the one controlling them!"

"It called him Master!"

"No," said Mo Ran. "No—"

But who believed that? Who would believe him?!

Shaking his head, Mo Ran took a step back. He was surrounded by those suspicious and hateful faces.

No...

He turned to look for Xue Meng, but Xue Meng was too far away. He hadn't seen anything that had happened. He looked to Madam Wang and Xue Zhengyong. Those two had indeed witnessed it, and their expressions were awful to behold. Mo Ran's mouth trembled. He wanted to speak, but didn't know what he could say in his defense.

A group of pawns surged out from behind Madam Wang. "Auntie! Look out!"

At his shout, the crowd turned. Xue Zhengyong sprang toward her immediately, but he was surrounded by pawns himself—he couldn't get to Madam Wang.

"Auntie!"

"Mom!"

There was a shrill metallic clang. It was Jiang Xi who had leapt from the crowd, Xuehuang in hand, to beat back the pawns surrounding Madam Wang.

"Shidi..." she said in shock.

Jiang Xi shot her a freezing look. "Use your eyes."

Master Xuanjing was squinting at a storm cloud on the horizon, its dark mass pressing closer and closer to Sisheng Peak. When he finally made out what it was, he dared not believe his own eyes. It wasn't until others began to turn toward that roiling black cloud that he cried, mustache quivering. "How could this be?! How many pawns are there?!"

The black chess pieces surged forward like the tide, an unending mass. Some were dead, some were alive, but all bore faces burned beyond recognition, mouths gaping and tongues torn out. They would never speak again even if they got their minds back. Behind them were beasts controlled by the Zhenlong formation, from dogs to snakes.

"Mo Weiyu!"

"Mo Ran..."

As the crowd turned to him once more, fear outweighed their fury. Those who had been pressing in on him took several steps back.

"Insane... Mo Ran, are you insane...?"

"How many chess pieces did you *make*?!"

Mo Ran opened his mouth. He wanted to say, *No, it wasn't me.* But who else could it be? The Space-Time Gate of Life and Death had opened again, and Taxian-jun had led his army of thousands back into this world. What was the difference between the two of them? They had the same memories and used the same spells. Mo-zongshi was just as skilled as Taxian-jun at the Zhenlong Chess Formation, and without any special commands, the pawns made by Taxian-jun would also acknowledge Mo-zongshi as their master. The slaughter of kin and the razing of cities, the use of forbidden techniques and the creation of thousands of enthralled soldiers—destroying the world and reducing all to naught—it was all his doing. All the blame fell squarely on his shoulders.

More pawns swarmed toward them, with no end in sight. They fanned out like ink on paper, drawing inexorably closer.

"What do we do?" someone cried, panicked.

"Mo Ran!" Mu Yanli snarled. "What do you have to say for yourself?! You planned this! I only wish Tianyin Pavilion had learned of this sooner so we could have had you executed!"

Black clouds obscured the sun, blanketing the world in darkness.

A bloody wind whistled through the mountain peaks. The horde of undead pawns was like a massive bell hanging high in the air, ready to come crashing down at any moment, to crush humans like ants and splinter the world itself.

Mo Ran's pupils shrank as he turned his face up to the sky.

The cultivators refused to give up. Some soared into the air on their swords to meet the enemy, while others stood their ground below. The clash this time was more intense, the air clotted with blood and screams. Heads rolled and intestines spilled into the dirt. But that black tide poured out from the horizon, on and on, striking fear into the hearts of all who stood against it.

"Dad! Mom!" Xue Meng's shout came from a distance.

Mo Ran whipped around. Xue Zhengyong and Jiang Xi were both covered in blood. There was too much of that furious crimson—it was impossible to tell whether it had come from themselves or their slain enemies. Xue Meng struggled mightily to make his way toward his parents, slashing a path through the undead with his scimitar, but he was one against so many.

"Xue Meng!"

Mo Ran started toward him, but Xue Meng looked away, conflicted. Xue Meng was trying to avoid him.

One of the Rufeng Sect revenants sprang at Xue Meng, sinking their sword into Xue Meng's shoulder. Blood streamed from the wound, dyeing his silver armor scarlet.

"Xue Meng… Xue Meng!" Mo Ran scrambled desperately toward him, but there were so many people between them, and Xue Meng was so far away. He couldn't… He couldn't get there in time…

Now that Xue Meng was injured, more chess pieces charged at him. His silhouette was swiftly swallowed up by the mindless Zhenlong puppets.

"Meng-er!"

"Meng-er!"

Hysterical screams tore from Madam Wang and Xue Zhengyong's throats. Mo Ran had never heard them shriek so miserably. His scalp prickled with foreboding. *Xue Meng...*

No. It wasn't supposed to be like this. There had to be a way— there had to be a way! Hua Binan wouldn't have sent Mo Ran to Sisheng Peak, setting up such a complicated scenario, merely to force him to watch as the sect was destroyed. What did Hua Binan wish him to do? What was it? What did Hua Binan want? What was this surprise meant to accomplish? What would bring an end to it, what would it take for him to be spared?

Realization broke over him. Mo Ran froze, heart pounding.

He finally understood. Hua Binan's ruthlessness, his insistence on ruining Mo Ran's reputation and pushing him into a corner— Mo Ran knew why he'd done it. Nangong Si had made the choice at Mount Jiao, and Chu Wanning had made it in that decisive battle in the past life.

He had no spiritual energy left...but he did have his core. He could feel that light glowing in his chest, pulsing alongside his heart.

Taxian-jun's crazed smile surfaced in his mind. *You're out of spiritual energy. If you keep going, your core will shatter. We both know how much you value your pride, Shizun. I think you'd rather die than become a commoner. Am I right?*

Mo Ran knew what he had to do.

Tears sprang to his eyes. Wrapped in the chaos of battle, Mo Ran felt suddenly calm.

In the past life, Chu Wanning had sacrificed himself, proving that putting the people before the self was not an empty phrase. Mo Ran seemed to once again glimpse Chu Wanning's pallid face in the instant before he'd shattered his own core. When his shizun thought he would die, his final words to Mo Ran were: "Choose compassion, don't hold onto hatred."

There was a rumbling *boom*, shaking the earth under the cultivators' feet.

"What happened?"

"What's going on?"

Everyone was stunned, dodging pawns as they looked for the source of the sound.

They didn't have to look for long. Where Mo Ran had been standing, a blazing light shone: not real flames, but the roaring conflagration of spiritual energy that appeared when a fire-type core burned itself out. Mo Ran was enveloped in their light.

Mo Weiyu. Emperor Taxian-jun of the past, the once-in-a-generation zongshi of the present. To bring an end to the calamity unfolding before his eyes, he'd detonated his own spiritual core.

Just as it had with Nangong Si and Chu Wanning, the shattering gave Mo Ran the greatest spiritual energy he'd ever wielded. His eyes were dyed scarlet by the flames, but there was no pain on his handsome face.

Who was he, in this moment? Could he cease to be the reviled Taxian-jun?

If he could, then he, too, wanted to be Chu Wanning.

Within his chest, his core splintered and melted away. The flames burned brighter, blazing past the clouds and illuminating the heavens themselves. In that moment, he sensed that clean and bright dream of his youth fluttering back into his heart. He saw Duan Yihan and Chu Wanning. He saw his mother stroking his cheek in the woodshed, saying, *Only repay kindness. Don't seek revenge.* He saw that youth outside Wubei Temple, carefully feeding him porridge from his cupped hand. *Slow down, there's more if you want it...*

In both of his lives, he'd wanted to be *good*. He'd failed to do so in the past life, and in this one, he'd grieved the events of that life for close to ten years.

How could he make up for it? He was tortured with yearning, day and night, but he didn't know how. If he were to say he'd once dreamed of saving the common people, who would believe him? He'd be mocked, berated, and derided.

He was Mo Weiyu, he was Emperor Taxian-jun. He'd made mistakes and he'd killed. Anything he did in recompense was useless and wrong. No one would forgive him.

Perhaps it was only in this fire, as his core shattered, as he sacrificed himself for that dream—as he took the same step Chu Wanning had taken in the past life—that he might gain the slightest reprieve. Only then might he have the right to cautiously say: "If I could, I too would want to be Chu Wanning."

Please, don't laugh at this wish of mine. Don't make fun of me. I know I'm dumb. For a long time, I had no one by my side. That's how I lived for two lifetimes, walking the wrong path for twenty years.

I'm so dumb. I don't know how I ended up in this hopeless darkness. I don't know how it came to this. When I think back on it, everything was a mistake.

I can no longer find Mom. Or Shizun.

Please. Hell is too cold. Let me go back, won't you...?

I want to go home.

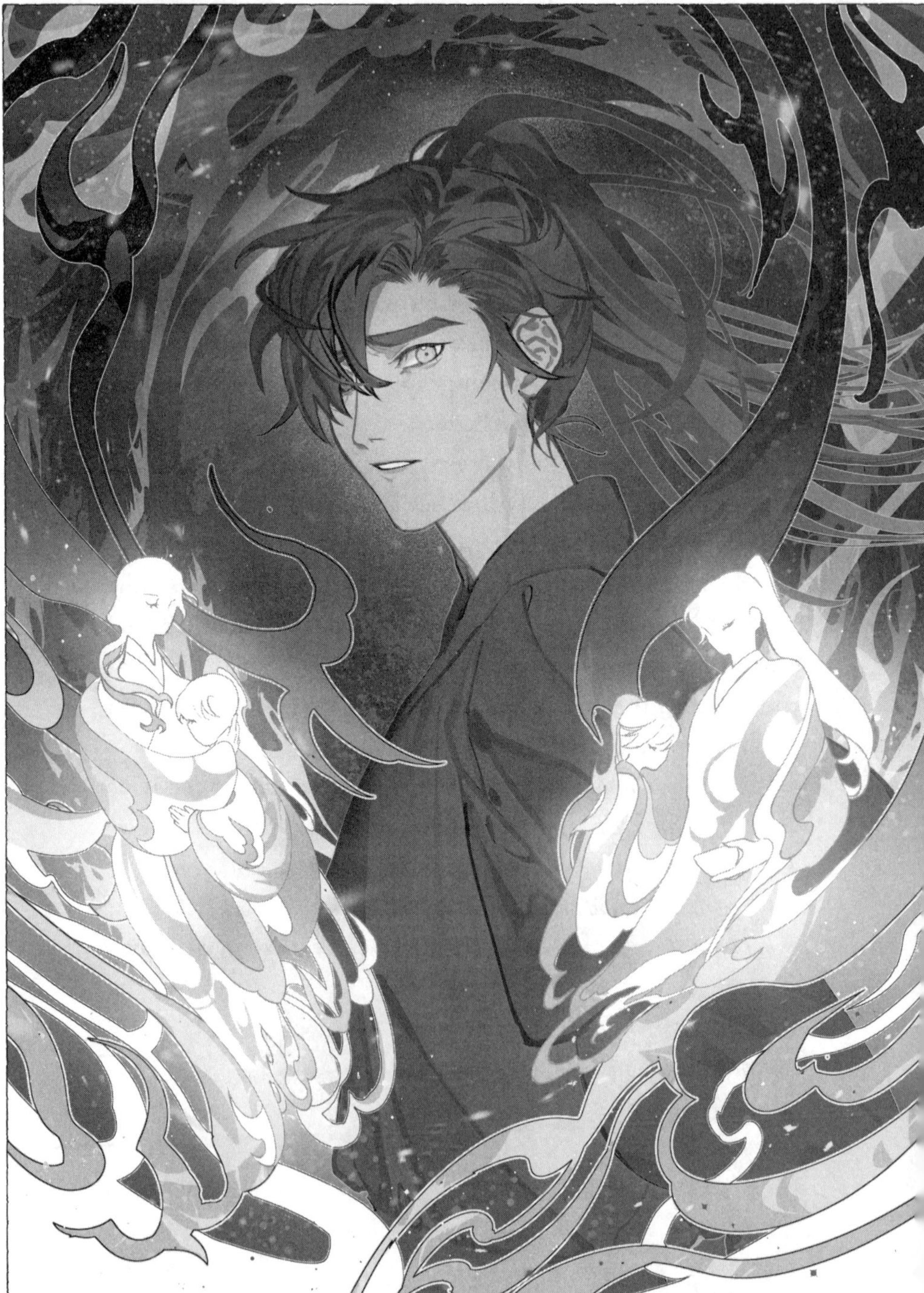

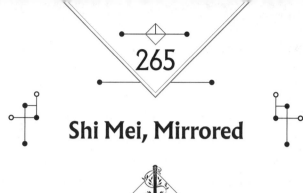

265

Shi Mei, Mirrored

WHEN A CANDLE burned out, only darkness lingered. When a fire went out, only ashes remained. Yet even darkness was once bright, and even ashes were once warm. Mo Ran too had once had days of light and warmth. But no one would know, and no one would care.

He had spent his last sparks of spiritual energy. He watched as the birds scattered and the undead soldiers crumpled, watched as the living regained their senses and the pawns fell apart. He saw the black tide about to swallow Sisheng Peak retreating and watched as the apocalypse was averted.

All of them thought him a despicable criminal, and he didn't disagree. But the demon had finally done something worthy of a god. Chu Wanning was his candle, and he had clumsily followed his light.

"Ge!"

"Ran-er!"

Fuzzily, he heard people calling his name. He saw Xue Meng stumbling forward out of the corner of his eye, saw Xue Zhengyong and Madam Wang breaking through the crowd and running toward him.

Their voices brought him profound relief. He showed his teeth, attempting to smile, but tears streaked down his bloodstained face.

He wanted to say, *I'm sorry, it's all my fault.* But his throat was choked with sobs, and he could only plead: "Don't hate me."

I really... I really loved all of you. I loved Auntie and Uncle, loved Sisheng Peak, loved this stolen warmth and stolen family. Auntie, Uncle, Xue Meng. Please don't hate me.

That dread army was beaten back. Mo Ran collapsed into the dirt.

When Chu Wanning had fainted from his wounds in the past life, his white robes had been stained with blood, but he had still seemed pristine. He and Mo Ran were not the same—Mo Ran had always been caked in filth.

In the moment before he lost consciousness, Mo Ran felt Madam Wang's soft embrace. "Ran-er," she cried, voice cracking with heartbreak.

He heard Xue Zhengyong confronting Mu Yanli. "A plot?" he was shouting. "What plot?! If he summoned these chess pieces, why would he go so far to save us?!"

He heard Xue Meng howling. "Don't touch him! Don't touch him! Don't take him away!"

Everything was a mess. Mo Ran wanted to explain—he had more to say, but he was so very, very tired.

He closed his eyes.

In Mount Jiao's Hall of Sages, the everbright lamps glowed steadily. The whale-oil candles were as thick and stout as bowls. Here, there was no light from the stars or sun. Only the candles weeping their waxen tears tracked the passage of time.

Shi Mei sat on the dais in a cloak of white fox fur. His forehead rested in his hand, eyes closed in meditative repose.

This had been Xu Shuanglin's preferred seat. Shi Mei had watched as Xu Shuanglin refined his Zhenlong chess pieces and created heaven and hell, wishing wholeheartedly to bring his shizun back to life. He'd found Xu Shuanglin terribly interesting. It was a shame he couldn't keep him around in the end.

Before Shi Mei lay an enspelled silk scroll, covered in flaring words and all manner of colored dots. This was the sand table Taxian-jun had created for the Zhenlong Chess Formation. Each black dot represented a black Zhenlong chess piece; silver connoted white pieces, and red the discarded pawns. The small squares scattered over the scroll represented their enemies. With this sand table before him, he had a clear view of the battle no matter where he was.

Shi Mei had unrolled the scroll upon the table but only glanced at it. He'd only set it up out of idle curiosity; he knew precisely what Mo Ran would choose. Taxian-jun would have had countless paths out of the snare, but Mo-zongshi had only one. There was nothing much to observe.

After a while, the doors of the hall opened. Soft footsteps rustled through the room. Shi Mei didn't look up. "You're here?"

A man's feet came to a stop upon the well-lit brick floor. He wore a snow-white cloak, the edge of his hood pulled low to shadow his face. He stood in the center of the hall with perfect poise. When he spoke, his voice was low but clear. "I just got word that Mo Ran shattered all of the pawns Taxian-jun created."

Shi Mei's eyelashes didn't so much as flutter. "Mn," he said peaceably. "It's not like he had much of a choice."

"Taxian-jun's body is falling apart. Those chess pieces he made started draining your spiritual energy ages ago. Now that Mo Ran's used his core to break them, you'll be free of them as well. This is a good thing."

"Oh?" Shi Mei smiled. "Are you worried about me?"

The man in white didn't answer. After a long beat, he asked, "What will you do next?"

"The plan hasn't changed." Shi Mei stirred at last. Stretching, he blinked open those peach-blossom eyes, and the whole room brightened with his smile. "Haven't we gone over this?"

"I know you've planned it out, but you must think this through. Mo Ran paid a heavy price to stop those Zhenlong pawns. These cultivators aren't idiots; there's no way they won't become suspicious."

Shi Mei smiled. "I know what you mean. Averting a terrible disaster for the cultivation world by shattering his own core—what a hero."

"Do you think the cultivation realm will interrogate their heroes?"

Shi Mei didn't answer right away. Still smiling, he wove his slender fingers together and propped his chin on top. "Don't you think Mo Ran's choice resembles Chu Wanning's actions in the past life?" he asked sweetly.

The man in white was quiet a moment. "Yes. A direct re-enactment, more or less."

"Then let me ask you this: When Chu Wanning was taken prisoner by Taxian-jun, how many people from the cultivation world cared? How many remembered him?"

Silence.

The smile on Shi Mei's face grew more radiant still. "Barely anyone, wasn't it? I've told you before. Xue Meng went everywhere seeking aid. In the beginning, there were people who shed a tear or two and promised to help him storm Sisheng Peak in a rescue mission. But what then? All those promises were empty air in the face of Taxian-jun's might. As time passed—as those feelings faded—those same people began to find Xue Meng irritating. When he next came begging, they changed their tune. How long has Chu Wanning been there, they asked. Who knows if he's still alive? Is it worth sacrificing people's lives for a man who might very well be already dead?"

The man in white shook his head. "No one knew what had happened to Chu Wanning. Mo Ran is right there in their midst, alive and well. Whatever their capacity for cruelty, they won't harm someone who just bled for the cultivation realm."

Shi Mei couldn't help a sigh. "Oh, you. You're still young—still naïve."

He rolled up the scroll on the table. The pawn markings had all turned red—out of commission. Unbothered, he stuffed it back into his qiankun pouch. "Everyone's noble when it doesn't touch their own interests. Their true nature emerges when it's their turn to suffer." His slender fingers knotted the string of the qiankun pouch. "To them," he said as he looked up, "Mo Ran might be an innocent man framed, or he might be a duplicitous villain. It'd be a shame to harm an innocent man, of course—but sparing a villain would bring bloody catastrophe down upon the entire cultivation world."

Seeing his listener rapt with attention, Shi Mei continued eagerly, "Perhaps he averted disaster by shattering his spiritual core, but too many things about him are suspicious. People are mistrustful by nature; their first priority is to rid themselves of anything that could pose a threat to them. This little detour won't change the outcome."

"Then you think Tianyin Pavilion will still take Mo Ran?" asked the man in white.

Shi Mei smiled. "Tianyin Pavilion is on our side, and everything's gone according to plan. Of course they'll take him. Once we have the shards of Mo Ran's spiritual core, Taxian-jun will be pliable again. With his strength, there's nothing we can't accomplish."

The man in white hesitated. "You've had control of him for close to a decade in the other world. What have you accomplished?"

Shi Mei froze, as if the man's directness had needled him. Frowning, he didn't respond for a long beat. "What do you mean by this?" he asked at last, eyes narrowed. "Are you questioning me?"

"No, I'm not." The man in white sighed. "We have the same goal in mind; I'm afraid no one on earth knows you better than I do."

Shi Mei's expression thawed somewhat, but his beautiful eyes remained fixed on the man's face as if assessing the truth of his words. Pursing his thin lips, he said, "It's good that you understand. Everything I've done is to take back what's ours. All of our sacrifices have been unavoidable."

"Of course."

"You're right, you do know me best," murmured Shi Mei. "In these two lifetimes, I've lived every day on a knife's edge. There's truly no one I can trust, aside from you." He paused. "Don't let me down."

Shi Mei's voice seemed to hover in the air like a butterfly after the words left his lips. A long, fraught silence passed before the man in white spoke once more. "There's a question I've been meaning to ask you," he said, placid.

"What is it?"

Overhead, storm clouds rolled in around Mount Jiao; leaves rustled on the slopes. The wind howled pitifully, like the wailing of a thousand displaced, wandering souls.

"I want to know what you sacrificed for our goal in the past life. Tell me the truth."

At this unexpected line of questioning, a furrow appeared between Shi Mei's brows. His eyes glinted. "Didn't I tell you ages ago? A few innocent people had to die, but this is to be expected. Just think about what we've gone through, and then you'll—"

"How many is 'a few'?" The man in white's soft yet determined voice cut through Shi Mei's answer, rendering him mute. His brows knit in a dark scowl, a look wholly uncharacteristic on his features. Shi Mei had always been mild and reserved, but it seemed he didn't care about baring his fangs in front of this man—as if his listener couldn't see the murderous intent on his face at all.

"A few is a few. Shall I make a registry of all the innocent dead so you can personally look it over?"

The man in white chuckled. "Enough," he murmured. "You know as well as I do that I won't be looking anything over anymore."

Silence stretched between them.

"I've always done my best to help you," the man in white said. "I've assisted you for years, ever since you found me and told me about the previous lifetime. When you concealed yourself within Guyueye, I did everything you asked of me from Sisheng Peak. Even when I felt confused and unsure, I knew your thoughts and goals were my own. For the sake of this mission of ours, I've long stopped caring whether I live or die. I never cared about sacrificing myself as long as we could succeed. I thought you were the same."

Shi Mei surged to his feet and paced around the room. "What do you mean by that? You say *you* stopped caring whether you live or die—are you implying I'm a coward who'd do anything to keep my life?" He shook out his sleeves, staring icily at the white-clothed man. "If you knew what kind of person I am, you'd never imply anything of the sort."

"I do know," said the man in white. "But I've been thinking—after you faked your death in the previous lifetime and stepped behind the scenes as Hua Binan, you had ten years to control the gu flower in Mo Ran's heart."

"Eight," Shi Mei corrected him. "Later, Chu Wanning split his souls and pushed what remained inside Mo Ran—thus giving him back some of his original nature. He was under my control for eight years before he killed himself, not ten."

"Okay, eight years then. In those eight years, you intensified the hatred in his heart and goaded him into committing all sorts of atrocities, but he drifted further and further from our original plan. Why didn't you stop him then?"

Shi Mei laughed from sheer anger. "Do you know how hard it is to create one Flower of Eightfold Sorrows?"

A pause. "I do."

"Do you know the enchantment would never work a second time on someone who's already had the curse uprooted?"

"I do."

Shi Mei wasn't smiling anymore. Fury flashed in his eyes. "Then what are you trying to say? What would you have done if it were you?"

The man in white paused, then sighed. "Haven't you decided for me?"

Shi Mei fell silent.

"I've never done those things or walked that path myself. I know I'd make the same choice if it were me in your place, but..."

Shi Mei narrowed his eyes, stalking down the stairs at the foot of the dais. He came to a stop before the man in white. "But what?"

"...I still have guilt on my conscience."

There was a moment of dead silence. Then Shi Mei grabbed the stranger by the lapels. His incomparably beautiful hand, with that serpent ring coiled around his delicate thumb, was now fisted tightly in the stranger's robes as tendons bulged from his fair skin.

"Guilt on your conscience? What difference is there between you and me? Everything we've done thus far—did you not plot each and every move with me? Did you not perfectly understand what each entailed? What happened to all the ruthlessness you had back then? Yet now you feel guilt? Why?" Every word came pushed through gritted teeth. "Is it because Xu Shuanglin saw you as a friend, although you lied to him every step of the way? Do you feel guilt because you taught him a fake Rebirth technique so he'd open the Space-Time Gate for us?"

"He never sold me out," the man in white whispered. "Even until death."

Shi Mei blinked, confusion and anger swirling in his eyes. "Very well—I did wonder what had you so worked up. What else? You saw those thousands of pawns and felt pity for them? You blame yourself?"

The man in white remained calm in the face of this outburst. "Did you never blame yourself? Not even a little?"

"You..." Shi Mei ground his teeth, madness and derision flashing in his gaze. He stared at the man before him for a very long time, as if gazing upon a colossal disappointment or a sickening traitor. Then, as if a truly cruel thought had come to mind, he burst out laughing. He unsheathed his venomous claws and drove them into the man's flesh. "Very well, very well. You've said so many pretty words, what with all your guilt and self-blame. But in the end, it's something else you're really upset about, isn't it?"

The glint in Shi Mei's eyes brightened at the sight of the man's brows furrowing in confusion. Like a vulture wheeling in the sky, hovering as he waited for his prey's final rattling breath before swooping down to dine.

"Coming to interrogate me like this—you believe you feel remorse after seeing all those Zhenlong pawns at work. You believe you feel regret after watching Xu Shuanglin die, but I know you.

I know your heart better than anyone—guilt and self-blame don't exist in you. You and I are equally cold and unfeeling."

That vulture's wings cast the long shadow of death, beating down lower and darker. "You feel no remorse at all. Stop fooling yourself."

He smiled once more, proud and composed. Shi Mingjing was always at his most graceful and poised when holding someone else by the throat. "If you ask me," he said slowly, "what you really mourn is the loss of your eyes."

Shi Mei whipped out the dagger at his waist. Using the hilt, he raised the hood of the man's white cloak until it fell back onto the man's shoulders. Beneath that fur-trimmed hood was a face of astonishing beauty, its exquisite features elegant beyond compare.

Face to face, the two men were identical—save that the white-cloaked Shi Mei's eyes were obscured by a white ribbon, a few tendrils of dark hair falling before it.

Shi Mei stared at the man, now stripped of his hood, and scoffed. "Shi Mingjing, take a good look at yourself. You only grieve that you've sacrificed more than I have. The situation on Mount Jiao was critical; to distract Chu Wanning, we had to use the last resort we discussed. With so many people watching, we couldn't just put on an act. You were blinded while I was unharmed. You're jealous."

"If I were jealous, I wouldn't have agreed to the plan in the first place. I wouldn't have prepared to sacrifice myself in the worst case. It doesn't matter which one of us survives to finish this, as long as one of us does. Why would I—"

Before he could finish, the other Shi Mei cut him off with a sharp, "Who's there?"

The dagger in his hand flew out, burying itself in a stone pillar. Shi Mei turned, voice cold. "Come out."

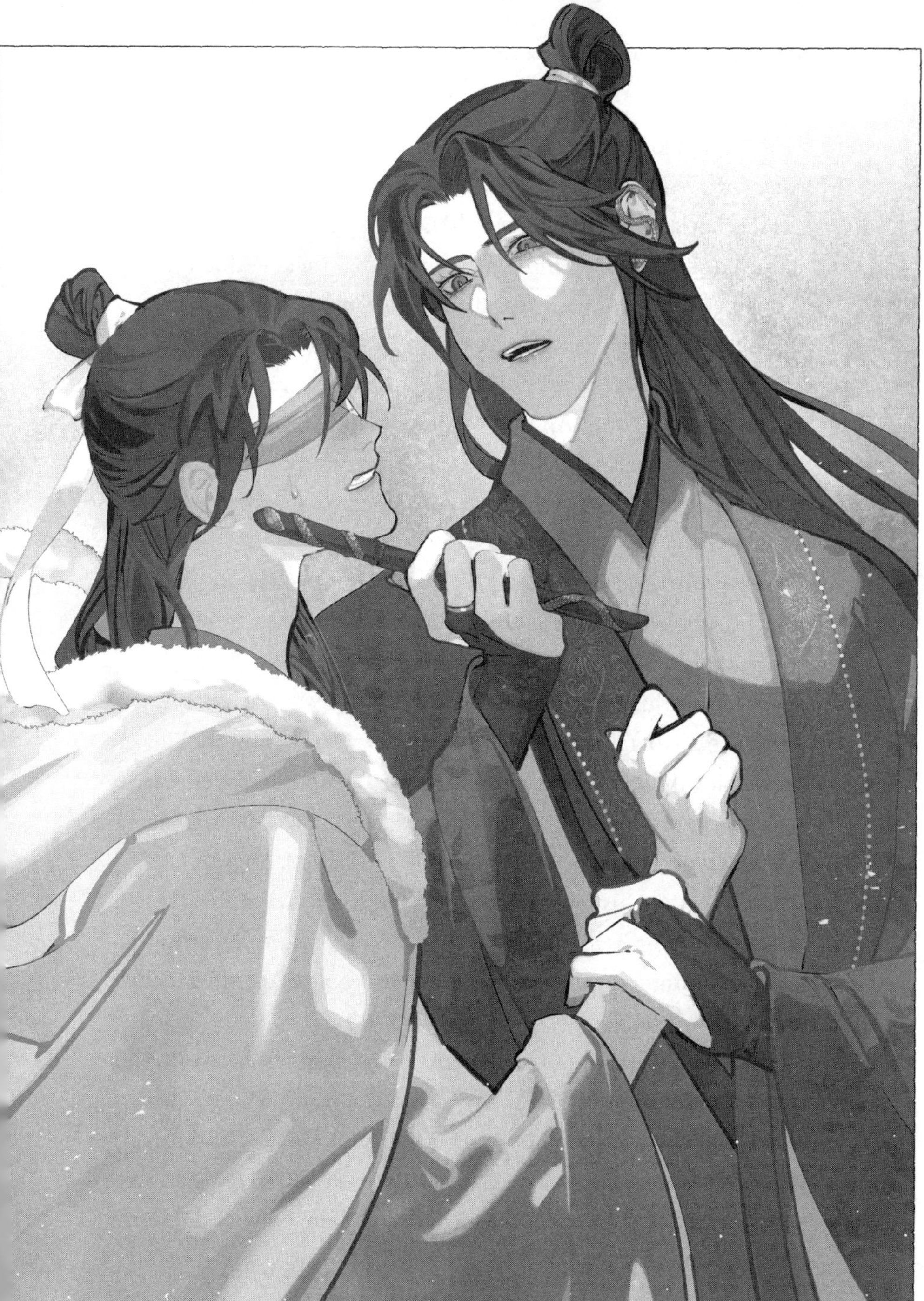

Huang Xiaoyue emerged from behind the pillar, looking much worse for wear.

He'd betrayed all the other cultivators on Mount Jiao in search of Rufeng's legendary hidden treasure chamber. Unfortunately, he'd triggered a mechanism and ended up locking his entire party inside the chamber. The treasure trove of Rufeng Sect contained all sorts of precious artifacts, sword manuals, and secret records—but it contained no food. All of Jiangdong Hall had become trapped inside. A bloody slaughter ensued, the strong quickly overpowering the weak. The sect members had consumed each other until only Huang Xiaoyue remained.

Some time after he'd eaten his very last disciple, Huang Xiaoyue at last struggled his way out of the chamber only to stumble upon this freakish tableau.

What was this? Two Shi Mingjings?

Huang Xiaoyue hadn't the faintest idea what he was looking at. The outside limit of his imagination was to assume they were twins; it would never occur to him that these were two Shi Meis from different worlds, united by the Space-Time Gate.

The longer he listened to their conversation, the more alarmed he grew. Huang Xiaoyue had always been sly and calculating; he saw almost immediately that he needed to escape. Yet Shi Mei had managed to catch him.

Shi Mei leveled him with a glare. "I was wondering who could have snuck in here. Looks like it's just an old rat." His gaze drifted down, registering the blood on Huang Xiaoyue's robes. "Blood? There are no animals on Mount Jiao. Where did all this blood come from?" He paused, comprehension dawning. "Human blood?" Every syllable dripped derision.

Sensing danger, Huang Xiaoyue whirled to run.

"Where do you think you're going?"

Like a hawk, Shi Mei soared through the air in a flutter of green robes and landed gracefully before Huang Xiaoyue. Those eyes as beautiful as misty rain looked up with a gaze cold enough to turn that mist to ice. "You must not know how I hate cannibals, old geezer."

They were the last words Huang Xiaoyue ever heard.

The stench of blood filled the hall. Shi Mei watched as Huang Xiaoyue collapsed, scarlet spurting from a fresh hole in his chest. Frowning in distaste, he wiped the blood from his hand. "Disgusting."

He turned and stared for a beat at the other Shi Mei, then softened his tone. "See that? Over these two lifetimes, there have been no shortage of beasts like Huang Xiaoyue in the cultivation world. The cards are due to be reshuffled. Don't overthink things. I told you I wouldn't let your sacrifices go to waste. Once our plan succeeds, I'll find a way to heal your eyes."

No response came. Shi Mei rolled his eyes. "Stop being so stubborn," he said dispassionately. "Fine, have it your way—I promise I won't harm any more innocents if I can help it. Will that do? Are you happy now?"

Some of the tension finally melted from the white-cloaked Shi Mei's stance. His lips parted as if to respond, but his other self was too annoyed to hear more. He stalked out of the ancestral hall without looking back.

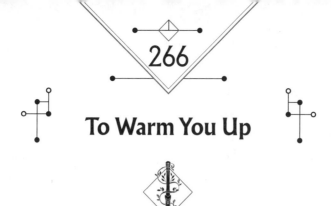

To Warm You Up

A T THE FOOT of Mount Jiao, hidden behind dense vines, a remote footpath wound its way up to Qingtan Palace, used by the Nangong clan when they came to the mountain to pay their respects to their dead. The palace was small, but its paths were rambling, and the garden was filled with dragon-blood flowers that glowed softly in the dark. Their bloom season had already passed, and only a scattered few retained their petals. From a distance, they looked like shattered stars bejeweling the velvet black of night.

Shi Mei strode into the depths of the garden, where a natural hot spring was nestled in the landscape. He disrobed, his bare feet pale as jade as he padded to the water's edge and looked down at his reflection.

The waters were hot, but his gaze was frigid. He reached a hand up to touch his chest—a large swath of flesh there had festered as a result of backlash from the forbidden technique. But now he could stop worrying: All was going according to plan, and soon, everything would get better.

He stepped into the water. The hot springs of Mount Jiao were imbued with the energy from the demon dragon, and bathing in them was spiritually nourishing. Shi Mei leaned against the wall of the pool and closed his eyes.

A rustling emanated from somewhere nearby. Eyes closed, Shi Mei called, "Who is it?"

Nangong Liu popped out of the shrubbery with a dragonblood flower tucked behind one ear. At the sight of Shi Mei, he smiled in delight. "Dear friend-gege, are you taking a bath? Can I help you at all?"

"No," Shi Mei said.

Nangong Liu scratched his head. "Th-then I'm going to leave, I'm going now. Otherwise, if you're naked and I'm not, it's not fair."

Through the curling mist, Shi Mei laughed. Deep within the springs, his face gleamed like the first sheen of ice in a Jiangnan winter: shining, fragile, and freezing cold. Those peach-blossom eyes fluttered open as he gave Nangong Liu a smile that was not a smile. "How so?"

"Because you're beautiful," came the frank reply.

"Oh... Does a little boy like you already know so much about beauty?"

"I'm five," huffed Nangong Liu. "I'm not little."

Amused, Shi Mei's smile deepened. "Okay, gege was wrong. Come here; let me ask you a question. Between myself and Taxian-jun, who do you prefer?"

"Dear friend-gege, of course." Nangong Liu said instantly. "Who is Taxian-jun? I don't know anyone with that name."

"Let me put it another way. Me and Mo Ran... He greeted you before. You remember him, don't you?"

Sucking his thumb, Nangong Liu gave the question serious thought and nodded.

"Whose face do you like better? Don't decide based on who you've known longer. I just want to know who you think looks best."

This time Nangong Liu couldn't give an instant reply. After more thought, he announced, "I still think dear friend-gege is the best."

This seemed to satisfy Shi Mei. "Oh? Tell me, what's wrong with him?"

"I...don't know."

"Then why do you like me better?"

Nangong Liu seemed hurt. "I don't know either... I just think you're prettier."

Shi Mei sank into thought. After a moment, he rose from the water and leaned against the edge where the mist was thin, revealing the graceful lines of his back. "Come here," he said with a smile, waving Nangong Liu over with a dripping hand. When he deemed Nangong Liu close enough, he straightened up, rising from the water.

"Aiya—"

Shi Mei laughed. "What's all the fuss? We're both men. There's nothing to be embarrassed about."

Nangong Liu scrubbed at his face. "M'not," he mumbled. "You got water in my eyes."

Shi Mei didn't care about his eyes. He grabbed Nangong Liu by the wrist and forced him to look at his body, baring that frightful wound on his chest. "Look at this. Are you afraid?"

That wound had festered badly and oozed pus. Nangong Liu scarcely glanced at it before turning away in disgust. "Yuck," he said, with the frank candor of children.

"Do you still think I'm pretty?" Shi Mei was still smiling, but his eyes were cold.

Rather than answer, Nangong Liu tried to struggle out of Shi Mei's grasp, but Shi Mei was strong. There was nothing he could do. Eventually, he teared up, voice quavering with fear. "L-let go of me. I don't like this."

"Take a good look."

"I don't want to—ah!"

Crack. Shi Mei's iron grip had dislocated Nangong Liu's wrist. Shi Mei's eyes flashed with resentment and dissatisfaction. "Didn't you just say I was pretty?" he asked, a manic light flashing in his eyes. "What, one little wound changes everything?"

"No..."

"Does the slightest imperfection make beauty revolting?" Shi Mei pressed closer. "Turn affection into disgust, longing into irritation?"

Nangong Liu couldn't help it—he burst into tears. "I don't get it, I don't get it! Let go of me, I want to go!"

His fussing worsened Shi Mei's poor mood. Storm clouds gathered in his eyes. He drew his hand back and slapped Nangong Liu across the face. "Imbecile. Get out." he said coldly, finally releasing his grip on Nangong Liu's wrist.

Once the sounds of Nangong Liu's sobbing faded into the distance, Shi Mei slunk back into the depths of the springs. His surroundings remained gorgeous, and the fragrance of dragonblood flowers in bloom yet filled the air, but his initial satisfaction had evaporated. In his heart was only fury, endless fury.

He punched the water's surface. After a great splash, the waves subsided, the ripples smoothing out to again show that reflection— still surpassingly soft and lovely, with a rotting wound over his heart.

Confusion and helplessness welled up to join Shi Mei's wrath. Leaning against the side of the pool, he tipped his head back and gazed into the sky.

"Everyone changes," he mumbled.

Just as seeds sprout and new buds swell; just as flowers unfurl their petals amidst green leaves to bloom, then die, then crumble into mud. Time's passage was marked by the change it wrought. Some would see their teeth sharpened, while others had their edges worn away.

"Everything changes..."

He wearily cupped a handful of water and rinsed his face. Comparing his past and present lives made the changes stark—but when did he step onto that dark road? When did the change become irreversible?

After dressing in a fresh bathrobe, Shi Mei bound up his inky hair and took that fragrant path back to the secret chamber on Mount Jiao. He stood at the door for a moment before pushing it open.

It was the dead of night. The lamps in the room had been snuffed out, leaving a single candle burning behind the gauze bed canopy. Shi Mei slipped silently into the room. All that marked his presence was the faint scent of soap from his bath, yet this was enough to wake the man behind the bed curtains. Taxian-jun's voice, rough with sleep, rang out. "Who's there?"

"It's me," Shi Mei replied with displeasure.

There was a short silence, then the sound of robes rustling as someone turned over on the bed. "How refined you are, Master," Taxian-jun sneered. "Eavesdropping in this venerable one's bedroom in the small hours of the morning?" He paused deliberately. "Not getting all hot and bothered, are you?"

Shi Mei's expression worsened. "You should learn to control yourself. None of us will have any fun if he winds up dead."

There was a faint hint of exhaustion audible in Taxian-jun's smug tone. "Master needn't worry. This venerable one doesn't have any strange kinks in bed—I prefer to keep things simple. No rambling, snakes, or blindfolded riddle games. No one's dying here."

Rambling, snakes, blindfolded riddle games—even an imbecile would understand whom he was talking about. Furious, Shi Mei flung the canopy aside as one might unsheathe a sword, ready to send sparks flying. Shi Mingjing's gentle visage came face to face with Taxian-jun's handsome mien. "You—!"

He froze before finishing his thought. He'd assumed Taxian-jun and Chu Wanning's long-awaited reunion would have culminated in debauchery. But upon drawing the canopy aside, what he saw was quite different.

Chu Wanning was sound asleep, cheeks flushed with fever. Taxian-jun lay beside him with his robes open, revealing a broad swath of pale chest. He held Chu Wanning in his arms, face gloomy as he stroked his hair. He looked simultaneously disdainful yet defiant, as if he'd never let go of the man in his embrace.

"What are you doing?" asked Shi Mei.

"What do you think this venerable one might be doing?" Taxian-jun shot back with utmost scorn.

Forget it, why argue with a corpse? Shi Mei closed his eyes, forcing himself to calm, but a tiny flame of fury still burned in his chest. He couldn't put it out. A retort slipped from his lips: "I hadn't expected Emperor Taxian-jun would still need his teacher's presence to sleep, even at his mature age. If you're not afraid of the dark, could it be that you missed being teacher's little pet?"

Shi Mei's jibe had the intended effect. Taxian-jun's eyes narrowed dangerously; he unconsciously moved to push the sleeping Chu Wanning aside, or perhaps even kick him off the bed. That would certainly make him look more imposing. But as he watched Shi Mei approach, he instead clutched the man in his arms tighter, sleeves flaring as he swept a hand over to cover Chu Wanning's face. He looked up, displeased. "What this venerable one does is no concern of yours."

"Watch your mouth." Shi Mei ground his teeth. "Don't forget who made you."

"Hanlin the Sage uses this fact to threaten this venerable one nearly once a day," said Taxian-jun icily. "I'm shaking in my boots."

"How dare—!" After so many snide comments, Shi Mei lost his patience. He jabbed at Taxian-jun's forehead and pushed in a thread of spiritual energy. "Gather Soul."

The words of the incantation dropped from his sensuous lips, but Taxian-jun's gaze remained determined and furious on him for a long time—so long that Shi Mei shuddered, feeling as if the man would finally escape his control. Sweat beaded on his forehead as he and Taxian-jun clashed in a silent battle of wills. Using nearly all the spiritual energy he possessed, Shi Mei shouted again: "Gather Soul!"

This time, Taxian-jun flinched. His eyes lost focus.

Panting, Shi Mei retracted his spiritual energy, clutching his aching chest as his vision went dark. Both his spiritual core and spiritual energy were weak due to his natural constitution. Regardless of how assiduously he cultivated, he was no match for a cultivator like Taxian-jun. When it came to medicines, he was a force to be reckoned with, but as soon as spiritual energy was required, he could barely hold his own.

Shi Mei closed his eyes in rest for several moments before he turned back to Taxian-jun. "I'll ask you once more. What were you doing?"

Subdued, Taxian-jun replied without inflection. "He has a fever. He's cold."

"So?"

This puppet who possessed only the cognizance soul from its previous lifetime answered blandly, "In this venerable one's arms, he'll be warmer."

Shi Mei stared at him. "Warmer?" His pale lips twitched and he burst out laughing, though his peach-blossom eyes held no mirth at all. "Mo Ran, are you mad? Feel the temperature of your skin—

what do you think you are? You're cold as ice all over—you're *dead*. You have no heart or lungs or warmth. You yourself are freezing cold; how do you intend to warm him up?"

Pain seemed to flash in Taxian-jun's hollow eyes, but it was a flicker only. He was merely a corpse, after all.

"Get up," Shi Mei ordered.

Taxian-jun didn't move. Brows furrowed, he sat still, struggling between his own willpower and Shi Mei's control.

"Get up!"

The command intensified. In response to Shi Mei's vicious tone, Taxian-jun finally obeyed. He rose slowly, his robes still loose and open. Chu Wanning's warmth lingered on his unmoving chest.

"Get out," Shi Mei said darkly.

Taxian-jun took a few shuffling steps, then came to a stop. "I have it," he said quietly.

"...What?"

"I do have it," he said with the same stiffness.

Shi Mei didn't understand. "What do you have?"

"Warmth." Taxian-jun slowly reached up to touch his chest, which had been pressed to Chu Wanning's skin. "It's warm here."

Shi Mei flinched as if stabbed, now furious. Nothing vexed him more than a misbehaving puppet. "Get the fuck out," he snarled.

Taxian-jun stepped forward again, but made it scarcely two steps before his face twisted. "No..." he muttered, clutching his head. Tendons protruded on his hands. He trembled, breathing hard. "This venerable one...refuses... H-how could this venerable one let you—" His eyes were screwed shut, his mind seesawing between focus and confusion, his memories flickering. He struggled again and again, tormented by two lifetimes. "—do as you wish?!"

His voice came to a shaking stop.

Shi Mei grunted, pressing a hand to his chest. Taxian-jun throwing off his control had unleashed a great wave of energy upon him. He stumbled backward, watching as Taxian-jun's eyes snapped open to reveal his bloodthirsty gaze. There was no hint of helplessness in those eagle-like eyes—only Shi Mei's own cool reflection.

Bone-pale, Shi Mei said slowly, "I see you're recovering faster these days."

Taxian-jun said nothing. His pupils flashed as he reached a hand out, panting shallowly, and summoned Bugui.

Shi Mei lifted his chin, his gaze running up along the blade until it landed on Mo Ran's predatory face. "What now? Are you angry? Do you want to kill me?"

That pitch-black blade flashed up, coming to a stop with its point against Shi Mei's snow-white throat. The movement was sharp enough to break skin, leaving a thin trickle of blood.

Yet Shi Mei didn't back down. "Your Majesty," he said scornfully. "My spiritual energy is the only reason you can even move. You'll die if you kill me, as I'm sure you're well aware."

Taxian-jun said nothing.

"It's true I'm no match for you in terms of power," Shi Mei continued. "But I advise you to think carefully whether you'd rather live like this or die in your escape."

Taxian-jun's hand was steady. After a beat, he withdrew Bugui and turned his face away.

Shi Mei reached up cautiously to touch the blood at his neck. "Fortunately, you're not an idiot."

Faced with Taxian-jun's silence, Shi Mei admonished him, "Don't pull this with me again. You know how things are between us." He glanced at Taxian-jun. "Right now you're like a rusty blade. I want to make you as useful as you were in the past, and keep using you as my knife. But you—you probably want to escape my control entirely and kill me."

Taxian-jun turned to stare icily at him.

"All these years, you worked for me in the other world," Shi Mei continued. "The crack left in the Space-Time Gate is too narrow for frequent travel, so I often sent you letters. But don't forget we also communicated telepathically through the gu flower. Of course I know what you're thinking. Don't be so surprised."

Taxian-jun finally spoke. "You seem to be going blind yourself. Where the hell are you looking that you see this venerable one surprised?"

Shi Mei pursed his lips in a scowl. "All right. If you understand the pros and cons of our arrangement, then simply endure the situation. We'll work together, and once everything is finished, we'll see if you manage to kill me, or if I obtain an undefeatable weapon."

"Looking forward to it," said Taxian-jun.

A low groan from Chu Wanning on the bed silenced both of them. The sound was as soft as a queen of the night flower blooming, but both men stopped their bickering and turned.

"Wanning?"

"Shizun—"

The erstwhile martial brothers stared at each other.

Taxian-jun glowered, then shifted his gaze from Shi Mei to the sleeping Chu Wanning. He spoke with affected carelessness. "He's had a fever for days, and he doesn't seem to be getting better. If it goes on like this, will he..."

The question died on his lips. Emperor Taxian-jun, butcher of thousands, stopped short of those final words. His lashes fluttered as his eyes closed.

But Shi Mei didn't care to beat around the bush. "Will he what? Are you asking if he's going to die?"

Perhaps it was a trick of the light; Taxian-jun's white face seemed to pale further. He compressed his lips, as if the word irritated him. "Will he?" he asked, carefully avoiding it again.

"Of course not. You underestimate the Beidou Immortal. Aren't you ashamed to ask this question?" Shi Mei arched a brow. "Who's responsible for this fever? Weren't you the one who took him like a starving animal?"

Taxian-jun's expression was beyond ugly. "He isn't me," he hissed. "Don't confuse me with that piece of garbage."

Shi Mei looked him up and down. "As it happens, I too think he's a piece of garbage. You know as well as anyone the lengths I've gone to. I tore open a great Space-Time Gate and brought you into this world to destroy that trash and help you return to ascendancy. Your Majesty," he said in a teasing singsong. "We're so very close to our goal. You also want a complete source of power—a powerful spiritual core—do you not?"

He regarded Taxian-jun as a hunting snake would, scarlet tongue flickering as he hissed sweet promises. He saw the desire in Taxian-jun's eyes, so he smiled, going in for the kill. "If you want to regain your full potential, behave a little." Venom seemed to shine on his teeth, and his eyes glinted eerily. "Our work goes more smoothly when you behave."

Taxian-jun fell silent, sweeping his sleeves back. "Enough." He pointed at Chu Wanning. "Let's talk about him first."

"What about him? He's merely had a shock from his soul returning to his body," said Shi Mei blandly. "There's not much to talk about. If you really want him to feel better, step outside."

Taxian-jun grew instantly wary. "What are you plotting?"

Shi Mei smiled. "Healing, of course."

"This venerable one will stay."

"That won't do," Shi Mei said. "Hanlin the Sage's healing arts are not for outside eyes." At Taxian-jun's silence, Shi Mei continued. "But it's fine if you wish to stay. I'll go. After all, Mister Emperor, you're so very powerful. I'm sure you know how to properly take care of him."

Taxian-jun's expression twisted into an ugly scowl. His spiritual power was harsh and domineering—completely unsuited to healing. In the past life, he'd had so many servants and doctors there had been no need for him to learn the art at all.

Shi Mei had wholly recovered his serenity. He watched him, smiling.

Taxian-jun couldn't stand to look at that smile. He turned around, jaw working as he avoided Shi Mei's eyes. His response came after a long moment. "Okay. This venerable one will leave, and you will heal him." He paused, and his voice went sharp. "But this venerable one will be right outside. If you dare..." The chill in his expression threatened a punishment worse than death. "If you dare touch a hair on his head, this venerable one will take your damned life."

Shi Mei let the threat roll off him. He smiled a little wider and waved Taxian-jun out.

After hovering at the door for a long beat, Taxian-jun at last left the room. Shi Mei stood in the secret chamber, finally quiet, and stared at the stone door he had closed behind him. Then he turned and walked over to that white-clad man. The mocking smile on his face fell away, in its place a calm yet utterly deranged expression. "Shizun," he cooed.

Step by step, he drew nearer. He had Chu Wanning in the palm of his hand—did it matter that Taxian-jun was outside? There were so many ways he could keep Chu Wanning from making a sound. By the time the emperor of the mortal realm returned, all his fury and cruelty would be futile. He'd have no one to blame but himself—for being so useless, so naïve, that he'd left his beloved in a nest of snakes for Hanlin to devour.

A slender hand drew the canopy aside. Shi Mei cast a gentle, ravenous gaze down onto the feverish man within. "This time, no one will interrupt us." Lowering himself onto the bed, he caressed Chu Wanning's face. "Come, Consort Chu. Let me master you, while your husband waits on the other side of the wall. Hm?"

267

Golden Dragon, Jade Pillar

SHI MEI PRESSED a sacred healing pill between Chu Wanning's lips, then sank his fine-boned fingers into his ink-dark hair like ten devilish white snakes. Lifting Chu Wanning's head, he pressed their foreheads together.

"Butterfly dreams haunt your slumber each night..." Quietly, he began to recite the incantation, but fell silent almost at once. He had intended to erase some of Chu Wanning's memories. This was one of his best-honed skills, which he'd previously used on Mo Ran. But perhaps Chu Wanning's souls were in too much disarray: It was entirely ineffectual.

"This might be rather difficult." Shi Mei sighed. He closed his eyes, then opened them once more, his sultry gaze now emanating a bewitching glow. He stared fixedly at Chu Wanning, then recited the incantation once more. "Butterfly dreams haunt your slumber each night; the past swept away, the present lost in misty mountains..."

This time it worked, but not perfectly. His spell fell like a boulder into water—there was a splash, but its ripples soon subsided.

No matter. A short stretch of time would suffice. When he and Chu Wanning were in the throes of pleasure together, he didn't want Chu Wanning's mind to be full of murderous intent. That wouldn't suit his tastes at all.

"Shizun, you've been asleep for so long. Isn't it time you woke up?" The murmured words had the force of a spell.

Chu Wanning's eyes fluttered open. Shi Mei's enchantment had done its work. His mind was fogged and stuck in the past life, his awareness reverted to the days shortly after Shi Mei had passed away. Mo Ran's grief from back then had wounded him so deeply he unconsciously yearned to change the past. His mind naturally drifted back to that period of time.

But a person's souls were an intricate thing. Souls from both lifetimes were crowded into Chu Wanning's body. Despite Shi Mei's spell, he wasn't quite lucid; his eyes were glassy, as if caught in a waking dream, and his memories were in disarray. He seemed to drift between wakefulness and sleep.

"Shi Mingjing?"

"Mn." Shi Mei's voice was gentle, a tenderness that hid all his twisted desires. "It's me."

Chu Wanning seemed exhausted. The fever had drained him; he made a soft noise of acknowledgment, then closed his eyes once more.

Shi Mei knew he was adjusting. He waited, unhurried, by his side. After a time, he heard Chu Wanning sigh, eyes still closed. "I must've been dreaming... I'm so glad you're still alive."

His mind was stuck in the time after the Heavenly Rift, Shi Mei knew, but he hadn't expected such sorrow from Chu Wanning. Shi Mei felt a rare pang. "You couldn't bear to see me dead?"

"You're so young...and so well-loved," murmured Chu Wanning. "It shouldn't have been you. I'm sorry..."

Shi Mei gazed at him quietly.

"I wish it could've been me. Then no one would grieve, at least."

The ache in Shi Mei's chest intensified, throbbing through his deadened heart. He remembered this feeling. He had felt it the first time he and Chu Wanning had walked home together, sharing an umbrella. In the following years, he'd schemed for ages in secret; those around him either died or drifted away. He had hidden himself in the darkness, pretending to be a heartless boulder. Eventually, he convinced himself he'd become stone.

It was not until this moment that, after so long, he vividly sensed the existence of his heart. It throbbed, it melted, it ached, it itched. He knew he shouldn't feel these emotions. Acid rain would corrode even stone, and soft moss would cause him to crumble.

But he couldn't help grabbing Chu Wanning's hand, heart pounding. Shi Mei opened his mouth, swallowing around his dry throat before he asked: "Then what about you? If I died, would you grieve? *Did* you grieve?"

Chu Wanning's sharp eyes were half-lidded. Beneath his long and dense lashes, those eyes held too much; Shi Mei stared into them hungrily, hoping to find some identifiable, concrete feeling within—but there was none.

Just as how water left alone remained water, and grain left untouched remained grain, only when kept in isolation would a singular emotion stay the way it was. But human emotions never arose in isolation. Shi Mei's death had caused Chu Wanning heartache, pain, self-reproach, and regret. All those emotions churned together like water stored with grain, a brew that had long fermented into something else entirely.

"Shizun," Shi Mei asked with single-minded fixation, "if you could do it all over again, would you do for me what you did for him? Would you sacrifice your own life to save mine?"

Silence.

"Would you?"

Chu Wanning's eyes were blank and dull. "Shi Mingjing..."

These three syllables were all he managed before his lips were brutally sealed. Shi Mei had awaited this answer so long, but when the moment of truth finally arrived, he dared not hear it. Didn't want to hear it.

He knew what Chu Wanning would say, Shi Mei thought. Resentment ricocheted through his heart. He kissed the man on the bed like a punishment. Chu Wanning was too stunned to understand what was happening until Shi Mei attempted to pry open his mouth with his tongue. Comprehension hit him like a dream shattering, and Chu Wanning's eyes flew open.

"Mngh!"

"*Shh*, quiet." Shi Mei panted, tapping Chu Wanning's throat to magically muffle his voice. "You taught us this spell; you said it would help us stay silent in dangerous situations. Did you imagine there'd come a day I'd use it for this?"

He didn't stop to take in the confusion and fury in Chu Wanning's eyes; his jealousy and hunger had pushed him past the bounds of rationality. "Did you know, Shizun? It's been two lifetimes. I've worked so hard, so carefully—I've never had a single day of peace."

He paused to tie Chu Wanning's wrists and ankles to the bed. "I'm not a normal person," he said through gritted teeth. "Considering what I have to do, I'm not *allowed* to be a normal person. But what does that matter? Even a puppet like Emperor Taxian-jun can do as he likes—why should I be the only one to deny myself?"

Shi Mei gazed at Chu Wanning struggling furiously beneath him, pain and satisfaction filling his heart.

"Now I understand. Whether in good times or bad, one must enjoy life to the fullest, Shizun." He bent over Chu Wanning, yanking Chu Wanning's clothes aside with desperate haste. "It's cost me so much to get here—shouldn't it be my turn to taste you? Think of it as a reward for your disciple, hm?"

Chu Wanning couldn't summon the strength to fight back; Shi Mei stripped off his robes with ease. Bathed in the chill air and the haze of the lanterns, the lean, muscular lines of his body were mottled with purple bruises Mo Ran had left behind.

Shi Mei's eyes darkened. "Really now," he murmured. "He did go a bit overboard."

He reached out and grasped Chu Wanning's chin, gazing into his phoenix eyes. Chu Wanning's gaze seemed veiled by mist; he was still trapped between dreams and reality, sensing that this was too absurd to be real yet too vivid to be fake. Combined with the chaos wrought by two lifetimes of memories flooding his mind, he couldn't respond.

"He and I are different." Shi Mei stared at Chu Wanning. His eyes softened, but within that softness was a hint of something darker. "He doesn't know how to make it good for you. Once you've tried me, you'll think no more of him."

He began to undress. He'd just bathed and was wearing only the bathrobe. It slithered quietly to the ground to expose a body as exquisite as fine jade. "Shizun..." he whispered, draping his weight over Chu Wanning.

Whether it was dream or reality, Chu Wanning could no longer contain his revulsion. He trembled from head to toe, face ashen.

"You're so warm..." Shi Mei knew the man beneath him would burst into furious castigation if he lifted the silencing spell, yet he couldn't resist caressing him as he breathed, "Will you be even hotter inside?"

"Shi...Mingjing!"

Shi Mei blinked in surprise. "You broke the spell yourself?" He lifted his eyes to stare into Chu Wanning's. "Oh, you. You really are..."

Chu Wanning's throat spasmed as he coughed up a mouthful of blood. "How dare you," he rasped. "Get the fuck away from me!"

Shi Mei fell silent, gazing down at the man beneath him. He really was too vicious, too stubborn, too unwilling to accept his fate and admit defeat. There was so much Shi Mei wanted to say, but none of it passed through his lips. In the end, he just smiled.

As Chu Wanning drew breath to snap at him again, Shi Mei clapped a hand over his mouth. Working quickly, he pulled out his own hair ribbon and tied it between Chu Wanning's teeth. "Since you can break the spell, I'll have to use this instead. Sorry, Shizun."

The sight of those dazed, wrathful, humiliated eyes inflamed Shi Mei. He bent to whisper in Chu Wanning's ear, "Remember now, you have to stay quiet no matter how good I make you feel. Your revered emperor is just on the other side of the door. If he hears you begging for me like a slut, do you think he'll be pleased?"

Shi Mei dragged his fingertips lower, drawing circles around every blue-black mark. When his touch drifted further down, Chu Wanning felt he had been skewered by humiliation.

His memories were a mess, and his awareness was stuck in the past life, before he'd discovered Mo Ran had fallen victim to a mysterious spell. In this state, he hated Mo Ran, but he hated his own shameless heart more. Despite his humiliation, his hatred, and his painful disappointment in Mo Weiyu, he couldn't help a thrill of pleasure when Mo Ran held him, when Mo Ran panted in his ear, when sweat dripped from Mo Ran's torso onto his bare skin. There were even a few instances, during the most frenzied of their entanglements, when he had sensed his own secret craving—for Mo Ran to never stop, to tear him apart, to pierce his soul through.

Those tempestuous trysts had given him an illusion of peace. When he lay wrapped in Mo Ran's arms, he'd sometimes feel as if none of those terrible things had ever happened. As if this man who entwined unceasingly with him might've loved him too.

But it wasn't the same with Shi Mei. He didn't know how he'd fallen into such a strange and vivid nightmare, but when Shi Mei laid his hands on him, he felt only fury and disgust. His stomach roiled at his touch—he didn't like it in the least.

Shi Mei's body differed from the one in Chu Wanning's memories. He was taller and stronger, yet still fair, with fine features, the lines of his muscles as smooth and elegant as if hewn from frosty jade. The scent on his skin was likewise clear and fragrant. It was nothing like the brute power Chu Wanning was used to.

Mo Ran's body was all he knew. Mo Ran's skin might've been pale, but hot blood surged beneath with a terrifying wildness. He radiated a pure masculinity like the blazing sun, capable of scorching the hearts of those it touched. Even though it sometimes smelled like blood, like iron—a hard, cold smell—his sturdy chest pulsed with warmth.

Chu Wanning's eyes snapped open. He twisted his wrists in his bindings, red welts blooming over the skin. Even the ends of his eyes were twin scarlet streaks of humiliation. But fighting was no use, and the thick furs spread on the bed would muffle any sound.

Shi Mei watched him with distant interest as he struggled like a trapped beast. "Why does Shizun waste his energy fighting?" he asked with an amused quirk of his lips. "Don't you believe I'll make you feel good?"

He lifted one of Chu Wanning's strong and slender legs, fitting his own hips between his thighs. His eyes darkened, ready to claim Chu Wanning as he'd dreamed a thousand times before.

Chu Wanning squeezed his eyes shut. He'd already bitten his lip bloody, and his nails were buried deep in his palms. All the muscles

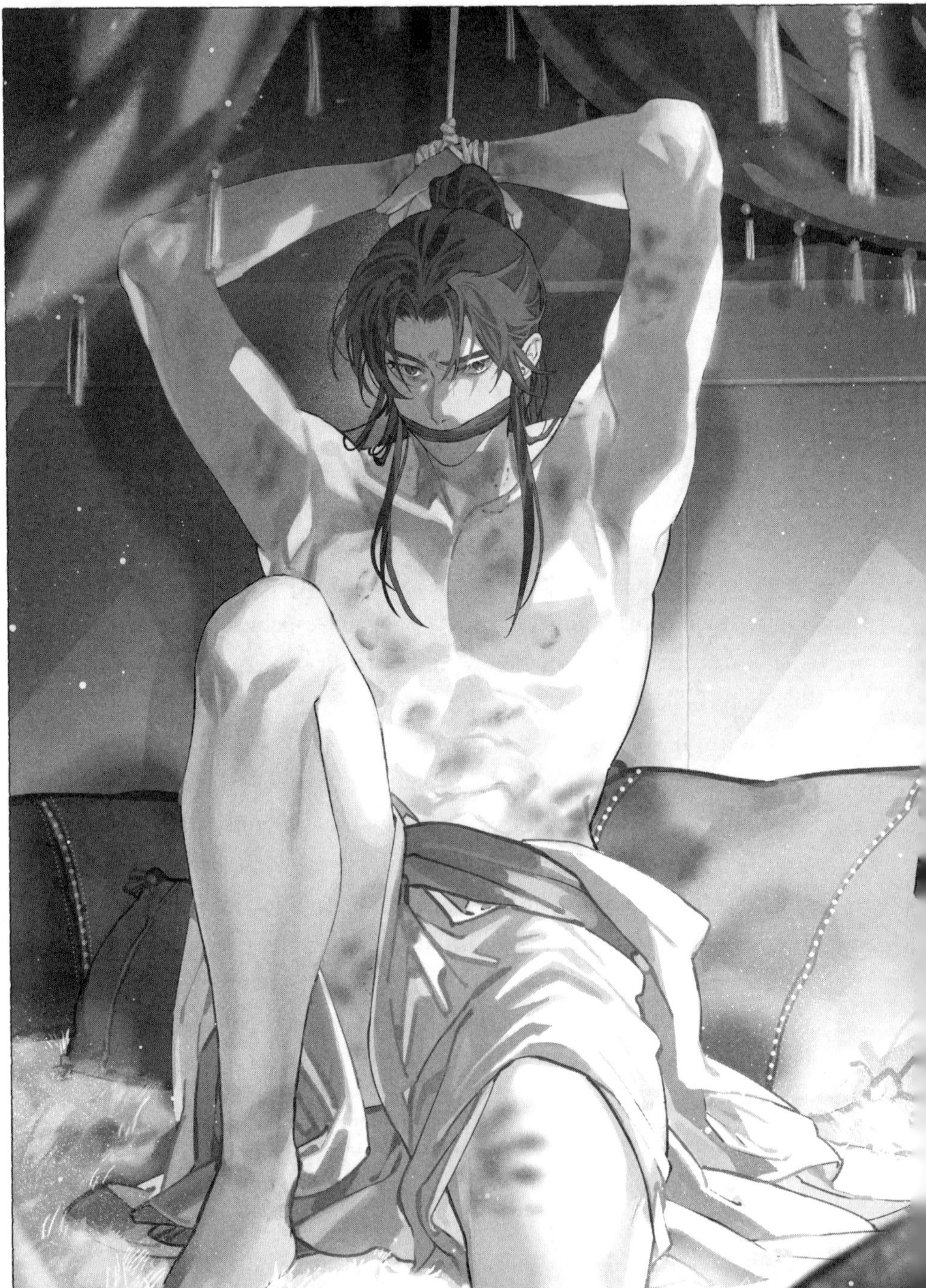

in his body were pulled taut, but not because he feared the pain of intrusion. Rather, what he felt was unbearable shame. Whether this was real or an illusion, it was far too humiliating.

If it was an illusion, he was ashamed of himself for dreaming it up. If it was real, he was ashamed of being so incompetent that two of his three disciples harbored such disgraceful intentions toward him.

He had always been the type to find fault in himself first. If it were just Mo Ran besotted, his desire might have been his own problem. But both Shi Mei and Mo Ran? Chu Wanning couldn't help wondering if he'd done something wrong or inappropriate— if he'd failed to live up to the role of a teacher—for two of his disciples to develop such base urges. Where did he go wrong, to suffer so?

He waited in tense silence, yet even after some moments, there was no movement from Shi Mei.

Chu Wanning slowly opened his eyes, dark brown pupils flitting up to Shi Mei, somehow frozen where he was. No hint of lasciviousness remained in his expression—instead, he looked almost comically aghast. Puzzled, Chu Wanning's gaze drifted downward, whereupon he saw something that truly beggared belief.

What...was that...?

That sensual atmosphere vanished without a trace. Chu Wanning felt as if he'd been struck by lightning.

Shi Mei's exposed member was, uh...g-gold?

It was so absurd Chu Wanning turned his head to keep from giving himself a headache looking at it. But after a few beats, he considered how strange this was. What kind of person had a golden dick?

Blanching, he forced himself to take another glance, facing the sight head-on.

This time, he got a good look. It wasn't that Shi Mei had loins of glittering gold, but rather that a little golden dragon had emerged at some point and coiled itself around Shi Mei's shaft. It was wrapped very tightly with its head stretched up and out, staring at Shi Mingjing in furious silence. The message was clear: It would crush the anatomy in its coils to a pulp should Shi Mei make any rash move.

Chu Wanning blinked. Shi Mei stared mutely.

The demon dragon bared its teeth at its unlucky victim and opened its tiny jaws in a shrill "Rawr!"

If not for his bound wrists, Chu Wanning would've put his head in his hands. He seriously couldn't bear to look.

At long last, Shi Mei spat, "What the hell is this?!"

The answer came in the form of the stone doors rumbling open, revealing Taxian-jun's countenance of displeasure. He strode through the doors with his arms folded over his chest, eyes sweeping over the shining golden dragon coiled around its jade pillar. Ridicule joined the threat in his voice as his thin lips parted in icy comment: "Miss, please get off the bed."

Furious with humiliation, Shi Mei didn't immediately take his meaning. "Miss?" he snarled. "Who are you talking to?"

"Oh, my bad." Taxian-jun squinted in scrutiny at the appendage within the dragon's coils. "It's Mister, after all. You're so small this venerable one couldn't tell at first."

That golden dragon's whiskers twitched as it bared its teeth to echo its master. "Rahhh!"

It was perhaps the greatest insult you could give a man. Shi Mei's vaunted composure wasn't sufficient to keep his face from flushing or the cords in his neck from protruding in rage. Even worse, he was fully undressed and tied up by a fucking miniature dragon no less. In this state, no display of anger would make him imposing, so he chose silence.

Emperor Taxian-jun strode into the room, coming to a stop before the bed. Leaning against the bedpost, he pushed his chin out. "Hua Binan, did you think this venerable one wouldn't know what you were up to as long as you made no sound?" He narrowed his eyes, scorn in every line of his handsome face. "You do think this venerable one is three years old, huh?"

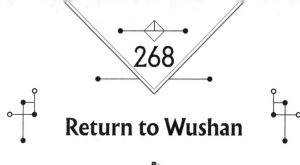

Return to Wushan

W ITH A GESTURE from Taxian-jun, the little dragon tightened its coils. Shi Mei paled, visibly pained, but his pride wouldn't allow him to drop his facade of calm. "Mo Ran, you dare to spy on me?"

Taxian-jun burst into laughter. "You jest. Tell me, what doesn't this venerable one dare to do?"

Shi Mei glowered.

"A quick introduction. This fine fellow is a vessel of the demon dragon of Mount Jiao, Wangli. It only obeys the commands of the Nangong clan." Taxian-jun cast him a sly glance. "To show such presumption with this venerable one's things in this venerable one's own territory—you must've really grown sick of living."

A vein pulsed at Shi Mei's temple, betraying what was certainly apoplectic rage. He'd never imagined the blood oath with Mount Jiao could be used in this fashion, and he was well and truly caught. He didn't dare push Taxian-jun, so he could only retort, "Take this foul thing away."

Taxian-jun stared openly at the object the dragon was coiled around before scoffing. "Then you'd better make sure you never take that disgusting thing of yours out again."

Already enraged by the interruption, Shi Mei rumbled darkly, "Who are you calling disgusting?"

"Whoever's tied up."

Chu Wanning stared.

Glancing at the bound Chu Wanning, Taxian-jun frowned and tried again. "Whoever's naked."

Chu Wanning was still staring. Having stepped in it twice already, Taxian-jun waved his hands. "This venerable one doesn't mean you."

"Mo Ran, you're ridiculous," Shi Mei proclaimed. Despite his words, he pulled his robe back on, then looked at Mo Ran again. "*Now* will you release it?"

"There's no hurry. Leave this room and walk away. Once you reach the back hills, it'll release you on its own," Taxian-jun said smugly. "But let this venerable one leave you with one reminder—if you ever think of touching this venerable one's property again...it already knows your scent. Even if you're beyond the bounds of Mount Jiao, it will find you and choke you to death."

Having no inhibitions made one unstoppable, and Taxian-jun's inhibitions could be counted in the negative. Shi Mei stormed out in a rage, leaving the emperor and the Beidou Immortal alone in the room.

Taxian-jun walked over to Chu Wanning and raised a hand—yet he saw that Chu Wanning's eyes, filled with sharp enmity, also shimmered with tears. Chu Wanning flinched away, no doubt reminded of Taxian-jun's violence during those long years as his prisoner.

Taxian-jun sighed inwardly as he brought his hand to Chu Wanning's forehead. Even he wasn't sure where this wisp of softness had come from. "Not so warm anymore," he said expressionlessly. "He might be useless, but his medicines are effective."

After a pause, he continued in cold tones. "I won't let that brute humiliate you again. No one is allowed to touch what belongs to this venerable one. You don't need to worry."

He had no clue Shi Mei had erased Chu Wanning's memories, temporarily returning him to the past life, and was thus oblivious to the shock that coursed through Chu Wanning at these words.

Mo Ran had called Shi Mei a *brute*...

Taxian-jun didn't notice Chu Wanning's expression. In fact, he'd avoided looking directly at Chu Wanning this entire time. He knew himself too well—if he looked too long at the sight before him, he'd lose control. There was no way Chu Wanning could endure any more rough handling in his current state.

In the past, he might not have cared. But he'd been so lonely in that other world for so very long. Unable to commit to either life or death, he was forced into this liminal existence as an incomplete revenant. Seeing Chu Wanning again seemed to have awakened some indistinct warmth in his frozen heart. He wasn't as rash as he used to be.

Taxian-jun untied Chu Wanning. Upon seeing the red welts on his wrists, he began to unconsciously massage the skin there, then quickly stopped when he realized what he was doing.

He really didn't know what was wrong with him.

The minutes dripped by. Shi Mei's spell began to weaken, and Chu Wanning's gaze again grew misty and unfocused. But even amidst the chaotic tangle of his thoughts, he pushed through the pain to speak through bloodless lips. "Mo Ran...he's back."

Whether it was dream or reality was no longer important. All that mattered was that Mo Ran's long-held wish had finally come true.

"So..." he rasped. "Don't feel hatred anymore."

Taxian-jun stared at him.

Perhaps because he thought the dream was about to end, Chu Wanning closed his eyes and extended a hand, chafed raw, to caress Taxian-jun's face. "Turn back."

Something seemed to collapse in Taxian-jun's heart. He stared at Chu Wanning, unblinking, confusion obscuring his features like a faint haze of clouds.

Chu Wanning furrowed his brow, voice rough with tears. "There's no way forward. Turn back... Stop heading down that path." He cupped Taxian-jun's face in his palm. Two lifetimes had left them both in ruins. The Beidou Immortal, his awareness flickering between two lives, gazed at the corpse of Emperor Taxian-jun. "Mo Ran," he rasped. "Why is your face so cold...?"

It's cold as ice. If I could, I'd be the candle waiting at the fork in your winter road. I'd burn my entire life up to light your way home. Why are you so cold...?

I don't know how long I can burn for you. What if my life is exhausted, what if I burn out? What if my flame is extinguished, but you're still walking into the darkness, refusing to turn back? What would I do then?

Chu Wanning's fingers trembled. He closed his eyes.

He'd ever been solitary in life, without friends or kin, and he didn't fear death. But what if he burned through all his remaining warmth yet failed to thaw Mo Ran's frozen heart? The idea roused a gnawing guilt. What if his flame were to go out, and that youth wanted to turn over a new leaf after, only to find himself unable to retrace his steps?

The thought of it made him yearn to live on, even for just one more day.

Maybe tomorrow, the ice would melt, and that man would turn around, walking out of the endless darkness into the light.

After the damage done by Shi Mei's spell and the turbulence of gaining two lifetimes' worth of memories, Chu Wanning spent the majority of the following days sleeping. When he briefly woke, his mind was muddled, and his sense of reality was scattered and incomplete.

Once Taxian-jun understood the reason behind it, he found Chu Wanning's confusion saved him a good deal of trouble. Chu Wanning was bewildered and easily placated. If Taxian-jun was too harsh one day, it was likely Chu Wanning wouldn't remember any of it the next time he opened his eyes. Because his memories were such a jumble, Chu Wanning always thought he was dreaming and thus let down his guard much more often.

A cat that scratched was interesting in its own way, but a big white cat snoozing in a soft, sweet ball was a rare sight indeed. He had to give it to Hua Binan—it was well done.

Every day, Taxian-jun asked Chu Wanning the same question first thing in the morning. "What do you remember today?"

And every day, Chu Wanning would frown and ask, "What?"

"Are your memories still stuck after our wedding in the past life," Taxian-jun would reply with uncharacteristic patience, "or are they at some other time now?"

At this point, Chu Wanning would probably say curtly, with a look of displeasure, "Mo Weiyu, what nonsense do you speak now?"

In the past life, Taxian-jun would've slapped him for his impudence. Now, Taxian-jun also raised a hand, but his movement slowed as he approached Chu Wanning's face, and his other hand followed. It didn't look like a slap at all—rather, he seemed to be cupping the other man's cheeks. He chuckled, satisfaction gleaming in his eyes. "Perfect. It'd be best if we could keep you like this."

He didn't want Chu Wanning to remember what had happened in his current life, or to remember the Mo Weiyu who'd become a zongshi. If Chu Wanning stayed in this state of befuddlement, it would be as though they had returned to Wushan Palace. They could spend their days and nights entwined no matter how much Chu Wanning hated him. His shizun, his Wanning, would again be his and his alone.

"Jealous of your own damn self," mocked Hua Binan. "You're pettier than a woman."

Jealous? thought Taxian-jun. *Impossible.* Anyone would grow accustomed to something that was around all the time, even if it was a dog or some random object. That was all.

On one particularly sunny day on Mount Jiao, Taxian-jun hauled Chu Wanning outside to sit with him beneath a flowering tanger-ine tree. He lifted his eyes to those little white flowers dotting the branches and sighed lazily. "Too bad they're not more fragrant. If only it were haitang."

Chu Wanning still thought he was asleep. "How are you so picky even in dreams?"

Taxian-jun rolled over on the grass, then shifted to rest his head on Chu Wanning's knee. They looked at each other, and Taxian-jun spoke. "This venerable one's always been like this. By the way, this venerable one is hungry. When we go back, make a bowl of congee for me. Egg-drop pork congee, but the egg can't be overcooked and the porridge shouldn't be too thick. A little bit of pork will suffice. You know how to make it, right? This venerable one's taught you how, many times."

Chu Wanning had no intention of complying, but between Taxian-jun's hauling him bodily toward the kitchen and his unceas-ing verbal cajoling, he was left with no other choice. Eventually he followed Taxian-jun into the ancestral hall.

The fire in the kitchen was readied, the rice was washed, and the water was warming up. Taxian-jun sat at the little table, chin resting on his hand as he watched Chu Wanning work at the stove, stewing in helpless irritation.

Thankfully, Chu Wanning thought this was a dream and hadn't put too much effort into his resistance. As for Taxian-jun, he knew this illusion would soon shatter, and so cherished it all the more.

The pot came to a boil, and the aroma of rice and meat wafted up from beneath the wooden lid. Taxian-jun folded his fingers beneath his chin. There was much he wanted to say to Chu Wanning, but there was no real point in voicing it. Nothing would change if he did. In the end, his lips parted, but the only word that came out was an indolent "Oi."

"Huh?"

What was he going to say? Taxian-jun didn't know. After some thought, he said solemnly: "Remember to add salt."

"...I did."

"Then remember to taste it."

Chu Wanning stared at him. There was a glint of relaxed mischief in Taxian-jun's eyes, so dark they looked purple. "Don't think of poisoning this venerable one with salt."

He came up behind Chu Wanning and glanced down into the pot. Without warning, he folded the man's warm figure into his arms. He nuzzled at Chu Wanning's temple, eyes drifting shut. "This venerable one still wants to torment you for the rest of your life."

"Mo Weiyu—"

Feeling Chu Wanning tense in his embrace, Taxian-jun held him tighter. He couldn't resist dropping a kiss on the nape of his neck, lashes fluttering. "What? This venerable one spent so much time teaching you the art of porridge, yet you won't make this venerable one a single bowl?"

This coarse logic reduced Chu Wanning to silence. With great effort, he dredged up some appropriately biting retorts, yet as soon as he tried to speak, his lips were soundly sealed against Taxian-jun's own.

When he held that flame, once lost and now regained, Taxian-jun returned to the warmth of the human world. Amidst the unremarkable scents of domestic life, this dead man walking kissed Chu Wanning freely and passionately, his freezing lips pressed to Chu Wanning's warm ones.

His shizun—his Wanning—his Consort Chu. No one could take him away, and he would never give him up.

Taxian-jun deepened the kiss, head beginning to spin as he pinned Chu Wanning against the table. He claimed Chu Wanning's swollen lips with abandon as his other hand reached up to slide off his clothes.

He'd often done things like this in the past. When he was in this kind of mood, he didn't care even if there were urgent petitioners outside. The wildest instance was one in which desire had seized him in the middle of the day, and he had indulged himself with the newly titled Consort Chu right in the council hall of Wushan Palace. Monks from Wubei Temple had come to bring his attention to the matter of the Drought Demon of the Yellow River and had constantly begged an audience. In irritation, Taxian-jun ordered the veil to be lowered to conceal them from view and allowed the monks inside. Past that gauzy canopy and its tinkling bead veil, he continued ravishing his own shizun on the lounge of patterned red sandalwood.

"Keep it down... I told them I summoned Consort Chu to save you some dignity." He panted atop Chu Wanning. "Make any noise and those bald donkeys will know you're the one in my bed."

"Mo Weiyu..." The eyes of the man beneath him were scarlet with shame. "You bastard!"

Taxian-jun snapped his hips harder in response, filth spilling from his lips. "Baby, that part of you down there is so hot and wet, so why is this part of you up here so bitchy? Hold back your moans, that's all."

When those oblivious monks came in, they beheld through the pale yellow gauze a blurred vision of Taxian-jun's broad back accompanied by a pair of willowy legs, weakly splayed and quivering with each of Taxian-jun's brutal thrusts. Those toes were pale and delicate, trembling like dew-laden lilies of the valley.

The monks' entreaties dissolved into incoherence, not that Mo Ran absorbed much of it anyway. All he retained was the sight of Chu Wanning pushed to his limits yet refusing to make a sound, tears streaming from reddened eyes. His body writhed, bucking as Taxian-jun fucked him to climax, body taut in suffering and suppressed pleasure, biting his lip bloody to remain silent—

It was too fucking arousing. The instant the monks left, Taxian-jun could no longer restrain himself. Hoisting one of Chu Wanning's limp legs up on his shoulder, he fucked him viciously from this new angle. "Wanning, you can let it out now. They're gone."

But Chu Wanning was delirious—his only thought was that he must keep quiet. Taxian-jun leaned forward to capture his bloodied lips, swallowing the taste of copper. "They're gone..."

He flipped Chu Wanning over, pushing him into the lounge and hammering deep into his slick hole. Without letting up for an instant, Taxian-jun reached around to grope at the smooth, firm planes of Chu Wanning's lean chest, throat bobbing as he gasped in the midst of feverish desire, "'S good? Gonna come for me?"

Damp strands of hair tangled over Chu Wanning's eyes; half his handsome face was covered by the mess they'd made of the cushions. Mo Ran's cock was simply too big; with each thrust, Chu Wanning felt his belly was going to be pierced through. He panted, lips parted, fingers fisted tight in the cloth.

The man behind him increased his pace, almost frenzied, until he finally came, burying himself to the hilt. Mo Ran knew where Chu Wanning was most sensitive, knew where to aim so each pulse of his thick, creamy release would hit right where it would make Chu Wanning shudder, make his scalp prickle, make him squeeze his eyes shut and moan. "Ah…"

Even then, Mo Ran was just getting started. It didn't take long for him to harden again, still buried deep inside the man trapped beneath him. Mo Ran flipped Chu Wanning over and stared at him, gaze dark through his own tangled hair, his eyes tracing a heated path over the expanse of his skin from his wet and hazy eyes to his bruised and bitten mouth. Lower, lower, until Mo Ran dove down and took one of Chu Wanning's nipples into his mouth.

Exhausted from their lovemaking, Chu Wanning let out a startled cry as one of his legs was raised up again, only to choke, gasping for breath, as that scalding heat pressed into him once more. "Ah… ah…" He shook his head and, unable to bear the sound of his own coarse moans, bit down on his own hand. Even then, the sounds of their filthy union couldn't be muffled; the frantic pace of their lovemaking had churned Mo Ran's seed within him into a sticky mess between his legs, the brisk slap of flesh on flesh lewd and wet, shattering the light in his eyes into glittering shards.

"Let go, stop biting yourself."

Of course Chu Wanning ignored him. He kept his teeth firmly set in his wrist, refusing to make any sound. Cursing under his breath,

Mo Ran braced himself against the lounge with one hand and grabbed Chu Wanning's arm with the other, pulling him almost off the couch. "Hold onto me."

"Wh-what...*ah*!"

Before Chu Wanning could react, Mo Ran scooped him bodily from the lounge and stood, driving Mo Ran's cock deeper as the weight of Chu Wanning's body sank to meet him.

Smiling softly, Mo Ran kissed him again. "You're not so heavy after all." Still holding him, he walked toward the inner hall.

But that swollen length was still buried deep inside his shizun. Whether purposeful or not, in this position, every step made Mo Ran's hot cockhead, sheathed inside Chu Wanning, press against his most sensitive spot. Every brush against it made his toes curl, yet he still childishly refused to speak or moan. He merely stared, black eyes fierce, at the disciple holding him.

"Why are you looking at me like that?" Mo Ran chuckled, coming to a stop and grinding upward. "You want this?"

Chu Wanning flinched.

It was humiliating, but his body had long grown sensitive to Mo Ran's ministrations. Chu Wanning's brows knit together, gasping softly as his cheeks flushed red. He could vividly feel the wetness dripping from where they were joined. Each of Mo Ran's movements made an increasingly bigger mess of them both.

Mo Ran fucked him like this for a while before growing impatient. He looked, eyes shadowed, toward the back hall he had been making for. Irritated at its distance, he pinned Chu Wanning down right on the icy floor of the great hall where court was held every morning. He couldn't wait any longer; the wet heat he was buried in felt so good. He shoved Chu Wanning down onto the stone, driving into him without mercy.

"Ah...ah..." In these wild moments, Chu Wanning felt as if his soul was leaving his body. Not even he could remain lucid amidst the current of this torrential entanglement. His legs dangled loose around Mo Ran's tight waist, and his body shook with every sharp movement of Mo Ran's hips. There were times when he felt he would die—that Mo Ran wanted to kill him, just like this...

Wushan Palace itself seemed to take on a wanton, disheveled appearance; the solemn imperial court was empty save for this pair of naked adversaries. Mo Ran panted raggedly, sweat trickling down the taut lines of his abdomen. He clutched his pleasure-drunk shizun tightly, driving in quick and hard from below. He heard Chu Wanning's low and suppressed murmurs and snatches of helpless whines.

"Wanning..." He captured Chu Wanning's parted lips in another feverish kiss. Exertion had left the veins on Mo Ran's neck bulging, his body as searing as his gaze. He nuzzled against Chu Wanning, their limbs tangling on the floor.

Amidst this lingering kiss and his punishing thrusts, Mo Ran pushed Chu Wanning hard against the stone, covering his mouth and nose with one hand and leaving only those glassy eyes visible.

He pumped twice more, then sank to his full depth inside Chu Wanning, toes going white with strain. "I'm gonna come... Wanning...here?"

Chu Wanning had been driven to the edge of insanity by Mo Ran's monstrous strength and vitality. His hands fell limp to the ice-cold stone, his limbs sprawled, wide and pliant, around Mo Ran as his body shook from mingled thrill and torment.

Mo Ran huffed, voice hoarse and eyes dark. He grabbed Chu Wanning's face and turned it toward him. "Here? Hm?"

The full head of him was pressed right against that deepest bundle of nerves in Chu Wanning's body; the merest touch made Chu Wanning's eyes fly open, revealing the humiliated flush at their corners.

He shook beneath Mo Ran, but was held in place by firm hands. Mo Ran breathed roughly into his ear. "Stop moving, baby, I'm close...ah..."

He groaned when his climax took him. That thick wetness flooded once more into the depths of Chu Wanning's overstimulated body. Chu Wanning spasmed as if struck by lightning, eyes closing in rapture.

"Wanning, does it feel good? Am I making you feel good?"

At such time, Chu Wanning could scarcely string two words together. Both scolding and rebuke were absent; his rational mind had fled long ago, his fine legs spread wide, his stomach filled with his own disciple's come...

Later, they had done such things often—on the great hall's throne, or the stairs, or against the wall. Taxian-jun's animal ferocity was a tameless, almost destructive force. When consensual, sex like this was all-consuming; despite the retaliatory and humiliating nature of the acts, it was mind-blowingly good.

In the present moment, in the depths of Mount Jiao, Taxian-jun stared into Chu Wanning's gaunt face. As he silently recalled those scenes, a perverse curiosity rose in his mind. Had Chu Wanning ever wondered why Song Qiutong had never conceived despite Mo Ran's prodigious appetites? He'd favored the woman at one point, but never found her quite to his taste. He wanted no children off Song Qiutong. Even in the throes of pleasure, he retained enough clarity to restrain himself: He never came inside her, ensuring she would bear no progeny of his. Perhaps as a result of the circumstances of his own birth, he felt that two people, unless they loved each other enough to spend a lifetime together, shouldn't beget any children.

But it was strange—he hated Chu Wanning so bitterly, yet he often thought that it would be welcome if his Consort Chu fell pregnant from the frequency of his visits. Was this his desire to dominate? To retaliate? To take possession? Did he crave this because it would be a punishment even more humiliating than physical disgrace?

He didn't know. In his ignorance, he dragged Chu Wanning down, again and again, into the abyss of sin and desire.

Never Leave Me

DIZZY WITH LUST, Taxian-jun yanked off Chu Wanning's belt sash. His robes fell away from his shoulders, revealing the bruises beneath.

Taxian-jun froze, his eyes dark yet searing, like two glowing embers in the ashes. After a stiff pause, he closed his eyes and sighed. "Forget it..." He would likely break Chu Wanning in half if he took him again right now. "I'll...let you off easy today."

There was an almost otherworldly silence in the kitchen as he released the man in his arms and refrained from taking any further liberties. Yet Taxian-jun couldn't resist leaning forward, swallowing hard as he kissed his lover's brows and eyes, trailing his lips down to the base of his neck, where he sank his teeth into flesh. Only then did he rise, yanking the man he'd shoved against the table up along with him.

The congee was ready, bubbling in its pot. Taxian-jun fixed Chu Wanning's clothes with a rough hand and cleared his throat, voice still husky and warm. "It's ready. Serve me a bowl."

His behavior baffled Chu Wanning. But the emperor's moods were often inscrutable, and Chu Wanning still thought he was dreaming, so he didn't ponder it deeply. In any case, having a proper meal was much more comfortable than being bent over the table to satisfy Taxian-jun's lust. Thus he opted to remain silent as he reached for the wooden lid.

"A big bowl."

"Trying to stuff yourself to death?"

The ghost of a smile flitted across Taxian-jun's face. "We'll see." He sat down at the table. He had a strong urge to step up to the stove and see what kind of damage Chu Wanning had done to the congee, but he had to keep up imperial appearances. Taxian-jun sat with appropriate poise, affecting an expression of refined disinterest.

When the bowl arrived before him on the table, however, Taxian-jun could no longer maintain his aloofness. It was both overcooked and watery. He didn't need to taste it to know the flavor was certain to be off as well—that terrible, familiar flavor that was forever beyond his reach.

"Eat," said Chu Wanning.

Taxian-jun stared at the little bowl for a very long time, stirring it without bringing the spoon to his mouth. Chu Wanning glanced at him. "It'll get cold if you don't eat it soon."

"Oh." He lifted the spoon to his lips, but after a moment's hesitation, he set it back down.

Chu Wanning finally seemed to take notice of his strange behavior. "What's wrong?"

"Nothing," replied Taxian-jun. He flashed a grin, devilish and disdainful. "It's so bad I don't want it anymore."

Chu Wanning stared at him.

"It's too stuffy in there. This venerable one is going to go get some air." He pushed the bowl away and rose to leave.

He was nearly at the door when Chu Wanning's voice rang out behind him. "If you don't eat it," Chu Wanning said with a tranquility born of enduring the same humiliation countless times, "I'll dump the pot."

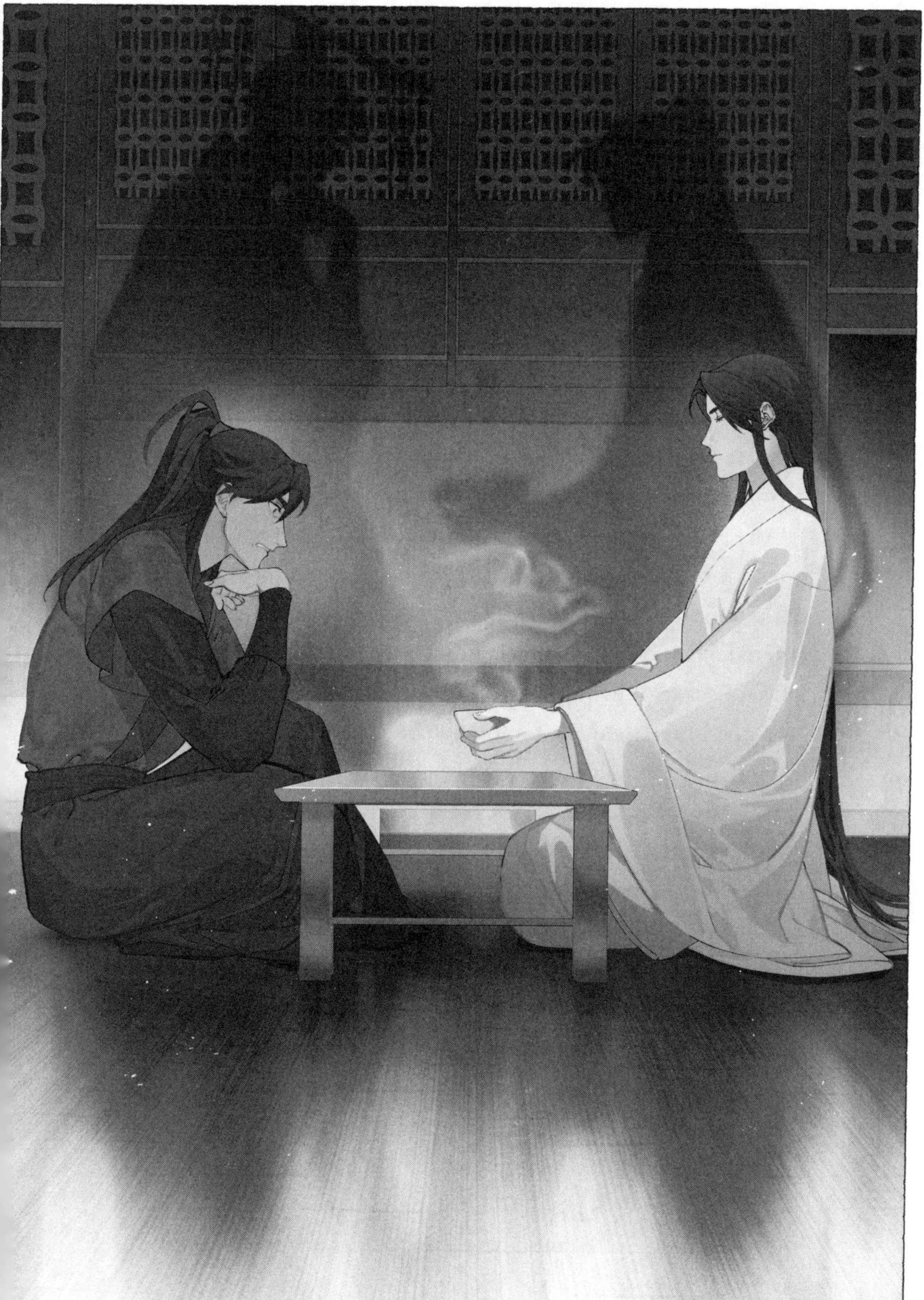

Most of what he made for Taxian-jun ended up wasted. It'd been the same since that first bowl of wontons was flung to the ground.

Taxian-jun whirled back around. "Don't touch it! I mean..." He cleared his throat in an attempt to hide his anxiety. "Leave it for now."

"What for?"

"None of your business."

Taxian-jun lifted the door-drapes and left the room. When he was safely beneath the eaves, he closed his eyes and heaved a gusty sigh. He was a corpse—no matter how greatly he resembled a living person, he wasn't one. He'd long since lost the ability to eat food.

After he'd killed himself at Wushan Palace, he was raised as a revenant by Hanlin the Sage. The sage had subsequently escaped to this world through the rift, but Taxian-jun had been left in that tattered old universe to carry out his commands for nearly ten years. In that decade of living as one of the dead, he hadn't eaten a thing. He'd never been a glutton for food, so he'd felt no regret. Until today, when that dreadful bowl of egg and pork congee was placed before him—only then did he feel the pang of this loss.

Why couldn't he still be alive? He'd waited so many years for this day, for a Chu Wanning who belonged to him alone. Now he couldn't even eat the congee Chu Wanning made for him.

What did Chu Wanning's congee taste like? Taxian-jun stood beneath the eaves with his eyes closed, trying to remember. After a long moment, he jerked up an arm to cover his eyes. No one could see the expression on his face—all that was visible were his pale, pursed lips and the clean lines of his jaw.

He lowered his arm and opened red-rimmed eyes.

His memory was poor, and he'd never been clever. If he could still taste, perhaps he could have recalled those memories. But his blood had cooled and his tongue was deadened. Even with the bowl of congee right before him, he couldn't remember what it tasted like. Now he'd never know.

Late that night, Taxian-jun went to look for Shi Mei.

By the cold pond before the ancestral temple, that peerlessly beautiful man stood with his pale feet bare, splashing in the cold water and sending up glittering droplets of light.

Shi Mei arched a brow at the sight of him. "It's a beautiful day," he said mockingly. "Yet instead of staying in the chamber with Chu-zongshi, Your Majesty has found the time to seek me out?"

Taxian-jun didn't bother with niceties. "Are you able to make this venerable one alive for a little while?"

Shi Mei looked him up and down. "Your status as a revenant shouldn't affect matters of the bedroom."

"That's not what I'm talking about."

"Hm? Then what *are* you talking about?"

"Eating," Taxian-jun said stiffly. "This venerable one wishes to eat."

Shi Mei's eyes darkened. "Your Majesty can't possibly want to eat those wontons?" he asked thoughtfully.

"No one makes wontons as good as my shige."

Shi Mei smiled. "There's a new one. To think you remember his existence today."

Taxian-jun's recollections of Shi Mei had been scrambled beyond recognition. Sometimes he had memories of the man, but most times he had no idea who he was. This mention of his "shige" today caught Shi Mei's attention. "Ah, but you spend all your time entangled with Chu Wanning on Mount Jiao. Don't you ever spare a single thought for your Mingjing-shixiong?"

Perhaps this was what they meant by "together, yet strangers still."

It took Taxian-jun a moment to respond. "You said this venerable one's body has too much yin energy, and that I shouldn't go find my shige before fully reviving with a new spiritual core. He's a water elemental cultivator; this venerable one would hurt him badly."

Shi Mei lied without blinking. "Indeed."

"So why did you bring up wontons?" Taxian-jun glared. "Don't you have any tact?"

Shi Mei smiled. "I was just wondering. Other than wontons, what food would make the Emperor Taxian-jun, connoisseur of a thousand delicacies, crave it so?"

Taxian-jun fell silent.

"What, you don't want to say? Then let me guess. Chu-zongshi cooked for you?"

Shi Mei found his answer in Taxian-jun's expression. "I heard Chu-zongshi of Sisheng Peak is a master in the kitchen," he said with a smile. "Capable of cooking the greatest charcoal. How curious that you'd eat it so happily."

This last cast a pall over Taxian-jun's already grim expression. "Just tell me if you can do it. Stop wasting my time."

"Of course there's a way, but I've already told you what it was."

Taxian-jun frowned. "What?"

"The same old thing," Shi Mei said gently. "The sooner we take Mo-zongshi's spiritual core, the sooner you'll return to life."

A tangerine blossom floated on the surface of the water. Shi Mei tapped it with his foot, catching the pristine blossom between his toes. Its petals were alabaster-pale, yet not even the flower could compare with the fair translucence of Shi Mei's skin.

Shi Mei looked smilingly down at the little bloom. "The sooner we work together to obtain that spiritual core and put it in you, the sooner I'll have access to your full strength. And the sooner you can eat whatever you want." He paused, looking up through soft lashes. "Then you can finally see the one you long for."

Faced with Taxian-jun's silence, Shi Mei concluded, "So I suggest you cooperate, Your Majesty."

"You asked this venerable one to massacre those cultivators at Guyueye, then made me summon an army of Zhenlong pawns to take down Sisheng Peak. This venerable one did it all. What else do you need from me? Just say it."

Shi Mei rubbed his hands together. "How refreshing. There's really not much more for you to do, save for one last thing."

"Tell me."

"Come with me to Tianyin Pavilion. The board is set for our final move. It's time to finish things."

Only then did Taxian-jun notice the golden-feathered pigeon perched on a branch behind Shi Mei—one of the messenger birds used by Tianyin Pavilion.

"Tianyin Pavilion contacted you?"

"They did." Shi Mei extended two slender fingers, a thin sheet of paper trapped between. "All good news. Everything's gone according to our plan. It's difficult indeed to play the hero—Mo-zongshi offered up his spiritual core to protect the cultivation realm, but no one's lightened his sentence because of it." He smiled. With a flourish of his fingers, the letter folded itself into a paper butterfly and flew toward Taxian-jun. "See for yourself."

"There's no need." Taxian-jun caught the butterfly but didn't unfold it. He stared, dark-eyed, at Shi Mei. "Just tell me when we start."

"The interrogation is in three days. Sentencing in another three."

"Six days?"

Shi Mei caressed the golden pigeon's wing, his countenance mild. In a blink, a snake's triangular head darted from his sleeve.

The animal sank its fangs into the bird's neck and swallowed the docile bird whole.

It happened so quickly. Nothing changed in Shi Mei's face—as if this was all entirely ordinary. He smiled and brushed an errant feather aside. "Exactly. We'll stay another three days on Mount Jiao, then go to Tianyin Pavilion to wait."

The feather drifted into the water. Ripples spread around it, destroying the reflection of the two men on the shore. "His spiritual core will make you unstoppable. Everything you want will be in your grasp."

Deep in thought, Taxian-jun returned to the secret chamber. Chu Wanning was already slumbering. It seemed he'd been reading, but had lapsed into exhausted sleep over the desk, his pristine white robes falling around him like a bank of fresh snow.

Taxian-jun stood beside him and watched him in silence. One man, one lamp, and one book. He'd seen all the glories the world had to offer, beauties of every color and kind and scenes of untold splendor. *It's only Chu Wanning. What's there to look at?* he asked himself, vexed.

But he still swallowed, impelled to lean down and take hold of this man, burying his face into the warm crook of his neck.

Chu Wanning stirred awake. Those phoenix eyes were mild and confused, yet when he remembered the cruelty of Emperor Taxian-jun before him, his gaze sharpened and chilled.

Taxian-jun watched the change, and the dissatisfaction and frustration in his heart multiplied like weeds. He couldn't stop himself from picking Chu Wanning up.

"What madness are you—mngh!"

The breath went out of Chu Wanning as he was shoved against the wall. Taxian-jun kissed him with passion and despair, lips roving from his neck to his mouth, and from his mouth down to his jaw. Panting, he asked, "Do you love me?"

Receiving no reply, he tried again. "Chu Wanning, do you love me?"

"What are you doing? Why are you..."

But Taxian-jun didn't seem to want to hear his answer. He simply wanted to ask; he didn't care what the truth might be. Or maybe the answer didn't matter—the road was long, and there was no turning back. No answer he could give would change a thing.

"If I weren't Emperor Taxian-jun—if I became a zongshi like you—would you choose to be with me? Would you be kinder to me?"

He bit down on the nape of Chu Wanning's neck, lapping at the broken skin as if he would drink his blood. As if this was the only way he could prove that the man in his arms belonged to him, and not to the Mo Weiyu who was different from him in every way. He lowered his lashes, and his voice went hoarse. "At the end of it all, do you still like the person he is more than the person I am...?"

"Mo Weiyu, what the hell are you talking about?"

Chu Wanning's memories were a mess. He only remembered the past life, not the present, so of course couldn't understand his raving. This was the only time he could belong to Emperor Taxian-jun alone.

Taxian-jun suddenly felt a terrible sadness. A bitter edge crept into the haughtiness in his voice. He nuzzled his lover, and at last quietly asked: "If I took his spiritual core...would you hate me even more?"

There was nothing one could change less than insecurity. Taxian-jun held Chu Wanning tight in his arms. "But you belonged to this venerable one first... Don't betray me."

Misery engulfed him. Perhaps a long loneliness would dull even the sharpest blade. "It's been eight years. Every moment he had you, I waited alone in another world."

Alone in Wushan Palace, with no one at his side.

"Don't leave me again. The first time, I at least had the ability to end things myself. But if you leave me a second time... I can't even choose to die." Taxian-jun furrowed his brow, darkness, madness, heartache, and obsession written in every line of his pale face. "I can't bear it. Not this time."

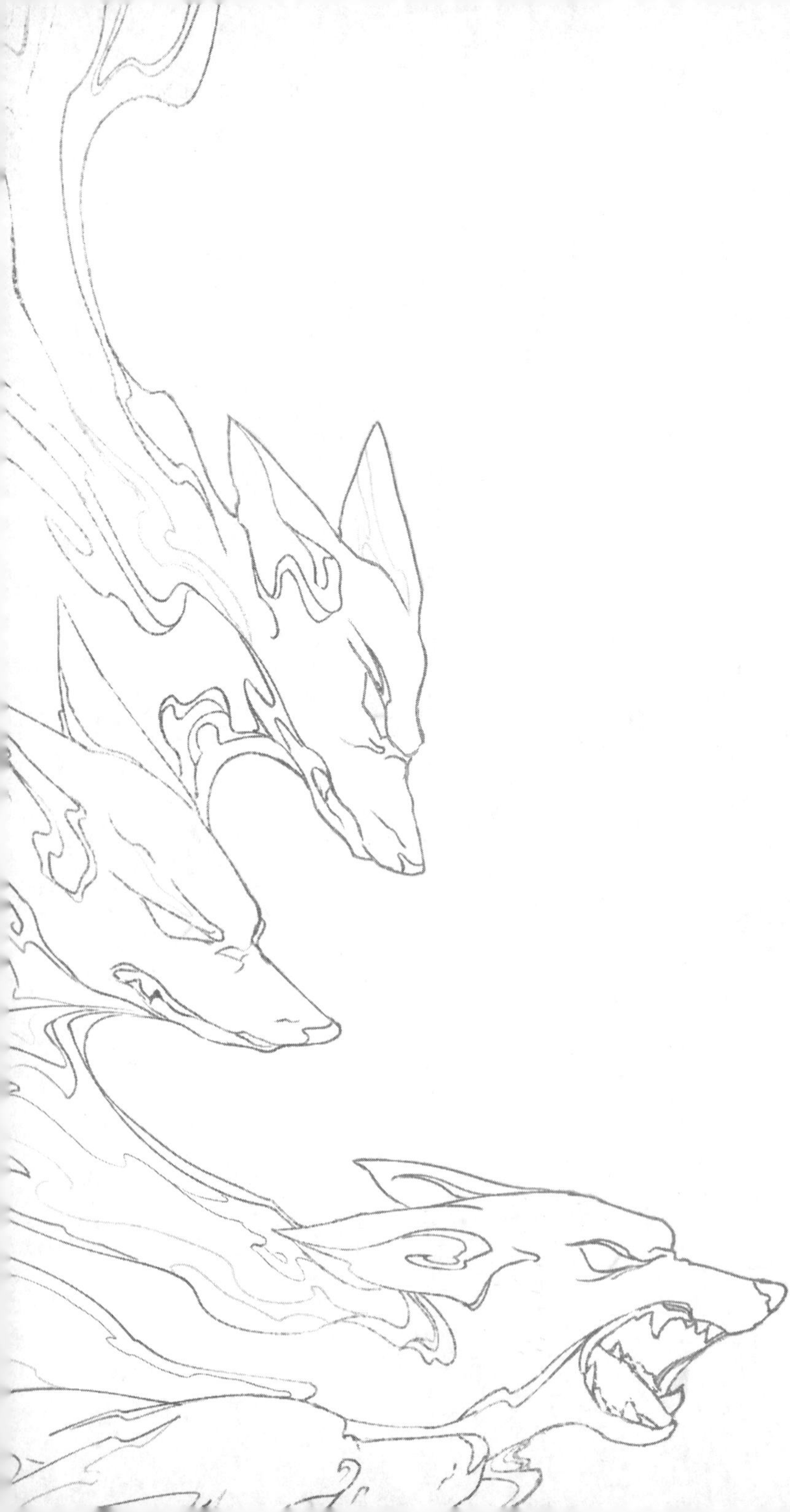

THE STORY CONTINUES IN
The Husky & His White Cat Shizun
VOLUME 9

Characters, Names, and Locations

Characters

The identity of certain characters may be a spoiler; use this guide with caution on your first read of the novel.

Note on the given name translations: Chinese characters may have many different readings. Each reading here is just one out of several possible interpretations.

MAIN CHARACTERS

Mo Ran
墨燃   SURNAME MO, "INK"; GIVEN NAME RAN, "TO IGNITE"

COURTESY NAME: Weiyu (微雨 / "gentle rain")

TITLE(S):

Taxian-jun (踏仙君 / "treading on immortals")

WEAPON(S):

Bugui (不归 / "no return")

Jiangui (见鬼 / literally, "seeing ghosts"; metaphorically, "What the hell?")

SPIRITUAL ELEMENT(S): Wood and Fire

Orphaned at a young age, Mo Ran was found at fourteen by his uncle, Xue Zhengyong, and brought back to Sisheng Peak. Despite his late start, he has a natural talent for cultivation. In his previous lifetime, Chu Wanning's refusal to save Shi Mei as he died sent Mo Ran into a spiral of grief, hatred, and destruction. Reinventing himself as Taxian-jun, tyrannical emperor of the cultivation world, he committed many atrocities—including taking his own shizun captive—before ultimately killing himself. To Mo Ran's surprise, he woke to find himself back in his fifteen-year-old body with all the memories of his past self and the opportunity to relive his life with all new choices, which is where the story begins.

Since his rebirth, Mo Ran has realized many things are not as they had seemed in the previous lifetime, a realization that came to a head after Chu Wanning's death while sealing the Heavenly Rift at Butterfly Town. During the five years of Chu Wanning's seclusion following his return from the underworld, Mo Ran wandered the land making a name for himself as Mo-zongshi.

Chu Wanning
楚晚宁 SURNAME CHU; GIVEN NAME WANNING, "EVENING PEACE"

TITLE(S):

Yuheng of the Night Sky (晚夜玉衡 / Wanye, "late night"; Yuheng, "Alioth, the brightest star in Ursa Major")

Beidou Immortal (北斗仙尊 / Beidou "the Big Dipper," title *xianzun*, "immortal")

ALSO KNOWN AS: Xia Sini (夏司逆 / homonym for "scare you to death")

WEAPON(S):

Tianwen / 天问 "Heavenly Inquiry: to ask the heavens about life's enigmatic questions." The name reflects Tianwen's interrogation ability.

Jiuge / 九歌 "Nine Songs." Chu Wanning describes it as having a "chilling temperament."

Huaisha / 怀沙 "Embracing Sand to Drown Oneself." Chu Wanning uses it rarely because of its "vicious nature."

SPIRITUAL ELEMENT(S): Wood and Metal

A powerful cultivator who specializes in barriers and is talented in mechanical engineering, as well as an elder of Sisheng Peak. Aloof, strict, and short-tempered, Chu Wanning has only three disciples to his name: Xue Meng, Shi Mei, and Mo Ran. In Mo Ran's previous lifetime, Chu Wanning stood up to Taxian-jun, obstructing his tyrannical ambitions, before he was taken captive and eventually died as a prisoner. In the present day, he is Mo Ran's shizun, as well as the target of Mo Ran's mixed feelings of fear, loathing, and lust. Unaware of Mo Ran's rebirth, Chu Wanning has been acting in accordance with his own upright principles and beliefs, which culminated in his death during the events of the Heavenly Rift at Butterfly Town. With the aid of Master Huaizui and Mo Ran, he returned to the world of the living, but only after five years in seclusion.

Chu Wanning's titles refer to the brightest stars in the Ursa Major constellation, reflecting his stellar skills and presence. Specifically, Yuheng is Alioth, the brightest star in Ursa Major, and the Big Dipper is an asterism consisting of the seven brightest stars of the same constellation. Furthermore, Chu Wanning's weapons are named after poems in the *Verses of Chu*, a collection by Qu Yuan from the Warring States Period. The weapons' primary attacks, such as "Wind," take their names from *Shijing: Classic of Poetry*, the oldest existing collection of Chinese poetry. The collection comprises 305 works that are categorized into popular songs and ballads (风 / feng, "wind"), courtly songs (雅 / ya, "elegant"), or eulogies (颂 / song, "ode").

SISHENG PEAK

Xue Meng
薛蒙   SURNAME XUE; GIVEN NAME MENG, "BLIND/IGNORANT"

COURTESY NAME: Ziming (子明 / "bright/clever son")
SPIRITUAL ELEMENT(S): Fire

The "darling of the heavens," Chu Wanning's first disciple, Xue Zhengyong and Madam Wang's son, and Mo Ran's cousin. Proud, haughty, and fiercely competitive, Xue Meng can at times be impulsive and rash. He often clashes with Mo Ran, especially when it comes to their shizun, whom he hugely admires. His weapon is the scimitar Longcheng.

Shi Mei
师昧　SURNAME SHI; GIVEN NAME MEI, "TO CONCEAL"

COURTESY NAME: Mingjing (明净 / "bright and clean")
EARLY NAME(S): Xue Ya (薛丫 / Surname Xue, given name Ya, "little girl")
SPIRITUAL ELEMENT(S): Water

Xue Meng's close friend, Chu Wanning's second disciple, and Mo Ran's boyhood crush. Gentle, kind, and patient, with beautiful looks to match, Shi Mei often plays peacemaker when his fellow disciples argue, which is often. Where Mo Ran and Xue Meng are more adept in combat, he specializes in the healing arts. In the previous lifetime, he died during the events of the Heavenly Rift at Butterfly Town, but in this lifetime, it is Chu Wanning who dies in his stead.

Xue Zhengyong
薛正雍　SURNAME XUE; GIVEN NAME ZHENGYONG, "RIGHTEOUS AND HARMONIOUS"

WEAPON: Fan that reads "Xue is Beautiful" on one side and "Others are Ugly" on the opposite.

The sect leader of Sisheng Peak, Xue Meng's father, and Mo Ran's uncle. Jovial, boisterous, and made out of 100 percent wifeguy material, Xue Zhengyong takes his duty to protect the common people of the lower cultivation realm very much to heart.

Madam Wang (王夫人) Wang Chuqing (王初晴)
SURNAME WANG; GIVEN NAME CHUQING, "FIRST LIGHT"

SPIRITUAL ELEMENT(S): Earth

Xue Meng's mother, lady of Sisheng Peak, and Mo Ran's aunt. Timid and unassuming, she originally hails from Guyueye Sect, having once been Jiang Xi's shijie, and specializes in the healing arts.

RUFENG SECT

Ye Wangxi
叶忘昔 SURNAME YE; GIVEN NAME WANGXI, "TO FORGET THE PAST"

SPIRITUAL ELEMENT(S): Earth

A disciple of Rufeng Sect, the adopted child of Rufeng Sect's chief elder. Highly regarded by the sect leader of Rufeng Sect, and a competent, chivalric, and upright individual. Noted by Mo Ran to have been second only to Chu Wanning in the entire cultivation world, in the previous lifetime.

Nangong Si
南宫驷 SURNAME NANGONG; GIVEN NAME SI, "TO RIDE," OR "HORSE"

SPIRITUAL ELEMENT(S): Fire

Heir to the now fallen Rufeng Sect. Died in the previous lifetime before Mo Ran's ascension as Taxian-jun. Died in this lifetime on Mount Jiao in an attempt to save his fellow cultivators. Has a complicated relationship with Ye Wangxi, his devoted childhood companion, and was engaged to Song Qiutong before the untimely fall of Rufeng Sect.

Naobaijin
瑙白金 NAO, "CARNELIAN"; BAI, "WHITE"; JIN, "GOLD"

Nangong Si's faewolf. Thrice the height of a human, with carnelian-red eyes, snow-white fur, and gold claws.

Song Qiutong
宋秋桐 SURNAME SONG; GIVEN NAME QIUTONG, "AUTUMN, TUNG TREE"

A Butterfly-Boned Beauty Feast who bore a resemblance to Shi Mei. After being rescued by Ye Wangxi, she joined Rufeng Sect as a disciple and was betrothed to Nangong Si. After the fall of Rufeng Sect, she was kidnapped to Mount Huang and killed by Xu Shuanglin. In the previous lifetime, Taxian-jun took her as his wife and empress after burning Rufeng Sect. She also shares a name with a character in *Dream of the Red Chamber*.

Nangong Liu
南宫柳 SURNAME NANGONG; GIVEN NAME LIU, "WILLOW"

Leader of Rufeng Sect and father to Nangong Si. Rumored to be the second-richest person in the cultivation world. Has a gifted tongue for flattery. Seems to have some negative history with Chu Wanning.

Xu Shuanglin (Nangong Xu)
徐霜林 (南宫絮) SURNAME XU; GIVEN NAME SHUANGLIN, "FROST, FOREST" (SURNAME NANGONG; GIVEN NAME XU, "WILLOW FLUFF")

The embittered brother of Nangong Liu and former disciple of Luo Fenghua. After faking his death, he adopted the false identity of Xu Shuanglin, under which he took in Ye Wangxi as his adoptive daughter and posed as one of Rufeng Sect's elders.

Nangong Yan (南宫严)

The ninth city lord of Rufeng Sect.

XIANGTAN

Duan Yihan

段衣寒   SURNAME DUAN; GIVEN NAME YIHAN, "CLOTHES, COLD"

Mo Ran's mother, who raised him on her own. Once a talented singer and dancer, famed as one of the twin goddesses of the riverbanks, she eventually had to turn to performing on the streets to earn money to keep Mo Ran and herself fed. Compassionate and kind despite the misery of her circumstances, she is described by Mo Ran as his first moral "lighthouse."

Xun Fengruo

荀风弱   SURNAME XUN; GIVEN NAME FENGRUO, "WIND, DELICATE"

A musician famed as one of the twin goddesses of the riverbanks. She had a rivalry-turned-camaraderie with Duan Yihan, Mo Ran's mother.

Mo Nian

墨念   SURNAME MO; GIVEN NAME NIAN, "CONTEMPLATION"

Madam Mo's son.

Madam Mo (墨娘子)

Proprietor of the House of Drunken Jade, a famed pleasure house in Xiangtan. Mo Ran takes his surname from her.

GUYUEYE SECT

Jiang Xi
姜曦   SURNAME JIANG; GIVEN NAME XI, "DAWN, SUNSHINE"

COURTESY NAME: Yechen (夜沉 / "deep night")

The aloof, haughty sect leader of Guyueye Sect. Rumored to be the richest person in the cultivation world. Despite his age, he looks to be in his twenties due to his cultivation method. His weapon is the longsword Xuehuang.

Hua Binan (Hanlin the Sage)
华碧楠 (寒鳞圣手)   SURNAME HUA; GIVEN NAME BINAN, "JADE, CEDAR" (HANLIN, "COLD, SCALES"; SHENGSHOU, "HIGHLY SKILLED, SAGE DOCTOR")

An elder of Guyueye Sect. Highly skilled at refining pills and medicines, and renowned as the finest medicinal zongshi around. He wears a hat and veil that reveal only his eyes. Beyond his medicinal skills, he also wields some talent with insects.

OTHER CHARACTERS

Mei Hanxue
梅含雪   SURNAME MEI; GIVEN NAME HANXUE, "TO HOLD, SNOW"

SPIRITUAL ELEMENT(S): Wood, Water, Fire (?)

A striking cultivator with pale gold hair and jade green eyes, Mei Hanxue is the head disciple of Kunlun Taxue Palace who stayed with the Xue family at Sisheng Peak for a short time as a child. He is skilled in various arts, including dance and playing musical instruments, and is an appreciator of wine and song. Known as "Da-shixiong" to the lady cultivators who flock around him, as well as by less flattering epithets to others, namely Xue Meng and Ye Wangxi. His weapon is the longsword Shuofeng.

Master Xuanjing (玄镜大师)
Abbot of Wubei Temple.

Master Huaizui
怀罪   HUAI, "TO BEAR, TO THINK OF"; ZUI, "SINS, GUILT, BLAME"

A monk of Wubei Temple. Renowned in the cultivation world for his choice to remain in the mortal realm despite having achieved enlightenment and being able to ascend to immortality. Master Huaizui has been in seclusion in Wubei Temple for over a century, and is reportedly able to wield the "Rebirth" technique of the three forbidden techniques. Despite his age, his physical appearance is that of a man in his early thirties. He wielded Rebirth, one of the three forbidden techniques, to bring Chu Wanning back from the underworld.

Li Wuxin
李无心   SURNAME LI; GIVEN NAME WUXIN, "'AN EMPTY STATE OF CONSCIOUSNESS' IN BUDDHIST MEDITATION"

Leader of the recently established Bitan Manor. A man in his fifties, with a pair of long, flowing whiskers. Smooth-talking and somewhat condescending to those he views as beneath himself. Lost his life in the assault on Mount Huang.

Ma Yun (马芸)
Sect leader of Taobao Estate. Rumored to be the third richest person in the cultivation world.

Liu-gong (刘公)
An elderly servant of Taxian-jun in his previous lifetime.

Mu Yanli
木烟离 SURNAME MU; GIVEN NAME YANLI, "SMOKE, TO LEAVE BEHIND"

The reclusive pavilion master of Tianyin Pavilion, as cold, competent, and commanding as she is beautiful.

Zhen Congming
甄淙明 SURNAME ZHEN; GIVEN NAME CONGMING, "WATER GURGLING, BRIGHT/CLEVER"

The thirteenth direct disciple of Li Wuxin. Ignorant, and ignorant of his own ignorance. His name is a homonym for the phrase "very smart."

Huang Xiaoyue
黄啸月 SURNAME HUANG; GIVEN NAME XIAOYUE, "WHISTLE, MOON"

Current sect leader of Jiangdong Hall, cousin to a former sect leader of Jiangdong Hall, and cousin-in-law to the previous sect leader, Qi Liangji.

Song Qiao (Jade-Hearted Lord)
宋乔 (化碧之尊) SURNAME SONG; GIVEN NAME QIAO, "TALL" (HUA BI ZHI ZUN, "LOYAL RULER WHOSE BLOOD HAS TURNED TO GREEN JADE")

COURTESY NAME: Xingyi (星移, "shifting stars")
The last zongshi from the Butterfly-Boned Beauty Feast tribe, who subdued a phoenix descended from the Vermilion Bird hundreds of years ago.

Sects and Locations

THE TEN GREAT SECTS

The cultivation world is divided into the upper and lower cultivation realms. Most of the ten great sects are located within the upper cultivation realm, while Sisheng Peak is the only great sect within the lower cultivation realm.

Sisheng Peak
死生之巅   SISHENG ZHI DIAN, "THE PEAK OF LIFE AND DEATH"

A sect in the lower cultivation realm located in modern-day Sichuan. It sits near the boundary between the mortal realm and the ghost realm, and was founded relatively recently by Xue Zhengyong and his brother. The uniform of Sisheng Peak is light armor in dark blue with silver trim, and members of the sect practice cultivation methods that do not require abstinence from meat or other foods. The sect's name refers to both its physical location in the mountains as well as the metaphorical extremes of life and death. Xue Zhengyong named many locations in Sisheng Peak after places and entities in the underworld because the sect is located in an area thick with ghostly yin energy, and he is furthermore not the sort to think up conventionally nice-sounding, formal names.

Heaven-Piercing Tower (通天塔)
The location where Mo Ran first met Chu Wanning as well as the location where, in his past life, he laid himself to rest. It's where Sisheng Peak imprisons the spirits and demons they exorcise.

Loyalty Hall (丹心殿)

The main hall of Sisheng Peak. Taxian-jun renamed it Wushan Palace (巫山殿) when he took over the sect.

Red Lotus Pavilion (红莲水榭)

Chu Wanning's residence. An idyllic pavilion surrounded by rare red lotuses. Some have been known to call it "Red Lotus Hell" or the "Pavilion of Broken Legs." In the previous lifetime, Chu Wanning's body was kept at the Red Lotus Pavilion after his death, preserved by Taxian-jun's spiritual energy.

Linyi Rufeng Sect
临沂儒风门 RUFENG, "HONORING CONFUCIAN IDEALS"

A prosperous sect in the upper cultivation realm located in Linyi, a prefecture in modern-day Shandong Province. Its seventy-two cities were burned to the ground by Taxian-jun in his lifetime, and by Xu Shuanglin in the present timeline.

Dragonsoul Pool (龙魂池)

The blood pool where a demon dragon's primordial spirit slumbers, and where Rufeng Sect makes sacrifices to the dragon.

Mount Jiao (蛟山)

One of the four great evil mountains of the cultivation realm, a relic of its bloody past. It also serves as the burial grounds for Rufeng disciples, earning it the moniker of Rufeng Sect's heroes' tomb.

Qingtan Palace (清潭宫)

A small palace on Mount Jiao, used by the Nangong clan when they came to the mountain to pay their respects.

Kunlun Taxue Palace
昆仑踏雪宫   TAXUE, "STEPPING SOFTLY ACROSS SNOW"

A sect in the upper cultivation realm located on the Kunlun Mountain range. Its name refers to both the physical location of the sect in the snowy Kunlun Mountain range and the ethereal grace of the cultivators within the sect.

Guyueye
孤月夜   GUYUEYE, "A LONELY MOON IN THE NIGHT SKY"

A sect in the upper cultivation realm located on Rainbell Isle. They focus on the medicinal arts. The name is a reference to the solitary and isolated nature of Guyueye—the island is a lone figure in the water, much like the reflection of the moon, cold and aloof.

Rainbell Isle (霖铃屿)

Not an actual island, but the back of an enormous ancient tortoise, which was bound to the founder of the sect by a blood pact to carry the entirety of Guyueye sect on its shell.

Wubei Temple
无悲寺   WUBEI, "WITHOUT SADNESS/GRIEF"

A sect in the upper cultivation realm. Disciples of Wubei Temple are monks.

Dragonblood Mountain (龙血山)

A mountain near Wubei Temple.

Taobao Estate
桃宝山庄   TAOBAO, "PEACH TREASURE"

A sect in the upper cultivation realm located in West Lake.

Bitan Manor
碧潭庄　BITAN, "GREEN POOL"

A recently established and up-and-coming sect in the upper cultivation realm. Barriers are *not* their specialty.

Jiangdong Hall
江东堂　JIANGDONG, THE SOUTH BANK OF THE YANGTZE RIVER

A sect in the upper cultivation realm. Qi Liangji became their new sect leader after the death of her husband, the previous sect leader.

Huohuang Pavilion
火凰阁　HUOHUANG, "FIRE, PHOENIX"

A sect in the upper cultivation realm.

Shangqing Pavilion
上清阁　SHANGQING, "TOWARDS HEAVEN"

One of the ten great sects, located in the upper cultivation realm. Shangqing Pavilion and Wubei Temple are the only two sects of the ten great sects to explicitly forbid sexual relationships and dual cultivation.

Tianyin Pavilion
天音阁　TIANYIN, "HEAVENLY/DIVINE SOUND"

An independent organization set up by the ten great sects that oversees trials and the imprisonment of criminals. They manage a prison that is reserved for criminals who have committed heinous crimes.

OTHER

House of Drunken Jade (醉玉楼)

A high-class pleasure house in Xiangtan, famed for its theater, star songstress, and food. It burned down not long before the events of the current timeline.

Name Guide

Courtesy Names

Courtesy names were a tradition reserved for the upper class and were typically granted at the age of twenty. While it was generally a male-exclusive tradition, there is historical precedent for women adopting courtesy names after marriage. It was furthermore considered disrespectful for peers of the same generation to address one another by their birth name, especially in formal or written communication. Instead, one's birth name was used by elders, close friends, and spouses.

This tradition is no longer practiced in modern China, but is commonly seen in wuxia and xianxia media. As such, many characters in these novels have more than one name in these stories, though the tradition is often treated malleably for the sake of storytelling. For example, in *Husky*, characters receive their courtesy names at the age of fifteen rather than twenty.

Diminutives, nicknames, and name tags

A-: Friendly diminutive. Always a prefix. Usually for monosyllabic names, or one syllable out of a two-syllable name.

DA-: A prefix meaning "eldest."

DOUBLING: Doubling a syllable of a person's name can be a nickname, i.e. "Mengmeng"; it has childish or cutesy connotations.

-ER: A word for "son" or "child." Added to a name, it expresses affection. Similar to calling someone "Little" or "Sonny." Always a suffix.

XIAO-: A diminutive meaning "little." Always a prefix.

Family

All of these terms can be used alone or with the person's name.

DI/DIDI: Younger brother or a younger male friend.

GE/GEGE: Older brother or an older male friend.

JIE/JIEJIE/ZIZI: Older sister or an older female friend; "zizi" is a regional variant of "jieije."

MEI/MEIMEI: Younger sister or a younger female friend.

Cultivation

-JUN: A term of respect, often used as a suffix after a title.

DAOZHANG/XIANJUN/XIANZHANG: Polite terms of address for cultivators, equivalent to "Mr. Cultivator." Can be used alone as a title or attached to someone's family name. Xianjun has an implication of immortality.

QIANBEI: A respectful title or suffix for someone older, more experienced, and/or more skilled in a particular discipline. Not to be used for blood relatives.

SHIGONG: Husband of shizun/shifu

SHIZHU: "Benefactor, alms-giver." A respectful term used by Buddhist and Taoist monks and priests to address laypeople.

ZONGSHI: A title or suffix for a person of particularly outstanding skill; largely only applied to cultivators in the story of *Husky*.

Cultivation Sects

SHIZUN: Teacher/master. For one's master in one's own sect. Gender-neutral. Literal meaning is "honored/venerable master" and is a more respectful address, though Shifu is not disrespectful.

SHIZU: Grand-teacher/master. For the master of one's master.

SHIXIONG/SHIGE: Older martial brother. For senior male members of one's own sect. Shige is a more familiar variant.

SHIJIE: Older martial sister. For senior female members of one's own sect.

SHIDI: Younger martial brother. For junior male members of one's own sect.

SHIMEI: Younger martial sister. For junior female members of one's own sect.

SHINIANG: Wife of shizun/shifu.

ZHANGMEN/ZHUANGZHU/ ZUNZHU: "Sect leader/Manor leader/ Esteemed leader." Used to refer to the leader of the sect. Can be used on its own or appended to a family name, e.g., Xue-zunzhu.

Other

GONG/GONGGONG: A title or suffix. Can be used to refer to an elderly man, a man of high status, a grandfather, a father-in-law, or in a palace context, a eunuch.

GONGZI: Young master of an affluent household, or a polite way to address young men.

YIFU: Person formally acknowledged as one's father; sometimes a "godfather."

Pronunciation Guide

Mandarin Chinese is the official state language of mainland China, and pinyin is the official system of romanization in which it is written. As Mandarin is a tonal language, pinyin uses diacritical marks (e.g., ā, á, ǎ, à) to indicate these tonal inflections. Most words use one of four tones, though some (as in "de" in the title below) are a neutral tone. Furthermore, regional variance can change the way native Chinese speakers pronounce the same word. For those reasons and more, please consider the guide below a simplified introduction to pronunciation of select character names and sounds from the world of *Husky*.

More resources are available at sevenseasdanmei.com

NAMES

Èrhā hé tā de bái māo shī zūn

Èr as in **uh**

Hā as in **ha**rdy

Hé as in **hu**rt

Tā as in **ta**rdy

De as in **dir**t

Bái as in **bye**

Māo as in **mou**th

Shī as in **shh**

Z as in **z**oom, ūn as in harp**oon**

Mò Rán

Mò as in **mo**ron

Rán as in **run**ning

Chǔ Wǎnníng

Chǔ as in **choo**se

Wǎn as in **wan**ting

Níng as in ru**nning**

Xuē Méng

X as in the **s** in silk, uē as in **weh**

M as in the **m** in **m**other, é as in **uh**, **ng** as in so**ng**

Shī Mèi

Shī as in **shh**

Mèi as in **may**

GENERAL CONSONANTS

Some Mandarin Chinese consonants sound very similar, such as z/c/s and zh/ch/sh. Audio samples will provide the best opportunity to learn the difference between them.

x: somewhere between the **sh** in **sh**eep and **s** in **s**ilk

Q: a very aspirated **ch** as in **ch**arm

C: **ts** as in pan**ts**

Z: **z** as in **z**oom

S: **s** as in **s**ilk

CH: **ch** as in **ch**arm

ZH: **dg** as in do**dge**

SH: **sh** as in **sh**ave

G: hard **g** as in **g**raphic

CHARACTERS, NAMES, AND LOCATIONS ●─○ 343

GENERAL VOWELS

The pronunciation of a vowel may depend on its preceding conso-
nant. For example, the "i" in "shi" is distinct from the "i" in "di."
Vowel pronunciation may also change depending on where the
vowel appears in a word, for example the "i" in "shi" versus the "i" in
"ting." Finally, compound vowels are often—though not always—
pronounced as conjoined but separate vowels. You'll find a few of
the trickier compounds below.

IU: as in **ewe**

IE: **ye** as in **ye**s

UO: **war** as in **war**m

APPENDIX

Glossary

Glossary

While not required reading, this glossary is intended to offer further context for the many concepts and terms utilized throughout this novel as well as provide a starting point for learning more about the rich culture from which these stories were written.

GENRES

Danmei

Danmei (耽美 / "indulgence in beauty") is a Chinese fiction genre focused on romanticized tales of love and attraction between men. It is analogous to the BL (boys' love) genre in Japanese media and is better understood as a genre of plot than a genre of setting. For example, though many danmei novels feature wuxia or xianxia settings, others are better understood as tales of sci-fi, fantasy, or horror.

Wuxia

Wuxia (武侠 / "martial heroes") is one of the oldest Chinese literary genres and consists of tales of noble heroes fighting evil and injustice. It often follows martial artists, monks, or rogues who live apart from the ruling government, which is often seen as useless or corrupt. These societal outcasts—both voluntary and otherwise—settle disputes among themselves, adhering to their own moral codes over the law.

Characters in wuxia focus primarily on human concerns, such as political strife between factions and advancing their own personal sense of justice. True wuxia is low on magical or supernatural elements. To Western moviegoers, a well-known example is *Crouching Tiger, Hidden Dragon*.

Xianxia

Xianxia (仙侠 / "immortal heroes") is a genre related to wuxia that places more emphasis on the supernatural. Its characters often strive to become stronger, with the end goal of extending their lifespan or achieving immortality.

Xianxia heavily features Daoist themes, while cultivation and the pursuit of immortality are both genre requirements. If these are not the story's central focus, it is not xianxia. *Husky* is considered part of both the danmei and xianxia genres.

TERMINOLOGY

BARRIERS: A type of magical shield. In *Husky*, a barrier separates the mortal realm and the ghost realm, and Chu Wanning is noted to be especially skilled in creating barriers.

CLASSICAL CHINESE CHESS (WEIQI): Weiqi is the oldest known board game in human history. The board consists of a many-lined grid upon which opponents play unmarked black and white stones as game pieces to claim territory.

COLORS:
WHITE: Death, mourning, purity. Used in funerals for both deceased and the mourners.
RED: Happiness, good luck. Used for weddings.
PURPLE: Divinity and immortality; often associated with nobility, homosexuality (in the modern context), and demonkind (in the xianxia genre).

COURTESY NAMES: A courtesy name is given to an individual when they come of age. (*See Name Guide for more information.*)

CULTIVATION/CULTIVATORS: Cultivators are practitioners of spirituality and the martial arts. They seek to gain understanding of the will of the universe while also increasing personal strength and extending their lifespan.

CUT-SLEEVE: A term for a gay man. Comes from a tale about an emperor's love for, and relationship with, a male politician. The emperor was called to the morning assembly, but his lover was asleep on his robe. Rather than wake him, the emperor cut off his own sleeve.

DRAGON: Great beasts who wield power over the weather. Chinese dragons differ from their Western counterparts as they are often benevolent, bestowing blessings and granting luck. They are associated with the Heavens, the Emperor, and yang energy.

DUAL CULTIVATION: A cultivation technique involving sex between participants that is meant to improve cultivation prowess. Can also be used as a simple euphemism for sex.

EYES: Descriptions like "phoenix eyes" or "peach-blossom eyes" refer to eye shape. Phoenix eyes have an upturned sweep at their far corners, whereas peach-blossom eyes have a rounded upper lid and are often considered particularly alluring.

FACE: *Mianzi* (面子), generally translated as "face," is an important concept in Chinese society. It is a metaphor for a person's reputation and can be extended to further descriptive metaphors. For example, "having face" refers to having a good reputation and "losing face" refers to having one's reputation hurt. Meanwhile, "giving face" means deferring to someone else to help improve their reputation, while "not wanting face" implies that a person is acting so poorly/shamelessly that they clearly don't care about their reputation at all. "Thin face" refers to someone easily embarrassed or prone to offense at perceived slights. Conversely, "thick face" refers to someone not easily embarrassed and immune to insults.

FAE: Fae (妖 / yao), refers to natural creatures such as animals, plants, or even inanimate objects, who over time absorb spiritual energy and gain spiritual awareness to cultivate a human form. They are sometimes referred to as "demons" or "monsters," though they are not inherently evil. In *Husky*, faewolves (妖狼) are a rare and expensive breed of wolf. Similarly, the feathered tribe are beings who are half-immortal (仙) and half-fae.

THE FIVE ELEMENTS: Also known as the *wuxing* (五行 / "Five Phases") in Chinese philosophy: fire, water, wood, metal, earth. Each element corresponds to a planet: Mars, Mercury, Jupiter, Venus, and Saturn, respectively. In *Husky*, cultivators' spiritual cores correspond with one or two elements; for example, Chu Wanning's elements are metal and wood.

   Fire (火 / huo)
   Water (水 / shui)
   Wood (木 / mu)
   Metal (金 / jin)
   Earth (土 / tu)

HAITANG: The *haitang* tree (海棠花), also known as crab apple or Chinese flowering apple, is endemic to China. The recurring motif for Chu Wanning is specifically the *xifu haitang* variety. In flower language, haitang symbolizes unrequited love.

INEDIA: A common ability that allows an immortal to survive without mortal food or sleep by sustaining themselves on purer forms of energy based on Daoist fasting. Depending on the setting, immortals who have achieved inedia may be unable to tolerate mortal food, or they may be able to choose to eat when desired. The cultivation taught by Sisheng Peak notably does not rely on this practice.

JADE: Jade is a culturally and spiritually important mineral in China. Its durability, beauty, and the ease with which it can be utilized for crafting decorative and functional pieces alike has made it widely beloved since ancient times. The word might evoke green jade (the mineral jadeite), but Chinese texts are often referring to white jade (the mineral nephrite), as when a person's skin is described as "the color of jade."

JIANGHU: A staple of wuxia, the jianghu (江湖 / "rivers and lakes") describes an underground society of martial artists, monks, rogues, artisans, and merchants who settle disputes between themselves per their own moral codes.

LOTUS: This flower symbolizes purity of the heart and mind, as lotuses rise untainted from the muddy waters they grow in. It also signifies the holy seat of the Buddha.

MEASUREMENTS: The "miles" and "inches" in *Husky* refer not to imperial measurement units, but to the Chinese measurement units, which have varied over time. In modern times, one Chinese mile (里 / *li*) is approximately a half-kilometer, one Chinese foot (尺 / *cun*) is approximately one-third of a meter, and one Chinese inch (寸 / *chi*) is one tenth of a Chinese foot.

MERIDIANS: The means by which qi travels through the body, like a magical bloodstream. Medical and combat techniques that focus on redirecting, manipulating, or halting qi circulation focus on targeting the meridians at specific points on the body, known as acupoints. Techniques that can manipulate or block qi prevent a cultivator from using magical techniques until the qi block is lifted.

MOE: A Japanese term referring to cuteness or vulnerability in a character that evokes a protective feeling from the reader. Originally applied largely to female characters, the term has since seen expanded use.

MYTHICAL FIGURES: Several entities from Chinese mythology make an appearance in the world of *Husky*, including:

AZURE DRAGON: The Azure Dragon (苍龙 / canglong, or 青龙 / qinglong) is one of four major creatures in Chinese astronomy, representing the cardinal direction East, the element of wood, and the season of spring.

EBON TORTOISE: The Ebon Tortoise (玄武 / xuanwu) is one of four major creatures in Chinese astronomy, representing the cardinal direction North, the element of water, and the season of winter. It is usually depicted as a tortoise entwined with a serpent.

FLAME EMPEROR: A mythological figure said to have ruled over China in ancient times. His name is attributed to his invention of slash-and-burn agriculture. There is some debate over whether the Flame Emperor is the same being as Shennong, the inventor of agriculture, or a descendant.

FUXI: Emperor of the heavens, sometimes directly called Heavenly Emperor Fuxi. A figure associated with Chinese creation mythology.

JIAO DRAGON: A type of dragon in Chinese mythology, often said to be aquatic or river-dwelling, and able to control rain and floods.

NÜWA: A goddess in Chinese mythology, said to have been the one who created humanity by shaping the first humans out of clay. A prominent figure in Chinese mythology, even outside creation myths.

PHOENIX: Fenghuang (凤凰 / "phoenix"), a legendary bird said to only appear in times of peace and to flee when a ruler is corrupt. They are heavily associated with femininity, the empress, and happy marriages.

VERMILION BIRD: The Vermilion Bird (朱雀上神) is one of four mythical beasts in Chinese constellations, representing the cardinal direction South, the element of fire, and the season of summer.

YANLUO: King of hell or the supreme judge of the underworld. His role in the underworld is to pass judgment on the dead, sending souls on to their next life depending on the karma they accrued from their last one.

PAPER MONEY: Imitation money made from decorated sheets of paper burned as a traditional offering to the dead.

PILLS AND ELIXIRS: Magic medicines that can heal wounds, improve cultivation, extend life, etc. In Chinese culture, these medicines are usually delivered in pill form, and the pills are created in special kilns.

PLEASURE HOUSE: Courtesans at these establishments provided entertainment of many types, ranging from song and dance to more intimate pleasures.

QI: *Qi* (气) is the energy in all living things. There is both righteous qi and evil or poisonous qi.

Cultivators strive to cultivate qi by absorbing it from the natural world and refining it within themselves to improve their cultivation base. A cultivation base refers to the amount of qi a cultivator possesses or is able to possess. In xianxia, natural locations such as caves, mountains, or other secluded places with beautiful scenery are often rich in qi, and practicing there can allow a cultivator to make rapid progress in their cultivation.

Cultivators and other qi manipulators can utilize their life force in a variety of ways, including imbuing objects with it to transform them into lethal weapons, or sending out blasts of energy to do damage. Cultivators also refine their senses beyond normal human levels. For instance, they may cast out their spiritual sense to gain total awareness of everything in a region around them or to sense potential danger.

QI CIRCULATION: The metabolic cycle of qi in the body, where it flows from the dantian to the meridians and back. This cycle purifies and refines qi, and good circulation is essential to cultivation. In xianxia, qi can be transferred from one person to another through physical contact, and it can heal someone who is wounded if the donor is trained in the art.

QI DEVIATION: A qi deviation (走火入魔 / "to catch fire and enter demonhood") occurs when one's cultivation base becomes unstable. Common causes include an unstable emotional state and/or strong negative emotions, practicing cultivation methods incorrectly, reckless use of forbidden or high-level arts, or succumbing to the influence of demons and evil spirits. When qi deviation arises from mental or emotional causes, the person is often said to have succumbed to their inner demons or "heart demons" (心魔).

Symptoms of qi deviation in fiction include panic, paranoia, sensory hallucinations, and death, whether by the qi deviation itself causing irreparable damage to the body or as a result of its symptoms—such as leaping to one's death to escape a hallucination. Common fictional treatments for qi deviation include relaxation (voluntary or forced by an external party), massage, meditation, or qi transfer from another individual.

QIANKUN POUCH: (乾坤囊/ "universe pouch") A pouch containing an extradimensional space within it, capable of holding more than the physical exterior dimensions of the pouch would suggest.

QINGGONG: Qinggong (轻功) is a cultivator's ability to move swiftly through the air as if on the wind.

RED THREAD OF FATE: The red thread imagery originates in legend and has become a Chinese symbol for fated love. An invisible red thread is said to be tied around the limb or finger of the two individuals destined to fall in love, forever linking them.

REIGNING YEARS: Chinese emperors took to naming the eras of their reign for the purpose of tracking historical records. The names often reflected political agendas or the current reality of the socioeconomic landscape.

SHIDI, SHIXIONG, SHIZUN, ETC: Chinese titles and terms used to indicate a person's role or rank in relation to the speaker. Because of the robust nature of this naming system, and a lack of nuance in translating many to English, the original titles have been maintained. *(See Name Guide for more information)*

SPIRITUAL CORE: A spiritual core (灵丹/灵核) is the foundation of a cultivator's power. It is typically formed only after ten years of hard work and study.

SPIRITUAL ROOT: In *Husky,* spiritual roots (灵根) are associated with a cultivator's innate talent and elemental affinities. Not every cultivator possesses spiritual roots.

THREE IMMORTAL SOULS AND SEVEN CORPOREAL SPIRITS: Hun (魂) and po (魄) are two types of souls in Chinese philosophy and religion. Hun are immortal souls which represent the spirit and intellect, and leave the body after death. Po are corporeal spirits or mortal forms which remain with the body of the deceased. Each soul governs different aspects of a person's being, ranging from consciousness and memory, to physical function and sensation. Different traditions claim there are different numbers of each, but three hun and seven po (三魂七魄) are common in Daoism.

THE THREE REALMS: Traditionally, the universe is divided into three realms: the **heavenly realm**, the **mortal realm**, and the **ghost realm**. The heavenly realm refers to the heavens and realm of the gods, where gods reside and rule; the mortal realm refers to the human world; and the ghost realm refers to the realm of the dead.

VINEGAR: To say someone is drinking vinegar or tasting vinegar means that they're having jealous or bitter feelings. Generally used for a love interest growing jealous while watching the main character receive the attention of a rival suitor.

WHEEL OF REINCARNATION: In Buddhism, reincarnation is part of the soul's continuous cycle of birth, death, and rebirth, known as Samsara: one's karma accumulated through the course of their life determines their circumstances in the next life. The Wheel of Reincarnation (六道轮回), translated literally as "Six Realms of Reincarnation," which souls enter after death, is often represented as having six sections, or realms. Each one represents a different "realm," or state of being, a person may attain depending on their karma: the realm of gods, asura, humans, animals, ghosts, and demons.

YIN ENERGY AND YANG ENERGY: Yin and yang is a concept in Chinese philosophy which describes the complementary interdependence of opposite/contrary forces. It can be applied to all forms of change and differences. Yang represents the sun, masculinity, and the living, while yin represents the shadows, femininity, and the dead, including spirits and ghosts. In fiction, imbalances between yin and yang energy may do serious harm to the body or act as the driving force for malevolent spirits seeking to replenish themselves of whichever energy they lack.

ABOUT THE AUTHOR

Rou Bao Bu Chi Rou ("Meatbun Doesn't Eat Meat") was a disciple of Sisheng Peak under the Tanlang Elder and the official chronicler of daily life at Wushan Palace. Unable to deal with Hua Binan's wretched tyranny after Taxian-jun's suicide, Meatbun took Madam Wang's orange cat, Cai Bao ("Veggiebun"), and fled. Thereafter Meatbun traveled the world to see the sights, making ends meet by writing down all manner of secrets and little-known anecdotes of the cultivation world—which Meatbun had gathered during travel—and selling them on the street side.

NOTABLE WORKS:

"God-Knows-What Rankings"
Top of the Cultivation World Best-Sellers List for ten years straight.

"The Red Lotus Pavilion Decameron"
Banned by Sisheng Peak Sect Leader Xue and Yuheng Elder Chu Wanning; no longer available for sale.

"He Who Failed as a People's Teacher"
No longer available for sale due to complaints filed by Yuheng Elder Chu Wanning.

2019 winner of the Ghost Realm's Annual Fuxi-Roasting Writing Contest

"Twenty Years on the Forbes Cultivation World's Billionaires Ranking and Still Going Strong: A Biography of Jiang Xi"

unknown reasons.

"

Orig

Dumb
↓
"The Husky & His White Cat Shizun"
Also being sold in another world.

...and others to come. Please look forward to them.